# THE KISS OF IMMORTALITY

Before I could protest, Johnny picked up a rather thick shard of crystal from the floor. "Here," he said with pride. "This could really hurt if you stepped on it."

He put one hand on the edge of the desk and stood up, gripping the glass in his other hand. When he dropped it in the wastebasket, I could see the small cut on his thumb, smell his blood in the air.

"You've cut yourself," I said breathlessly.

"Yeah, but it's not too bad." He put his thumb into his mouth and sucked on the wound.

"Ah." A groan inadvertently escaped my lips and the hunger within me raged like a fever through my body. My voice grew deeper, more husky. "Don't do that. Hold out your hand and let me see," I ordered, moving closer to him.

Reluctantly he held his hand out and I cradled it in my own two hands. Our eyes met and he was caught. Before I even knew I had reacted, I pulled him to me. He tensed, then relaxed and smiled, wrapping his arms around me as I kissed him, stroking his thick black hair.

My mouth found his neck and my instincts reacted immediately.

I sunk my teeth deep into the vein and his blood washed into my mouth, filling my body with warmth and energy.

Books in the Vampire Legacy series by
Karen E. Taylor

BLOOD SECRETS
BITTER BLOOD
BLOOD TIES
BLOOD OF MY BLOOD

Published by Pinnacle Books

# THE VAMPIRE LEGACY

# BITTER BLOOD

## KAREN E. TAYLOR

PINNACLE BOOKS
Kensington Publishing Corp.
http://www.pinnaclebooks.com

ZEBRA BOOKS are published by

Kensington Publishing Corp.
850 Third Avenue
New York, NY 10022



First Printing: October, 1994
First Pinnacle Printing: September, 2000
10 9 8 7 6 5 4 3

Printed in the United States of America

*Dedicated to Pete with undying love*

# ACKNOWLEDGMENTS

The support network for the Vampire Legacy novels is seemingly endless. Once again, I'll try to mention everyone involved. Thank you to: Cheri, Elise, and John, for their invaluable proofreading, often on short notice; to Paul, whose expertise on cemeteries and the seduction of barmaids was very helpful; to the ladies of the neighborhood (again); to Sherron, for her promotional advice; to my editor, John Scognamiglio, at Zebra Books; and to Cherry Weiner, my agent. But the real stars are my family, for their support, their love, and their understanding. Thank you all.

# Chapter 1

I shook the cold rain from my heavy woolen cloak as I entered the pub. That the place was nearly empty was not surprising. Although the sun had been set for nearly half an hour, it was still early, too early, for most of our regulars and certainly too early for the tourists. Two men, hunched over their bitter ale, glanced at me from the bar. To my acknowledging nod, they gave a brief grunt of greeting and returned their full attention to the contents of their mugs.

Idly, I moved behind the bar, still groggy from my nightmare-interrupted sleep. I gave the counter a cursory sweep with the dishcloth, then poured myself a large glass of port. Sipping gratefully, I leaned back into the shadows, my eyes greedily searching the dark street outside for passersby.

Business had been bad recently. And while I did not need the money, I did miss the tourists. The wine helped, but it would not be long before I had to feed, at any cost. The hunger possessed me fully, its grasp stronger, more savage each waking moment, seeming to grow proportionately with the intensity of the dream. Two years ago I had sought freedom from that grip to discover too late that there would be no deliverance for me, only a deeper traveling into the inhuman soul—mine or his, it made little difference.

A light touch on my arm drew me, shuddering, out of my thoughts and back to the present.

"Someone walking on your grave, Dottie?"

I looked up at the ruddy face of my one-time boss, now my partner and smiled slightly. "I imagine so, Pete," I said, reaching below the bar to hand him a crumpled pack of Players. He followed the same routine every night before leaving the pub. He would smoke one cigarette, drink a glass of stout, and count the money in the drawer before making his way home to wife and family.

I poured him a drink and handed it to him as he sat on his stool, counting the day's take. The cigarette dangled from his upper lip, and he squinted up at me through the thick smoke.

"Thank you, darlin'. What did I ever do before you came?"

I laughed. "You lost money, just the same as we do now. How was business today?"

"Could have been better, Dot. But you know how I'm not one for complaining." He shut the cash drawer, stubbed out his cigarette, and reached for his coat on a hook behind the bar. "Now, you, I worry about. Tending this bloody place night after night—it's not right for a young thing like you. Close up early tonight, Dottie, and go out and have some fun. Get some roses back into your cheeks."

I reached over and protectively pulled his lapels up closer to his neck. "Pete, you are a dear, but I really enjoy the nights here, with no crowds, no pressure. And in any event, I don't know anyone here well enough to go out with them."

He gave a brief, angelic smile, but the feigned expression of innocence did not fool me; try as he might, he could not disguise the glint of mischief in his eyes.

"Now, that reminds me," he started in his slow, matter-of-fact way. "Bless me if there wasn't a young chap in here a little earlier, asking after you." He began to rummage through his pockets, absently patting and prodding them. "Seems to me I wrote his name and number down somewhere. A Yank, did I tell you that? He said he knew you in the States. Awful anxious, he was. Now, if only I could find that paper . . ."

I folded my arms and leaned against the bar, waiting for him to complete his act as patiently as was possible. Pete, for all of his sixty-plus years, was more of a child than I had ever been, a lover of surprises and practical jokes. Finally he produced a wrinkled, grubby piece of paper with a flourish, and I held my hand out to receive it.

"Thank you, Pete. Have a nice evening."

"You, too, darlin'." With a wink he left, whistling an old music-hall tune as he went through the door.

I shook my head and regarded the paper, folded and lying in my trembling hand. There was only one person who knew my current location. Two years had not been enough time to forget him, or the taste and feel of him, yet those years had merely reinforced my reasons for leaving.

Mitch was better off without me; I had believed it then and I believed it now. I was not the same woman I had been; I was changed and not, I thought, for the good. My desperate strike for freedom had failed. I had not driven away the dark spirit. Instead, by giving him death, I had allowed him entrance to my soul and will. Sometimes in my loneliest times, I held him close, savoring our shared passion and pain. We were one in his death, as we had never been in life—it was his whispering voice I heard during the hunt, his cynical pleasure I felt when I fed.

I did not hear the door open—its cheerful little bell had not announced a customer—but suddenly he was there, leaning across the bar, one eyebrow raised and a sardonic smile on his face. "How lovely you look tonight, my dear. How about a drink for an old friend?"

"Dammit, Max. Get the hell out of here."

His body wavered and shimmered, dissolving instantly into the shape of one of our regulars, very surprised and slightly belligerent. "All I want is a drink, Dot, then I'll leave you alone."

"Oh, God, I'm so sorry. I thought you were someone else." I gave him a bright smile and pushed a glass in his direction. "This one is on the house."

He took the drink and my apology good-naturedly. "Thanks. You don't seem too chipper tonight. You feeling all right?"

"I am fine, thank you. Just a little tired, that's all."

He shrugged and moved away from the bar to sit at a table, and was joined a few minutes later by a few of his friends. I shoved the note unread into my apron pocket and tended to the business of the pub.

Later that evening my long wait for tourists finally paid off. A group of six, loud and embarrassingly boisterous, arrived one hour before closing, quickly driving out the regulars. I singled out the likeliest candidate, tall and broad-shouldered, with a bold look in his eyes that caused my body to tighten in anticipation. I smiled at him as I took their orders and served their drinks, offering him a glass of port. When he questioned me, I leaned close to him. "For later," I whispered, "for endurance." He drank it in one gulp, shuddering slightly at its bitterness, and immediately asked for another.

"He's ours now, my little one," the cynical voice in my mind prodded. "Don't wait too long."

I did not. So desperate was I for this man that I issued last call almost immediately. My invitation to him to stay and help close up was met with unabashed approval from his friends, and soon we were alone.

I locked the door, dimmed the lights, and walked back across the room. He joined me behind the bar as I was counting the money in the register. "Aren't you afraid I might steal that?" he questioned with a crooked smile as he helped himself to another glass of port.

I laughed, low and sensually, as I put the night's profits in the safe. "There's not enough here to even be tempting." I gave him a warm, appraising glance. "And somehow I don't think you're interested in my money."

"You sure are right about that, babe." He crossed over to me and put an arm around my waist. "When you're finished here, let's go back to my place." He mentioned the name of his hotel and I nodded my agreement, leaning closer to him.

His grip tightened. "I don't think I caught your name. . . ."

"Dorothy . . . ah, just Dorothy. And yours?"

"Oh, I get it. No last names, right? Then I'm Robert, Robbie to my friends."

"It's wonderful to meet you, Robbie. You'll never know how much."

"But I'll bet I can guess." He pulled me closer and kissed me; my teeth grazed his lip, drawing one intoxicating drop of blood. I savored it and probed with my tongue for more. My hands were wrapped about his waist. I slid my nails slowly up his spine and he shivered, took his mouth away from mine, and looked down at me.

"God." He was breathing heavily, and small beads of sweat appeared on his brow. "You really want this bad, don't you?"

I moaned in answer, and his face grew fierce, full of passion. His hands grasped my waist and he lifted me onto the narrow counter behind the bar, pushing against me forcefully and insistently until I encircled his body with my legs.

He kissed me again and slid his hand down the back of my jeans, kneading the flesh of my lower back. His skin was so warm, so alive. I had to have him now.

"Wait," the voice inside urged. "Let's play a little first."

"I don't want to wait," I protested aloud, and reached up to loosen his tie and unbutton his shirt.

"Neither do I." He lifted my sweater over my head and threw it on the floor. While he nuzzled my breasts, he struggled unsuccessfully to untie my apron. With an exasperated sigh he spun it around on my waist and began to unfasten my jeans. I pulled his shirt off and he ground his groin into mine. Putting my tongue to his skin, I traced a delicate path to his neck and gently nibbled there while he eased my pants down around my knees.

There was a pounding in my head and my gums tingled, signaling the growth of my canines. I was ready; it had been too long, entirely too long. The pounding increased, louder and more demanding.

Abruptly, he pulled away; I lost my balance and lurched up against him.

"What was that?" His voice was angry, suspicious.

"Nothing," I purred, wrapping my arms tightly around his neck. "Come back to me, make love to me."

"No way," he said, wresting himself away from me and putting his clothing back into order. "There's someone at the door."

"They'll go away. I need you, Robbie."

"Forget it."

I was trembling with my unsatisfied need. Quickly I fastened my jeans, put my sweater back on, and walked over to him, where he was putting on his coat. Gently, I laid my hand on his arm and rubbed my head on his sleeve. "Robbie, please, what's wrong? We can go somewhere else if you like, please . . . you can't leave me like this."

The knocking at the door continued, more urgent now.

"Nothing doing, babe. I've heard about this scam before. How much would it have taken to pay off that guy out there—the witness to your 'rape'—five hundred, maybe an even thousand? No thanks, you may be the sexiest bitch I've seen in this country, but you're still too rich for my blood." He pushed me away from him and opened the door. "She's all yours, pal," he said to the figure standing hesitantly in the doorway. "I barely touched her."

"Damn," I swore under my breath as the door slammed. The little bell jangled, discordant in my ears. I rubbed my hands along my jeans. "Well?" I addressed the man whose shadowed face was unrecognizable, even to me. "This had better be damned important."

"Deirdre?" The voice sounded embarrassed, and vaguely familiar. "What was that all about?" He stepped forward into the dim light of the room.

Instantly, I knew who he was—the mysterious Yank visitor Pete had told me about, whose name and number were on a crumpled piece of paper in my apron pocket. And it was not Mitch. Disappointed at that realization, I understood that my dread at meeting him again would have been overruled by my strong desire to see him, hold him, make love to him one more time.

"Hello, Chris," I said to the man who had inherited Mitch's features and build. He had aged in two years, I thought; lines of worry creased his face and he looked like he hadn't slept in weeks.

"Deirdre, it is you, isn't it? I barely recognize you."

"Yes, it is I, in the flesh," I said with no trace of a smile. Were my changes so apparent, even in the darkness? My hair was still almost black, but I had let it grow to its original length. That could not have made much of a difference to him. And although I had not aged, I knew that my mirror revealed me to be harder, coarser, debased somehow by my inhuman instincts.

"Your eyes look funny, they're . . . well, they're almost glowing." I could hear fear in his voice, a reluctance that had never been there before.

"Don't be silly, Chris. The light in here is deceptive." I reached over and turned on one of the switches behind the bar. "There now," I said reassuringly, squinting slightly against the glare, "is that better?"

"Yeah, I guess so." He paused for a moment, and when he continued, his tone was slightly sullen. "I hope I didn't interrupt something important. That guy sure shot out of here like a bullet. And do you always wear your apron backward?"

I reached down to my waist, twitching the apron around to its proper position, but ignored the unspoken questions about Robbie's presence. "Would you like a drink? On the house, of course." I smiled at him, but he refused to meet my eyes.

"Sure, why not? I'll have a beer."

I motioned him to a table. "Sit down," I said, opening two bottles of beer from the refrigerator, "and I'll join you."

He watched me intently as I walked out from behind the bar and sat down next to him. Without a word he took the bottle from me and drank, quickly and furtively, as if to fortify himself against some dire event. His hands, I noticed with surprise, were shaking. But then, so were mine.

"Now, maybe you would like to tell me how you came to be here and how you knew where to find me. Did your father send you?" The emotion I tried to disguise in my voice was not just frustration over the interrupted feeding.

"No." His voice sounded choked, overhung with anger and grief. "No, he didn't send me. But I found your address while I was sorting through his papers and knew that I should come to see you. . . ."

My heart sank. He was dead. I could feel it. I could see it in Chris's face. Jesus, I wailed inside, Mitch is dead. He died and I could have stopped it, but I didn't. I had the power to keep him with me forever, and I did nothing.

"Mitch is dead." My voice, flat and toneless, did nothing to express the despair that the stating of those words caused.

"Oh, no," Chris was quick to protest. "It's not that, honest. It's just that, well, he's bad off, Deirdre. I don't know what's wrong, nobody does. But I think he's dying." He took one more drink of his beer, then set the bottle back on the table softly. His eyes finally held mine and his voice, so much like Mitch's, fell gently on my ears.

"And I think only you can save him. You must save him, Deirdre. Come back to him."

# Chapter 2

"So"—I motioned Chris to a seat on the dark-patterned sofa in what I once would have called my parlor—"what exactly is wrong with him?"

My voice wavered on the last word, and he looked up at me with a start. He had been occupied in studying the room; I could almost see it through his eyes. The furnishings were pleasant enough, though somber in tone—the room large and well-proportioned, the windows draped in heavy burgundy velvet. But the room itself was impersonal, no photographs or mementoes were displayed, as if its inhabitant had no life. It was a cold room, silent and dreary, like the rest of the house, with the feel, if not the actual appearance, of emptiness and decay. A fitting residence for one of my kind, I thought.

"Pretty dreary, isn't it?"

He shrugged. "No, it's very nice, really. Just not what I imagined." Chris still seemed uncomfortable with me or with his mission, I couldn't tell which. Perhaps it was just embarrassment at meeting his father's lover after two years, at being alone with me, in this house, lacking Mitch's presence.

I did the best I could to make him feel at home. "You know, Chris, I hurried you out of the bar and over here without giving you a chance for another drink, or maybe a meal. Are you hungry?"

He gave me a quick smile, reminiscent of the younger

man I knew. "Yeah, you know me, always hungry. How about you—"

He stopped abruptly and the smile dropped from his face, replaced by a painful grimace.

I covered his embarrassment. "I haven't been shopping for food in several days, but I could probably find something. . . ."

"Deirdre, you don't have to do this."

"But you're my guest; I want to make you comfortable."

"No, I mean you don't have to lie to me, pretend to be something you aren't." He looked at me then, and the knowledge of what I was seemed to be reflected in his eyes.

I took a few steps back, retreating closer to the doorway, not wanting to threaten him in any way. "So, he told you. And made you believe it."

He jumped up from the couch, his hands clenched. "Yes, I believed it. I had to believe it. It's true, isn't it?"

"Yes, Chris, unfortunately, it is all true. But I fail to see how any of this will help your father. You say he is dying; can you tell me why?"

"Dammit, Deirdre, don't you understand?" He screamed his anger at me, and I withdrew from him further. "I already told you, no one knows what's wrong. If anyone knew why, they would stop it." Suddenly his anger was replaced with sadness; he sat back down on the couch with a flop and lowered his voice. "Shit, the last time I saw him, he didn't even know who I was. Just sat there in the crazy ward, humming some old song, in his damned institutional pajamas, his damned institutional slippers. He won't even talk about it anymore; it's like he's already given up, already let them devour him, from the inside out."

"Who?"

He gave me a cool, intent stare so like his father's, I wanted to cry.

"The ones like you, of course. The other *vampires.*" He fell silent and rested his head in his hands, rubbing his eyelids. When he finally looked up at me, his face was flushed. He had said the word with such vehemence that it seemed an obscenity echoing in the room. Perhaps it was obscene to him; it was to me. I stood within the doorway and regarded him solemnly.

"There are no others like me. There was only Max, and he's dead." Even as I said it, my voice wavered and the doubts I had felt over the past two years began to reassert themselves. Was Max really dead or had he somehow survived? The thought was absurd. I knew he had died; he had died by my hand. Had I not felt his life drain from him, slowly and painfully? His presence in my current existence was spiritual only. My dreams and visions of him were merely mental aberrations, a guilty conscience, my own self-induced punishment for his murder.

Tense and nervous, I gripped the door frame, my nails gouging out pieces of the woodwork. "No," I said now with more conviction. "Max is dead and buried. He can't be the cause."

Chris wasn't listening to me, wrapped up as he was in his own thoughts. "Dad used to visit his grave, did you know that?" He gave me no time to respond, but continued bitterly. "But how could you know? You very conveniently disappeared off the face of the earth. Oh, I know why you did it." He gave me a quelling look to forestall the protest I had begun to make. "Even Dad said he understood your feelings. I guess you can justify anything if you try hard enough."

He paused as a distracted look entered his eyes and a sad smile crossed his face. "He used to go there every day and read the tombstone you so generously provided.

He even made sure that your daily gift of roses was received. Dad always said that as long as those kept coming, he knew you were still alive and might come back someday."

I edged slowly into the room and sat down in a chair facing him. He barely noticed my presence. Nervously, I plunged a hand into my apron pocket, came upon the half pack of cigarettes, and lit one without thinking, simply to give my trembling hands something to do. Chris looked over at me, and his small smile disappeared.

"All those roses for that dead son of a bitch, and nothing for my father, not even a letter or a call. He loved you, Deirdre, loved you more than you'll ever know or deserve, and you gave him nothing."

Nothing. I sat and considered his words as I smoked my cigarette. How simple the situation must seem to him from his perspective of youth. Reality was much more complicated than Chris wanted to see; the moral and ethical reasons that drove me to this country, the decisions of life, death, and immortality were more important than my petty loves.

"Love be damned." Max's voice rang inside my head. "We're hungry. Take him," the seductive tones urged. "He's young, healthy, and would make excellent sport. His blood is rich, his skin tender. We must feed *now.*"

I crushed out my cigarette and stood up, moving slowly toward Chris. He raised his eyes to mine, and was caught in my gaze. I walked over to him, gripped his shirtsleeves, and pulled him off the couch. We were so close that I could see the throbbing of the veins in his throat, smell the salty odor of his sweat and blood.

"Yes," the voice hissed. "*Yes.*"

His eyes began to glaze over. "Chris"—the whispered words seemed to force themselves from my throat as I reached one hand up to stroke his cheek—"did your father not warn you of vampires? Or are all Greers born idiots, thinking to tame the supernatural with their talk of love? It didn't work for your father and it will not work for you. And you, my dear boy, will pay the penalty he owes me."

That dark voice, echoing in this room, startled me. Did I speak the words? I couldn't tell from Chris's appearance, for although his eyes were opened wide in terror, his gaze was uncomprehending. His fright could easily be due to my proximity or his contact with the inhumanity of my stare, which suspended him—a prisoner to my hunger. With an extreme effort of will I drew my eyes away from him and closed them tightly, to seal the death and corruption inside.

As his labored breathing began to return to normal, I stood, blind and swaying, still holding on to his shirt. Finally I eased my eyes open and caught his bewildered stare. "No," I said, shaking my head, my voice muffled slightly by the growth of my teeth. "No, I will not."

I released him and, moving to the window, pulled open the heavy draperies. Just a glimpse of the dark night streets helped to soothe my nerves and calm my internal tremors. I knew then that it was not just Mitch who was being devoured from within. Perhaps with my return, we could both be healed.

"Deirdre?" He sounded hesitant and confused, obviously with no memory of what had just occurred. "What's wrong?"

I pressed my hands against the cool glass and sighed. "Nothing, Chris. Do you have a return ticket?"

His answering nod was reflected in the window; I turned around and gave him a weak smile. "Cash it in. I'll make arrangements for us both."

"Then you'll come back? You'll help Dad?" The sadness that had haunted him all evening was replaced suddenly by a look of hope, of happiness.

I wished fervently that I could capture some of his

youthful optimism. "Yes," I said deliberately, "although I can't promise that I'll be able to help or cure him. But I will come back."

I was not sufficiently recovered or prepared for his headlong rush across the room and his exuberant embrace. "Thank you," he said into my ear. "Thank you."

I took a deep breath and held it, then pushed him away from me, so quickly that he stumbled, grasping the top of a chair for support.

"Never, never do that again," I spat out at him through my bared teeth.

His eyes widened at the sight of my canines, and he paled. "I'm sorry . . . I didn't think . . ."

"You had better start thinking." My voice was harsher than I intended, and he cringed. "You interrupted my feeding tonight and I'm hungry, very hungry. You must understand who you have recruited for your cause. I am not an angel of mercy, but an angel of death. Don't forget that, ever."

He nodded and looked at me helplessly. "What should I do?"

"Tonight, go back to your hotel room and lock your door. Get a good night's sleep and call me tomorrow at sunset. We'll make our plans then."

He walked to the door, removed his coat from the rack, and put it on. The dejected slope of his shoulders wrung my heart. I hadn't meant to be so hard on him.

"Chris," I called softly, and he turned to me. "I didn't intend to frighten you. You're safe as long as you keep your distance." I smiled again, and he relaxed at the disappearance of my fangs. "Sleep well."

I allowed myself ten minutes before I followed him out onto the street. At this hour most of the bars and restaurants that I normally frequented would be closed, but it was imperative that I feed now. When I thought how close I had come to taking Chris, not once, but twice, I knew that I had to find someone quickly. Fortunately, I knew exactly where to go.

The hotel lobby door was unlocked; I slid past the sleeping clerk and consulted the guest register. I avoided the elevator, taking the stairs instead. Once outside his door, I stopped and listened carefully. He was in there, sleeping and alone. I knocked on the door tentatively, then louder, until his slightly drunken voice rasped out. "Who's there?"

"Room service," I called seductively. "Open the door."

I heard his cursing, the rustling of bedclothes, and the click of a light switch. He opened the door a mere crack, but wide enough for me to insert my hand and push it open. "What the hell?" He was wrapped in a towel, his hair falling slightly over his forehead, his eyes still unfocused.

"Room service, Robbie." I moved closer to him and shut the door behind me. "I want you," I whispered, "and there are no witnesses here. No scam, no rape. Just you and me. How about it?"

His eyes, confused at first, lit in recognition. He'd had quite a bit more to drink since he left me; I could smell it, heavy on his breath. His inhibitions were gone, and a broad smile crossed his face as he dropped his towel. "Sure, babe, come on in."

"I already am in," I said, leading him to the bed.

"So you are," he began, but I pushed him down, violently. "Hey," he protested, "that hurt."

"I don't want to hurt you, Robbie. Just lie still and I'll give you an evening you'll never forget." I straddled him, and he raised his hands and joined them behind his head.

"I'll bet you will." He was with me now, ready, and

watched with a lazy smile as I removed my clothes. He reached for me. "Not yet," I warned, and turned out the light.

He shifted under me, and rolled me over, resting his weight on his arms. I could see his smile gleam in the near darkness.

"Now?"

"Now."

He entered me abruptly and I gasped, startled at his suddenness. But it didn't matter. I hadn't sought him out for the satisfaction of sex; I had come for his blood.

"Is it good?" he asked, his breath warming my ear.

"Good," I purred through my clenched teeth, "but I know how to make it better." Growling, I pierced the surface of his neck, and his blood flooded into my mouth and throat, spreading its rejuvenating warmth. Greedily, I drew in that precious liquid and he groaned, the pain of my bite overridden by his passion. I drank, overwhelmed as always by the miracle of stolen life, almost unaware of his continued frantic thrusts, his incoherent grunts, until he reached his climax, silently shuddering.

I continued to pull on him, long past satisfaction, for the mouth that drank was not entirely my own. Two hungers were being fed, one much darker and deeper than mine. The pulse of my victim slowed; the naked flesh bearing down on mine grew flaccid and unresisting. With alarm I felt his heartbeat falter; I forced my mouth away from his neck, rolled him over, and switched on the light.

He was so pale, so lifeless. Even as I told myself that I had gone too far, I heard the insatiable laughter in my mind.

"That was good, my love. But why stop so soon? He's strong; there is more to be had."

"Any more and he would be dead." The disgust in my voice was not directed at Max alone. If this man died, I would be the one left with the blame. Brushing my hair back, I laid my head on his chest. To my relief, his heart was still beating; he was young and would probably be strong enough to live.

I sat up and slapped Robbie's face, none too gently; his head bobbed back and forth on the pillow. Finally he sighed, opened his eyes, and looked at me.

"Don't go," he said weakly. "That was wonderful. As soon as I get my strength back, we could do it again."

I looked down at him in loathing. The entire situation was pitiful, and the fact that he was begging for more, ludicrous. I wanted to laugh, but the sound that escaped my lips was more of a choked sob. I brushed my bloody tears away and began to get dressed.

When I was fully clothed I sat next to him and took his head into my hands, relieved to see a natural color returning to his skin. The glance he gave me seemed aware and alive.

"I'm feeling better now. Let's do it again." His voice had regained some of its strength and I felt reassured as I met his eyes.

"We can't do it again, Robbie. We never did it at all. You see, it was all a dream."

"A dream?" he repeated stupidly.

"Yes, it was just a dream, and tomorrow you won't remember it or me. Do you understand? You don't know me; you've never met me. I'm just a dream."

"Just a dream."

He was asleep before I closed the door. I hoped that the suggestion would take hold, but it really made no difference. Tomorrow night at this time Chris and I would be out of the country. Soon I would be with Mitch.

Tears began flowing again as I took to the streets. I hurried through the night, wrapping my cloak tighter around a body that never felt the cold, in the futile attempt to warm the soul within.

# Chapter 3

I didn't turn on the lights when I arrived at my house; instead, I locked the door and climbed the stairs, dropping my clothing as I went. In the shower, I set the water at its hottest and attempted to purge my mind and body of all their contacts that evening: the remains of sex and the taking of blood, the tears, the thoughts of Mitch and love.

The room filled with a billowy steam, obscuring the pale moonlight. I watched it curl and dance, tried to imagine what it would be like to merge with the mist, to transform myself as legend said I could. Before he died, Max had hinted of powers as yet undeveloped and undiscovered within me, beyond human understanding. But in the past two years I had made no attempt to cultivate these mysterious powers; the thought of abandoning what little humanity I had for the unknown terrified me absolutely.

The idea entered my mind that now might be the time to experiment, in an attempt to reach my true powers. But as I ran hands over my naked, tangible flesh, feeling the familiar curves of breasts and thighs, I denied the seduction of those thoughts, taking comfort in what I still had. This body, although corrupted by its appetites, was untouched by age and death. I would fight to keep it as it was; it was all I had left of my lost human life.

"And so you deny your birthright and refuse my gift." From out of the mist he came to me, his white, undead flesh glistening with drops of moisture. His face was tender, almost loving, and he reached his arms out to me, forgiving, pleading.

"Oh, Max." I gasped the words. "I'm so sorry. I didn't want to kill you, but you gave me no choice."

He smiled at me, the pointed tips of his canines showing briefly, his hard, muscular body gleaming through the steam. His left side bore a scar, presumably unknown for one of our kind, a small, jagged cut marring the perfection of his skin.

A part of me wanted to touch him, feel the tissue that had somehow formed over his death wound, but instead I backed away from him, putting my hands up in denial. "You gave me no choice," I repeated, my justification sounding hollow even to me.

He threw his head back and laughed, as if his death were of no importance. "I know, little one." His voice was steady and smooth, reassuring. "I asked too much of you; it was too hard a test. Just come to me now and I'll make it right for you."

I took a step in his direction and he caught me in his arms. His eyes glinted in the mist, revealing his true intentions. His mouth came down on my neck and with his bite he infused me with the chill of death and of the grave. I felt the heat of my body flow into him; his every touch burned my skin with an intense cold. Crying out in pain, I slumped against the shower wall, feebly pushing him away as I slid down into the tub.

When I opened my eyes, he was gone and the water had run cold. "Damn," I swore, shivering as I stood up and turned off the tap. I wrapped myself in a large towel, went into my bedroom, and lit the fire laid in the hearth.

The flames soon gave the room an appearance of

warmth and normalcy, but still I sat, shaking and trembling with the spiritual cold he had inflicted on me. Tonight had been one of the strangest I had spent since Max had died. True, I was accustomed to his presence in my mind, had come to expect his appearance during the hunt and my feedings. But he had never seemed so real before, so alive. And he had never touched me, except in dreams, nor had he attempted to touch the living through me. Was the arrival of Chris the catalyst, the final event that unbalanced my mind? Would I eventually go mad, out of control, to be hunted down and killed like a rabid animal? I felt sane, but no doubt so did a thousand others who justified their actions by the authority of the voices in their minds.

"Damn you, Max," I said aloud. "You're supposed to be dead. Why don't you act it?"

There was no answer; my phantom chose his own time. I laughed at my own fancy. I knew Max was dead. I did not believe in ghosts and I did not truly believe that he had taken possession of me. I thought myself to be a rational, relatively modern creature, however ridiculous that seemed, and knew that there must be a rational explanation, both for me and for Mitch.

"Mitch," I whispered, "I'll be there soon." I sat staring at the flames, and the thought of him calmed me and the unnatural chill finally subsided.

Relaxed, stretching my body before the fire, I did something I had not allowed myself to do for two years. I called his features to mind, his intensely blue eyes, his hawklike nose, the small wrinkles that formed on his face when he smiled. I remembered his hands, their strength and slightly rough texture, molding themselves into my cool skin; his body, scarred but beautiful, lying warm and alive next to mine. I could taste him now, his flesh and blood, hear his voice in love and in anger.

Why did I ever leave him? And when I returned, would I have the strength to leave again?

"Damn," I swore again, and went to the window. I could sense the approaching dawn, and knew that I must sleep. From force of habit I pulled the blinds down, closed the heavy drapes, and climbed into bed, wrapping the covers around me. The warmth of my rejuvenating body enclosed me, and I focused entirely on the life and vibrancy now coursing through my veins. Oblivion came quickly, and I slept.

The cemetery gates swing open soundlessly. The gravel paths pull me forward and I follow as if in a trance, allowing them to lead me to the grave that I long, and dread, to find. In my tightly clenched fist I hold a rose, his rose; the thorns drive themselves deeply into the flesh of my palm. My blood, so long ago violated and invaded, contaminated beyond redemption, drips on to the earth, blackening its once-pure surface.

There is no need to call his name; the blood calls for me, drawing him up close enough to draw me down. The moist smell of rotting flesh assails my senses, so much death and corruption surrounds me. I open my mouth to scream, but it fills with the soil of his grave and I drop deeper into his domain, helpless in the power of his grasp.

Suddenly my limbs are free, and I am cleansed from the stench of the grave. I hover, disembodied, in a clear, starlit sky over an expansive field. It smells green and young and beautiful, and I inhale its fragrance deeply.

But I am not alone. Above me hangs another shape, darker and more defined. It swoops; I struggle to avoid it before it merges with my soul. Too late, the shock of penetration overcomes me and we are one. I am forced to see through his eyes; his voice, my voice, speaks words of reassurance.

"Do not fight me, my love," it advises. "It will be made right."

Far below, unaware of our approach, lies a body reveling in the warm spring night. She is naked but unashamed, young, beautiful, and wholly desirable. We circle above her, then descend with the currents of the wind, slowly spiraling down, until she senses our nearness and opens her eyes.

She smiles and opens her arms to us. I want to warn her, to tell her to run and hide, but the lightning shock of recognition makes it impossible for me to speak.

"But see," his voice urges. "See how it was for me."

And I am in his mind. I see how I was, for it is my human self who lies before us on the altar of our hunger. She draws me to her and I want to take her for myself. She is so young, so alive, and her knowledge of that life is childlike and pure. Oh, how I long for that innocence again, and so I claim her. And in that claiming, that rape of myself, the innocence is lost.

Her tears are mine as I break through the surface of the grave and lie panting, sobbing, on the violated earth.

When I awoke the next afternoon it was shortly before sunset. I shook my mind clear of the dream images; already vague and fading, they left only a faint residue of sorrow and bitterness. With a sigh I turned myself to the tasks ahead of me.

I remained in bed and phoned the airport, reserving two one-way tickets on the next flight back to America. The departure and arrival times were perfectly timed. On my previous trip I had been forced to take a private jet to avoid any touch of sunlight; on my return, it seemed, the night would fly with me. Even with unexpected delays, we should still arrive in the evening hours, allowing me ample time to find a secure daytime resting place. I wondered with a fleeting smile if my old suite of rooms would still be available.

When the travel arrangements were made, I got up from bed and went to my closet. Most of my clothing was unsuitable for this trip, designed as it was for the seduction and capture of my unsuspecting victims. It was always my habit to start each segment of my life with a new identity. Everything from my existence as Deirdre Griffin had been discarded, traded in for clothing to fit my new persona. Finally, I removed two pairs of jeans and a few loose-fitting sweaters and threw them on the bed, along with contact lenses and the few personal items that were always with me: several old books, some letters, and a relatively new acquisition, the scrapbook detailing my life compiled by Larry Martin. I did not look through the book, but placed it on the bottom of the suitcase, shuddering at my remembrance of our final confrontation.

Poor, maddened Larry, who in reaching out for immortality, demanding vampire's blood at the cost of my life and his sanity, had ended his life with Mitch's bullet through his heart. I had not escaped unscathed: the shot had gone straight through Larry and grazed my shoulder. He had died, pinioning me to the floor with his body, his blood staining my clothes and skin. My physical wound had healed quickly, but for some reason his death still haunted me. Not as much as Max's did; still, I knew that I shared the responsibility of guilt, perhaps even carried the largest portion. Larry would never have lost control of his emotions or his mind but for me. I led him along the path to his death as surely as if I had pulled the trigger myself.

Yet, I thought, rationalizing the event once more, had

he lived, I would now be dead. Mitch's arrival had saved my life, and now I would attempt to do the same for him.

Covering the book with my clothing, I closed and locked the suitcase, then dressed. When I checked my image in the mirror, I laughed softly to myself. If Deirdre had any friends remaining, they would hardly recognize her in this outfit: black leather miniskirt, black knee-high boots, and black lace hose. And although the effect was softened slightly with a pale peach angora sweater, I doubted that my fashion-designer acquaintances would approve. But Mitch might, I thought with a mischievous grin as I surveyed the view of my body from the back.

If, my mind cautioned, he could be healed; if he could be returned to his former self; if he wanted me back in his life. I only had Chris's word on the endurance of his love. There had been no contact between us since the day I received his letter telling me he could not accept the conditions of my life. And although I fully understood his decision, knew it had been his only logical choice, my feelings for him remained unchanged. Even after two years of trading my body for sustenance from strangers, I still felt his blood in my veins, calling to me, crying for his presence.

I jumped nervously when the phone rang, then picked it up.

"Wake-up call." Chris's voice sounded cheerful and normal.

"Hello, Chris. Pack your bags, we leave at nine tonight."

"Great. Somehow, I knew you'd help. He'll get better, you'll see. Just having you there should make a huge difference to him. He's missed you so much."

"Well," I said noncommittally, "I suppose we will see about that soon. Just meet me at the pub around seven;

we can leave from there. I have a little business to conclude."

After hanging up with Chris, I neatened the bedroom and bath and went downstairs, gathering, as I descended, the clothes I had discarded on the stairs last night. Rolling them all into a ball, I threw them into the front closet, found my cloak, and wrapped it about my shoulders. After checking to see that the back door and the windows were locked and secure, I put the one extra front-door key into my pocket, picked up my suitcase, and went out into the street. I looked back at the dark house for just one moment, wondering if I would ever return. This place had never seemed like home to me; I could leave it with no regrets, no memories. It had been nothing more than a stopover—a rest from my travels.

When I arrived at the pub, Pete and several of our regulars were playing darts. He looked up at me, and the smile on his face faded slightly when he saw my suitcase. He left the game and came over to me.

"Going away, Dottie?"

"I'm afraid so, Pete. You see, that young man who stopped by yesterday is Mitch's son."

He nodded knowingly. He had no idea of what my life had been before I had arrived at his door in response to his advertisement for a barmaid, but I had mentioned Mitch and our attachment.

"So he wants you back. Not that I blame him, he should have sent for you a long time ago. He's a lucky fool, this Mitch of yours." He picked up my suitcase and set it behind the bar. "And when do you leave?"

"Tonight." I shrugged off my cloak and hung it on the hook, replacing it with an apron. "You see, it's an emergency and too complicated to explain right now, but when I get back, you can have the whole story."

He returned my smile. "I'll hold you to that, darlin'.

And what am I to do while you're gone? Where could I find as good a partner or as juicy a barmaid as you?"

"I am sorry, Pete," I began, but he laughed and gave me a fatherly pat on my behind.

"Now, don't you worry one minute over what I'll be doing. Sure and I'll miss you, but I'll manage fine. As long as you don't want to cash in your half of the business."

I matched his lighthearted tone as I opened the cash drawer and looked at the small amount of money it contained. "What, and miss out on all this profit? No, Pete, you will not get rid of me that easily."

"Good, then you can return to your Mitch with my blessings. But you be sure to tell him now that I said he should make an honest woman out of you."

I reached over and gave him a small hug. "I don't think there's much of a chance of that, but thank you for saying it." I handed him the extra front-door key. "Look after my place while I'm gone."

He nodded and turned his back to me for a minute, busying himself at the bar. When he turned around his eyes were slightly wet and he held up a full glass of stout for a toast.

"Listen, boys," Pete's voice echoed in the nearly empty room, "our little Dottie's going away." His announcement was met with laughter from the customers. We hadn't made any attempt to keep our conversation private, so they had overheard every word. Still, it was just like Pete to make this an occasion for celebration. "Drinks on the house."

By seven o'clock the party was getting out of hand. Pete was leading the growing crowd in a second rendition of "Knees Up, Mother Brown" when Chris entered. The bell on the door clanged in a tone of finality, and the singing stopped. I introduced Chris and made my good-byes quietly, with a word for each of the regulars and a long kiss for Pete that caused them all to hoot and applaud. With a courtliness that belonged to another age, he solemnly consigned my suitcase to the waiting cabbie, and clapped Chris on the shoulder.

"Take care of our Dorothy, young man. And Dottie, you come back soon, darlin'."

I hugged him one more time and got into the cab. Chris moved around to the other side and slammed his door. As we drove off, I turned and gave Pete a final wave, watching until he went back inside, then settled into my seat and sighed.

"Deirdre"—Chris reached over and lightly, tentatively, touched my arm—"are you okay?"

I looked at his young, eager face and felt a poignant wave of sadness. "Over a hundred years of good-byes—you'd think I would be used to it by now. But every time it hurts."

The cabbie gave a small chuckle. "If you're a hundred years old, lady, then I'm the Prince of Wales. The airport, right?"

"That's right, Charlie," I said with forced cheerfulness. "We need to make a nine o'clock flight."

Three hours into the flight, when most of the passengers were asleep, I became aware that Chris was watching me, the window reflecting a thoughtful expression on his face. We had eaten dinner—rare prime rib for me, seafood for him—and drunk numerous glasses of wine. Our conversation had been commonplace, merely a relating of personal events happening over the past two years. We both avoided the mention of Mitch, or the plans we should be making for our return. After our meal he had occupied himself with magazines and a paperback detective novel, a taste he and his father shared, I noted with a small smile. And I had watched out the window, thinking of nothing but the clear black sky and the clouds below us, billowing and curling.

I turned away from the night and smiled at him. "It is a beautiful night for flying, don't you think?"

He nodded. "Yeah, but planes always make me a little nervous. How about you?"

"Nervous? No, I feel perfectly at home right now." I spoke mostly to put him at ease, but realized as I said it that it was true. The overhead lights were dimmed, with only a few reading lights to illuminate the darkness. Well fed and rejuvenated, my body was satisfied, and my mind content to contemplate nothing but the warmth of the cabin, the faint human scent of the passengers, and the night sky outside. "I could fly like this forever."

"Well," Chris said with a wry, almost bitter smile, "I'm glad someone is enjoying themselves."

"Chris, I'm as worried as you about Mitch."

He looked down at the book on his lap, folded down the corner of a page to mark his place, and slid it into his coat pocket. "Deirdre, we need to talk about this before we land. There are things you need to know."

"Fine, Chris, go ahead."

He threw me a doubtful look and glanced around the plane. The passengers nearest us were sleeping, but he lowered his voice to a near whisper anyway. "I know you insist that there are no other vampires, just you and Max, but you must know that's impossible. There have to be others."

"I don't deny their existence, Chris. Of course I know that somewhere there must be others. I just can't see that they would have any relevance to Mitch or me."

"That's exactly what Dad thought—until they began coming to him at night, tormenting him, deviling him." His eyes darted restlessly before returning to me. "I, well, I don't quite know how to say this without it sounding callous or hard. I don't really mean it that way, honest, but that's why Dad didn't contact you himself. He was determined to take it on, to keep it from you so that you wouldn't be involved in any way."

"Involved in what, Chris?"

He clenched his fists, and his voice grew louder. "But you are involved, aren't you? And in taking the responsibility for your actions, my father is being punished. It's your place, Deirdre; you're the one they want. So, I came to get you, hoping that you would still have enough humanity to respond."

"And I did, it would appear." I reached over and laid my hand on his trembling arm. "I'll help all I can, you know that."

"Yeah," he said, shrinking away from my hand, "and that only makes it worse, somehow. You see, I haven't really brought you back to just save Dad. The others, they want the one who killed Max, and right now they think it's Dad. But when you arrive, I don't see how even you can hide your involvement." Chris looked at me, his eyes shining with unshed tears, his face showing fear and guilt. "Oh, God, I'm sorry. They want you dead, Deirdre, and I've brought you to them."

# Chapter 4

I began to laugh, softly at first, then louder, with only a small trace of hysteria. Chris looked at me in disbelief, and a stewardess rushed to our seats.

"Miss, ah, Grey"—she consulted her passenger listing—"we'll be landing in less than three hours. Would you like another drink? Or maybe a pillow or blanket? Most of our passengers find that resting is a good way to pass the time."

"I understand," I said, still choked with laughter. "I am sorry, and yes, I would like another glass of wine. Thank you for asking."

Her arched brows told me she thought I had already had enough, but she dutifully fetched my drink. After she left I took one long sip and, sufficiently calmed, turned to Chris. The expression on his face had changed from guilt to embarrassment. I smiled in my most reassuring manner, but he relaxed only slightly.

"Look, Chris, I think it is very sweet of you to be concerned about me, but I can take care of myself. And if I can't"—I shrugged—"well, I'll deal with that if it happens." I turned my face to the window again. "It wouldn't be that great a loss, after all."

He wasn't meant to hear my last words, but his ears were sharper than I thought.

"How can you say that? Doesn't your life mean anything to you at all?"

"Chris," I sighed, forcing my gaze away from the night sky, "I'm old and tired. I have led an interesting life, if you can call it that. I've lived through three major wars, and more historical events than you can remember. Everyone I have ever known or loved has died or will die, while I go on virtually forever. And what sort of legacy do I leave? A few dresses on a rack somewhere, a couple of pages in some lousy scrapbook, or maybe just a hazy memory locked inside the head of some man I met in a bar, someone I subsequently and cold-heartedly drained of a portion of his blood so that I could live." I shook my head slightly. "No, Chris, it would not be that great a loss."

"But what about Dad?" His tone of voice was indignant and belligerent, his expression and question displaying such a youthful ignorance that, unexpectedly, I grew angry.

"What about him? He wants no part of me, a fact he made quite plain in the letter he sent less than two years ago. I would be a sorry fool if I believed anything else."

"Oh." Chris gave me an odd look. He opened his mouth and shut it quickly, as if he wanted to say something else, then thought better of it. He shook his head instead. "Why did you agree to come back with me?"

I sat quietly for a moment, listening to Max's laughter echoing in my head. "Now's the time, my dear, to give him the speech. You know, that one about how the future doesn't matter, about how you have to be with the man you love. You were quite eloquent about it once, if I remember correctly."

"Just stay out of it," I murmured, turning my face to the window.

"What?"

I looked back at Chris and gave him a half smile. "You are right, Chris." Laughing softly at my own folly, I continued. "It seems a shame that over a century of living did not make me smarter, but where your father is concerned, I am a fool. Now"—I reached over and gently smoothed his hair—"settle back and get some sleep. I have some thinking to do."

It was raining when we landed in New York, a cold rain, soft but insistent. Due to a technical problem at the gates, we had to walk from the plane to the terminal, and although the airline supplied umbrellas, we were still completely soaked by the time we got inside. The airport was crowded; somehow I had managed to forget just how many people lived in New York. We arrived at the baggage claim, and I was trembling, not with the wetness of my clothes and hair, but with the overwhelming presence of so many humans. My senses were deluged by the odor, the jostling, the warmth of these living bodies all pressed together. I leaned against the wall and rubbed my hands over my face, feeling faint and exhilarated at the same time.

"You okay?" Chris came over to me, our suitcases in hand.

I nodded weakly. "Can we go now?"

He led the way through the airport, and eventually we burst through the front doors into the night. I sighed my relief; he hailed a taxi and we got in.

"Where are you staying?"

I looked over at Chris. "I haven't made any arrangements yet. I had thought I might go back to my old place."

He reached into his pocket and handed me a set of keys. "Dad's place is empty right now. Why don't you stay there for a while?"

I looked at the keys and hesitated.

"Go on," he urged. "Why spend the money for a hotel? I'd feel better knowing you were there. Besides, I live just a few blocks away; it would be more convenient."

"Fine," I agreed, "but just for now."

When we arrived at Mitch's apartment, Chris walked in with me and opened the door. It was exactly as it had been when Mitch lived there. Except for the musty, unoccupied odor that lingered in the air, it was as if he had just stepped out for a moment.

"I hope it's okay." Chris glanced around doubtfully. "I cleaned up the best I could."

I looked at the room, the books neatly lined up, the tables dusted, the vacuum cleaner tracks on the carpet, and felt a small shiver of déjà vu. "I see that you Greers are all the same."

"What?"

"Oh, nothing." I gave a small laugh at his confusion but did nothing to explain myself. The similarity to his father was almost uncanny: the neatness, the expectation of my arrival was so much like Mitch's attitude that I could almost feel his presence.

"Well"—Chris moved nervously toward the door—"if everything is okay, I guess I'd better be going. I'll call you tomorrow and we'll go see Dad."

"That would be fine. Call around sunset. I assume there are visiting hours at night?"

"Seven to nine," he informed me. "We should probably leave here no later than six."

"Great. See you then. Good night."

He closed the door and I heard him go down the stairs and out the front door. The cab door closed, the motor surged, and he was gone, leaving me alone with my memories.

For a time I wandered through the apartment, studying the rows of books, amazed once more at their variety. Idly, I ran my finger down the spines of the books, then went into the kitchen. The refrigerator was empty except for two bottles of wine. Silently thanking Chris for his forethought, I poured myself a glass from one and carried it and my suitcase into the bedroom.

This room was also clean—too clean, it seemed to me, but I restrained the urge to open my valise and throw the clothes about. Instead, I opened the closet and looked at Mitch's clothes. A faint smell arose from them, and I closed my eyes for a minute to isolate the aroma, to breathe it in more deeply, to fill my lungs with the odor of him.

"Damn." I turned away from the closet and left the room. All at once I felt restless and trapped, and knew that I could not sleep there that night. Tomorrow during the sunlight would be soon enough. I picked up the phone and called a taxi.

The cemetery gates were locked and the graveyard was surrounded by a tall, heavy fence. Smiling to myself about the old joke, I reached down and grasped the padlock in my hand, looking up and down the street to see if I was being observed. There was no one in sight. I had sent the cab driver away, and who else in their right mind would be visiting a cemetery at night? Who, indeed, I thought with a small laugh as I pulled the lock apart, pushed open the gates, and closed them again behind me.

Walking quickly, I passed through the older section, where the tombstones were tilted at odd angles and the ground gently rounded. As if from a great distance, the noises outside the gates seemed muffled and indistinct. Even the sounds of my passage were muted; the scratching sounds of my boots on the gravel were no more than a whisper in the night.

I had received directions to the grave site when I had purchased the plot, and as I entered the newer section,

I recited the landmarks to myself. "Three trees clumped on the right, two benches and a water faucet, then the third grave to the left." It turned out to be nothing like my dreams, but then, I thought with a shrug, what is?

The granite marker stood tall and proud, bearing the simple inscription over which I had commiserated for much too long, especially when one viewed the final result: his name, the date on which he died, and one word, "Father." I had considered many inscriptions—some were humorous, some slandering or sentimental—but realized finally that my feelings about Max were too confused, too convoluted, and had settled for that one relationship. It made little difference that somewhere else lay another much-loved person under that same title; his earthly remains had long since gone to dust, and Max, I reasoned, was truly the father of the creature I had become.

I stood for a long time, contemplating his grave. I waited for his voice in my mind, his step on the path, the emergence of his grasping hands. There was nothing but silence. Feeling oddly at ease, I sat down on top of his grave and leaned against the tombstone. The grass was icy and the stalks pushed themselves into my stockings, but the earth remained still and I was alone.

"Max." I addressed him solemnly, my quiet voice forcing strange echoes from the surrounding stones. "I want to make peace. We have paid for your death. Both Mitch and I have paid. Let it go. Let *us* go."

There was no response, not even a glimmer of his presence. I laughed softly at myself, for I already knew that he chose his own time, his own appearances. But still I sat for some time, thinking, weighing the actions of my past, searching my mind for any alternatives that could have been chosen over his death. I came to the same conclusion as always: he had given me no choice; his death had been unavoidable. And although I regretted the deed and missed his presence as acutely as I would a piece of my own body, I knew finally that, given the same situation, I would kill him again.

I rose from the ground slowly and with a sigh. This was as much peace as I would realize, tonight or any other. There was nothing here for me; there never was. I brushed away the dead leaves that had adhered to the back of my cloak. As my hands touched them, they crumbled, but the brittle crunching sounds they made did not disguise the approaching footsteps. I stiffened and remained standing with my back to the path, not really wishing to face this apparition.

"Deirdre?" There was surprise in his voice, and recognition. "It is you, is it not? It's been a long time."

I relaxed. The slightly accented voice seemed vaguely familiar, but it was not Max's. I turned around.

I knew that we had met before, but I could not quite remember his name. He was distinguished, handsome, and his clothing spoke softly of old money. I pulled my cloak together and folded one arm over it, ashamed of my own apparel, suited more for the life I led in England than the one I had led in America. But I gave him a gracious smile and extended my other hand to him. "So nice to see you again, Mr., ah . . ." I felt myself blushing, wishing I could remember his name.

"Lange. Victor Lange."

Even before he said it, his name and the situation surrounding our meeting came back to me. The recollection caused me to shiver slightly. He had been the one to give me the final clue that enabled me to discover who Max really was. I regretted his role in the affair. Eventually Max would have dropped his shield and let me know himself. Perhaps his death could have been avoided. I looked at him with an uncertain smile, wondering if he knew he had been indirectly involved in the killing of his friend.

He took my hand and raised it to his mouth. His lips moved delicately over my knuckles and he laughed. "But of course you wouldn't remember me. We met only once, and that, briefly."

"I do remember you, Mr. Lange. After all, it's been only two years. But I am surprised that you remember me."

He dropped my hand and smiled at me. "How could I ever forget someone like you? Besides, I've been waiting for you. Max said you would come here sooner or later. I walk here often, watching for you."

I jumped, startled. "Max said?" I questioned him, my voice raised to a higher pitch than normal. "But Max is—"

"Dead," he interrupted, his charm lost suddenly in the flare of anger. "A most regrettable occurrence." His eyes glittered in the moonlight and I, barely aware of my reaction, backed away a few steps from him. He noticed my movement, and his expression and voice softened. "Forgive my poor use of the language, I didn't mean to alarm you. Max never actually said it to me. It was merely a part of the stipulations of his will: that I should watch for you after his death."

"His will? But what has that to do with me?" I gave him a suspicious glance. "Or you, for that matter?"

Victor threw his head back and laughed loudly. "How like Max to not tell you. He was always such a secretive bastard, wasn't he? I won't keep you in suspense any longer, Deirdre. I am executor of his will and you, well, you are a very rich lady."

"Rich?" I shrugged slightly. "I was rich before. How much did he leave me?"

"Everything he had, my dear. You are his sole heir."

I stared at him in shock for a second, then repeated in disbelief, "His sole heir?"

Victor nodded, smiled, and took my arm. "I knew he

hadn't told you, although I advised him to many times over. Max always insisted that he had all the time in the world, that he would explain everything at the right moment." He began to walk back down the path, gently urging me along.

"Well," I said, hoping that the bitterness I felt did not show, "that moment never came."

"No." His tone was noncommittal as he pushed the front gates open, giving first the padlock and then me a quick, curious glance. "Careless of the caretakers to leave these unlocked."

"But so convenient for late-night visitors."

He gave me a shrewd look, then smiled and patted my arm. "You can't imagine how good it is to see you alive and well. When you disappeared after Max's death, I was very worried."

"Why would you be worried?"

He did not answer the question right away. "I left town on business the very night he was murdered. By the time I returned, Max was buried and you were gone. Without a trace, I might add. I'm afraid I may have jumped to the wrong conclusion, not that it matters at this point."

I looked at him expectantly, but he seemed deep in thought. "And that conclusion was?" I prompted Victor.

He shook his head briefly and gave a small, angry laugh. "It does seem ridiculous now that I consider it again. I rather thought that Greer had killed you also. And hid your body."

"Mitch Greer? Why on earth would you have thought that?"

Victor shrugged. "As I said, it doesn't matter at this point. What is important is that you are here now, and safe. We'll need to get together sometime soon. I have many papers for you to sign. Where will you be staying?"

"At a friend's apartment." My privacy was still a major

concern, and I saw no need for Victor to know where I would be—especially that I would be at Mitch's place. There was too much I did not know about him and his anger at Max's death was still strong. The vehemence with which he said Mitch's name proved it. "I'll call you at the Imperial, if that's suitable."

"Fine." He waved and a car pulled up to the curb. The driver emerged, nodded to us, and opened the back door. Victor motioned for me to enter, but I shook my head.

"I think I'll just stay around for a while and go home later. It's a lovely night."

He glanced at the sky and smiled his agreement. "If I were thirty years younger, Deirdre, I would be pleased to stay and keep you company. But watch yourself; this is not exactly the best neighborhood around."

I stood on the curb and watched as they drove away. After they were gone from sight, I glanced back once more at the quiet cemetery, then began to walk slowly in the direction of Mitch's place. Three blocks away I hailed a taxi and rode back home.

# Chapter 5

To my surprise, I did sleep that night and the rest of the next day as well. And although I dreamed, it was not of Max. Mostly I dreamed of Mitch, of the days and nights we had shared, of sunlit times together that were pure fantasy. All the same, I knew how he would look in the sunlight, his eyes lightened, squinting slightly, his hair reflecting shimmers of gold and silver. They were peaceful dreams of laughter and love, with no taint of blood or death. I woke with a smile on my face.

Stretching luxuriously, enjoying the smell of the clean sheets, I tested my hunger response. When thoughts of biting and drinking aroused no response, no growth of the canines, and no inner raging, I knew that I would remain sated for the next few days. I had fed only two nights ago and fed well.

I shuddered slightly at the thought of Robbie, his urgency, and my own needs. Having remained celibate for more than twenty years until I had met Mitch, it had been alarmingly easy to fall back into promiscuity. His final denial of me, and the presence of Max, had pushed me into my old ways: the trading of sex for blood. And although each time I found myself repulsed, sickened by the bartering, I did have the feeling that this way was more honest, more fair. My victims got what they wanted, as did I. But it had never occurred to me how I would explain the situation to Mitch—I had never expected to see him again.

I rose and dressed in jeans and a sweater and went out to the kitchen to pour myself a glass of wine. I had almost finished it, when the phone rang.

"Hello." My voice was tentative; I felt like an intruder here, without Mitch. I need not have worried, however, for it was Chris, right on schedule.

"Hi, it's Chris. Did you sleep okay?"

"Fine, thank you."

"Well, I just wondered; I called last night when I got home, but there was no answer."

"I went out for a walk."

"Oh." His voice sounded tense and disapproving. I guess he assumed I was out feeding already.

"Just a walk, Chris, nothing else."

"Oh." The intonation was different this time, embarrassed maybe, or apologetic. I laughed slightly, thinking that actually he had made the adjustment to the truth about his father's lover fairly well considering the enormity of it all.

"Something funny?"

"No, Chris, not really. Will we be leaving soon?"

"Yeah, I'll be by in about fifteen or twenty minutes." He paused for a second. "But that might not be enough notice, I'm sorry. Can you be ready?"

"Of course. See you then." I hung up the phone and rushed into the bathroom to apply my makeup and contact lenses.

After I had coaxed some color into my pale complexion, inserted a pair of green lenses, and brushed my dyed black hair, I stepped back and studied the results in the mirror. "Not too bad," I said aloud with only a bit of a frown, "but first thing tomorrow night I need some clothes and a new dye job."

"I don't know, my love, I've gotten used to the color. It makes you look more the part."

There was no reflection in the mirror, but when I swung around, Max was leaning in the doorway, his lips curved in the condescending smile I remembered so well. The outline of his body was hazy though, and when I looked at him straight on, he seemed to fade in and out of my vision.

"Go back to hell, where you belong, Max." I pushed past him as if he weren't there. And he wasn't. Still, my breathing had quickened and my pulse raced slightly. Hurriedly, I picked up my cloak and bag, turned out the lights, closed and locked the apartment door.

Chris was waiting, parked a few yards down the street. He blew the horn when I walked down the steps and waved to me. I waved back and got into the passenger side.

"You okay, Deirdre?"

"Yes, why?" My voice was raspy, and I coughed to cover it up.

"Well, I don't know, you look a little pale."

"Is that supposed to be a joke?" I snapped in response.

"Oh, no, not really. Forget it, okay?"

He drove in silence for a while, concentrating on the traffic, ignoring, as much as possible, my presence in the car. Finally he cleared his throat and glanced over at me.

"You know," he began hesitantly, "I seem to keep saying the wrong things to you. I don't mean to make you angry; it's just sometimes I don't know what to say. I've never been in the presence of someone like you."

"But you have, Chris. We spent some time together before I left town. Can you remember how you treated me then?"

"Yeah." A reluctant smile crept over his face. "We

played pool. You skunked Dad every game. He really hated to lose." The smile faded. "But it's all different now that I know."

"It shouldn't be, Chris. I'm exactly the same person I was then."

"Are you?"

"Yes," I said, but my voice lacked conviction. "Yes," I said again, stronger this time, and with more defiance. "I am the same."

"Okay," he agreed, turning into the parking lot of a large hospital. "If you promise to not be too touchy about it all, I'll try just a little harder to forget."

When he finally found a parking space, he turned off the engine and the lights. I reached over for the door handle, but his touch on my arm stopped me.

"Deirdre, before we go in, I think you should know a little of what to expect."

I nodded. "Tell me."

He looked out the window intently; his voice was soft and pained. "He probably won't know you, most likely won't even acknowledge your presence. Dad hasn't spoken coherently for about two months now. He eats only when they feed him and he has absolutely no contact with reality—a total withdrawal from everything around him."

He sighed and continued. "We've tried all sorts of stimulation for him, but nothing works. Physically he checks out okay; other than looking like hell and having lost about thirty pounds, he's in excellent health. But mentally, he's gone." He choked on the last words, and I could see the glistening of tears in his eyes. "He may never get back to normal, never be what he once was. But if we can get a reaction from him, just one reaction, they think they might get somewhere."

I closed my eyes, letting the blackness enfold me, wrapping myself in the starkness of Chris's words. One of the first things that had attracted me about Mitch was his sharpness—the alertness in his eyes, the feeling that he was totally alive and a hunter, akin to me. The fact that he might spend the rest of his life in an autistic state was unthinkable, obscene. I wanted to cry, wanted to rage and scream against the fate forced on him. And I knew that should he prove unredeemable, those who had driven him to this extremity must pay with their lives.

Wearily, I put my hands up to my face and sighed. Was I always to be at odds with the others of my kind; would I never find rest from revenge and murder? When I lowered my hands and opened my eyes, Chris was staring at me, expectantly waiting for some sort of response.

"Dammit, Chris, I told you before I can't work miracles. You tell me that for over a year and a half he's been in the care of some of the best psychiatric experts in this city and yet you seem to expect that I can succeed where they have failed. Don't lay this entirely on my back. His case just might be as hopeless as they all think."

"But don't you see, it's not entirely hopeless—it can't be. He's holding on for something. He's still alive, and where there's life there's—"

"No," I interrupted. "Don't preach that adage to me. I've been dead so long, I've forgotten what life is like. But I will try, Chris. I will do my best to get a reaction."

"It may take a while, and a lot of visits. It could be months or even years." He looked over at me questioningly, pleading for my understanding, my cooperation.

"What the hell," I said vehemently, repeating words I had said to his father not long ago but somehow an entire lifetime away. "I have all the time in the world. Shall we go in?"

I hate hospitals; so many memories are evoked by

their appearance and odors, recalling death and war and sickness. This place was no different from others I had been in: It had the same sickly-sweet disinfectant smell, the sour odors of sweat and urine. But it was clean, sterile, and almost cheerful in an infantile way. Brightly colored posters and prints decorated the otherwise stark white walls, and the nurses' station where we checked in was gaudily trimmed for an early Valentine's Day.

Most of the patients were aged, tired, and confused, walking the halls in a shuffling old-man gait, mumbling soundlessly to themselves. I shuddered at the sight of them, at the ravages of time, disease, and unkindness. Knowing that most of them had been toothless babies long after I had reached the age of sixty made me feel uneasy, guilty. I yearned to run back down the hall and hide in the darkness of the night.

Chris must have felt my hesitation, for he put a gentle hand on my elbow and steered me into a central room. A nurse greeted him by name and with a smile. I ignored their quiet conversation, concentrating instead on a search for Mitch. He wasn't there; I couldn't feel the slightest suggestion of his presence. Then as I half turned to Chris and the nurse, hearing her say to him that no, there had been no change while he was away, I saw him, and the shock of his appearance sent a terrible chill through my spine.

I had already observed the tall, too slender form standing at the grated-over window. He had laid his face against the grill, and his hands were splayed out beside him, grasping at the wire, scratching to get out into the night. His hair was totally gray and my eyes had passed over him, almost discarding him, until he turned to the side and I saw his profile.

"Dear God." I gasped at the change in him and took a few tentative steps toward him. My movement attracted his attention for just one second; his haunted, non-focused eyes touched mine, then flew away. He shuffled over to a nearby chair, and as he walked, he spoke, the words too quiet for me to hear. But there seemed a familiar rhythm to the movement of his lips, and I looked over at the nurse questioningly.

"Go ahead," she urged me, "try to speak to him. He's not violent."

The room seemed endless, but eventually I stood right in front of Mitch. He remained staring at the floor, and I discovered that he was not speaking, but singing.

" 'Into the ward of the clean, whitewashed walls . . .' "

"Mitch."

There was no response from him, but the song continued. " 'Where the dead slept and the dying lay . . .' "

"Mitch," I said, louder this time. "It's Deirdre, I'm back. Can you hear me?"

His eyes moved from the floor and fastened on my face. There was no recognition, no spark to show me that this was the man I loved. But his voice grew more agitated, louder, as he sang the next lines. " 'Wounded by bayonet, saber, and ball, somebody's darling was borne one day.' "

I knelt in front of his chair. His eyes followed me and he jumped and shivered as I grasped his warm hands between my cold ones. I did not speak this time, but sang with him instead.

" 'Somebody's darling, somebody's pride, who'll tell his mother where her boy died?' "

After the first four words his voice faltered and stopped, but I continued, feeling slightly foolish. His eyes darted nervously, trying to avoid my face, but eventually I drew them back to me and still holding on to his hands, gently urged him out of the chair. He was trembling violently under my touch, but that merely encouraged me, and I spoke his name again.

"Mitch."

This time I connected. I knew he heard me and understood; his hands tightened on mine and he whispered my name. Then before I could react, he quickly dropped my hands, formed a fist, and silently punched me in the jaw, striking me with such force that I fell to the floor.

As I pulled myself up, shaking my head and gingerly feeling my jaw, I saw him running from the room, pursued by a nurse and two orderlies.

I stood, swaying in the air slightly, oblivious of the uproar Mitch's action must have been causing around me. The noise level in the room rose and, as if from a long distance, I could hear the laughing and crying and shouting of the rest of the patients in the room. But my eyes were fastened on the door through which he had disappeared.

What the hell did you expect, you fool, I thought. A passionate embrace, a warm welcome-back kiss? His eyes had been the eyes of one who looked on hell, and I had helped to put him there.

I looked over to where Chris stood, open-mouthed, staring at me. The nurse who had been talking to us came over with a piece of gauze, dabbing at my bleeding lip, making her apologies over and over. Irritated, I shrugged her away and gave Chris a small, bitter smile, wincing somewhat with the pain.

"Tell me, Chris, was that enough of a reaction for you, or shall we try again?"

# Chapter 6

"Oh, my God, Miss . . ." the nurse began.

"Griffin."

"Miss Griffin, I would never have expected that to happen. No one here would have. Mitch has never shown any tendency toward violence the entire time he's been here. I just can't imagine what got into him."

"I did."

She gave me a strange look. "What?"

"Never mind, it doesn't matter."

"I hope you understand that we can't be held liable for this event. I mean, if we thought he would hit you, we would never have let you approach him. It's not a case of negligence, and I sincerely apologize for your discomfort. Shall I get a doctor for you?"

I laughed. "I don't need a doctor, thank you. And I promise I will not sue you. I believe I finally got what was coming to me."

Puzzled, she cocked her head at me, obviously wanting more information. I chose not to elaborate. Her obvious fawning was beginning to anger me.

"Think nothing more of it." The finality in my voice drove her away, and I went out into the hallway to find Chris.

Since there was no sign of him, I assumed he had gone to Mitch's room; I found a small waiting area and sat down. Picking up a newspaper, I began to catch up on current events. I was thoroughly engrossed in the crossword puzzle when a shadow fell across the page. "Jesus," I swore under my breath, afraid to look up, not knowing who it was. Mitch, come to take another shot at me, perhaps? Maybe my very own personal ghost, here to gloat over my disastrous choice of loving a human? Who it was made no real difference to me. I had no desire to see or talk to anyone else this evening.

"Just go away and leave me alone." I sounded surly even to myself, but didn't care. "I've had trouble enough for one night."

"I'm sure you have, but it's important. Please?"

And because I did not recognize the voice, I glanced at the speaker. He was tall and dark with a fresh-scrubbed sincerity in his face, his jacket and stethoscope identifying him immediately.

"Ah, one of the resident white-coats. I told the nurse I didn't need a doctor."

"Miss Griffin." He smiled broadly, ignoring my bad temper. "I'm John Samuels, Mitch's doctor. My friends call me Sam."

He extended his hand and I reached up to shake it. "Dr. Samuels," I said coolly, "what can I do for you?"

His smile faded only slightly. "You may have already done it. I just wondered if you could spare a little of your time and talk to me about Mitch. There's so much going on here, I can't tell you how excited we all are. He's talking again—a little disoriented, true, but that's to be expected—but, good God, he's talking clearly and lucidly."

His enthusiasm was contagious. Reluctantly I returned his smile and agreed. "I have nowhere else to go, Doctor, and nothing but time on my hands. I am at your disposal."

"Thank you."

I rose from the chair. He smiled and escorted me to his office.

As he settled in behind his desk, I sat uncomfortably, glancing casually around his office. He gave me a long, appraising look, then reached into the top drawer, extracting an ashtray, a pack of cigarettes, and an engraved gold-plated lighter.

"I won't smoke one now," he said with a guilty look. "It just calms me to have them here." Then he laughed. "I know, you think that as a doctor I should have more control, more sense, don't you?"

"I think nothing of the sort. You are human; you may do as you like."

"Why did you say that? 'You are human.' What does that mean?"

I shrugged. "Oh, you know what I mean." My voice sounded relaxed and even, betraying none of my inner turmoil. "It has been a rather extraordinary evening, as you well know. As for me"—I smiled encouragingly—"I don't mind if you smoke, provided you share."

"Fine." He offered the pack, I took one, and reached for the lighter. "Allow me," he said graciously, and quickly struck the flame. I cupped my hand around his as I lit the cigarette, inhaled deeply, then sat back and looked at him.

"Miss Griffin," he began tentatively, "your hands are shaking."

"So?"

"Well, if I had a suspicious mind, I might begin to wonder why you are so nervous and so hostile."

"How fortunate for me"—I couldn't hide the sarcasm in my voice—"that you do not have a suspicious mind. Can I be honest with you, Dr. Samuels?"

"Absolutely, but call me Sam, please."

"Well then, Sam, I do not like hospitals or doctors. It's nothing personal; I am sure you are very good at what you do, I would even be willing to believe that somewhere beneath your charming bedside manner lies a real person." I took another drag on my cigarette, then reached forward to flick the growing ash away. "Right now, however, I would like nothing more than to leave. It seems quite apparent that my presence is a disturbing influence on Mitch." My voice broke on his name and I looked away from Sam's intent gaze.

"And you were hurt by his reaction, surprised?"

"Not surprised." I paused for a minute and thought. "Not at all. The entire event merely confirms what I suspected."

He said nothing, but reached over and lit a cigarette for himself. He kept the lighter in his hands and tapped it on the desk, turning it over, reading the inscription. Finally he looked up at me. "Well?"

Suddenly the anger and frustration I had been reining in since I arrived exploded. "Dammit, he threw me back into the world almost two years ago, forcing me to live the kind of life that even you, with your undoubtedly keen insight into the human psyche, cannot imagine. His son coerces me back with the story that only I can save him. And then to be met with such hatred, such pain." I pressed my fingers against my eyes to prevent the flow of tears. "I never meant for him to be hurt." My voice softened, and Sam leaned forward to catch my words. "I wanted him, I loved him. Love him, more than I have ever loved any man, and this is what my love did to him." I lowered my hands and balled them into fists.

"Miss Griffin." The doctor's voice was compassionate, warm, and I relaxed. When I opened my hands, there was a slight smell of burnt flesh, and I looked down with surprise at the stub of the cigarette crushed between my fingers. I dropped it into the ashtray.

His concern for me showing in his face, Sam stood up and moved toward me. "Did you burn yourself?"

"No."

"May I see?"

"No." Petulantly, I put my hands behind my back.

"Miss Griffin . . ."

I looked at him for a minute. "Oh, what the hell. Call me Deirdre. If I stay here much longer, you will manage to worm out all my deepest secrets." I smiled at him, honestly this time, for I was beginning to like him. "Damn, you are good at this doctor thing, aren't you?"

He flushed at my praise and sat back down at his desk. "Yeah, I'd like to hope so. Do you feel better?"

"Yes, I think so."

"Then maybe we can start over. Deirdre"—he nodded at me, acknowledging my permission to use the name—"how long ago did you and Mitch meet?"

"Two years ago, just a few days after Thanksgiving."

His head jerked in surprise. "Is that all?"

"Yes, why?"

"No reason, I just had the feeling that your relationship was of longer term than that."

"Does it matter?"

"Not really. And you left the country when?"

"New Year's Eve."

"The same year?"

I nodded and he reached over and put his cigarette out. "So you knew each other only a short time."

His statement seemed like a question. "Love at first sight?" I suggested in reply with only a small tinge of sarcasm.

"Could be." Sam met my eyes, and I saw a cautious admiration begin to form. "Do you mind my asking how old you are?"

I tried to evade the question, but quickly searched my

memory for the last recorded age for Deirdre Griffin. "What possible difference can that make?"

"None, I suppose. I hope I didn't offend you."

"Not at all, Sam. I'm thirty-eight."

He looked unconvinced. "I'd have guessed from your appearance that you were younger, but your eyes are older, somehow. You're an interesting case, Deirdre."

"Case?" I jumped up from the chair.

"Oh, sorry. I didn't mean that, it's just an expression we use around here. Please sit down again."

"Actually, I would like to leave now. I would be happy to come back and talk again sometime if you think it will help Mitch."

"Even if it doesn't, I'd like it."

"Are you flirting with me?"

He hung his head. "Yeah, I guess I am, maybe just a little."

I extended my hand. "Well, I'm flattered. Thank you."

Before Sam could shake my hand, Chris entered the office. "Deirdre, I'm so glad I found you. It's wonderful. He's better, really better. He wants to see you, wants to know if you're still here. I told him I'd find out."

I sighed, knowing that I could not face Mitch again, so soon after his initial and forceful rejection of me. "Tell him I'll come back tomorrow night. I have to go now."

"Wait!" Chris came after me. "I'll drive you home."

"No, you stay here with your father. I'd like to be alone."

Some habits die hard. For one of my kind, they can often be the only things that keep you alive. So I was not really surprised to discover that my walk led me that night to the Ballroom of Romance. More amazing was the fact that the club was still in business and open.

There was no crowd waiting at the door; its popularity as a night spot must have waned during the years I was away. The doorman was unfamiliar to me. His expression of bored disinterest was apparent as he pulled open the entrance.

Inside, everything was exactly as it was when I had left. The tables, the bar, the dancers—nothing had changed. I caught myself scanning the dance floor for someone I knew and stopped immediately. Who did I expect to see? Max? Larry? Dead, they are dead, I reminded myself, and would not return. Pushing gently through the group of people standing near an empty seat, I laid my bag down on the bar and ordered a drink.

I thanked the bartender for the prompt service when he brought my wine. At the sound of my voice the man tending the other end of the bar turned and glanced at me. His eyes narrowed, as if to focus more clearly in the dim light.

"Miss Griffin?" He recognized me and came over. "It is you. I thought so. Long time no see, huh?"

"Yes, it has been a while. How are you?" I could not remember his name, but I remembered quite plainly the scornful attitude he had shown me in the past. Now, however, he was pleasant, courteous, and respectful.

"Fine, thank you. Can't complain, I suppose. Can I get you something?"

I pointed to my full glass and shook my head. "But you can do me a favor, if you would."

"Anything for you, Miss Griffin. It's nice to have you back."

I listened for a sarcastic note in his voice and found none. I smiled at him. It was nice to meet someone I knew before who had no ulterior motives, no hidden resentment, no open hatred. "Well," I began, "I would like to look around a bit, you know, for old time's sake."

"Be my guest." He threw his arms wide in a welcoming gesture. "You're the boss."

"Thank you." I picked up my wine and headed toward the door that led into the offices and lounges behind the club. This too had not changed. I had a strange feeling that if I waited here long enough, I would see a younger Deirdre walk these halls, her intended victim in thrall, willing to follow, to give her what she wanted. I shivered slightly, then walked without hesitation to Max's office.

The room was dark, but I did not bother to put on the lights. There was no need; my night vision was good enough to see that it was exactly as Max had kept it. And I knew this room so well, I could find my way through it blindfolded.

I closed the door and leaned my face up against it. They had replaced either the entire door or the wood panels within it, for there were no gouges in the wood to show where the makeshift stake had entered, no indication that a living being had once hung impaled there, spewing its life on the floor. Even the carpet was new; there had been too much blood spilled for the stains to be removed. Nothing in this room gave any sign that a battle for life had been waged within its walls. It was sterile and empty, but still I searched for his presence. Surely he would be there if he were anywhere.

"Max." I whispered the name at first, then said it louder. There was no response. I took a drink of my wine and walked across the room to sit on the couch. "Dammit, Max, just like always. When I don't want to see you, you come around, and when I would like to talk, you're unavailable. It seems to me you're even less reliable dead than you were when you were alive."

I set my glass on the table, kicked off my shoes, and

lay down on the white leather sofa, staring at the ceiling. Unexpectedly, I began to cry, my sobs quiet, absorbed by the dark, lonely walls. I cried for myself, for Mitch, for all those I had loved now dead, and I cried for Max.

When I finished, I curled up into a ball and slept.

A soft moaning in the corner wakes me. Rising from the couch, I go to him, but it is too late. Mitch is dead, his face stretched in pain, gaunt and aged, his skin white and bloodless. The fang marks on his neck are mine.

"Deirdre." Max's voice causes the fine hairs on the back of my neck and arms to rise. I make no movement, but stand with my back to him, trembling.

"Deirdre." The name is a command; I am his, I always was. I turn around.

"You are dead, Max," I say, and look upon him. The flesh on his bones is shredded, rotting, and decayed. His finely sculptured face is now nothing more than a skull, but the mouth opens and talks.

"Deirdre, come to me. I am not dead."

I move forward one timid step. "Not dead?" I see the stake piercing his rib cage, see the wood of the door behind him splintered with the impact of the killing blow. "No." I cannot deny the evidence of my eyes. "You are dead."

"Not dead, my love, for you still live and I am with you." One skeletal hand grips the implement of his death, but the other beckons. "Come to me."

My legs walk toward him, my body obeys him. But my mind is screaming, I am screaming.

His arm grips my shoulder and pulls me to him, the opposite end of the stake is positioned over my heart. The point penetrates my flesh, breaking the bones, the ribs, and finding its rest deep within my chest.

"Peace," he whispers as he holds me close, lovingly. "Peace and death."

There is no peace for me, no death. There is only the unavoidable pain and the sound of my voice, shrill and sharp, screaming.

"You are dead."

# Chapter 7

"Deirdre?"

Disoriented, and feeling drugged, I sat up from the couch and saw the figure of a man outlined in the doorway.

"Max?" I whispered the name.

"I think you were having a bad dream." The voice was reassuring and I relaxed. "Close your eyes and I'll turn the lights on."

When I opened them again, Victor Lange stood there, smiling at me. "They told me out front that you were here. Did I disturb you?"

Standing, I smoothed my clothes. "No, actually I am very happy to see you. I was having a nightmare."

"Want to talk about it?"

"Not really." I met his eyes briefly, then turned away. "What are you doing here?"

"Oh," he said casually, walking around to the desk and setting his briefcase down on the top of it. "I stop by from time to time to check over the accounts. I trust you have no objections."

"Objections? Why would I object?"

Victor looked at me with amusement, then turned the latches on his case and the lid sprung open. "Because you own the Ballroom now. Or at least you will when the papers are signed."

"I own the Ballroom." It took a moment for the fact

to sink in, then I laughed, a sharp, scornful laugh directed at no one but myself.

"Do you mind if I ask why you find it funny?" Victor's voice had lost its pleasant tone, acquiring instead an angry, resentful edge, as if I were laughing at him.

"Honestly, Victor"—I choked back the rest of my merriment—"it is nothing you said. It is just that, well"—I thought for a minute, then continued—"the entire situation seems ludicrous to me. That Max should leave me the club, and that this room, a room I never wished to see again, along with everything else he owned, belongs to me. That the employees here, most of whom treated me as if I were a leper, should now be employed by me. And that, somehow through his death, Max found a way to bind me to him forever." That final word wavered in the air. Suddenly, I did not want to laugh.

Victor gave me an odd glance, then proceeded to shuffle through his briefcase. After he had gone through the entire stack of papers, he shook his head and looked back at me. "I'm sorry," he said with a gesture toward the desk, "but I don't seem to have the necessary papers here for you to read. Perhaps you would let me give you the gist of his will. There's no intent to bind you in any way. There are, in fact, certain provisions should you not wish to accept his possessions. But before we discuss that, I'd like to clear up one misunderstanding. Max left you everything for one simple reason: He wanted to take care of you."

I made a small sound, a derisive chuckle.

He came out from around the desk and, standing in front of me, gently clasped my chin in his hand and moved my head up to meet his gaze. "Max loved you more than anything in the world." Victor's eyes seemed for a second to glaze over with pain and sadness. Then they cleared and he smiled. "You should be flattered and comforted to know that he chose you. That above all others, he chose you to receive his legacy."

I pulled away from him, uncomfortable with his direct stare. Walking over to the table, I picked up my half-filled glass and drained it. I did not like the thoughts of any of this. Max's legacy to me was nothing more than an infinity of loneliness and estrangement. It could not be sweetened by material things; love could ease it, but that seemed something I would never achieve. When I spoke again my voice was small and tight. "And if I do not want his legacy?"

"As I said, there are provisions. His estate was to be held for you for twenty-five years after his death. Had you not turned up by then, all of his assets would have been transferred to an organization known as The Cadre. The same is true if you refuse. But I urge you to consider this carefully; you'll be turning your back on an enormous fortune. Something that could support you quite luxuriously for centuries."

"Centuries?" I gave a nervous laugh. That would be fine, if I could only live that long."

"Ah"—Victor smiled—"just a figure of speech, you understand. I merely wish to impress upon you the vastness of his wealth."

"Oh."

Victor walked over to the window and pulled the drapes aside, looking out. "We'll have snow later on tonight," he remarked flatly, then turned back to me. "And although I know that you're a night owl, I'm afraid that it's getting a little late for me. Can we make arrangements to meet tomorrow, or the next day? I'll bring the papers and you can review them at your leisure."

"That would be fine," I said, cautiously studying his movements. It bothered me that he seemed to know more about me than he should, but it was obvious that he had been a close friend of Max's. And despite his many flaws, Max had never once risked the exposure of what I was. "Trust him," the voice in my head whispered, and I complied. "When would you like to meet again?"

"Here, tomorrow night, say around eleven. I still have The Imperial to run, you know."

He went to the desk and retrieved his briefcase. "May I escort you somewhere?"

I nodded and walked with him out of the office. When we reached the door to the bar, I turned to him and disengaged my arm from his. "Actually, Victor, I think I would like to stay here for a while, in the club. I could use another glass of wine and some company."

"I'm sure you could." We went into the bar, and he took my hand. "Good night, then, till tomorrow."

Although I had told Victor I desired company, it was not really true. Being present in a crowd of humans was enough for me. But as I started my fourth glass of wine, a man stopped at my table. I looked up at him, taking in his expensive suit, manicured hands, his unnaturally even teeth exposed in a seductive smile.

"Hi." For an opening statement, it was unimpressive.

"Hello." I tried to be cordial, but resented his intrusion on my thoughts.

"Are you Deirdre?" At my nod, he pulled up a chair and sat down. "Fred sent me over, said you might like to meet me."

"Fred?"

"You know, the bartender."

I looked over to the bar and the man I had recognized waved at me with a knowing look. "Oh, Fred." I gave a small, sardonic smile. He was trying to make up for his past rudeness now that I was his boss. So much for the lack of ulterior motives.

I shrugged and looked the man over again. Fred must have learned a lot from watching Max arrange my meetings; he certainly had a feel for the kind of man I preferred. And although I should not have been hungry, my appetite awakened instinctively. Maybe I should give Fred a raise, I thought, and smiled at the man again, this time warm and welcoming.

"Did he happen to say why I might want to meet you?" The question was abrupt, but my voice was low and husky and he took no offense.

"No, just that you're new in town and seemed lonely."

"Make that newly back in town, and you would be right. And lonely? Well, you are here now, so how could I be lonely?" I wet my lips and crossed my legs under the table, lightly brushing his leg with my foot. "Would you like to dance?"

His name was Ron Wilkes, an attorney with an elegant condominium in the best part of town, a wonderful stock of wine, and an enormous round bed complete with red satin sheets. After we spent an hour consuming two bottles of his best Merlot, he seemed extremely drunk. I feared that he might pass out before he got around to seducing me, but he eventually led me to his bed.

When it was all over, I lay on my back, his head nestled on my shoulder and his arm heavy on my stomach. I wiped my mouth and stared at the mirrored ceiling, trying not to recall how long it had been since I had made love to a man who was not drunk, trying not to recall who that man was. It did no good. Mitch's face was etched on my memory, his body permanently bonded to mine. I sighed and Ron stirred briefly.

"Deirdre," he murmured, and reached his hand up, brushing against my nipple.

"Ron, I have to go now." I shifted away from him, but he pulled me back.

"Don't go just yet." He was still strong, still aware—I had taken only a small amount of blood, more a token than a meal—and he was not as drunk as I had thought. Pushing himself up on one elbow, Ron gave me a sleepy smile. "That was wonderful."

Looking up at his face, I felt a strong surge of guilt. Coming here with Ron had been a purely instinctual reaction. I had not needed his blood, had not needed to feed. It had been unfair of me to use him this way; he had not deserved it. His only mistake was being in the wrong place at the wrong time. And my mistake was in not taking enough from him to leave him open to my suggestions. I decided that I would have to bluff my way out of this one.

"Yes," I agreed languidly, stroking his hair, working my way down to the small mark at the base of his neck. He flinched slightly and I gave a nervous laugh. "But I am afraid you'll have to keep your shirts buttoned for the next week or two. I got a little carried away."

He fingered his neck delicately and gave me a searching look. "You bit me?"

"Yes." I could see the blush creep over me through the mirror.

"I thought so." I tensed at his words, but there was no fear or alarm on his face, just a satisfied smile. He plumped one of the pillows, rolled over, and sat up, drawing the sheet over us both. "Actually, it was a unique feeling. Very erotic. And well worth it."

I laughed, relieved. "I'm glad you think so."

"Would you like to do it again?"

I found his blasé attitude rather shocking. "What, bite you?"

"Among other things, yeah."

I sat up and threw back the sheet. "Some other night, Ron. I really do need to leave."

"Okay. Can I call you?"

Gathering my clothes, I shook my head and began to get dressed. "I'm staying with a friend right now, and I forget the number. But I have your card; I'll call you."

"That'd be great." He got out of bed and went for his clothes. "Let me drive you home."

I zipped my jeans and smoothed the sweater down over my hips. "No, it's late and you need your sleep. I'll take a cab."

"If that's what you want." He came over and gave me a small hug and a kiss on the forehead. Then, with his arm still around me, he walked me to the door. "See you soon, huh?"

Victor's weather prediction was correct. The streets were slick and the sidewalks lightly dusted with newly fallen snow. By the time I reached Mitch's brownstone, my cloak was almost completely white, and since I had no body heat to melt it off, practically frozen stiff. I hung it over the shower in the bathroom and pulled a chair up to the window, watching the snow until the sky began to lighten. Then I pulled the drapes closed and crawled into Mitch's bed.

My deep, dreamless sleep was interrupted shortly after three the next afternoon by the insistent ringing of the phone. I ignored it at first, but still it kept ringing. Finally I dragged myself from the bed and answered.

"Deirdre, did I wake you?"

My pulse jumped at the sound of his voice.

"Mitch." I whispered the name, fearing that it might not be him.

"Hi."

I smiled, thinking how he always paused in conversation, collecting his thoughts and choosing the words carefully. I waited and he continued. "Look, I'm, well, I'm really sorry about last night. I don't quite understand what happened, what could make me do that to you. I barely even remember it, except that they're all talking about it here."

"I'm sure they are." A trace of amusement crept into my voice and I laughed, rubbing my jaw in remembrance. "It was quite a greeting, Mitch."

"Yeah." He paused again and I closed my eyes, imagining him, not as I saw him last night, but as he was before. I could almost see him run his fingers through his hair in a tired gesture, almost see the glint in his blue eyes. "They said I knocked you flat. Are you okay?"

"I'm fine, Mitch, not that it much matters. But how are you?"

"I don't know. I feel normal, I guess. They tell me I've been here for over a year, and that seems right. I can remember most of what went on, but almost as if it were a dream, or something that happened to someone else. And when I woke up this morning I barely knew where I was. The whole thing is so strange."

"We need to talk about this, Mitch. You must try to remember what happened to you so that we can fight it, so that it won't happen again. Can you arrange some privacy for us this evening? This isn't the sort of thing we want to discuss in the presence of your doctors."

"Well . . ." His voice was evasive, uncertain. "I'm not sure that they'll leave us alone. I think they're afraid I might hit you again. But come anyway, come as soon as you can." There was a pleading in his voice that twisted my heart.

"I'll be there by seven. And Mitch?"

"Yeah?"

Taking a deep breath, I began, rushing my words together, to say what I didn't want to say. "I don't want to make this situation any more difficult for you. I am pleased that you seem to be doing better and will do anything I can to help you. Anything at all. But be assured that when you are fully recovered you won't need to worry about my presence. I'll go and let you live a normal life again."

"Deirdre, I . . ."

"No, Mitch, you know this is how it must be. Don't deny it. There's no place in your life for me. We both know that." I let my tears fall unchecked, but was pleased that there was no sign of them in my voice. "I'll see you tonight."

I hung up the phone before he could say anything more. Rolling on to my stomach, I buried my head in the pillow. It was totally absurd for either of us to believe that our relationship could have any better an outcome than it had two years ago. Nothing had changed; I remained what I was and ultimately Mitch would not be able to live with the truth of my existence.

"Then why are you here?" Max's deep voice resonated in my mind. "There are many others to be had and much sweeter blood to drink. You're still so young, so naive. Let me show you what awaits you."

Suddenly my mind was filled with a whirl of exotic images: men and women as carnal vessels of lust and hunger, flesh pressed against flesh, bodies and limbs intertwined, the salty flavors of skin and sex, the forbidden rush of blood, the flooding of the blood, overwhelmingly sensual in its taste, its power.

"Let us go, my love," he urged. "Let us go now. We could leave tonight. I know of places we could go where no one would ever find us. Places where we would be treated as gods, places where we could establish our own dynasties. There is nothing for us here. *Nothing!* But the world outside is waiting and if we leave I can be with you always, to teach, to experience, to live."

My body responded as if he were there; his breath was hot on my neck, his fingers tracing the bones of my spine. I could feel his strong hands grasp me, his nails penetrate my skin, his hungry mouth fasten on me. Max's passion and urgency were mine. I writhed and shivered in torment under his dominance.

I rolled over again, my back arched, my breath escaping in quick, frantic gasps. "No!" I cried, pressing my fingers against my eyes until hot red spots appeared beneath the lids. But still the images continued, flowing through my senses. I pressed harder, as if to tear the thoughts from my mind. Finally, the pain brought me back to myself and drove him away. Then, when my blurred vision returned and the red spots faded, I got up from the bed. Trembling, I walked down the hallway and stepped into the shower.

# Chapter 8

After the shower I wrapped myself in a towel and went back into the bedroom. Opening my suitcase, I looked over the clothes I had brought with me. None seemed suitable, so I went to the phone and dialed a number I remembered well.

It was picked up on the first ring, the voice crisp, professional, and unfamiliar. "Griffin Designs, Ms. McCain's office."

"I would like to speak with Betsy."

"May I tell Ms. McCain who is calling?" The tone of voice was curt and the last name was emphasized, as if I had no right to use the given name. The secretary's attitude annoyed me, and I had no desire to publicize my presence, but I supposed it could not be helped.

"Deirdre Griffin."

There was a slight pause, as she remembered me. "Of course, Miss Griffin. I'll put you right through."

Before I could even react to the change from rude to gracious, Betsy McCain's brisk voice burst through the phone.

"Deirdre, what a surprise. I'd no idea you were back in town. How are you?" I was surprised at her warmth. We had become acquainted only at the sale of Griffin Designs, and although by the end of the deal we had each admitted to a grudging admiration of the other, I would never have considered her a friend. Still, her reception of my return was welcoming.

"Fine, Betsy. And you?"

"Better than ever." I heard her take a sip of something, and she continued. "Business has been hectic, but wonderful. Your last show was so good and we had all those orders to build on. I'm afraid I did have to make some changes though. And I've not been able to capture the Griffin romance, or so the critics say." Her voice had a brittle and sly edge. "I, er, I don't imagine you'd consider signing on for a while as a consultant, you know, just while you're here?"

"No, I'm sorry. I won't be in town for too long."

"Too bad. Anyhow, what have you been doing?"

I almost told her the truth and smiled as I imagined what her reaction would be. Well, Betsy, I've been in Europe, draining the blood from tourists. Remembering her as cold-blooded and calculating, I suspected she might even approve. I laughed at the thought. "Oh, nothing of much interest, traveling mostly. But I wonder if you could do me a small favor."

"Anything, Deirdre. I still feel a little guilty, but only a little, mind you, that I bought you out so cheap. I don't mind returning the favor, provided it is a small one." Her statement was not entirely humorous, and I admired her honesty.

"Well, you see, I came back in a bit of a rush and wasn't able to bring much with me. I need some clothes—you know my taste and size—and a hairdresser. And I would like them to come to me. I realize this is a little unorthodox, but I'm expecting some rather important calls and don't want to leave my apartment." The lie came easily to my lips. I was accustomed to covering up my lack of daytime appearances. "I would be happy to pay extra for your inconvenience, of course."

Betsy barked out a short laugh. "No inconvenience,

Deirdre, but of course you'll pay extra. How soon would you like all this?"

"Is this afternoon too early?"

"No problem." She took another sip.

"And while you're at it, could you send some coffee along? I haven't had any time to shop at all."

"Okay, decaf or regular, ground or whole bean?"

"Ground, I guess, the other doesn't matter."

"Fine. Now, where are you staying?"

I told her and expressed my thanks. "You're a real lifesaver, Betsy. It's wonderful of you to do this."

"Oh, hell, Deirdre, it's not often that a fashion great comes to me for help. I'm delighted, I really am. See you soon."

By the time the doorbell rang, I had managed to dress and brush my teeth, but had no opportunity to apply any makeup to liven my pale complexion. It really doesn't make any difference, I thought as I cautiously opened the door to four women, one of whom was Betsy McCain.

She was exactly as I remembered her, dressed in an extremely tailored suit, her short, dark hair perfectly groomed, her handshake firm.

"Jesus, Deirdre, what the hell have you been doing to yourself? You look like death warmed over."

I laughed. "You haven't changed, Betsy. Still as blunt as ever, I see."

To my surprise, she looked embarrassed and a slight blush crossed her face. "I'm sorry, I didn't mean anything by it."

"I know. And you are right, I do look terrible." I turned to look at the women she had brought with her. One of them made a move to open the drapes. "No," I said, harsher than I intended. "Don't open those. I have a headache"—I lowered my voice a bit—"and the sunlight makes it worse."

Betsy gave me a quick look, then nodded at the women. "We have some extra lights in the car, bring those in." Then she glanced over the apartment with an amused smile on her face. "Not quite what I would expect of your place, Deirdre. It's nice, but somehow it's just not you."

"Mitch lives here."

"Oh." Her eyes sparkled at the mention of the name. "I remember, he's that sexy policeman you were dating. Are you still seeing him?"

"Yes." I didn't feel inclined to relate the story to Betsy McCain. She seemed friendly enough, and although it would be a relief for me to have someone to confide in, I knew I could not indulge in that luxury. My last female friend had been brutally murdered, a direct cause of our relationship. "And I'll be seeing him tonight. So you'll have to work magic."

Betsy stood smiling behind me as we both looked into the mirror. My hair was as close to its original auburn as was possible, my nails manicured, and makeup had coaxed a delicate color into my complexion. She had brought with her eleven outfits, mostly dresses, and for that night we had chosen a winter-white wool sheath. It was, I thought, too short and too tight, but Betsy assured me it was a perfect fit.

"Well," she said over my shoulder, "what do you think?"

"Much better."

"Much better, my ass. You looked like a hag when I came and now you're gorgeous. I doubt that your Mitch will be able to control himself."

I began to laugh. "I hope you're wrong. Last night he knocked me out."

"What? He hit you?"

"Yes," I began, then saw the expression on her face. "Well, no, I mean, he did, but it isn't like you think. He wasn't himself last night."

She nodded knowingly. "Funny, he didn't seem the type. Drinker, huh?"

"No, he isn't a drinker. It is just that, oh, hell, Betsy, it would take much too long to explain."

She put her hand to her hip. "I've got the time."

I glanced at the clock. "Some other time. I'm supposed to meet him at six."

"Okay." She seemed reluctant to leave. "Just don't take any shit from him. No one is worth it."

"I know."

"Anyway, Deirdre, this was fun." She met my eyes with her customary directness. "I know you don't really like me much; no one does. I'm far too outspoken, too brash for most people to take. Some of that is a defense, I guess, and some of that is just the way I am. But I really appreciate your calling me. Maybe we could meet for lunch sometime if you're not too busy. I have a good head for business, but I just don't have the flair you do. Do you think you could help me out a bit?"

"I would be happy to do that, Betsy. But make it dinner instead. We could go to The Imperial again, I suppose. My treat, of course."

"Well, of course, you didn't think I'd pay, did you?" The ungracious words were softened by a sincere smile, and she slowly walked to the door. "Can I give you a ride somewhere?"

"No, I'll take a cab." Walking over to her, I put my hand on her arm. "Thank you so much. You've been wonderful, and I think you do have a flair all of your own. When shall I make reservations for dinner?"

"I don't know, let me check my calendar first and then I'll call you. Will you still be here?"

"Yes. Oh, and Betsy don't forget to let me know what I owe you."

"Hell, Deirdre, even you know me better than that—I never procrastinate when money is involved. Why, I'll probably write up your bill just as soon as I get back to the office." She laughed and closed the door behind her.

By the time I arrived at the hospital, I was shaking with nervousness. I paid the driver and got out, looking reticently at the front doors. Coward, I admonished myself, and forced myself to mount the steps and enter. Slowly I walked down the corridor and stopped at the nurses' station.

"May I help you?"

I was relieved to find a different nurse on duty. This one I judged to be in her early thirties, with baby-fine blond hair. She could have been pretty, but the expression on her face as she studied me was extremely unpleasant. At least, I thought, I won't have to accept countless apologies again. "I'd like to see Mitch Greer."

She looked up at me, the eyes behind her glasses narrowed and skeptical. "Are you a relative?"

"No, I'm a friend."

She removed her glasses and gave me a scornful look. "I'm sorry, Mr. Greer is not receiving visitors this evening. Perhaps next time you could call ahead and verify visitation procedures."

"But he's expecting me. And I was here yesterday evening and there was no problem then."

She shook her head and turned back to her papers. "Well, that was yesterday, wasn't it? Tonight is tonight."

Stepping away from the counter, I stood for a second, watching her, attempting to gain my composure. "Excuse me," I said with a cold politeness, "then would it be possible to speak with Dr. Samuels?"

"Consultation hours are during the afternoon, from three to four, for family only." Each word seemed to punctuate her sudden and inexplicable dislike of me.

"Damn." I swore quietly. I moved closer to her and said in a louder tone, "Excuse me again, and I really hate to bother you, but may I use your phone?"

She pointed with her pencil toward the entrance. "Pay phones are in the lobby."

"Fine, thank you so much for your help." The sarcasm seemed lost on her. She made an unintelligible reply and returned her attention to the papers spread out on the desk. Exasperated, I turned away and began to walk back down the hall. I figured I could call Chris; he could get me admittance. But I had come to see Mitch, and see him I would, if I had to climb up the wall and break through his window.

"Deirdre?"

I spun around and faced Dr. Samuels.

"It is you, I thought so, but you look different. What did you do?"

I shrugged. "Nothing much. This is how I looked when I knew Mitch before. I thought it might help."

"You look great. Why did you ever change?"

I looked at his face, smiling at me with admiration, and smiled back. "It's a female thing," I said, knowing he would never understand my need for establishing a new identity. "Sometimes we just need to look different."

"But you're leaving? Don't you want to see Mitch?"

Although I was ready to explode into anger, I controlled my reactions. "Of course I want to see Mitch. But I was informed that I had not followed the proper procedures. I was just about to phone Chris to see if he could help."

"You could have asked for me."

"I did. 'Consultations from three to four for family only.' " I mimicked the nurse's condescending attitude.

Sam laughed. "Oh, I understand. Jean must be on duty this evening. Don't worry, I can get you in."

He escorted me back down to the nurses' station. Jean looked up at him. "Oh, Dr. Samuels, there was some woman here." Then she saw me standing behind him and stopped abruptly.

"I know, Jean. She's to be allowed to see Mr. Greer. This is Deirdre Griffin." He made a gesture of introduction in my direction, but Jean merely stiffened at the mention of my name and refused to meet my eyes.

"She's not on the list. And she's not family."

"An oversight on my part, Jean. I'm sorry you were inconvenienced."

Then Jean gave me a long, cold stare. The scorn that she had in her eyes earlier was replaced by hatred. "There are proper procedures"—she addressed me, without any trace of apology in her manner—"and it's my job to make sure that they are followed."

Sam's voice was considerate but cool. "Yes, well, thank you, Jean. We all know how dedicated you are to your work." He gave her a token smile and nod in dismissal, and we walked farther down the hall. Until we entered his office, I could feel her eyes follow us, and her surveillance made me uneasy.

I dropped my cloak and purse on the closest chair. "What the hell is her problem?" My voice was light, but inwardly I was still seething.

Sam shrugged. "Damned if I know. She's a stickler for the rules, but will usually bend a little every now and then. Unless she's jealous of you."

"Why on earth would she be jealous? I've never met her before." And never want to again, I added to myself.

"Well, Mitch has been here for a while, and she

started working only about a week after he was admitted. So I guess she feels there's a sort of tie between them. In any event, she's always been immensely interested in his case. Or so she maintains. The gossip from the other nurses is that she has a case on him."

"A case on Mitch?"

Dr. Samuels's eyes ran over my body in a quick complimentary glance. "Pretty ridiculous really. And it would have to be one-sided on her part. After having known you . . . well"—he shrugged, a look of compassion on his face—"I guess it's not pleasant seeing your fantasies dissolve right in front of you."

I looked away. His scrutiny of me was becoming uncomfortable. "May I see Mitch now?"

"Yes, of course." He moved to the door. "You want to see him, and here I stand, holding you up. He's in number seventeen, about ten rooms down, on this floor. Would you like me to take you?"

I nodded. "Please, if you would. I don't mind admitting that I'm just a little apprehensive about this meeting."

He began to walk briskly, and I followed at his side. "Everything will be fine, Deirdre. Mitch and I talked today, after he called you, and I know how much he's looking forward to seeing you. I'd be very much surprised if anything like last night occurs again."

My stomach twisted as he knocked on the door numbered seventeen. And when it was flung open, I jumped back in alarm. Sam held my arm gently but firmly. Reluctantly I lifted my eyes to Mitch's face.

He was still thin and gaunt, aged beyond the two years we had spent apart. But his eyes had lost their haunted look; they were crystal-clear and intensely blue, even more than I had remembered.

"Mitch." The name half choked me, and I was only

vaguely aware that Dr. Samuels had dropped my arm and was awkwardly backing away.

Then Mitch smiled at me, and I forgot the rest of the world. There were no doctors, no nurses, no patients. There was only Mitch. His arms came around me and he held me to him tightly, possessively. I began to cry softly onto his chest. He rocked me back and forth, comforting me with the warmth of his hands, the sound of his voice. Our bodies felt as if they were fitted to each other. We had both been broken, shattered by events out of our control. And now we were one, united again, through the same chain of circumstances.

As he stroked my hair with his weakened fingers, once so strong and calloused, I knew that although I had tried to purge myself of him, tried to forget what we had shared, our bond was unbreakable. He would be forever in my blood, my soul. And as his mouth came down on mine, I realized, too, that I was lost, that I could never again leave him while he lived.

# Chapter 9

"What the hell are you doing back in town?"

We were sitting side by side on Mitch's narrow patient's bed. Nothing had been said after he kissed me; he merely led me by the hand, sat us both down, cupped my face in his hands, and stared at me, searching, questioning me with his eyes. I wondered what he was looking for—did he expect to see signs of love or age, joy or sorrow? When he finally did speak, I started guiltily, not needing any words, wanting nothing but his gaze on my face.

I reached a hand up and stroked his cheek. "What strange greetings, Mitch—not 'How have you been,' or 'I missed you,' or even 'Long time, no see.' No, that would be too easy. Instead, I get hit and then I get profanity." I smiled at the mischievous grin that my words caused. "Do you think that's fair?"

He grew serious. "Fair has nothing to do with it. You shouldn't be here."

"And why not?"

He picked up my hand and put it to his mouth, glancing warily at the partially opened door. "For a lot of reasons, most of which we can't discuss here. It's too dangerous in this city, for you especially. Even so"—he put his arms around me, hugging me tightly to him, breathing the rest of his words into my ear—"I'm glad you came. God, I missed you so. You just can't imagine."

"I think I can, Mitch." I stretched up to kiss him, but out of the corner of my eye I saw a figure in hospital whites standing hesitantly in the doorway. I tensed and pulled away as Jean entered the room. She held a plastic pitcher of ice water in one hand, and a set of clean sheets were draped over her other arm. Bustling around the room efficiently and briskly, she placed the pitcher and one glass on the table next to the bed. The ice cubes clattered and the water slopped over the lip. Ignoring the spill, she stood, holding the bedclothes, staring down at us expectantly.

I remembered what Sam had said about her earlier, and I hid my half-smile on Mitch's shoulder. He kept his arm around me, not willing to move.

"Can I help you, Jean?" His voice was courteous and warm. Of course, I realized, he would have no idea of what she felt about him, or me, and I assumed that she could be a dedicated caregiver if properly motivated.

"Clean sheets, Mr. Greer." She held them forward and I could smell their fresh, starchy odor.

"But they were changed only this morning. Besides, I have a visitor."

"So I see."

He seemed not to have caught the suppressed anger I heard in her voice and he continued. "This is Deirdre Griffin, my, ah, fiancée." I glanced at him sharply on hearing of the unexpected escalation of our relationship. His only reaction was to tighten his grasp on my shoulder. "And Deirdre, this is Jean, one of the best nurses this dump has."

"We've already met."

She ignored my comment but beamed at his praise. "I do the best I can." Flushed and smiling, Jean seemed almost pleasant. Then her expression dropped and she gestured at us. "But visitors should be seen only in the lounge, and I have work to do."

Mitch's voice contained a gentle teasing. "Dr. Samuels said we could meet in here. And you can change the sheets after visiting hours just this once, can't you?"

"I guess so." She hesitated a moment, then placed the sheets on the pillow, lightly brushing against Mitch's arm as if by accident. But I knew better; I saw the glint in her eye as she walked away. "Visiting hours are over at nine sharp," she said, giving the door an angry push. It banged noisily against the wall. "And all doors are to remain open."

Mitch shrugged apologetically. "I think she's having a bad day. Now, where were we?"

He kissed me again, a long and hungry kiss, and I responded in kind. When it was finished, he glared at me. "Now, why the hell are you here? And how did you know where I was?"

"Chris came for me. He said you needed me."

Mitch grimaced. "Why, that little—I expressly asked him not to contact you. When I was still coherent, I told him that you were not to get involved." He ran his hand through his hair, a puzzled expression on his face. "At least I'm pretty sure I told him. I seem to have lost track of a lot of things, including time."

"What is the last thing you remember, Mitch?"

He looked at me, and I could see the pain enter his eyes. "About three months after you left, they started coming to me. At first I thought I was dreaming because they came only at night, while I was in bed. Then suddenly they were there, everywhere, after dark, watching me, laughing at me, their teeth pointed, dripping blood." He shivered and stopped talking abruptly, staring at the bare white wall.

"Mitch?" Alarmed, I grabbed his arm and shook it. "Mitch?"

He jumped and turned to me again. "Sorry, did I drift off?"

I nodded. "Like you were in another world."

"It is another world, Deirdre. Why didn't you ever tell me?"

"Tell you what?"

"How terrible they are. How inhuman."

"Mitch," I said as softly as I could, attempting not to betray the rush of panic I felt at his words, "I don't know who they are. The only other one like me who I knew was Max, and he's dead."

"Is he?" His eyes showed doubt and uncertainty.

"Yes, he is dead, Mitch. He can't threaten you anymore. You must believe that."

If he took any reassurance from my words, he didn't show it. "You see, that's just it. I didn't know what to believe anymore. Finally, I came to the conclusion that I had just flipped out, gone completely crazy. There was no evidence of what I knew, of what I saw, and yet they were there with me, inside my head, mocking and torturing. I eventually got to the point"—and he lowered his head, not looking at me—"that I wasn't sure that you existed either. My memories of you were vivid, but so were the others, the ones that plagued me, the ones no one else saw, no one else believed in."

"But Chris knew me."

"I wouldn't listen to him. I shut him out, because if you were real, then so was all the rest of it. I think I really wanted to believe I was crazy. It was safer that way."

"And you wrote me the letter."

"Letter? I didn't write to you. I wanted to at first, but you said six months and I waited. I guess I just couldn't hold out against them that long."

"But I received a letter from you."

Mitch shook his head. "I wish you had, but it wasn't from me. I didn't write. I know that for sure. What did it say?"

I got up from the bed and walked over to the window.

"It said that you couldn't accept my life, that you could never see me again."

"Oh, God. Deirdre, I'm so sorry, I didn't have any idea."

I turned and gave him a bitter smile. "How could you have known, Mitch? You didn't send it."

"Even so, you should've known that I wouldn't have said that."

"And why not? You said so yourself, we're terrible, we're inhuman. Why would anyone in their right mind want to take that on themselves? I had no choice but to walk into it willingly." I shook my head. "No, Mitch, it made perfect sense then, and it makes sense now."

Mitch sighed wearily and lay back on the bed. "Let's not fight about it now." He rolled over on his side and bent his knees, patting the open space on the bed. "Come here."

I settled in next to him. "You look tired, Mitch. You should try to get some sleep. I'll come back tomorrow night and we can talk some more then."

"Yeah," he agreed, stifling a yawn. "It's been a pretty busy two days."

Tenderly, I reached over and stroked his hair. The texture of it on my fingers was soothing, and the gesture seemed to calm him. He closed his eyes and gave an appreciative moan, then opened them again, sat up, and kissed me on the jaw.

"What's that for?"

"To make up for last night?"

"Oh, last night, forget it. It didn't hurt for long. But maybe you could tell me why you did it."

He smiled ruefully. "It was the only way I could be sure you were real." His expression grew thoughtful. "That, plus the fact that you're so bloody contrary, showing up when I least expected you. And when I saw your face, I felt such a strong rush of anger, not so much at you, Deirdre, as at the circumstances, at the sheer impossibility of what you are. Well, I just lashed out without thinking. Do you forgive me?"

"Mitch, my love"—I gently pushed him back on the bed and kissed him—"if you get better, I will forgive you anything. Sleep well."

I stood over him for a moment until his breathing deepened and he began to snore softly. Then I wiped my tears away and walked out of the room, turning out the light as I left.

The door to Dr. Samuels's office was partially opened, and I hesitated briefly, then knocked. "Come in," he called. His voice sounded weary, but his smile was broad when he saw me and he gestured to a chair.

The ashtray, cigarettes, and lighter were on top of his desk; one lone, unlit cigarette was tucked alongside the blotter.

"I'm sorry, did I disturb your evening ritual again?"

"What? Oh, you mean smoking. Actually, I usually do one only before I'm ready to leave. But this"—he picked up a cigarette and rolled it over in his fingers, "this one is my third. I'm afraid that you've provided all of us with an interesting dilemma.

"How so?"

He slid a packet of papers over to me. "This represents testing done on Mitch just six weeks ago."

I looked at the tests, page after page of neat circles. "But every answer is exactly the same—he took only the first choice."

"Exactly. Did you know that some days we couldn't even get him to hold a pencil?" He didn't wait for my answer but pulled more papers from the top of the stack. "And these are the series I gave him today."

I could not read them, but saw that each question was

answered with a different filled-in circle. "And the results?"

"Perfectly normal. Absolutely within the range of accepted psychological adjustment. Oh, Mitch has his fears and insecurities like all of us, but even they are normal. In many cases, fear is a healthy reaction. I like to say it keeps us from getting too cocky about our position in this world."

"And what does Mitch fear?"

Sam gave me a strange look, almost crafty. "What do you fear, Deirdre?"

His direct question threw me off guard, so much that I almost told him the truth. I fear the sunlight, I fear discovery. There are days when I am more afraid of life than death. And mostly I fear dead vampires who will not stay dead but live on in your mind and soul.

"Strangers, lack of privacy, and doctors who ask questions that they should not."

"Fair enough," he said, acknowledging my caustic tone. "I guess it's not really relevant anyway. But you must admit the fact that before you gave your very glib answer, there were darker fears that surfaced. You know it and so do I. I saw it in your eyes."

"And Mitch? After all, he's the patient, not I."

He picked up his cigarette and lit it, offering the pack to me. I shook my head and he went on. "Mitch is afraid of what he should be, especially when you consider his line of work. Senseless violence, blood, and death figure quite high in his current profile. But"—he went through his papers again, choosing one particular sheet—"when he first came here, when he was still reasonably coherent, he was very vocal about his problem." Sam took a drag on his cigarette and slowly exhaled. "Vampires. Or, as he put it 'those goddammed bloodsucking creatures in the night.' They had invaded his mind, he said, they were torturing him, punishing him for some crime."

I reached a trembling hand across the desk for the cigarette pack. "I think I will have one after all."

Sam nodded. "I thought you might. It's all pretty weird, don't you think. Why would a grown man be so afraid of mythical creatures? But you should know that through it all, while he was raving about 'them,' he was trying to protect you."

"Protect me?" My voice cracked a bit, and I cleared my throat. "What do you mean?"

"He didn't want them to find you. He said they would kill you if they knew where you were. We tried to find you, thought you might be able to help, but no one seemed to know where you had gone. Oh, Mitch knew all right, but he wasn't telling."

"Excuse me, Sam, this is all very interesting, but I'm afraid I don't quite get the point." My voice was even, but I lowered my eyes so he couldn't see the anger and sorrow I knew they must have held. "Mitch is getting better; you should be happy that he is recovering, not constantly worrying over what caused his problem."

"No"—his voice grew loud, and he got up from the desk and closed the door, standing with his back to it—"you don't understand. I am happy, thrilled, even ecstatic over his miraculous recovery. But don't you see, that's my point. In all my years of practice I've never seen a miraculous recovery. I don't believe in miracles, Deirdre. So there has to be some other answer."

"You sound just like him."

"Who?"

"Mitch," I said simply, smiling as I remembered so many of our conversations where he denied so many things, including coincidence and supernatural beings.

"Deirdre"—he crossed over to me and took my hands—"you see, that's why I need your help. You hold so much of him inside you. I need to understand what happened to you both so I can determine if he is truly healed, so that I can in good conscience sign his release. You must tell me everything. You owe it to Mitch, and you owe it to yourself."

Although I was still wary of his questions, I was moved by his argument. And if telling the story would hasten Mitch's release, I supposed that an edited version would not do much harm to any of us.

Sam stood, holding my hands, awaiting my answer. I pulled away from him and picked up my bag and cloak.

"Fine," I agreed, "but could we go somewhere else? Hospitals make me uncomfortable."

# Chapter 10

When Dr. Samuels found out that I was staying at Mitch's apartment, he decided it would be a good idea to meet there. His movements as he drove in traffic were cautious and careful, a totally different style from Mitch's assured competence. But then, Mitch drove a dingy, broken-down sedan, and Sam's car was a new foreign sports model. He seemed quite proud of it, so I politely complimented him on it. When we pulled in front of Mitch's place, he seemed reluctant to leave it parked at the curb.

Sensing his apprehension, I turned to him. "Perhaps we should have taken a cab."

"No, this'll be okay, I guess. I'll just set the alarm."

"It will be fine," I assured him, "and if not, it's only a car after all. I assume you have insurance."

"Of course I have insurance. Doesn't everybody? Don't you?"

"No, I don't own a car. And I don't believe in insurance."

He gave me an incredulous look. "What do you mean, you don't believe in insurance? You must have some, life insurance at the least, or property insurance."

"I own nothing I value that much."

"Not even your life?"

I laughed. "It should really be called death insurance, being merely a bet with the company that you won't die before they get enough money from you. The only way you win is by dying sooner than they plan. And"—I winked at him as we went up the stairs—"I do not plan on dying."

"Deirdre," Sam said as I opened the door and we entered Mitch's apartment, "you are one strange lady."

"Make yourself at home," I called to him as I went into the kitchen. "But I'm afraid I don't have much to offer you in the way of refreshments. Would you like coffee or wine?"

"Coffee, I guess. And I hate to be rude, but I'm sort of hungry. Have you got anything to snack on?"

I realized that I really should bring some food into the apartment for appearance' sake, even though I would never eat it. "No," I said idly, "I haven't had time to go shopping since I arrived." I began to brew the coffee. "I hope you don't need cream or sugar in this."

"Black is fine."

I stood in the doorway of the kitchen while the coffee dripped and saw Sam studying the rows of books. "A pretty impressive collection, isn't it?"

"Yeah." He pulled out one volume. "*The Annotated Dracula.* Why am I not surprised?"

"Oh, come now, Sam, you'll find that book on a lot of shelves. You shouldn't make too much of it."

He shrugged, then turned to look at me. "I know, how about a pizza?"

"Pizza? I told you I have nothing to eat here."

"No, I mean order one. You do have a phone, don't you?"

"Very funny." I gestured to the phone sitting on the end table. "Be my guest."

He dialed a number. "I'll have a large, um, hold on a second"—he put his hand over the receiver—"Deirdre, what do you like on yours?"

"Nothing. I don't eat pizza."

"Not at all? Why not?"

I crossed my arms and leaned against the doorjamb. "I'm allergic to tomatoes."

"This place makes a great white pizza, then. Just dough, cheese, toppings, and spices."

"Garlic?"

He smiled at me. "Yeah, lots and lots of garlic—it's wonderful."

"No thank you, I'm not really hungry."

"Okay, it's your loss." He completed his order, gave them the address, and hung up. "Why do they always say twenty minutes? Just once I'd like to call and have them tell the truth."

I shrugged, went back into the kitchen, and came back out with one mug of coffee for Sam and a glass of wine for me.

"You're not having coffee?"

"No, sit down, please." He settled into the one armchair. I sat down on the couch, took a sip of my wine, then set it back down. "Now, what would you like to know?"

"Everything you can remember would be good." He fumbled in his suit-coat pocket for a moment and brought out a small tape recorder. "Would you mind if I taped this? I take terrible notes, and my handwriting's so bad, even I have trouble reading it."

I glanced at the machine in doubt. If I should make a mistake and say the wrong thing, I would have to get the tape from Sam somehow. It would be easy to tamper with his mind, but I didn't trust modern technology; it was not susceptible to my wiles.

He sensed my hesitation. "You'll forget it's running after a while, really. And it's much better for me. Please?"

At my reluctant nod, he pushed the record button. The machine made a soft whirring sound. I picked up my wine, took another drink, and cradled the glass between my hands.

"I met Mitch three days after Thanksgiving, two years ago, at the Ballroom of Romance. He was investigating the death of Bill Andrews and wanted to question me about him."

"Bill Andrews was a close friend of yours, then?"

"No, we had just met the night he died. We were mere acquaintances, really."

"Then why did Mitch see fit to question you?"

I frowned and bit my lip. This was more difficult than I had expected it would be. Any bare telling of the story would be bound to put me in a bad light, and I could not fully explain. I gave Sam a sharp look, thinking that I didn't have to care about what he thought of me. This was all to help Mitch.

"Rumor was, around the club, that Mr. Andrews and I had shared an intimate evening before his death." My voice was dispassionate, matter-of-fact.

"Did you?"

I sighed and gently set my glass on the end table. "Look, Sam, this is difficult for me. Those few weeks were an extremely painful experience not just for Mitch, but for everyone who lived through it. And it is not a pretty story, I promise you. But it would ease the telling if you saved your questions until later."

"I'll try, but you've got to understand that it's in my nature to ask questions. That's why I do what I do."

"Then just close your eyes and pretend you're hearing a story about people you do not know, people who do not exist."

I stood up and walked to the bookshelves, stopping slightly behind him as he sat in the chair so that I would not have to watch his face. Hesitantly, I began.

"There were three more murders, two of them following fairly quickly after Andrews's, all with the same cause of death. Oddly enough, they had been drained almost completely of their blood, with no visible signs of violence other than two small punctures on their necks." I stopped for a minute, waiting for some sort of comment from him.

Sam nodded his head, and gave a clinical, "Uh-huh, go on."

"Well, since I knew all but the last murder victim, Mitch jumped to the conclusion that somehow I was involved. That I was the connecting link between them."

I paused again, editing the story, knowing that I could not tell him that Mitch's conclusion was true. That would incriminate me too deeply, raise too many questions in Sam's curious mind. "As it turns out, it was all a coincidence. The only link I had with any of it was Max."

"That would be Max Hunter, the famous 'Vampire Killer'?"

"So you do know something about all this?" My question sounded petulant; if he knew the story, why should I have to relive it?

"All I know is what was in the papers at the time. When Mitch was admitted, I did the required research, of course. I can show you the file sometime if you like. But I assume there is a lot more to tell than what appeared in print."

I gave him a skeptical look and he continued as if to justify himself.

"I was out of town, doing my internship at the time. So I missed all the excitement. And there really was very little published about the case."

I walked across the room, picked up my glass and drained it, then went to the kitchen for more. When I returned, his eyes followed me intently. "So Mitch found this Max Hunter, and killed him. And that should have been the end of it all. But it wasn't, was it?"

I gave him a sharp look. "Sam," I said firmly, "please try not to interrupt. It's very distracting."

"Sorry, I forgot."

An uncomfortable silence enveloped us, but Sam kept his promise for a while and said nothing else, waiting patiently for me to continue.

"In between the third and fourth murders, something completely unpredictable happened that threw everyone a curve. Gwen"—I hesitated on her name—"my personal secretary, was also brutally murdered. And although her death was completely different from the others, there seemed to be a connection." I stopped and paced the room, finally ending back on the couch, not looking at him but staring into the depths of the wineglass.

He urged me on, reminding me with a small cough of his presence. I jumped, startled, pulled abruptly out of my private retreat into the past. I had almost forgotten he was there.

"We found her, Mitch and I, in my apartment. She had a wooden stake driven through her heart." I turned my eyes to him and noticed his sickened expression. "Yes, you are right," I said, interpreting his look, "it was possibly the most grotesque display of violence I had ever seen. That alone would have been enough to drive a sane man crazy." I put my head into my hands to hide my red-tinged tears. "You cannot imagine the amount of blood Gwen's small body had possessed. It had sprayed all over the room, pools of clotting, sticky blood everywhere you looked."

As I sobbed, I felt a gentle touch on my hands; Sam was offering his handkerchief. I accepted it, blotted my eyes, rolled it into a ball, and tucked it into the side of the couch.

The doorbell rang and we both jumped. "I think your pizza has arrived," I said, and he answered the door.

While he was completing his business with the delivery man, I went to the bathroom and splashed water over my face. I was not surprised when I came out and saw the pizza sitting on the kitchen counter, unopened, permeating the apartment with its nauseating odor. Even a human with a strong stomach would have had a difficult time eating during this story.

I poured the rest of the wine into my glass and sat back on the couch to finish the story. "It turned out that Gwen's death was unrelated to the other murders. Max did not kill her."

"Who did?" Sam asked with a rueful smile.

"A young man by the name of Larry Martin." I suppressed the shiver caused by his name. "But I don't think we need to discuss that situation at all. The only reason I told you was so that you could have a feel for the kind of horror Mitch experienced."

"And you too." His voice was sympathetic and compassionate. "Was she your secretary for very long?"

Does it make a difference? I wanted to shout at him, finding myself angry with his clinical questions. "Yes," I said curtly, "I had known Gwen for almost ten years. She and Max were the only friends I had."

"And Max? What happened there?"

"Max died the same way Gwen did. Only this time we were present for the actual event." I looked away from him, hoping he could not hear the lies in my voice. "Mitch killed him in the line of duty. It was a case of self-defense, really. Max had broken Mitch's arm, smashed his knee, and was trying to kill him. I don't even know how Mitch managed to drive the stake in; he had lost a great deal of blood, and Max"—I shuddered now, remembering the writhing body I impaled on the door, the groping hands, the blood flowing from the wound and pooling on the floor—"Max was strong and he struggled a great deal. But people fighting for their lives often do miraculous things. Mitch overcame him and Max died."

My final words echoed through the room, mocking me.

"So at the end Mitch had come to believe that Max was a true vampire."

I shrugged. "Mitch thought that Max believed he was. Max was literally a bloodthirsty killer. What difference does it make what Mitch believed about why or how Max committed his crimes?"

"And what do you believe?"

I gave him a steady look. "Max Hunter was my best friend. He had been my lover, looked after me like a father, guided my career, and was probably the single most important person in my life." My words seemed to shock him. It was incongruous to speak of a murderer in such glowing terms, but I kept my gaze on him as I continued. "He was also the most cold-hearted, manipulative bastard who ever lived. He deceived me the entire time I knew him. And I believe that no matter what he was, the world is a better place without him."

"But did either of you have any proof about him?"

"Proof? We heard his confession before he died."

"And that's another thing. If Mitch did not think Max was a vampire, why did he kill him the way a vampire should be killed?"

I gave a short laugh. "Quite honestly, the choice of weapon was just another one of life's strange coincidences."

"And what were you doing when all this happened?" He frowned as the words escaped his lips, as if he realized that they would be damning to me.

I allowed my anger to show. "I was there, what was I to do? Max was, oh, dammit, Max was just Max. I don't believe that I could say anything that could make you understand Max. He was larger than life, a romantic hero in the classical sense. Arrogant and egocentric, he often thought of himself as a god. And I'm not so sure that he was wrong. But he couldn't accept the fact that I could love a"—I just barely stopped the word "human" from escaping my lips—"another man. When Mitch and I realized that Max was the murderer, I begged him to let me handle it. Mitch was too stubborn, too proud, to accept my help."

My criticism of Mitch seemed to anger Sam. "And what in hell do you think that would have accomplished? What would have kept Max from killing you?"

I gave him a direct stare. "Max did not want me dead. He would never have hurt me physically in any way."

"Just the same"—Sam shrugged—"I think Mitch did the right thing, not allowing you to confront him alone."

"Had I gone alone, there would have been no confrontation." No, I told myself, there would have been no confrontation, since I would easily have succumbed to Max's demands. It was only Mitch's trust in me that enabled me to break the bonds imposed on me. "For all the good it has done me. I'm right back where I was, stuck between the two of them." I muttered the last words but did not repeat them at his request. "I didn't want the two of them to meet, would have done anything possible to avoid being involved in an death of either of them. Max had forced the issue to an impasse, so that there could be only one alternative—his death or Mitch's. And I loved Mitch. There was no other choice." I stopped on that last word. I had said too much, and if Sam had been listening carefully, he would have been able to hear my admission of murder. But he ignored my last comment—perhaps he wasn't as good a listener as he thought.

"And you left the country so soon afterward. Why?"

I stood up suddenly. "This discussion has reached its end, I think. Why I left is, quite frankly, none of your business. And I am tired."

He accepted my rebuff calmly and nodded, finally taking a sip of his coffee. "Damn coffee's cold"—he headed for the kitchen and opened the cardboard box—"and now so's the pizza."

I tried to match his commonplace tone, as if I really had been telling a story about strangers, not people I knew and loved. "There's more coffee, and you can reheat the pizza."

He began to rummage through the cabinets, opening then slamming them closed; dishes and pans rattled and clanked. Eventually, I heard the sound of the oven door creaking open. "It'll be ready in about five or ten minutes, in case you've changed your mind."

I glanced at the clock; it was only slightly after eleven. "No, I don't . . . oh, no."

"What's wrong?" Sam came out of the kitchen.

"Nothing really, but I just remembered I had an appointment this evening."

"At this time of night? With whom?"

"Victor Lange, executor of Max's will."

He gave a low whistle. "No kidding? Max left you something?"

"No, Sam." I tried to smile, but what appeared on my lips was more of a grimace. "Max did not leave me something—he left me everything."

I paused a moment while he let my statement sink in. "I suppose I should call him and reschedule."

"I would if I were you. If you don't mind my asking, how much do you get?"

Laughing, I answered him. "After all the questions you've asked this evening, another one could hardly matter. Especially in such a trivial area. I don't really know how much, but I understand it is a fairly large fortune—that is, if I choose to take it."

"Choose to take it? Why wouldn't you?" Sam's tone betrayed his incredulity.

All traces of laughter disappeared from my voice, and I looked at him with disappointment. "You heard the story, but you didn't listen, did you? It comes from Max." I turned my back on him and dialed the number of the Ballroom of Romance.

"Victor Lange, please, Deirdre Griffin calling," I said when the phone was answered.

I waited for a moment until Victor picked up the line. "Deirdre, you're late."

"I know, Victor, I'm so sorry. We'll have to meet at another time; I'm involved in another matter right now."

Victor chuckled. "I'm sure you are. Max once mentioned your proclivity, but I wasn't sure I believed him."

I resented his tone. "It's not what you think, Victor." He laughed again. "Whatever you say, Deirdre. By the way, there was a friend of yours here tonight, asking for you. Someone by the name of Ron. Ring any bells?"

"Damn," I said coldly. "I told him to wait for my call." I thought for a minute. "I would appreciate it, Victor, if you could discourage this kind of activity. Is he still there?"

"I don't know. Shall I check?" His voice still held amusement, and I grew angry, not so much at him as at myself for causing this situation.

"Dammit, no. I'll deal with him later."

"As you wish. Would you like to make another appointment?"

"Tomorrow night, same time, same place?"

"Fine, only don't stand me up again, Deirdre. Have some compassion for an old man."

I hung up the phone and turned around to find Sam staring at me.

"Trouble?" he said, a puzzled expression his face.

"Nothing that I can't handle, thank you." I was sorry to see that my hard tone caused a touch of pain in his eyes. With a lighter voice I joked, "Now, is that your pizza I smell burning?"

"Oh, shit!" He went for the kitchen. The oven door squeaked again. "Thank God, it's not too bad. I never eat the crust anyway. I'm starving, how about you?"

"No, really, I don't—" I started to insist again, but a blaring siren sounded from the street. "What the hell?" I asked, but Sam came running from the kitchen and headed toward the door.

"It's the car alarm." He was outside before I could say anything, and I quickly followed him.

Sam stood at the curb, yelling obscenities at the shadowy figure tearing down the street. I held my ears to keep out the sound. When the thief was out of sight, he went around to the shattered driver's window and reached in to shut off the alarm. The acrid smell of blood and further obscenities from Sam's mouth assaulted my senses at the same time.

"Oh, shit, I cut myself. Goddamned car thieves. Goddamned stinking neighborhood. Goddamned stinking car."

"Shall I call the police?" My voice was trembling; the odor of his blood was so close, so compelling. "Or an ambulance?"

"No to both. Do you suppose Mitch has a first aid kit?"

"I don't know."

"Well, let's at least go inside and see what sort of damage I've done."

I glanced at him hesitantly as he came around the car and toward me. His shirt was streaked with red and his arm dripped small crimson drops. My nostrils flared, my teeth grew sharp, and the hunger awoke. "Blood," the voice inside hissed with glee. "We don't want him around anyway, do we, my dear? We could have him now; take him inside. We could answer all his questions in one simple step." Laughter that was not mine rang in my head.

"Oh, Jesus, not now, please not now, just go away," I whispered to him.

"Deirdre, are you okay? You're so pale—don't tell me you faint at the sight of blood?"

My nervous laughter echoed back from the surrounding buildings as I tried to drown out the inner urgings. "Of course not, Sam. I used to be a nurse." My voice sounded soft, breathless. I tried to pull my glance away from his arm and that precious blood dripping on the sidewalk. I didn't dare breathe as I walked past him to the brownstone's entrance. "Come inside." My back was to him and I licked my trembling lips. "I'll see what I can do."

His wound turned out to be little more than a superficial scratch. And to my relief, when his arm was rinsed in cold water, the bleeding stopped. I ran the water in the sink to flush away all traces of his blood. Then I lightly daubed the cut with antibiotic cream and wound his arm with gauze that I had found. My trembling subsided, and when I had finished I was able to give him a smile, with unsharpened teeth. "All better."

"Thank you. That was very well done. Are you really a nurse?"

"Some time ago I served as one, yes."

"Can't have been that long ago, Deirdre. You aren't that old."

"Well, it seems like a long time ago." I shrugged. "You know how it is."

"Yeah." He looked at me and began to laugh.

"What's so funny?"

"Nothing, I guess." He continued to laugh, almost

giggling. "What a strange evening it's been. As I said before, you are one strange lady."

"I am what I am."

"Yeah, well, aren't we all?"

I gave him a twisted smile. "No, actually, Sam, I don't think so."

He stared at me for a minute, all traces of his laughter gone, then he checked his watch and shook his head. "Look at the time. How did it get so late? I'd better go now. Do you mind if I take the tape home, make some notes, and talk to you later? I can't really think after midnight."

"That would be fine. I'll see you tomorrow night."

"Can you make it earlier? I have plans for the evening."

I shook my head. "Absolutely not. I have plans for the day."

"The night after that, then. But I assume you'll be visiting Mitch."

"Yes, during the evening." I laughed. "At least I will be there if Nurse Jean isn't on duty."

"Don't worry, she knows who you are now. She'll let you in."

"If you say so."

He began to make a move to the door. "Oh, Sam!" I stopped him before he could get out. "Take your pizza, please."

The disgust I felt must have shown, because he started laughing again. "You know, I don't think I've ever met anyone with such an aversion to plain, simple pizza as you."

I went to the kitchen, put it back into the box, and handed it to him with a half smile. "Enjoy."

Sam took the box, then laid it down on the table near the door. His expression was serious again. "Deirdre, I want to thank you for talking to me this evening. Everything you've told me will be a big help, and if his rate of improvement continues, I think I can promise that Mitch will be released soon."

I put my hand out, but he surprised me and put his arms around me in a brief embrace. Ignoring my gasp, he kissed me lightly on the lips, then moved away and picked up the pizza box. "Thanks again, Deirdre, and good night."

After he had gone, I closed the door, locked it, and went into the kitchen to open the window. It took almost an hour to rid the apartment of the smell of burnt garlic pizza. And by that time I had also purged my senses of the smell of Sam's blood.

# Chapter 11

My dreams bring me once more to the cemetery. This time I am spared the trip through the dirt of his grave. He is waiting for me, lounging indolently against his tombstone, smiling at me, the tips of extended canines and white skin gleaming in the moonlight.

Wordlessly, I hand him the rose I carry, and with a courtly bow he takes it from me, delicately inserting it into his breast pocket.

Although I know it for a dream, I also sense that it is real; he is real and he is solid flesh once more. I find my voice and speak.

"What is it to be this evening, Max? More blood? More death, and torture, and guilt?"

He holds out his hand and I reach for it, touch it. He draws me to him. Our hearts beat to the same rhythm. Enfolding me in the black silken wings of his dark soul, he whispers to me.

"Nothing so simple, my love. You have more painful lessons to learn than that. Tonight I will show you youth, my youth and my lost innocence."

The world spins around us, a giddy, sickening whirl. A heavy, tangible mist swirls around us, and we are engulfed in that mist, then disembodied, thinned and carried by the cold night wind.

Candles are burning and a large hearth glows with the dying embers of a fire. Above the hearth hangs a tapestry coat of arms. At first I think the room is empty, but my eyes are directed to a young man, dressed in fine dark velvet, who sits hunched over a piano.

No, an inner voice supplies, a clavichord; the piano does not yet exist.

The music the boy plays is sweet and pure, and something about the way he holds his head is familiar. Then, still playing, he turns his head briefly to glance at a woman entering the room. A smile curves his lips as he returns to the music, finishing it with a feverish intensity. When the last chords fade from hearing, he shakes back his long black hair and rises from the bench.

I gasp at my recognition of him, and although I have no body, no physical presence in this place, his eyes come to rest where I would be standing, as if I called his name. His face is still flushed with the fervor of playing, the eyes light and shining with an eagerness that even after years of looking on those same eyes, I have never seen before. His finely sculptured face is the work of a master, Bernini perhaps, or Michelangelo, but immature, or incomplete, as if the artist had neglected the last few chisel strokes that would imprint the true character.

Intently I study the young man, no more than fifteen or sixteen years of age, and the incongruity becomes clear. It is Max before the many centuries heaped upon his flawless features the blemishes of pride and arrogance, murder and blood—Max before the inheritance of the curse of vampirism.

"No," I cry, voiceless in this ancient place. "No." That so fine a creature could be so absolutely corrupted is an evil almost beyond comprehension.

"You see," he replies, an irony in his voice, unheard in the young one's, as he talks quietly with the other person in the room. "I was once your equal. I walked proudly in unity with my fellow men and humbly before my God." And the irony is replaced by sadness as I feel him direct our eyes to the woman. "My mother"—his tears are hot on my face—"an angel among women."

I look at her; through my vision she is a normal, middle-aged woman, her hair graying. Her thin frame seems fragile, and although weighed down with the volume of her clothing, she holds herself erect with pride and effort. Her face is creased with worry, sorrow, and laughter, and her light eyes are circled beneath with heavy shadows. But in Max's view she is beautiful, and his memories of her become mine. I remember her calm voice, her clarity of thought, her many loving acts, as if she were my mother. And I feel his pain when she coughs quietly, yet persistently, into a small silk handkerchief.

"She is dying." Max's voice confirms my thoughts. "In two years she will be gone." He turns on me in bitterness. "You are not the only one to have lost your loved ones over the centuries. But listen now, you must learn who I was to learn who I became."

Suddenly we are no longer observers of the past. We are merged with the youthful Max, buried deep within him.

"Madre." I grasp her hands within mine. "You were to rest. Go back to your bed; I will come up to say good night later."

"No, my son." She smiles, and the knowledge of her impending death saddens me. "This will be your last night under this roof as my son. When next you return you will no longer be my Maximilian, my dearest boy." She wipes her eyes. "But do not think that I am unhappy with your choice. You will do well in your vocation. You must remember to make me proud, and to celebrate your first Mass for me."

"Mother, I will."

She reaches up and gently touches my cheek. "Now play for me."

I obey and sit down at the instrument again. It is strange to look down on hands that are not mine, playing from memory music I do not know. And yet it feels right. Max's young fingers move across the keys; the music comes from deep within me, flows through me, filling and purifying my corrupted soul with unexpected joy.

The scene begins to blur before my eyes and the mist engulfs us, pulling us away.

"Please, just a few minutes more," I cry. I do not want to leave the music or the room, filled with so much love. It could be a home for me; it *is* my home. "I want to go back."

There is no one to answer my plea, for suddenly I am in the cemetery, alone, in my own body once more, pressed against the cold earth of his grave.

When I woke, I could not remember where I was, much less who I was. "Max?" I whispered, trying to sense his presence within me. There was no response. I shrugged off the covers and walked down the hall to the bathroom. As I stooped over the sink, splashing water on my face to alleviate the confusion and grogginess caused by the dream, my stomach tightened in panic. What if I looked into the mirror and saw, not my face, but his? And would I know the difference?

Trembling, I reached behind me for a towel, dried myself, and slowly dropped it, revealing to my relief the familiar features of Deirdre Griffin.

"Jesus, what a dream." Tensely I laughed at my fears. "You are you," I assured my mirror image. "Who else would you be? And Max, a priest? Deirdre, you have had some strange dreams in your life, but I believe that one will take first place." The sound of my voice provided some comfort, but my eyes quickly darted around the room, looking for the familiar ghost.

I jumped when the doorbell rang and without thinking went to answer it. Checking through the peephole, I saw Chris standing there and realized that I was naked.

"Chris," I called through the door, "I'm unlocking the door, but give me a minute before you come in."

"No problem."

I undid the latch and ran back to the bedroom, closing the door behind me. In the closet was Mitch's green terry-cloth robe and I put it on, tightening the sash. As I heard the door open, I quickly ran a brush through my unruly hair, and pinched my cheeks to give them a little color.

"Deirdre," Chris called, "are you decent?"

"No." I came out of the bedroom and smiled at him. "But I am dressed."

"Very funny." He acknowledged my attempt at humor with a weak smile, but I noticed he was furtively surveying the apartment.

"Are you looking for something, Chris?"

"No." Then he met my eyes and blushed. "Well, yeah, I guess I am. Didn't you have a guest here last night?"

"Yes, I did."

"Is he still here?"

"No, he is not. How did you know someone was here?"

He blushed again. "I stopped by last night, you know, to celebrate with you about Dad's recovery. But before I could ring the doorbell, I heard voices. I guess you decided to have your own private party." His voice sounded harsh and strained, but any anger I felt at him dissolved when I saw his sad, disappointed face.

"You should have come in, Chris. It was only Dr. Samuels, and what we talked about concerned you also. I assure you it was not what you call a private party." I mimicked his tone, and to my surprise, he laughed.

"I'm sorry, I didn't really know what to think. You know, with you being what you are and all, well, I jumped to the most obvious conclusion."

His implied judgment of the way I lived was beginning to anger me. "Chris," I said sternly, "first I am going to make us some coffee. Then it is time you and I sit down and have a little talk about what I am."

He gave me an evasive look. "Coffee'd be great, but Dad is waiting for us."

"This will not take long, and I promise you that Mitch will understand. There are things you should know, things he cannot or will not tell you."

He shrugged, but followed me to the kitchen, taking two mugs from inside a cabinet and leaning back against the counter. "I didn't imagine that you'd drink coffee," he said with a glance that betrayed a fearful curiosity.

"Fine, we will start with that. I can drink almost any substance. I do not gain nourishment from it, but my system can accommodate it. Solid food is another matter, however. Rare meat is about the only food I can digest. Even that is not easy, but I can do it if I have to."

"Why would you have to? What possible difference could it make to you?" He sounded genuinely confused.

"That brings us to the next of the unpleasant facts of my life, Chris. Every day, every night, I am forced to deceive the rest of the world, carefully disguising my instincts into a façade of human behavior. So if socially I am called upon to attend a dinner, I must eat. Not every time, true, but often enough so that I do not call attention to my differences."

"But what are you afraid of? What can hurt you?"

I gave him a sharp glance, but his face was innocent and open, showing nothing more threatening than simple concern.

"Not everything you read in the books is true, of course. A stake through the heart worked well for Max." I shuddered as I made the statement, thinking that it really did not seem to work that well. He was still haunting me. "Prolonged exposure to sunlight would probably also do the trick. But I am not repelled by crosses or crucifixes."

"Garlic?"

I laughed. "It is true that I have a great aversion to garlic, but it was something I felt when I was still human. So for me, yes, garlic is an effective deterrent. For others like me, I cannot say."

"Still human?" He gulped on the words. "Exactly how long ago was that?"

"One hundred and twenty years ago, give or take a few. Apparently based on the information I gleaned from Max before he died, I am quite young for one of my kind."

He shivered and turned away from me.

I went to the coffeemaker and filled the two mugs, pushing one into his hand. "Here. Now, shall we go sit down?"

He nodded and we went to the living room. I sat in the armchair and he chose the couch, studiously avoiding my eyes. "Chris." I said his name to get his attention and he jumped slightly. "What I have to tell you now is the worst of it. I must ingest at least one pint of human blood each week to feed myself. This is not something I can do without. If I allow the hunger to build, the instincts will take complete control over me, forcing me to feed whether I want to or not. There is no substitute for human blood; its taking is a necessity, and cannot be overruled. This is the first and foremost commandment in my life, one you must never forget. Rest assured, however, that my feeding does no permanent harm to my victims."

He sat silent for a while, drinking his coffee, staring off into space. When he asked his next question his voice was weak, hesitant. "But doesn't everyone you bite become a vampire when they die?"

I looked at him in shock. "Good heavens, Chris, no. Where on earth did you get that idea?" My honest laughter calmed him, and his voice grew stronger.

"You know, I read it in books."

"Can you imagine what would have happened by now if that fact were true? There would be no humans on the earth—everyone would be like me. The escalation on that would surely rival the current inflation rate."

"Yeah." He gave me a sheepish grin. "I guess I just wasn't thinking."

The levity of our exchange was a welcome relief to the tension, but there was more I had to say, even though I knew he would not like it.

"Chris, you must listen to me, this is very important. I love your father as much as possible given the incredible circumstances surrounding us. I will try to do nothing to hurt him while I am here. But I must feed, I have no choice. I do promise you that I will not do it here, in his apartment." I looked up from my coffee cup and met his eyes, holding contact with him as firmly as possible. "You must not be jealous for him. You must not ask questions about how I take my sustenance and you must not tell anyone what I am."

"I promise."

"And you must not come back here until I have fed again." I counted back to the last night I spent overseas. "It has been five nights now, and I want you to stay safe. Tonight will be fine, I will be in total control and we can go to the hospital together. But tomorrow I will go out and do what I need to do. It does not concern you, and"—my voice grew harsh—"it does not concern your father."

"But"—Chris sounded petulant—"he's doing so well. What'll I tell him?"

"You need tell him nothing. He knows what I must do."

He nodded, drained his coffee, and looked over at me. "Thank you for talking to me. I can see how hard it is for you to talk about it, and I appreciate your honesty. Plus, I'd never have had the guts to ask you those questions if you hadn't brought up the subject first."

"You must not be afraid of asking, Chris. I will answer if I can." Setting my empty cup on the table, I stood up. "Now, give me a minute or two to get dressed, and we'll go."

In the bedroom I checked the closet, found and put on a pair of black leggings and a red knit tunic that buttoned down the front, applied some makeup, and brushed my hair one more time. My standard high-heeled black pumps were in the living room by the door. I walked down the hall and stepped into them. Chris was still sitting where he had been when I had left, his legs stretched out and his head resting on the back of the couch.

"Chris?" The tone of my voice was tentative, almost plaintive.

"Yeah?" He picked his head up, rubbed his eyes, and glanced over at me.

"Well, tonight, as I already explained, should be a safe night. I was hoping that perhaps, after visiting hours, we could go somewhere. I don't sleep well these days and would enjoy the company."

"Sure, what would you like to do?"

Eager to return to the previous relationship I had enjoyed with Mitch's son, I said the first thing that came to mind. "I thought maybe we could play some pool."

His relaxed laugh was a relief to me. "Yeah, sure, we could do that. Just go easy on me, okay? I don't like losing any more than Dad does."

# Chapter 12

Mitch was dressed and waiting in the lobby when we arrived. Chris had seen him first and had run ahead, taking the front steps two at a time. I stopped just outside the door and watched them through the glass, smiling sadly to myself at their hugging and back-pounding. Only when Mitch's eyes sought mine over Chris's shoulder did I enter. Even then I held back guiltily, embarrassed somehow at the truths the three of us now shared. If Mitch had not moved away from Chris, if he had not given me the slow, sensual smile that lit up his blue eyes, I might well have turned around and walked away. But he held out his arms to me and I went into them willingly.

After our embrace, Mitch kept one arm around my shoulders and looked at Chris. "Well, did you bring it?"

"Oh, shit, I'm sorry, Dad. I meant to stop, honest, but I forgot."

"That's okay, Chris. I just figured that was why you were late." Mitch stopped a minute, dropping his arm from me and giving Chris a stern glance. "If you didn't get it, then why are you so late?"

Chris gave me an uncomfortable look. "Well, you see, Deirdre and I, we were talking, you know, and I—"

"I was explaining to Chris the facts of life, Mitch. Whatever it was he forgot, I take complete blame."

"The facts of life?" Mitch laughed. "He could probably tell us a few things about that subject, I bet."

Chris blushed bright red, and I felt sorry for him. "No, Mitch, the facts of my life."

"Oh." Mitch stopped laughing and nodded. "That's different. No problem, Chris. I was only joking with you anyway."

"What was he supposed to get that was so important?"

Mitch gave me a sheepish look. "My dinner—the food here is the worst. But it's really not as important as it seemed earlier, when I talked to you, Chris." He stopped for a minute, holding back the good news as long as he could. "They're letting me out tomorrow."

"Tomorrow?" Chris and I both said it at the same time.

"That's wonderful, Mitch. I'm so glad."

"But it's awful soon, isn't it, Dad? I mean, aren't they afraid you might have a relapse? Not that it's not good news or anything, but how could they have made that decision so quickly?"

"Chris, if I didn't know you better, I'd swear you were trying to keep me here. But those were my questions too. Dr. Samuels maintains that I am better. Hell, anyone can see that I'm better. And apparently he had a talk with Deirdre and she helped to ease his mind on a lot of things. I'll still have to check in on a regular basis." Mitch paused and gave a small grimace. "It's a lot like parole, as it turns out. But as long as I stay the same or continue to improve, he says that I'll be fine."

He reached over and patted Chris on the shoulder. "So you see, everything's going to be okay. Now, maybe you could run out and grab me something to eat anyway. I'd like to have some time alone with Deirdre."

"Mitch, is that fair? We'll have plenty of time alone when you're released." I shot Chris a quick glance to see if Mitch's order upset him. Oddly enough, he had a huge grin on his face.

"All right, Dad! Now I know you're back to normal." Chris walked to the door, turned, and waved. "Be back in about an hour. See you then."

Mitch took my arm and steered me down the hallway. I tensed as we passed the nurses' station, but Jean was nowhere in sight. When we got to his room he closed the door, a slow smile spreading across his face. "For obvious reasons, it doesn't have a lock. We'll just have to take our chances."

"Chances on what, Mitch?" Trying to maintain a teasing quality to my voice was difficult, for the boldness of his words, his glance, almost took my breath away. I felt a rush of excitement, along with the heat of an embarrassed blush, flowing through my body. In lieu of an answer, he moved one of the visitors' chairs in front of the door to prevent its opening, then reached over and turned out the light.

Surprised at his daring and fearful of discovery, yet strangely elated, I stood quietly, half afraid to move or speak. Then suddenly I did not care where we were, or who was likely to walk in on us. Mitch was back and we were together in spite of all the obstacles that fate had heaped before us, and that was all that mattered.

His first touch was a tentative, delicate stroking of my cheek with the back of his hand. I drew in my breath, silent and shivering, as his fingers traced their way along the base of my neck. He pulled me to him and kissed me, and the delicacy of his touch was soon abandoned. His hands grew rough and demanding, exploring my body, his kisses covering my face and neck. Finally he broke away and looked down on me with a shaky smile.

"Deirdre?" The whispering of my name gave me chills, and I could not speak. But I could give him the answer we both wanted. With trembling fingers I reached up and began to unbutton my tunic. Only when I unfastened the bottom button did I look up.

Mitch made no move, he only smiled as I began to work on his shirt. My hand brushed against the heated flesh of his chest, and he flinched slightly and sighed. When I tugged his shirt out of his pants and undid the last button, he pulled the tunic down over my arms and unfastened my bra.

His mouth nuzzled at my shoulder and I gasped. He moaned quietly as he worked his way down my breasts and stomach, and knelt to ease my leggings and panties down my hips and legs. He supported me with one arm, and obediently I followed his silent urging to lift first one leg and then the other. When I was completely naked, his mouth and hands fastened on me with hunger and passion.

Oblivious of our surroundings, I called his name again and again, flinging myself against him when he stood up. His eyes, reflecting the moonlight streaming in the windows, met mine, and he scooped me up and carried me to the bed. Hurriedly he removed his own pants and we lay naked, side by side, our mouths and bodies rediscovering each other.

After what seemed an eternity, or a second, he entered me and his breath on my neck was labored and hot.

"Deirdre, oh, God, Deirdre," he said. "I've waited so long."

I said nothing, but clasped him to me, careless of his crushing weight, careless of my sharp nails and teeth. Abandoning all thought, I felt my body pulled into the vortex of passion, swirling ever upward into him, into the union of our bodies and souls. I loosened my grasp. "Mitch," I whispered hoarsely, "look at me."

He supported himself on his arms above me and opened his eyes. The merging of our glances was electrifying, a more intimate moment than any we had ever experienced. The strength of that look alone brought our building orgasms to their peaks. I shuddered and cried, feeling myself dissolve in his arms. He collapsed against me, sobbing and spent, his fingers tangled in my hair.

When our breathing returned to normal, he rolled from me and started to dress. I threw back the sheets and picked up my clothing to do the same. As I buttoned my tunic, I began to laugh, and his questioning look only intensified my amusement.

"Something funny?" Mitch sounded mildly indignant. "It's sort of an inappropriate time to get the giggles, isn't it?"

"Oh, no, Mitch, it's not that." I went over to him and put my arms around him. "That was wonderful beyond words. It's just that"—and I started to laugh again—"I was wondering if Jean would be the one to change the sheets tomorrow."

"What does that have to do with anything?"

"Nothing, really. But she doesn't like me very much and I'm sure that this episode would only reinforce her bad opinion of me." I shrugged and slipped my shoes back on. "It makes no difference to me; the thought simply struck me as funny. Now, you should probably unblock the door and put the light back on."

Mitch smiled and nodded. "I love you," he said almost as an afterthought, walking over to move the chair and turn on the lights. He had not yet put his shirt on, and when I saw him in full light, I wanted to cry at the way his body had been wasted; those years apart had been harder on him than on me. He carried the reminders of our separation like battle scars, his hair gray, his normally tight muscles slack, and the flesh of his chest and back scarcely concealing the bones underneath. And when I saw the few reddened scratches on his back, I tensed and swore.

"Damn." I said it quietly, but he heard and turned to me.

"You've got it wrong, Deirdre. The correct response is 'I love you, too, Mitch.' Try it out, will you?"

"No, I didn't mean that. Your back is all scratched. I'm so sorry."

He craned his neck to look over his shoulder. "Am I bleeding?"

"God"—I took a short breath—"I hope not. Come here."

I ran my fingers gently over him. "Does this hurt?"

"No, it feels good," he said, then winced when I came into contact with one particularly nasty-looking scratch. "Well, maybe not good, but it feels right. Sort of like getting your first hickey. You're trying to hide it when all the while you want to shout out, 'Look what I got.' "

Worriedly, I checked his neck, then breathed my relief. "You're lucky in that respect, Mitch. No marks for Sam to wonder about during your release examination."

"And your examination results? Will I live?"

I put my arms around his waist and laid my cheek against his protruding shoulder blades. "Without a doubt, my love. Now, get your shirt on. Chris should be here soon."

"I like that, the way you've started calling me 'my love.' But you still haven't said it."

Giving him a small push so that he would turn around and face me, I put my arms around his neck and smiled up at him. "I love you, too, Mitch."

Chris arrived with their dinner about fifteen minutes later. I could hear the rustling bags and smell the greasy odor of cooked meat long before his tentative knock sounded outside the open door.

"Come on in," Mitch called, and Chris poked his head in with a slightly curious glance at the two of us.

"I hope you didn't mind waiting. The, um, line was pretty long." He walked into the room and set the bags on the bedside table. Mitch went for them immediately and unwrapped two of the sandwiches, an ecstatic smile on his face. He held the burgers up to his nose and inhaled deeply.

"Now I know I've died and gone to heaven. What else could I possibly ask for?" His tone was smug, satisfied, and the look he gave me betrayed what had occurred while Chris was gone.

Embarrassed, I felt myself blush. "If you two don't mind, I'll let you eat in peace. I could use some fresh air."

"You'll be back, won't you?" A pleading note entered Mitch's voice, belying his former confidence. I moved over to him and kissed him on the cheek.

"Of course I will. Enjoy your dinner."

I did not go outside, but continued down the hallway. When I got to the barred window, I stopped and looked out on the night. It was snowing again and a draft came through the cracks in the molding. Inhaling deeply to remove the odor of food from my system, I saw the reflection of one of the patients, shuffling toward me. He did not enter one of the rooms as I expected, but came right up behind me and spoke.

"Nice night, ain't it?" His voice was nasal, high-pitched, and monotonous.

"Yes, very beautiful." I didn't turn around, expecting he would quickly lose interest in conversation and go about his way. Instead, he put his hand on my shoulder and said again, "Nice night, ain't it?"

"Yes," I said louder, "it is a nice night."

"You're his girl, ain't you? The cop's girl? He killed someone, did you know that? Drove a stake right through the poor bastard's heart. I was here when they brought him in. I heard him talk about it all. He's crazy. We're all crazy here, but he's worse 'n us. He believes in vampires." His hand tightened on my shoulder, his grip unexpectedly strong. He was working his way into the story and the monotone he first used had become more vivid as he continued. His deep-throated laughter caused a shiver down my spine, and suddenly the hallway seemed too long, too far from the rest of the hospital.

"He's a crazy one, he is. He believes in vampires, I heard him." I watched him through the window, his mouth working, as if chewing on his words, his eyes losing their hollow and glazed appearance, growing in cunning and comprehension. "Maybe you're a crazy one too. Tell me"—his voice deepened, becoming more cultured, more familiar—"tell me, my dear, do you believe in vampires?"

I looked again at the reflection in the window. I had never seen him before, did not recognize his face. But when I spun around to confront him, to compel him to leave, Max stood before me. It was Max dressed in the hospital pajamas, Max with his robe hanging askew, one end of the sash dragging on the floor.

"Dammit, Max, go away and leave us alone. That's all I ask."

His face acquired his usual semisarcastic expression. "You should know by now, Deirdre my love, that I will never leave you. You are mine, even Greer cannot change that. Although"—he gave a nasty, knowing smile—"the sex is good, I must admit that. Perhaps that was the attraction I could not understand before. But he'll grow old, wrinkled, and impotent, as all humans must. And what will you do then?"

I made no response, but shoved past him and slowly

walked back to Mitch's room. The back of my shoulder blades itched, as if his gaze on me were a tangible thing. Then the feeling retreated and his presence seemed to evaporate. All that remained was the patient's original voice following me down the empty hallway, whining, and begging for an answer. "Nice night, ain't it?"

Mitch and Chris were sitting on the bed. They had finished their meal and were talking quietly, but the conversation had stopped abruptly when I approached the door. I didn't bother to ask them what they were discussing; I had heard my name mentioned by both of them before I entered, and their nuances of tone had not been wasted on me. Both had been angry, but Chris's voice sounded defensive, resentful. Dammit, I thought, I'm getting tired of justifying my existence, of apologizing for what I am.

"Feeling better?" Mitch smiled at me as I approached him, his eyes lit with his special way of looking at me.

"Yes," I lied without much conviction, "the walk helped clear my mind. But I'm afraid that I have to go now. I have some things to tend to if you're coming home tomorrow." I ignored the way Chris tensed at my remark, concentrating instead on Mitch's expression. He seemed disappointed, but not upset.

"Well, if you have to go . . ."

"I do. But I'll be eagerly awaiting your arrival tomorrow."

I moved over to the bed, and Mitch stood up and put his arms around me. I returned his hug and gave him a light kiss on the cheek. "Until tomorrow, then, my love." I turned to Chris and held out my hand. Reluctantly he stood up and shook it, then sat back down again without saying a word. Giving Mitch one final look, I walked out the door. To my relief, the patient who had spoken to me was no longer in the hall, and I hurried out the front doors.

# Chapter 13

There was a crowd standing around the entrance of the Ballroom when I arrived. The doorman I had seen previously still looked bored, but this night he was at least making an effort to examine the IDs of the patrons. I gave him a nod as I entered, and he caught my arm.

"Card?" he questioned, not looking up at me.

"Excuse me?"

"Driver's license, proof of age?"

"I'm afraid I don't have anything of that sort with me."

He gave a grunt. "Then you can't go in."

I was being jostled by the people behind me and thought that I should have gotten the key to Max's private entrance from Victor. The doorman let several people who had their cards ready go in ahead of me. Although I attempted to follow them, his arm extended across the door, blocking my entrance. I reached over, grabbing his wrist in my cold clasp, and he looked at my face.

"Now," I said with only a trace of the anger I felt, "do you recognize me?"

"No." He gave me a belligerent stare. "I don't. And I can't let you in, it's the rules."

"And, tell me"—my voice was almost a whisper, but it

silenced the complaints of the crowd behind me immediately—"who makes the rules? The owner?"

"Nah, I never met the broad. I take my orders from Mr. Lange."

"Then be so kind as to tell Victor that Deirdre Griffin is here."

He laughed a bit, obviously unable to place the name. "And who the hell are you that I should run your errands?"

I leaned over toward him and smiled, not very pleasantly, into his face. "The broad who owns this place."

"Oh, shit," he said, and his arm dropped.

"Exactly. And you and I will get to know each other later. Be here."

"Oh, shit, Miss Griffin, I didn't mean to give you a hard time or anything, I was just doing my job, you know. We've had some trouble with underage drinkers, and I was to card everyone who tried to get in. No exceptions."

"I understand, and you are doing a good job of it." I let go of his arm and gave him a real smile. "Don't worry, you won't be fired."

He rubbed his wrist. "Thank you, Miss Griffin. I really appreciate—"

I interrupted. "Now, tell me, is Victor here?"

"Yeah, back in his, or I mean, your office."

"Thank you." I moved past him and entered the bar. The music from the band was deafening; I had not yet adjusted to the pace and noise of life in New York. I shook my head slightly and headed toward the offices.

Once again the eerie feeling of déjà vu overtook me, and timidly, for fear of waking too many ghosts, I knocked on the closed door.

"Come in." Victor's voice carried well into the hall.

I opened the door and went in. "Hello, Victor. I'm a bit early, perhaps that will make up for last night."

"Deirdre." Victor crossed to me and kissed my hand. "It's so nice to see you. You're looking well." His eyes glinted with amusement. "I do hope you're enjoying your visit."

"Well"—I shrugged, not meeting his eyes—"it's not so much of a visit as it is a return home. I did live here for ten years, after all."

"Do you plan to stay, then? I'd always received the impression from Max that you were a bit of a Gypsy, that you never stayed in any one place, or with any one person, too long." He chuckled to himself and walked around the desk, sitting down in front of his open briefcase.

His attitude angered me. I didn't take kindly to jokes about my lifestyle from someone I did know, much less someone who was practically a stranger. I walked to the desk, leaned over, and looked down at his face, longing to slap the smile from it. "Victor, it seems to me that you did not receive the one impression of me from Max that I would most like to emphasize." Quickly and threateningly, I slammed the lid of his case down. He jerked his fingers away and looked at me with a shocked expression. I met his eyes and continued. "The one thing that I value most is my privacy. And what I most abhor are personal questions of any kind. If you and I are to continue in any relationship, business or otherwise, you must understand this. I dislike comments or judgments about my life from anyone. Max presumed upon a long-standing relationship; you and I do not share that same history."

Victor lowered his eyes, seeming to study the grain of the leather briefcase before him. "I'm sorry, Deirdre. I didn't mean to intrude upon your privacy; that would be the last thing I would want. And I do understand that you might think we don't know each other very well. But I feel as if I do know you, through Max." He raised his face to me again and I saw a sadness in his expression. "God, the way he talked of you, he made you seem so real to me. Through his love and admiration of you, I grew to admire you, maybe even love you a little myself. And now that he is gone"—Victor's voice acquired that slight, thin edge of anger it always did when he mentioned Max's death—"it seemed natural to me that as his best friend I should proceed as he would wish, providing support for you, the only woman he ever loved."

I wanted to laugh at this archaic and trite speech, to scoff at his expression of Max's love for me, but something in Victor's tone of voice, his complete sincerity and truthfulness, caused tears to well up in my eyes. I brushed them away with the remains of my anger. "Now I'm the one to be sorry, Victor. I meant no offense, and I hope you'll take none." I gave him a smile and sat down in front of the desk, my hands folded demurely on my lap, my voice soft and confidential. "One of my biggest problems is, I suppose, a fear of familiarity. There have been too many occurrences in my life of which I'm not proud, and I don't care to have them bandied about or made into humorous conversation. Max and I shared an unusual relationship, and now that he's gone, I'm not sure that I wish to pursue another of the same sort. I hope you can understand that this is not directed at you personally, and that you can forgive my harsh words."

"Please consider yourself forgiven, Deirdre. And please, if you can, consider me your friend. I've no reason to hurt you and every reason in the world to wish you well. Perhaps we have more in common than you would expect."

I laughed at this statement and gave him a hard stare. "Like what?"

"Well"—he shrugged and gestured around the office—"we are both owners of fairly successful night spots that have managed to stay in business for years. For this city, that should be enough."

I nodded. "That may be true, but I also have part interest in a failing pub."

"There you go! I've had a few flops over the years myself. Not that it matters, of course, but sometimes the ones that don't do so well are the ones we most enjoy." He stood up and walked to the window, pulling aside the shade, then sighed and turned again to me. His eyes were guarded now, his expression serious. "But there's something else we share, something that I know you feel, deeper than anything, a tie that could bind us together if you wish it to."

I tensed at his words, unsure of the point he was making, but thinking again that he seemed to know too much about me. As before, the voice deep within me urged me to trust him. I listened to it unwillingly, wanting to get up from my chair, leave the room, and never see Victor Lange again.

He was watching me intently, as if he sensed my inner conflict. "Go on," I said with more sharpness than I intended. "What sort of bond could you and I possibly share?"

He hesitated a moment. "I don't want to bring back bad memories, Deirdre, nor"—he gave me a calming smile—"do I wish to invite your anger again." Victor laughed and rubbed his hands together. "You're pretty formidable when you're angry. I might have lost some fingers earlier, and they might not have grown back."

How odd he is, I thought, but said nothing and let him continue.

"No, I don't wish to upset you, and although I understand completely why you're so sensitive about this matter, I must speak of it."

With every word he spoke I grew more nervous. He knows what I am, I thought, but, how could he? Max would not have told him, and I was surely discreet enough in my dealings with humans that he should have no inkling of my true self.

"What we share," Victor continued, "is something more important than businesses or restaurants. You attempt to hide it, but I know you feel it too."

"Please get to the point, Victor. What is it that I feel?"

"Outrage and anger at the ending of a good man's life. Grief and loneliness now that he is gone. Our bond is Max—the loss of Max, and our love for him."

He must have mistaken my breath of relief as a derisive comment and he looked at me sternly. "Oh, I know what it sounds like when I say that I loved him, but I did. He was like my son, my brother, a comrade-in-arms, so to speak. And I know that you are grieving for him too. This we share, and just maybe we can help each other through it."

"I am over it, Victor." My voice seemed strong and confident, hiding my internal trembling. "It's been two years since Max died, and I have dealt with his death. It's time to move on."

"Are you over it, Deirdre? Truly?"

I lowered my eyes to hide my confusion. This was not the conversation I had feared, but it was painful enough. How could I possibly explain to Victor what Max's death had done to me? I didn't trust him enough to confide in him about the visions, the dreams, the nightmares. How could I explain that I regretted the death more than I would ever have expected? And how could I tell him that I would murder his friend again, given the same circumstances?

"Yes," I said. "I am over it." I glanced at my watch impatiently, seeming even to myself cruel and callous. But it was getting late, and I had to feed tonight. I was determined that Mitch's release tomorrow, and our reunion, would not be marred by my need for blood. "Now, do you have some papers for me to sign?"

Victor looked at me, his eyebrows raised in surprise. I felt even more reprehensible than before. He had poured out his soul to me and I had returned his confidence with my petty concern about an inheritance.

"Yes," he said coolly. "I have the papers. Have you decided yet whether you will accept or not?"

"No, I thought I should review them first."

Victor nodded brusquely. "That would be wise, of course." He walked over to the desk and opened his briefcase, removing a folder and handing it to me. "Here, take them with you and read them at your convenience. You should have your attorney review them also. And if you have no attorney, I can recommend one for you."

His tone was businesslike and impersonal, and I suddenly regretted my treatment of him.

"Victor," I started, "I am sorry."

"Think nothing of it, it doesn't matter."

"Oh, but it does. To me, it does. You are right, of course"—I gave him a quick glance to see if he was looking at me—he was staring with pain at the folder clutched in my hands, "blood money" his glance said—"I haven't gotten over Max's death and it would be a help to talk with someone about it. But not now, not tonight; it's still too raw, too painful. Give me some time, please."

Finally he smiled at me, a sad sort of smile that did not reach his eyes. "We can talk again, anytime, whenever you feel ready. Keep in touch." He closed and locked his briefcase and walked toward the door. He stepped out, then abruptly turned around. "And don't worry, any secrets you wish to guard will be safe in my confidence. Trust me."

I watched him walk out the door, then went over and

sat at the desk, laying the folder down in front of me. "I trust you, Victor, all right," I muttered, "but only about as far as I can throw you." I opened the folder and attempted to read the first page. It might as well have been in a foreign language for all that I understood. Deciding to accept Victor's offer of an attorney, I pushed the papers over to one side of the desk.

I opened the top desk drawer and idly rifled through its contents, feeling like an intruder in Max's office. Everything was organized, neatly lined up in little compartments and boxes that I almost hated to disturb. Nevertheless, I lifted everything out and spread the entire contents of the drawer over the desktop. Even with Max's curious black scrawl labeling some of the items, the collection was oddly impersonal; there remained no imprint of the man. I picked up the silver letter opener, remembering it as part of a gift I had given him when the Ballroom had opened, remembering a time when Max had stood, turning it over and over in his hand. When I had asked what he was thinking, he had said sadly, "Silver for werewolves and wood for vampires."

I wondered now, as I did then, what he had meant. We had been quarreling; maybe he was threatening me. Or, and the new thought came into my head only because I knew now what he was, maybe he was threatening to take his own life. At the time, though, I had been too wrapped up in my own concerns to question him. So many things he could have told me, so many things I could have learned from him had I but asked; all this knowledge was lost with his death. And there was no one to blame but myself, and my complacency, my goddamned preoccupation with independence.

I laughed bitterly at my thoughts; I had never been independent. When I looked back at our relationship I could see now that Max had always called the shots, had always directed my actions, subtly and shrewdly manipulating my emotions, my habits, my view of the world. Hell, he's doing it even now, I thought, from the grave.

But he had miscalculated at the last, underestimating the love that Mitch and I had shared. A shiver went through me when I considered how close I had come to killing Mitch, how I had nearly acted on Max's order. How could he have failed to know how I would react? Max knew me, probably better than I knew myself. What fatal flaw in his thinking had led him to push me to my limits?

Two years of thoughts about Max's death, and I still had no answers. The visions and dreams of him merely posed more questions. I laughed again, humorlessly. I could almost believe they were a true contact with Max, that a portion of his soul or his being was communicating with me in this way. He was certainly as demanding, as infuriating, as when he was alive.

"And all of it is getting you nowhere, Deirdre," I said, and began putting the drawer contents away, holding out only the letter opener, a key ring, and a small black address book. I stood up and walked over to the couch where I had laid my purse, and put the items inside. Then I went behind the office bar. The shelves contained only glasses and the refrigerator was empty.

"Damn," I swore, wanting a drink to fortify myself against what I had to do this night. Somewhere out on the dance floor was a man, with warm flesh and hot blood, I would have to seduce and upon whom I had to feed. There was no other choice, it had to be done tonight. And I knew what would happen: the darker self would take control of my emotions, and my body, so recently touched by Mitch in love, would be possessed by someone I did not know, and did not like. It was the greatest of all obscenities, and it was the life I now led.

I looked around the office. I was wrong in thinking that Max had made no impression here. While I lived, so did he. I carried him with me as surely as I carried his heritage, his inheritance.

"Damn you to hell, Max Hunter, for all your gifts to me. I don't want any of them." I gave the bar an angry shove, and to my surprise it toppled over and hit the floor. The crystal glasses jumped and shattered, spreading thousands of shimmering fragments across the room. I walked over them; they crunched under my shoes, like the frozen grass in the cemetery where Max was buried. I took my purse from the couch, turned out the lights, quietly shut the door, and went out to the club, where a man I did not know waited.

# Chapter 14

The band was not playing and most of the people that had been dancing were now gathered around the bar. I hesitated briefly, not wanting to push my way through the crowd, until I realized that, at least until I declined Max's offering, I was the owner. I stepped around the back of the bar, lifted the counter, and walked up right behind Fred, lightly putting a hand on his shoulder.

"Shit!" He jumped and spilled the drink he was pouring. When he saw it was me, he smiled apologetically. "Oh, hi, Miss Griffin. I didn't know you were here." As he talked, he deftly wiped the bar and served a new drink without batting an eye. "Busy tonight. Just like old times, huh?" I stood for a moment, watching him, admiring his technique. "So," he said, handing out another glass, "what can I do for you?"

"A drink would be nice."

He reached up and removed a wineglass from the overhead rack. "The usual?" At my nod he filled it with the rich deep red wine I preferred. I drained it while he watched and handed it back so he could refill it. "Bad day? We could talk about it. I'm good at that, you know."

"I'm sure you are, Fred. But some other time, if you please. Right now could you get someone to sweep out the office? I am afraid I knocked the bar over."

He stopped and stared at me. "You did what?"

I laughed. "Knocked over the bar in the office. There's broken glass all over the floor."

"You are having a bad day. No problem, consider it done. Anything else?"

"No, not really. I think I'll mingle for a while."

"Oh, that reminds me. Ron is here."

"Ron?" At first I didn't place the name, but Fred gave me a knowing smile and a shrug of his shoulders.

"You know, Ron, from the other night. You must've made quite an impression on him. He's been hanging around ever since, looking for you."

"Great."

Fred didn't miss the sarcasm in my voice. "I could have him thrown out if you want me to."

"No, that won't be necessary." As I thought further about the situation, I decided that Ron presented an ideal solution. I knew him already, had even gone to bed with him once. A second time would not hurt, and this time I could rectify my previous mistake, taking enough blood to leave him open to my suggestions. I smiled at Fred, feeling the tingling sensation of hunger begin. "Actually," I said, my voice husky and low, "I want to see him again very much. Where is he?"

Fred pointed him out for me. Picking up the bottle of wine and two glasses, I moved across the dance floor to where Ron sat waiting at my regular table.

"Hello, stranger," I whispered as I slid into the chair beside him. "Where have you been?"

"Deirdre." He leaned toward me and kissed me on the lips. "You are here, then. They told me you weren't here tonight. I've been looking for you."

"So I've heard. But I've been rather busy the past few days. And I told you I would call."

"Yeah." Ron reached over and touched my hair, separated and held a lock under his nose, inhaling the scent of it, rubbing it over his neck and cheek. "But I missed you. I guess I didn't really believe you would call." He stopped a minute and looked at me. "Hey, you changed your hair color, didn't you? It looks nice."

"This is my real color anyway."

"I knew that."

I jumped slightly at his remark. "How could you possibly know what my natural color is?"

He gave me a sly smile and a wink.

"Oh, I said, suddenly angry at his blatant attitude. "Of course." Restraining the urge to slap his face, I gave him a direct stare. He was grinning at me, but not maliciously and not as if he had deliberately intended to embarrass me. After all, I reminded myself, if you are going to play the tramp, you must expect to be treated as one.

I forced a smile before he could notice my uneasiness and poured us each a glass of wine.

He hesitated before sipping it. "I'd planned on staying sober enough to enjoy your company. But I guess one glass won't hurt." He held up his glass and clinked it against mine. "To the most intriguing woman I've ever known."

We talked for a while, small talk mostly. His conversation centered around his private law practice. Mine was about the sale of Griffin Designs, and a brief description of my stay abroad.

"Deirdre, I can't believe you just walked out of a thriving business. What on earth were you thinking of? Didn't you have anyone to advise you?"

"No, it wasn't that. It was time to leave, so I left."

"That easily? No second thoughts?"

I laughed a bit. "Well, not about selling out anyway. The sale itself left me with enough money to relocate and live off comfortably for many years."

"And what will you do when that runs out? Don't you have any provisions for retirement and old age?"

"My thoughts on old age, Ron, are unrepeatable. But I assure you, I am well endowed."

"I know." I blushed; his comment had nothing to do with my financial situation. Then he gave me an appraising glance, checking out my clothes, my jewelry. "So, you're rich too?"

I gave his hand a small tap. "What a question to ask, Ron. Does it make any difference?"

"No, not really." He moved closer to me, rubbing his leg against mine. "I'd want you even if you hadn't a penny to your name. But if you ever need a good attorney, you might just keep me in mind."

"Well, now that you mention it," I started to say, but stopped when I noticed Fred, standing next to my shoulder.

"Miss Griffin," he said, nodding at Ron, "your office is finished. Should I lock it up again?"

"No, I expect to be back in later on. Thank you."

"Oh, and I restocked the bar for you, including a new set of glasses." His eyes sparkled with repressed laughter. "But I wouldn't go barefoot for at least a couple of days if I were you. It was a real mess."

"Thank you, Fred. I really appreciate it."

"No problem."

Ron glanced at me when Fred left. "You have an office here? I knew you were a regular, but an office?"

Laughing, I stood up and took his hand. "It's not exactly mine yet, but that doesn't matter." He got to his feet, and I pulled him to me. I had procrastinated long enough; it was time for me to get to the point. I gave him a seductive smile, kissed him on the neck, and whispered in his ear, "I suspect that one of the sofas opens into a bed. Would you like to come see?"

We made our way down the hall, and I opened the door of the office and flicked the lights on.

Ron whistled appreciatively. "This is your office, huh? Just exactly what do you do here?"

"I don't know yet, but apparently I own the place."

He gave a small gasp and stopped in midstride. I caught a knowing gleam in his eye before he recovered his composure. Then he turned away and walked to the bar. "So," he said, his tone casual, confidential, "you're the one Max Hunter left all his money to?"

I was astonished at Ron's mention of that name. "Did you know Max?"

"Me?" He hesitated and looked up from the bottle he was opening. "Oh, God, no. I don't run in such rarefied circles. Of course, I've been coming to the Ballroom for a while, so I knew who he was. And he must have known me by sight at least, but it would be stretching the fact to say that we knew each other." He pulled the cork out and poured two glasses. "Did you know that every attorney in this city has been hoping to discover the missing heiress? And I run into you by chance." He laughed and walked over to me to hand me the drink.

"To the richest woman you know?" I anticipated his toast.

"Easily," he said, his voice warm and sensual. "But as I told you before, that doesn't matter. I do okay for myself. Oh, I guess I could always use a little more, but I'm not some gigolo out looking for a free ride."

I looked at him warily. "No?"

"No way. I do have ulterior motives"—he gave me a sincere smile, practiced, perhaps, but still honest—"but they have nothing to do with your money. Now, drink your wine like a good girl and turn out the lights."

I did as he asked and crossed the room, feeling foolish and dirty. I allowed him to embrace me, stood motionlessly while he unbuttoned my sweater. He put his arms around me and his hands caressed my bare skin. But I felt nothing, no hunger and no arousal. We need this man, I urged myself, we need his blood. I closed my eyes and stretched up to kiss him, trying to pretend that he was Mitch. It didn't work; my senses were too deeply developed and he didn't taste or feel the same. I nuzzled his neck, hoping to awaken my feeding instincts, and he moaned, but there was no answering response in my body or mind.

"Damn." I pushed him away from me, walking over to the window, my hands clutching the open edges of the sweater. Silent tears began to flow down my face.

"Deirdre?" His voice seemed to travel a great distance to reach me. I ignored his presence, as if that would make him leave me alone. "What's wrong? Are you crying?"

I didn't answer. Ron came up behind me and put his hand on my shoulder. His touch was gentle, reassuring, more like the touch of a friend than a lover. *Please be a friend,* I silently begged him, *I've had enough lovers.* I needed someone I could trust, someone in whom I could confide. And although that type of relationship was impossible for me, I responded to his delicate urging, turned around, and let him hold me while I cried.

He stroked my hair, and when the sobbing subsided, he cleared his throat softly. "Feeling better?" he asked, his voice subdued. "Want to talk about it?"

"Not really." I sniffed and went to the bar for a couple of napkins to wipe my face. "I am sorry, Ron. It's nothing personal, but it's just no good. I can't do it, not with you."

He laughed nervously. "Sure sounds personal to me, but don't worry. Do I look like the kind of guy who needs to force himself upon crying women? It's just that the other night was special, different. I thought you felt the same."

"I'm glad it was special for you, but for me it was a mistake." Ron's eyes grew angry, and I tried to make amends. "No, I don't mean that the way it sounds. I like you, very much it turns out, but since I'm already emotionally involved with someone else, the entire situation is too difficult for me to handle. I'm not very good at interpersonal relationships; you can probably tell that. The words never come out right."

"If you are involved with someone else, why did you bring me back here?"

"I thought I could at first. But then, when we were talking and I got to know you better, I found that it was impossible."

"And the other night?"

"Well, I didn't know you that night, you were anonymous. That plus the fact that my other relationship didn't seem to be working out." I smiled ruefully, and rubbed my jaw in remembrance.

"So who is this other guy? Some rich s.o.b. like Hunter?"

"Oh, God, no. Not at all." I looked over at Ron and smiled shyly. "Actually he's a policeman."

He gave me a long, unfathomable look. "A cop? You're joking, aren't you?" He paused a bit, then continued. "No, you're not, are you?" He began to laugh, instantly easing the tension in the room. "No one, especially you, would joke about that. Fell for the uniform, did you?"

"He is a detective; I've never seen him in uniform."

"But you've seen him out of uniform enough times to do the trick, I suppose. Speaking of which, close up your sweater, please. If nothing is going to happen, I'd like not to be reminded of my failure all evening." He spoke pleasantly, his anger gone. "And I guess I might as well drink myself blind. Care to join me?"

I nodded, fastened the buttons, and, walking to him, accepted another glass of wine. My eyes caught his and I began to giggle, then laugh boisterously. He looked puzzled but eventually joined me, and we both stood like a pair of idiots laughing at nothing.

"I think it was the bit about the uniform," I said when I could speak. "It struck me as funny. This has been a most interesting evening." I took a sip of the wine and looked at him in a new light. He was right; he wasn't looking for a free ride. And he seemed to be someone I could trust. Walking over behind the desk, I picked up the folder containing Max's will and held it out to him. "Now, shall we get down to business?"

"Business? I thought you didn't want to."

"No, not that kind of business. I happen to be in the market for some legal advice. Can you recommend an honest lawyer?"

"I'm not sure whether it would be a wise move for me to represent you," he said as he hesitantly walked toward me.

"Why not? I'll pay you well."

"I don't need your goddamned scraps, Deirdre. I'm not some snarling mutt panting after the first bitch in heat I find." He put his arms down at his sides, his fingers tensed and splayed out. "You don't want to sleep with me. Okay, I can deal with that. But you don't have to offer me compensation. Quite frankly, I don't think I like the games you're playing with me."

"Ron." I moved around the desk and touched his arm. "I haven't been playing games. I like you and I trust you." He pulled away from me and refused to meet my eyes, but I continued. "That doesn't happen very often. I require legal representation and I think you could perform the job to my satisfaction. You may choose to turn the offer down, but I hope you won't. I need your help."

When he raised his head, his eyes looked sad. "I've always been a sucker for ladies in need," he said with a reluctant smile. "And you say you're not good at handling people. Let me have some time to think it over, and check on the professional ethics involved. Can I let you know tomorrow?"

"That would be fine, Ron, thank you." I wrote down Mitch's address and phone number on a scrap of paper and handed it to him. "This is where I'm staying and the number there. Don't lose it, I suspect the number is unlisted. Any time in the late afternoon would be a good time to call."

He folded the paper carefully and put it into his coat pocket. "I'll guard it with my life. And I'll talk to you tomorrow, then. Good night." He began to extend his hand, then shook his head with a grin and put his arms around me. "What the hell," he said, kissing me lightly on the lips. "I think you just bought yourself an attorney."

# Chapter 15

The buzzing of the intercom interrupted my second attempt to read Max's will. Tentatively, I pushed the button on the phone. "Yes?"

"Miss Griffin? This is Fred. I hope you don't mind the interruption, but I saw Ron leave and figured it would be okay."

"What is it, Fred?"

"Johnny said you wanted to see him. He's about ready to go home now and said that you told him not to leave until you talked. He's a bit shook up."

"Johnny? Who the hell is Johnny?"

"The doorman. Shall I send him back?"

"Oh, the doorman, I forgot all about him." I sighed. I wasn't really ready for another personal encounter. "Yes, Fred, go ahead and send him back."

A minute later Johnny stood knocking at the open door.

"Come in, Johnny, and close the door behind you, please."

He walked in gracelessly, a gangly youth, probably no more than twenty-one or -two. He seemed so much younger here in my office; not occupying the position of authority at the door had robbed him of his maturity. He had a thick crop of black hair that fell forward into his eyes as he sat on one of the chairs and stared down at the floor. Not wanting to make this meeting too formal, I walked around and sat on the edge of the desk, my legs crossed, one foot idly swinging.

"So, Johnny, how long have you been working here?"

"About six months," he muttered.

"And do you like it?"

He looked up at me, "Yeah, it's a good job. And I don't want to lose it, Miss Griffin. It's just not fair of you to fire me for not recognizing you." His face acquired a sullen expression, making him look even younger. "I mean, I didn't know who you were, I was just doing what they said I should." He glanced back at the floor as if something caught his interest there.

"I am not going to fire you, Johnny. Actually I suppose I should be flattered that you thought I was young enough to need identification." I had expected he would look up again, but still he stared at the floor. I grew annoyed at his lack of attention and leaned over the desk to see what was occupying his attention. "Is something wrong?"

"No," he said, getting up from his chair and kneeling on the floor. "But there's something shiny under your desk. Let me get it for you."

Before I could protest, he reached and picked up a rather thick shard of crystal. "Here," he said with pride, "this could really hurt if you stepped on it."

He put one hand on the edge of the desk and stood up, gripping the glass in his other hand. When he dropped it in the wastebasket, I could see the small cut on his thumb, smell his blood in the air.

"You've cut yourself," I said breathlessly.

"Yeah, but it's not too bad." He put his thumb into his mouth and sucked on the wound.

"Ah." A groan inadvertently escaped my lips, and the hunger within me that had not appeared with Ron raged like a fever through my body. My voice grew deeper, more husky. "Don't do that. Hold out your hand and let me see," I ordered, moving closer to him. Reluctantly he held his hand out and I cradled it in my own two hands. Our eyes met and he was caught. Before I even knew I had reacted, I pulled him to me. He tensed, then relaxed and smiled, wrapping his arms around me as I kissed him, stroking his thick black hair. My mouth found his neck, and my instincts reacted immediately. I sunk my teeth deep into the vein and his blood washed into my mouth, filling my body with warmth and energy.

"More, take more," the inner voice coaxed. Max's presence was strong, and his craving for life pushed me further, urging me to gorge myself upon this young body. "Drink," he whispered with a dark joy. "Take it all, take it all."

Johnny's grip on me began to weaken, and I could feel the strength fading from his limbs with each swallow I took. His body trembled against mine.

With a great effort of will I slowed on the pulling of Johnny's blood, gradually weaning myself of its intoxicating taste. Removing my mouth, shuddering at the shock of its removal, I tried to ignore the inner wail of disappointment and anger, concentrating instead on the live warm body I held against me. Johnny swayed slightly; his eyes were closed, his mouth curved into a small, sensual smile. I moved away from him, held his face in my hands, and called his name softly.

"Johnny, open your eyes." When he did, I continued. "Nothing happened here. Can you remember that? Nothing happened."

"Yeah," he agreed, "nothing happened. I feel funny. Can I sit down?"

I smiled at him. "Sit. Let me get you something to drink."

When I came back with his drink, his eyes were more focused and the dreamy expression had faded from him.

"Here," I said kindly, handing him the glass, and watched him drink it in one gulp. "Do you feel better now?"

"Yeah, I guess so. What happened?"

I laughed, attempting to put him at ease. "You cut yourself, remember?"

He nodded slowly. "It's kind of funny, the sight of blood never bothered me before."

"Well"—I shrugged—"these things do happen."

"Yeah." He still sounded confused, but stood up abruptly. "Can I go now?"

I made eye contact with him again, and he showed no fear, no recognition of what I was. "You most certainly can, Johnny. Thank you."

"For what?"

"Why, for being so diligent in your work."

He returned my smile. "Gee, thanks a lot, Miss Griffin. See you later, huh?"

Hoping that would be the last of the interruptions that evening, I returned to my desk and the reading of the will. I advanced only a page, however, before there was another tentative knock on the office door.

"Damn," I said under my breath, then louder, "come in.

"Am I interrupting?" Fred walked halfway into the office.

"No, what the hell, come on in, everyone else in the world has been here tonight."

He gave me a quizzical look. "You really are having a bad day, aren't you?"

I gave an exasperated smile and pushed my hair back from my face. "No, the day was fine. It's the night that's been a problem. Honestly, how did Max ever get anything done?"

Fred laughed. "Max never slept and was almost always here, day and night. Most places like this never see the owner; they have managers and assistant managers to handle the day-to-day affairs. But Max did everything himself. We all wondered when he would break . . ." His voice trailed off.

Max's death and the murders he had committed to earn him that death were public knowledge. That he truly was what the papers called him in jest, the Vampire Killer, had been kept secret. I knew the effect his deeds had upon my life and Mitch's, but had never given any thought to what others might think. It might prove interesting to get Fred's version of the story.

"You think it was the tension, then, the pressures of his life, that drove him to kill those people?"

Fred smirked. "I think the man was crazy; you only had to work for him for a month to see that. But I'd never have believed him a killer." He gave a small chuckle. "I wouldn't have thought he'd want to dirty his hands that way."

"So you believe he was innocent?"

"Hell, no, I think he did it. Don't you?"

"I know he did it, Fred. I heard it from his own lips, and Max, for all his faults, rarely lied to me." I laughed bitterly. "There were many things he didn't tell me, but when he spoke, he spoke the truth."

Fred nodded. "Yeah, he was like that. It was always the things he didn't say that got you." He glanced around the office and shrugged. "Anyway, I guess it was bound to happen, but it sure was strange, both him and Larry being carried out of here dead. And you know, the place was packed for months afterward, people sneaking in to visit the cellar and the office as if they were shrines or something. You'd think they'd stay away after all that, but we were turning them from the door in droves." His eyes shifted away for a minute and then came back to rest on me. "Speaking of the door, you did a good job on Johnny."

"Excuse me?" I jumped at his comment and knocked the folder on the floor. "What about Johnny?"

Fred moved down on his hands and knees to help me pick up the scattered papers.

"Be careful," I warned him, "there may still be some glass down there. Johnny found a piece and cut himself."

"No problem." He handed me the papers and I put them into the top drawer.

"What about Johnny?" I repeated, eager for his answer.

"Well, I don't know what you said to him, but whatever it was, it worked. He walked in like he was going to his own hanging and he walked out with a big smile on his face. We've had trouble with him before. He's not exactly the smartest person alive. I mean, he does pretty good as long as he doesn't have to make any decisions on his own. Anyway, I think he thought that you were going to fire him. I take it you didn't."

"No, of course not. I'm not legally the owner yet, so I'm sure that any decision of that nature would be a little premature."

"Not the owner? But Max left the Ballroom to you. How could you not be the owner?"

I saw no need to discuss with Fred the possibility of my declining Max's estate. "I haven't signed the papers yet."

"Oh, if that's all, that's no big deal. Anyway, I don't want to take up much more of your time. I just wondered if you'd like me to get the staff together tomorrow for a meeting, you know, to meet you."

"So that I won't be turned away again for lack of identification?"

"Yeah." He gave me a broad smile that I returned. "Is tomorrow too soon, do you think?"

"Probably. Tell me, who's been employed here the longest?"

"That dubious honor belongs to me, Miss Griffin. I was the first person Max hired. I've always hoped to be the one to lock up when we close for the final time."

"Look, call me Deirdre, please. This Miss Griffin address is beginning to annoy me. It makes me feel positively ancient."

He gave me a sly look. "As if anyone would think you were old. I don't believe you've aged a day since the first time I saw you."

"Inside, I feel like Methuselah. But let's forget about age. Tomorrow evening I want to meet with you about how the Ballroom is being run and how you would like to change it. And if you have any suggestions about an appropriate manager"—I gave him a calculated look, thinking he would probably want the job, and, that even if I didn't like him very much, he would be good at it—"please say so. I don't plan on devoting my entire life to this place—one night a week should do just fine."

"Great," he said, and went to the door. He turned around again before leaving. "You know, Deirdre, I've sort of been dreading your return, hoping that you wouldn't come back. You and I never really clicked before, and I blame a lot of that on Max's attitude toward you. You were untouchable—none of us was allowed to refer to you by anything other than Miss Griffin, as if you were goddamned royalty or something. Jesus, I remember a time when a waitress was fired on the spot for some derogatory remark about you. She didn't say it to Max, of course, but he heard everything, saw everything. Lange's a lot like that too. But you seem different, warmer maybe, more approachable, or"—he gave an ingratiating smile—"maybe you're just better looking than I remembered." Then he shrugged, seeming embarrassed. "Well, anyway, that was a pretty long speech. I really only wanted to say that I'm glad you're back now, and I hope you'll stick around for a while."

"Thank you, Fred. Good night."

By the time I arrived outside Mitch's apartment that night, it was after three. The night was cold and clear and the moon was full. I rummaged around in my purse and found the crumpled pack of Players I had brought from England. One cigarette was left—it had lost a little of its tobacco, and was crooked—but I straightened it out with my fingers. Sitting down on the steps of the brownstone, I lit it and inhaled both the smoke and the night air deep into my lungs. I stretched my legs out in front of me, enjoying the feel of the tightening muscles and the warmth of Johnny's blood flowing through my body, rejuvenating and energizing. This is the best time, I thought, when the overpowering hunger is gone, the hunting successfully completed, the feelings of youth and life renewed.

I should have gone into the apartment, but the night seemed peaceful and I remained sitting on the steps. The smoke from my cigarette curled thickly into the still air; I blew on it playfully and, as the smoke dissolved into nothingness, replayed the evening in my mind.

It had been a strange night, to say the least, and a busy one. Of all the events, the one that I tried to hold closest was the fact that Mitch had indeed recovered. That, I reminded myself, was the reason I had returned. Even if things didn't work out between us, and I still didn't see how they could, he was cured. I had helped him recover his life. His demons had been effectively dismissed, even though mine were still snapping at my heels, tearing at my throat. I sighed and tossed the burning cigarette into the street, watching the flurry of sparks as it hit. Then I stood up, brushed off the back of my cloak, and reached in my purse for the key to the door.

I was not surprised, just slightly annoyed, when I heard the approaching footsteps. "Hello, Max," I said curtly, crossing my arms and turning away from the door slowly. "I was wondering when you would show up."

I looked into the face of a total stranger; his forehead was dotted with beads of sweat, his eyes darted nervously, searching the dark street. "I ain't no Max, lady. Gimme your purse."

He grabbed at the bag; my hand shot down and held his right wrist in an unbreakable grip. "No, it's mine. But I will give you some money if you want."

"Give, like hell. I'll take what I want." He tried to wrench away from me, but finding himself securely held, he reached around and fumbled in his right-hand pocket with his free hand. I tightened my fingers around his wrist in warning and twisted his arm slightly. "On second thought"—I smiled warmly in his face—"I don't believe I have any cash at all." He shifted back and forth on his feet, his left hand still in his pocket. "I don't suppose"—I felt the cracking of bones as I continued my pressure on his wrist—"you would accept a check."

He didn't answer, but gave a feeble whimper. His face was now drenched in sweat and his eyes filled with pain.

"No." I smiled at him again and he shrank away from me. "I didn't think so." One final twist ensured that his arm would be immobilized for a while.

"Jesus, you bitch, you broke my arm." He stood his ground indignantly, cradling his wrist, tears streaming down his face.

"So I did," I said pleasantly, climbing the steps and removing the key from my purse. "You should have someone look at it. Go home now. And find another line of work." I turned away from him with an amused laugh and opened the door. "You don't seem to be smart enough to handle petty robbery."

The insult must have been the final straw. I heard the shot and felt the burning pain of the bullet enter my left shoulder. I could hear his rasping breathing, and the echoing retort of the gun. The smell of gunpowder was thick in the air.

Anger rose up within me, a terrifying, inhuman anger that I knew to be entirely my own. How dare he try to hurt me, I thought, and then, he must pay for this wound.

I spun around slowly and he was still standing two steps away, amazed perhaps that I hadn't cried out or fallen down. He held the gun awkwardly in his left hand. I kicked it away roughly, breaking his other wrist in the process. Then I reached down, grabbed the fabric of his coat, and held him up to my face. Our eyes made contact, and I smiled at him once more, this time with canines fully exposed.

"You stupid bastard," I hissed at him. "I gave you a second chance. You should have taken it and run." His eyes rolled in his head and he whimpered again. "And now it's too late."

"Whatcha gonna do?" His voice was hoarse with fright. The combination of the smells of his fear and my own blood was intoxicating. I laughed, and his answering shudder was gratifying, fueling my instincts.

I shifted my grip, holding him with one hand and stroking his greasy hair with the other. "Why, lover," I purred deep in my throat, "I only want to kiss you good night."

His terror intensified my feeling of elation and anticipation. His feet kicked feebly as I dug my fingers into his hair, roughly pulled his head over, and pierced his neck with my fangs. Although I was not hungry, my anger fueled my instincts and I fed on him for a while, leaving him with more than enough blood to survive. Then I dropped him. His limp body rolled down the steps and he groaned softly when he hit the sidewalk.

# Chapter 16

When I entered the apartment I went to the bedroom window. My attacker was slowly pulling himself up from the pavement, looking around, I assumed, for his gun. I knocked on the window and he looked up at me in fear, his eyes rolling slightly, then took off at a slow run. I gave a small laugh while I watched him disappear into the night. "That felt wonderful," I said, and stood for a moment, savoring the elation of my victory. "Just like being a god."

When the words escaped my lips, the joy I felt suddenly turned into abhorrence for both the deed and the thoughts that accompanied it. Was this how Max had started his killing spree, with the thrill that complete power over human beings could bring? "No," I said to my reflected image. "I will not be like Max."

I turned away from the window, wincing at the pain caused by the movement. This wound will have to be dealt with very soon, I thought, and pulling off my cloak and sweater, went into the bathroom and looked at the wound in the mirror.

There was a blackened hole in the back and a small amount of bruising on the front of my shoulder. I had bled a little, evidenced by the slight trickle of dried blood traced on my back, but my body, strengthened by two feedings, was already healing. Unfortunately, the bullet was still lodged inside. I could feel its alien presence there, a small, nagging pain that I knew would have to be removed. But, I thought as I stiffly twisted my arms around, I wouldn't be able to do it myself.

"Damn," I addressed my image, "who the hell am I going to get to do this?"

Mitch would be home tomorrow, but I hated to burden him so soon after his release. And any type of hospital was totally out of the question. I prodded my shoulder but could not feel where the bullet had lodged. If I had, I would have cut it out myself from the front.

I took off the rest of my clothes, went into the bedroom, and slipped on Mitch's robe. I picked up my cloak and sweater, examined the holes in both garments, and tossed them into the wastebasket with disgust. I jumped at the sharp twinge the movement caused me. Using my arm was painful, and I had no idea what sort of limitations the injury might impose on me. The bullet would have to come out, that much was certain.

On my way through the living room I picked up the Yellow Pages, then went to the kitchen, opened the second bottle of wine, and poured myself a large glass. Sitting at the table, I leafed through the pages of doctors' numbers. Only a very few made house calls, and I knew none of them. The only doctor I knew at all was Sam, and he could be of no help. I looked up his number anyway, and sat for a while, drinking and staring at the sky through the window. Dawn was still hours away, but I needed to take care of the situation soon.

"What the hell." I got up and went to the phone. "He owes me for the story I told him the other night." I dialed the number and a surprisingly alert voice answered on the second ring.

"Sam, this is Deirdre Griffin. I am sorry to call so early. Did I wake you?"

"No, I'm on early shift this morning. But what are you doing up already? I thought you were a night owl."

I laughed nervously. "Actually, I haven't been to bed yet."

"Oh." There was a slight pause. "Is something wrong?"

"Well, yes. I was wondering if you could recommend a doctor for me. I have a bit of a problem here."

"Deirdre, if it's an emergency, you should call for an ambulance right away. Better still, I'll call one for you."

"No!" I interrupted. "No ambulance. And it's not really an emergency. But I need to find someone who makes house calls, someone who can be trusted, someone who can get here soon."

"Sure sounds like an emergency to me. I'll be right over."

"But it's not a mental problem, it's physical."

"I'm a psychiatrist." He paused, then continued when I didn't reply. "That means that I'm a physician too. And although I don't usually make house calls, I've got to admit that you've got me intrigued. I can be there in twenty minutes; can you hold on till then?"

"Yes," I said, wondering how I would answer the questions I knew he would ask. "Thank you, Sam. I really appreciate it."

"Don't mention it. Now, explain the situation, please, just so I know what I need to bring with me."

I thought for a moment. If I told him what was involved, he would never come. He would insist on an ambulance and a trip to the hospital. And that could be deadly for me. "We'll improvise; trust me, it'll all be fine."

"Okay." I could hear his reluctance. "But I'll bring my bag anyway. See you in a bit."

I hung up the phone, went back to the kitchen, and poured another glass of wine. I had no idea whether any type of anesthetic would work on me, and I could not allow him to put me to sleep in any event. We would have to do it without any sort of painkiller. I drained the glass, refilled it, and began to make a pot of coffee. Sam would probably need it.

I did not bother to dress, and when the bell rang, answered the door in my robe. Sam smiled, hesitated in the doorway, then entered, quietly closing the door behind him.

"Coffee?" I suggested timidly.

He gave me a curious look. "I thought you had a problem. Let's get to work first."

"Fine." Appreciating his no-nonsense approach, I reached up and dropped the shoulder of the robe. "I have a bullet lodged in here somewhere"—I indicated the bruise—"and it's in a bad position, so that I can't remove it myself."

He dropped his coat on the floor and looked at me in amazement. "Remove it yourself? Are you crazy? Besides, it can't be anything recent. May I?" I nodded my permission and he reached over and touched my shoulder, examining the front and back. "I can see that you were shot, but from the healing I would say that it was at least a month ago." He pulled me over closer to the light. His hands were warm and firm against my flesh. "The blood is recent though. Were you doing something to reopen it? And why wasn't the bullet removed when it happened? Jesus, Deirdre, this is even stranger than I expected. I can't just cut you open here in this apartment. You need to go to the hospital."

"Absolutely not, Sam. I will not go to a hospital. If you can't help me, then I will find a way to do it myself." I pulled the robe back up and tightened the sash. "Thank you, I'm sorry I disturbed you."

Sam laughed, but sobered immediately when he saw

my serious expression. "You're not joking about this, are you?"

"No." I managed a small smile. "I am not joking. I was shot this evening"—I looked at the clock—"oh, just about an hour ago. I can show you my clothes for proof if you like."

I walked into the bedroom and retrieved my sweater and cloak. "It would not have been a problem had the bullet exited, but"—I came back into the living room and handed him the garments, wincing at the pain—"unfortunately it has not. It must be removed."

Sam poked his finger through the bullet holes in my clothes, smelled them, then looked up at me in confusion. "I guess it did just happen," he admitted reluctantly. He set the clothes down on the couch. "And as far as removal of the bullet, well, I can't argue the fact that it should come out. But I'm not really a surgeon and I'm hardly equipped for an operation. I have nothing but novocaine, and that won't do much good. And even if I had something stronger, I couldn't do anything here. What if there were complications?"

"There will be none. I can promise you that. I heal very quickly." I pitched my voice at its most persuasive level.

"But"—he gave me a doubtful look—"Deirdre, I can't. It's unthinkable."

"If something goes wrong, you may call an ambulance and have me put into the hospital. That should prove to you how certain I am that we can handle it here."

"Well, I don't know."

"Sam." I looked into his face and caught his eyes. "I could find a way to convince you. But I would much rather have you uncontrolled and free of any suggestions, willing to do this because I have asked you as a friend."

"And if I don't do it?"

"As I said before, I will do it myself. Look, I am sorry. It was a mistake to call you, I realize that now, but I knew no one else to call. Now that I think it over, I see that it is better that you not get involved in my life any further. Just forget about it. It is of no importance." I held out my hands to him, trying but failing to hide the grimace of pain caused by the movement of my arm.

"Okay, I'll do it," he said abruptly.

"You will?" I was surprised. I had expected him to question me further, but did not really expect him ever to agree.

"Yeah, I will. I think I know you well enough by now, to believe you when you say you'll do it yourself. At least this way, you have a better chance. And when the complications arise, I'll check you into a hospital, where you belong. But"—he gave me a sly smile—"if everything goes the way you say it will, you owe me a complete explanation of all of it. I listened to that tape again and I know there are things you wouldn't tell me."

I eyed him suspiciously.

"Come on, Deirdre, if you want me to do surgery here, you'll have to trust me completely. Anything you say will be kept in strictest confidence."

I still hesitated, then finally nodded. "Where shall we do it?"

Sam glanced around the apartment. "If you're sure about no hospital"—he looked at me for confirmation and I nodded again—"then the kitchen table is probably the best place."

I picked up my ruined clothes from the couch, and when we went into the kitchen, put them into the trash can there. Sam cleared the few things on the table, set his bag on the counter, and opened it. He wiped the tabletop with a piece of gauze and an antiseptic solution. When he finished, I climbed on the table and lay on my stomach, my head pillowed on my folded arms.

Sam moved my arms to my sides and pulled the robe off my shoulders, tucking it in around my waist. Probing the wound again, he gave an acknowledging grunt, turned to the sink, and washed his hands. I tilted my head so that I could watch his preparations. He wiped the counter with the same antiseptic solution and laid out his instruments. When everything was removed from the bag, he put on a pair of rubber gloves and picked up a syringe. "This will probably sting a bit, but I think I can give you enough to dull the pain. Hold on."

He swabbed my shoulder with alcohol, and I felt the needle slide into my skin, felt the warmth of the novocaine spread through the area. He gave me several shots, and when he was done, he wiped the area again. I gripped the edge of the table tightly and he gave me a small pat on the shoulder blades. "Relax," he said with assurance, "it will all be over soon."

"That's what I'm worried about." I rested my head on the table and my voice was muffled slightly.

"It's still not too late to get you to a hospital."

"No."

"Okay, then, here we go."

"There is one thing you should know before you start, Sam."

"Great, now you tell me. What is it?"

"You'll have to be quick. Make your cut as deep as possible, so that you can get to the bullet in time."

"In time for what?"

"Well, before I start healing again."

Sam laughed humorlessly. "Oh, sure, don't worry about it. Now, this will probably hurt a little. Are you ready?"

"Yes."

The novocaine had not worked, but I had expected that. His incision was sharp, clean, and painful. I held my breath and bit my lip as I felt the probe deep inside my shoulder, a cold metal intrusion. I stifled a shiver as he worked his way to the bullet. I felt his breath warm on my neck, felt the twist of the instrument as he searched.

"Ah," he finally said with satisfaction, "I've got it." He dropped the probe and the bullet into the sink. "You okay?"

"Yes," I replied, my voice wavering only slightly. "That feels much better already."

"Sure it does." I heard the skepticism in his voice. He applied pressure to my shoulder with one hand, and reached into his bag with the other. "Now, we'll probably need a few sutures here." He lifted the wad of gauze he had been pressing onto me and peered under it. "Well, maybe only a little tape." There was a long pause, and I heard him draw in an astonished gasp. "Jesus," he said, "I don't believe it."

"What, Sam?"

"Jesus," he said again, and pulled away from me.

I wiggled the robe back onto my shoulders and sat up on the table, fastening the sash, licking the blood from my bitten lips. "What's wrong, Sam?"

His face was ashen, his expression fearful. He backed away and I slid off the table and grabbed his shoulders. "Thank you, Sam. That was very well done." I smiled at him, but he simply stared at me in shock.

"Jesus." His eyes touched me briefly, then lowered, and he pushed away from me, his hands, covered still with the gloves, now coated with my blood, held extended to keep me away. "What the hell are you? You . . . you're not normal, not natural, your shoulder—"

Calmly, I interrupted him in the hope of staving off his growing panic. "I told you I healed quickly."

The tone of my voice seemed to help. He still kept his distance, but relaxed his arms. "Heal quickly, my ass. It's almost as if nothing ever happened to you, certainly no one could tell that you'd just been operated on. Hell, I'm not even sure you were, although I was the one who did the cutting." He gave me an appraising glance, calculating, I thought, what could have caused this extraordinary healing. It was almost as if I could hear the possibilities being listed, then being denied in his mind.

I stood quietly, not moving, waiting for his next response, knowing that nothing in his background or training could ever have prepared him for this moment. When he did speak, his voice was soft and full of doubt.

"Maybe I should take another look at that shoulder. I mean, the light's not so good in here; I could've been mistaken." Sam approached me slowly and still I did not move. He pulled the robe back cautiously, then whistled slightly through his teeth. I could feel his hands trembling as he examined me thoroughly, prodding at what was only minutes ago a fairly deep incision. "Does this hurt?"

"No, not at all. You did a wonderful job. Much better than I could ever have done. It was quick and clean, but"—I gave him a glance out of the corner of my eye—"the novocaine was a waste of time."

"You felt everything?" He stripped off his gloves and dropped them into the sink with disgust. His voice was strained, almost angry. "If I'd thought that you could feel it all, I'd never have done it. I'm sorry, it must have been awful."

I shrugged. "It doesn't matter now, Sam. It's over."

"Jesus, Deirdre." He swore again and slumped down into one of the kitchen chairs.

"Coffee?" I suggested again. "Or perhaps you would like something stronger?"

"I doubt that you have anything here actually strong enough to handle all this. Besides, I have to get to work soon. Coffee will be fine." Some of his natural humor had returned to his voice, and he managed to give me a weak smile as I handed him a full mug.

"I hope you like it black," I said as I turned away and poured a cup for myself. "I don't have any cream or milk."

"I know," he said smugly, "I remember from the other night that you have no food here at all. I must admit that I'm surprised you even have coffee."

"I like coffee."

"Oh." He took a sip and watched me over the rim of his cup. "Well?"

"Well what, Sam?" I tensed, anticipating his question.

"Aren't you going to tell me? You owe me that, don't you think?"

"I am very grateful for your assistance, Sam, but what would you like me to say?"

He gave a bitter grunt. " 'What would you like me to say?' " he mimicked my question. "What the hell do you think I want to hear, the goddamned weather report?" He shook his head and took another drink of his coffee, staring into the darkness of the cup. "You're not human, are you?"

"I suspect that would depend on your definition of human, Sam," I said gently. "I personally like to think that I am as human as any other person."

His head shot up. "Don't bullshit me, Deirdre. I get that every day from sick people who feel the desperate need to deny their inner selves. I don't know who you are, or even what you are, but I'd be willing to bet everything I have on the fact that you're not crazy and not human."

"Yes," I said with a sigh, sitting down across from him, "you are right, Sam, I am not crazy."

"And?"

"And I'm not human."

The silence was filled by the ticking of the clock. I glanced up at it and so did he.

"Alien." The word came out so quietly that he cleared his throat and said it again. "You're an alien, aren't you?"

"An alien?" I repeated, laughing in disbelief.

"Yeah, you know what I mean, an alien, outer space and all that. So where do you come from?"

"I do know what you mean, Sam." My tone of voice was light and teasing. "I just wasn't expecting that particular question. Actually, I come from Kansas."

"Kansas?" He seemed even more confused.

"Yes, you know, Kansas—the Midwest, farms and fields, Dorothy and Toto."

"But if you're not an alien, what are you?"

I tilted my head at him encouragingly. "What do you think? I should imagine you know enough about this situation by now to figure it out on your own."

He took a long drink of his coffee, and as he swallowed I saw the blood drain from his face. He was quick to put the facts together and come up with the proper conclusion, however unlikely and unsavory it was. He jumped up from the table and knocked his half-empty mug on the floor. "Jesus." The fear returned to his voice, and the easiness we had managed to reestablish dissolved instantly. "You're a goddamned vampire."

# Chapter 17

"Actually," I said to Sam while I wiped the spilled coffee from the floor, "I am not entirely sure about the damnation, but you are correct about the other." He had retreated, but no farther than the kitchen doorway, when I had risen to get the towel. The expression on his face indicated his own internal war: part of him wanted to run, and the other wanted answers. When he spoke, I was relieved to discover that the second impulse won.

"But how could it be possible?"

I got up from the floor and threw the coffee-soaked towel into the sink along with his blood-covered gloves. "I am afraid that I have no answer for that, Sam. I am what you said; that is a fact. But as for its possibility? I don't know any better than you."

"But a vampire is a mythological creature, a folktale, no more real than the bogeyman, or unicorns, or fairies."

I gave him a serious look. "Is it so much harder to believe than the other fact that you so readily wanted to accept?"

He paused a moment and thought. "But alien visitations are fairly well documented and have been reported by so many different types of people. It seems more real somehow, more measurable by scientific methods."

"And you accept scientific methods, of course." My quiet voice took on a scornful tone. "But have you ever stopped to consider that folktales might have a basis in truth, might be the same kind of documented accounts from hundreds of years ago?"

He gave me a sheepish look. "No, not really, I can't honestly say that I ever gave it a second thought. Some things fit into reality, and others do not."

"And even now you don't believe me, because I don't fit into your idea of reality."

He cleared his throat. "I don't want to believe you. I wish from the bottom of my heart that I didn't have to believe you." Sam stared at me for a time and shook his head. "But I do believe you. Only now I don't know what I should do."

"Why should you have to do anything?"

"Well, well . . . but you're a vampire." His voice acquired a higher pitch and cracked on the last word. "There must be something I should do."

"Sam, listen to me. What I am is no danger to you or to anyone else. I lived in this city for ten years, and in all that time the blood I took was never missed." He shuddered at the mention of blood, but I continued. "Generally, I take less than you would donate at a blood bank. I do no harm to others. You can check on the facts if you want. The only people killed here in that fashion were killed by Max."

"Max." He said the name emphatically in remembrance, from my story the other night. "Max was a vampire too?"

"Yes."

"Then Mitch"—his eyes drifted to my face and stayed there—"Mitch was telling the truth."

"Yes. And you should take a lesson from him. If you were to let on to others what I am, you would be treated the same—institutionalized for years. Not a soul would believe you."

Sam laughed, more to relieve his tension than to express humor, and began to gather his instruments and pack his doctor's bag. "And does Mitch know about you?"

"Yes, Mitch knows." A smile crossed my face thinking of him. "And he doesn't seem to think that I'm a threat to the general public. Let it go, Sam." I moved to him and put a hand on his arm gently. "You can't do anything about this situation." Meeting his eyes, I drew him into me as much as possible. "And you really don't want to."

"No," he said directly, "I don't. But I want to talk more about it, document your case, if only for my own satisfaction." He smiled at me honestly, with only a trace of fear. "What an opportunity. Interviewing a real live mythological creature. I wish I'd brought my recorder."

"Well, Sam," I said with a twisted smile, "although it's not all it is cracked up to be, I will do my best to satisfy your curiosity. But it will have to be some other time." I glanced over my shoulder at the window. The first streaks of dawn were appearing in the sky. "You have to go to work, and I have to go to sleep. I'll see you out."

He gingerly picked up the gloves from the sink, wrapped them in the towel, and put them in the garbage. When he picked up his bag, we walked into the living room. He retrieved his coat from where he had dropped it on the floor and put it on. "When can I call you?"

"Later on, maybe in a few days. I'd like to get reacquainted with Mitch, spend some uninterrupted time with him. We have a lot to catch up on."

"What will you do when I leave?"

"Go straight to bed and sleep until Mitch comes home. He'll be released today, won't he?"

Sam laughed. "At this point, Deirdre, I've no good reason to hold him. Apparently, there was never anything wrong with him." He shook his head again and walked to the door. As he opened it he turned to me and his voice seemed strangely enthusiastic and youthful. "Jesus, vampires, who'd have thought?" he said, and went out.

After pulling the drapes and securing the apartment for the duration of my sleep, I went into the bathroom and removed my robe. Sam had done a good job on my shoulder, I thought as I twisted my arm around. It was still sore, but I knew that the slight stiffness and bruising would be gone by the following day. The scar from the incision, however, would require a little longer to heal. I hung the robe on the door hook, walked down the hall, and crawled into bed.

I open my eyes to an unfamiliar darkness, and the pain in my shoulder has worsened greatly. I feel the presence of others in near proximity, but I have been robbed of all my heightened senses. I am blind in this night—hurt, bewildered, and weak beyond relief. Panic strikes me and I attempt to scream. The sound that escapes my lips and lungs is a deep, rattling moan.

We are dying.

The voice echoes within my mind, and as I recognize it, I relax inwardly. Although I am still caught up in the grip of fear and pain and death, I know that I dream. And because I am Max, I know that this body I now occupy is older than the other I inhabited; it is hardened, embittered by ten long years of privation. I have served as priest and comrade on the battlefields of this holy war.

The mind of the younger Max knows nothing but the cause he has supported. He is shielded from our thoughts, from his thoughts, from the remembrance of another twenty blood-filled years of war. He is the present, I am the present. And I have served, my pain-ridden senses cry out, I have been found worthy of these deeds done for God. And now I will die. But even in the face of death there is a lightness of spirit, a satisfaction in the ministry for church and Savior. There is also a deep sadness for works that must be left unfinished—this is what I regret, not death itself.

The light from a lantern bobbles in the distance and moves toward me; I peer through the darkness to see who approaches.

"Brother," the figure addresses me in a heavily accented Spanish. "Dying is difficult when much work for the Lord remains to be done." There is an irony in the voice, but I respond to the words because they mirror my own thoughts exactly.

"I do not fear death," the whispered words rasp from my dry throat, "for I go to my God."

"But should there be a way to save you for future works, would you undertake it, though the path be strewn with hardships?"

I nod, and the pain of this movement causes my head to spin. I see the glint of a knife, but I am held by the gaze of his eyes as he makes a movement too fast for me to follow. A strong arm encircles my shoulders and holds my body in an upright position. I black out for a minute, and when next I am aware, a bitter tonic is flowing into my mouth; I choke and swallow. The medicine's taste is familiar, and something in my mind, alien, yet familiar, screams a warning.

"Do not drink," it cries, "for the salvation of your soul, do not drink."

But I cannot control my reflexes. With each swallow the taste becomes less repulsive, growing instead seductive and sweet, like the finest wine. My body blazes with heat, a healing warmth floods through my system. Infection, pain, and death all fall away from me, and I am man perfected, healthy, alive, and, the warning voice sobs, human no more.

The man wraps the sickroom blanket around my shoulders. The smell is offensive, but I welcome the warmth, for my body has suddenly grown cold. "Come with me," he says with a biting laugh. "You do not belong here anymore."

"You are a saint," I gasp, bewildered and awed by my complete recovery from death. "An angel from God, come to work a miracle. In nomine Patri, et Filii—"

He interrupts me with another laugh. "That is enough of that. Now, come."

Docilely, I allow him to lead me away from the life I led. He whispers counsel to me as we walk, his strong arms support me as I stumble, overwhelmed by the array of sensory stimulation I am now receiving. The stars are so bright, clearer than I had ever noticed before. I can smell so much more in the night air, and the texture of the ground beneath my bare feet is rich and firm.

I finally become aware that we are riding in an open carriage; he drives the horses hurriedly, cursing and whipping them on. When we arrive at the house, it is still dark, but I feel the approach of dawn, and catch some of his panic and fear. I do not want to enter that house, but he reaches up and throws me over his shoulder, carrying me as if I were dead. All the while, he is speaking, his voice soft and commanding. I cannot fully grasp the meaning of his words, but they frighten me and anger me. They drop heavily into my soul, and the coldness of death sinks once again into my body.

We enter a darkened chamber. I can see that it is unfurnished but for two coffins. He puts me onto my feet and stares deeply into my eyes. I cannot look away.

"I have prepared a place for you. Today you shall sleep here and tomorrow night I will explain all." He smiles and I shudder at the malice in his face, at the sharpened teeth he displays. But I obey him and lie down in the box he has opened.

When the lid is closed upon me, I want to cry out, to leave the empty place to which he has brought me. But his command holds me, and as I sense the sun rising, my eyes close of their own volition. Of his words, only one remains in my mind and I carry it into sleep with me. "Nosferatu."

A swirling inner rage overcomes me, wrests me from the transformed body of Max, and I stand again disembodied. I am not alone, for I feel his breath and hear his voice, heavy with hate and regret. Somehow the young and the old Max have merged together, the two voices combined in a cry that rings in my ears and causes a chill to caress my spine.

"I want to die. I should have died. Dear Father in heaven, let me die."

I woke shivering, echoing Max's words. Not yet recovered from the dream, I was startled by the touch of a hand on my head, stroking my hair. I sat up quickly, snarling and hissing. "You bastard," I whispered vehemently, "what have you done to me?"

"Deirdre? Deirdre, what's wrong? Wake up, please, wake up."

The name seemed unfamiliar at first, but the pain in the voice finally reached me, and I realized who and where I was. I opened my eyes to find Mitch hovering over me, his expression hurt and uncertain.

"Oh, God, Mitch, I'm sorry. I didn't realize it was you."

"I understand from Dr. Samuels that you had a rough time last night. And I really didn't want to wake you." He leaned down and kissed me warily on the cheek, his eyes betraying his fear. "But you seemed to be having one hell of a nightmare."

"Thank you." My voice was dry and rasping. I brushed the hair from my eyes, cleared my throat, and tried again. "I was. How long have you been here?"

Mitch looked over at the clock on the bedside table. "Oh, about an hour or so. It's wonderful just to have you here and watch you sleep." A loving smile crossed his face, and he sat down on the bed next to me. "You have the face of an angel, Deirdre. But when you started thrashing around, muttering and crying, I thought you'd be better off awake. You can go back to sleep now if you like; the sun won't set for a couple of hours."

"Nonsense, Mitch, now that you're here, why would I want to sleep?"

"Then do you want to talk about it?"

"Talk about what, Mitch?"

His mouth twisted, and I recognized the slight edge of jealousy in his voice. "Talk about what happened last night between you and Dr. Samuels."

"Oh, that." I reached over and touched my shoulder. As I expected, the soreness was gone, but I could trace a thin scar where there had been an incision. Then I took his hand and pulled it over so that he could feel the skin. "He told you nothing?"

"Not a word. Just that everything was okay, that I wasn't to worry, but there had been a slight emergency last night and you would probably be a little tired today." He peered at my shoulder. "So what happened?"

"Some unlucky mugger chose the wrong victim."

"You were mugged?" He lost his pout and grew instantly concerned. "Where? You really should be more careful."

I laughed, and gave him a sharp look. "You should know better than anyone that I have very little to fear from someone not armed with a wooden stake. I was right outside this apartment and he surprised me; I suppose I wasn't paying attention. But I can assure you he got the worst of the exchange. All I received was a bullet in the shoulder that unfortunately I could not dig out myself."

"Did you call the police?" He seemed personally affronted that this had occurred.

"No, I didn't."

"Why not?"

"When he left, he had two broken wrists and was missing about a pint or so of blood. I really didn't want to have to explain that to your friends at the precinct. And I believe he'll probably be a little reticent about attacking a lone woman in the future."

Mitch laughed. "I guess so. You really broke both his arms?"

"At first I broke only one. I hoped that he would take the hint and leave me alone. But then he shot me, and it hurt. I got angry and, I'm afraid, a little carried away."

"And you told all this to Dr. Samuels?"

"No, Sam never asked how it happened. I asked him to remove the bullet, and he did."

"In the hospital?"

I gave a small laugh. "You know how much I hate hospitals, Mitch. I wouldn't allow myself to be admitted. We used the kitchen table."

"Bloody hell, Deirdre. You let my psychiatrist perform surgery on you on my kitchen table?"

I shrugged and smiled. "What difference does it make? Yes, your kitchen table. I'll buy you a new one if you like."

"No, that isn't the point. Didn't it hurt?"

"It hurt like hell. But it's over now."

"But, Deirdre . . ."

"Hush, my love." I put one finger to his lips and

traced my other hand slowly up his shirtsleeve until I reached his neck. I pulled his head toward me so that our faces were only inches apart, and smiled. "Now, do you want to talk about my operation," I whispered, "or do you want me to welcome you home?"

# Chapter 18

"Deirdre?"

"Hmm?" I murmured lazily, my head resting on Mitch's chest, my fingers gently stroking the faint scars on his right arm, the visible memories of his confrontation with Max.

"I think Dr. Samuels may suspect what you are."

I raised my head and met his eyes. "Why? What exactly did he say?"

"Well, he never came out directly with any accusations. But he asked some really strange questions during our exit interview—all about vampires—did I still believe that they were real, did I have any guesses about how they would survive in modern times, how would they live, what would they look like?"

I gave a small chuckle. "And what did you say?"

He matched my smile. "I lied shamefully, of course. You'd have been proud of me. But"—Mitch paused a moment, combing his hair back with his fingers—"he seemed disturbed by my answers. He acted strange, almost as if he were disappointed that I denied everything. And from the look in his eyes, I think he suspects. It could be a problem."

"No, it will not be a problem. And you are wrong, he suspects nothing. He knows."

"How on earth could he know? And what do we have to do about it?" His voice was edged with anger, not directed toward me, I thought, but toward whatever peril Sam's knowledge might contain.

I stroked his cheek to calm him. "Don't worry, my love. I plan to do nothing about Sam. He knows only because I told him and I trust him with the truth. He is no danger to me, or to us."

"Us." His voice was soft now, he took my hand and kissed the palm. I closed my eyes and savored the sensation as his warm mouth sent a shiver up my spine. "I like the sound of that." His mouth moved up to the soft, delicate skin on my wrist. "And what do you plan to do about us?"

"An interesting question, little one." My body tensed and my eyes flew open at the sound of Max's voice. I glanced around the room and saw him, lounging indolently in the doorway. "What shall we do with your human lover? Transform him? No, I can tell you don't like that idea. Marry him? Why not? The three of us could be very comfortable together."

*Go away,* I urged him silently, aware of Mitch's growing confusion. *Just go away and leave me alone.*

Max laughed so loud that I thought it was impossible that Mitch would not hear. But he seemed oblivious of the unwelcome presence in the room.

"Deirdre? What's wrong? I don't mean to pressure you about our relationship, but I can't seem to help myself. It was hell those years without you. I can't bear the thought of losing you again. I told you before that I don't care what you are or what you've done. I love you and I want to marry you."

"Mitch." I tried to keep the anger from my voice, for it was not directed at him. "I don't want to talk about this now. Later, perhaps, when we are alone."

"Alone?" Mitch sat up and looked around. "Who else is here?" He gave a small nervous laugh when he saw nothing, then relaxed and ruffled my hair. "Deirdre, we are alone."

"I—I—I know," I stammered, upset at my error and outraged at Max. "I meant after we've spent more time together alone."

*Dammit, Max, get the hell out,* I thought to him. *You're not wanted. Go away and leave us alone.*

Max threw his head back and laughed, undaunted by my anger. I could do nothing in this situation but endure his presence, and he knew it. Then his eyes softened and he nodded toward me. "I'll come back, little one, look for me." His figure faded and he was gone.

I sighed and continued to stare at the empty doorway. Mitch reached over and waved his hand in front of my face.

"Deirdre, are you okay?"

I pulled my eyes away from where Max had been standing and turned my attention back to Mitch. "I've been away and you haven't been well. I think we should wait awhile, take it one day at a time. A lot of things have happened to the both of us while we've been apart."

"Nothing has changed for me, Deirdre." His voice was sad. "I thought you felt the same."

"I do, Mitch, I do." I kissed him. "But, well, there are a lot of things you don't know, about me and how I have been living."

"You could tell me."

"I could and I will." I got up from the bed, pulled a pair of jeans and a sweater from my suitcase, and began to dress. "But I can't talk about it now."

"What are you doing? Are you going somewhere?" Mitch was growing angry, and there was nothing I could do.

"I have to go out."

"Just like that, huh? Welcome home, Mitch, and then you're off again?"

I walked over to him and sat down on the bed. Smoothing his hair, I held him close to me. "I do love you, Mitch. You must believe that or we'll never be able to come to terms in this relationship. And I will be back tonight. But right now I have some business to tend to."

He started to reply, but the phone rang and he answered. "Yeah," he said with a suspicious look at me, "she's here. And who the hell are you?"

He grunted and held his hand over the mouthpiece before handing the phone to me. "Some guy named Ron. Sounds young and handsome. I suppose he's the business you need to see about?"

"Jesus, Mitch, he's my attorney."

"Oh," he said, handing me the phone with a shrug and a sheepish smile. "I'm sorry."

"Hello, Ron." My voice sounded tired and irritated. "What can I do for you?"

"You know." His voice was warm and intimate and I stood up, turning my back to hide my embarrassed blush from Mitch's keen eyes. "But," he continued, "I assume that's still out of the question. Was that your cop who answered?"

"Yes."

"Thought so. He sounds like a cop."

"Excuse me, Ron, but did you call for anything specific?"

"Yeah, sorry. I just wanted to let you know that I did some checking around and I can accept your job without a conflict of interest."

"You know, Ron, I have been meaning to ask you, what sort of conflict could there be?"

"Well"—his voice sounded evasive—"there's the other night, for one thing."

I laughed. "You have a hell of a set of professional ethics if that's all it is."

"The Bar does tend to frown on relationships with clients." He stopped abruptly, and I knew there was another reason he did not want to mention.

"And?"

"And what?" Now Ron sounded defensive.

"And there's something else. I can hear it in your voice."

There was a long pause, and Ron sighed. "Well, I have, in the past, done some work for The Cadre, and since they inherit everything if you decline, I thought there might be a problem."

"Oh." That made sense to me. "What exactly is The Cadre?"

"An international organization of entrepreneurs." The answer came readily to his lips, as if it were rehearsed, but I hardly cared one way or the other.

"So," Ron said, his tone relaxed again, "when should we get together? I'll need to read over the will."

"I have to be at the Ballroom sometime tonight." I winced at Mitch's intake of breath and glanced at the clock. "How about nine or so?"

"That'd be great." He hesitated. "Ah, you aren't bringing your friend along, are you?"

"Oh, no," I insisted. "I don't think that would be wise."

"Good," Ron agreed. "I wasn't looking forward to meeting him anyway."

"No, I suppose not. I'll see you later, Ron. Thank you for calling so promptly."

I hung up the phone and looked over at Mitch. While I was on the phone he had slipped his pants on, and was standing by the window.

"The Ballroom? Why on earth are you going there?"

I moved behind him, put my arms around his waist,

and rested my chin on his shoulder. We stood there for a while, not speaking, but watching the glistening rain on the early evening streets.

"Well? Aren't you going to answer me?"

"It's the ultimate joke." I smiled and kissed the bare skin of his shoulder. "Max left everything to me in his will, including the Ballroom. I'm his sole heir."

"No kidding? Who'd have thought?"

"Not me. But he did, so now I have to struggle with that as well as everything else. He never did me any favors, and even from the grave he's making trouble for us." I didn't try to disguise the bitterness in my voice. "Max is the dirtiest bastard that ever lived."

"Was."

"What?"

"Max was the dirtiest bastard that ever lived. But he's dead now, Deirdre, and he can't hurt you anymore." Mitch turned around and held me close to him. I wanted to cry, but instead I hugged him back, then broke away abruptly.

"You are right, I suppose. It's just hard for me to believe he's dead."

"Well, he is," Mitch said determinedly, "and I don't want to talk about him anymore. I thought we were rid of him two years ago. Let's quit dragging him back. Okay?"

Was that what I was doing, I wondered, causing his presence by my thoughts of him? "Fine," I agreed, trying not to let my skepticism show. "And now, the sooner I go, the sooner I can get back. Get some rest, my love." I attempted a sensuous smile. "You'll need it when I get back."

Mitch followed me out to the living room but stopped me as I started to walk out the door. "Where's your coat?"

"My coat? Why?"

"It's pouring out, you'll get soaked."

I laughed. "It hardly matters to me."

"But it does to me. It's bad enough that you have to leave just when I get here, but if you think I'm going to let you back in here dripping wet . . ."

"You can towel me off at the doorstep when I get back."

"Now, that's a tempting offer—" Mitch started toward me with a boyish grin.

"Anyway," I interrupted him, "I don't have a coat. I brought only one with me, and it's now in your kitchen trash."

"Why is it there?"

"Bullet hole,"

"Oh, yeah, I almost forgot about that incident. Look, maybe I'd better come with you tonight. Just give me a minute or so to finish dressing, and I'll be right with you."

"No, Mitch, you should stay home." I tried to say it as gently as possible, but it came out as more of an order than a request.

"And what the hell does that mean? That I'm not good enough to be seen out in public with you?"

"I never said that, Mitch. I just think that you should stay home; you haven't been well." I knew he was getting angrier with each word I said, but there was nothing I could do. He could not accompany me tonight, or any night when I met with Ron. The anger he felt now would be nothing compared to what he would feel if he ever learned what had transpired between me and my newly hired attorney. "No," I repeated. "You should take it easy tonight. It's your first night home, and you need your rest."

"And that's another thing, Deirdre, while we're at it. I haven't been sick and there's absolutely nothing wrong with me. This is the second time tonight you've used my health against me. You won't talk about making a commitment to this relationship because I haven't been well. You won't let me come with you anywhere because I haven't been well."

"And all of that is true, Mitch." I held my position at the door, although I really wanted to hold him and comfort him. "You haven't been well."

Suddenly, it was as if all the anger and frustration he had been feeling for the past two years boiled over at once. "Bloody hell, Deirdre. And if I haven't been well, as you so delicately put it, then maybe you can tell me whose fucking fault it is." I cringed away from his obscenity. I knew he never used that word unless under a great strain, but he ignored my reaction. "I can tell you whose fault it is. This whole situation is your fault. You and all the other goddamned bloodsuckers out there got me into this, and now I can't ever get out. I wish to hell I'd never heard of vampires. I wish to hell I'd never fallen in love with you! I'm sick to death of the whole thing."

He stood staring at me, panting slightly, and I watched the anger slowly drain from his eyes, to be replaced by sadness and remorse. But it was too late; the words had been said and he could not unsay them. And I could not deny their truth, not to him or to myself.

There was nothing I could say, nothing I could do to change this moment. This was the moment I had spent most of my life avoiding, the inevitable moment I knew would come when I first fell in love with Mitch. Why did I ever allow it to go this far? Why did I ever let him into my life?

I could only stand and look at him, no more than three feet away from me, and more than a century out of reach. And when I felt my eyes begin to tear, I turned my back on him.

"Good night," I whispered softly, and walked out into the wet darkness of the night.

# Chapter 19

By the time I got to the Ballroom I was completely soaked. But the walk in the rain had cleared my mind, if not my sadness, and I felt prepared to face the evening. I walked through the crowd, ignoring the curious stares of the people that I passed, and stood at the bar.

"Fred."

He looked over at me and stifled a small laugh. "I guess it's still raining out, huh?"

"Yes." I smiled back at him. "I'll be back in the office. Bring me a towel or two, will you? And get someone to relieve you here. We need to talk."

"Sure thing." He took off his apron and headed out the other side of the bar.

"Oh, and Fred?"

"Yeah?"

"If someone by the name of Mitchell Greer shows up or calls, I'm not here. You haven't seen me and don't know when I'll be in next. Make sure the doorman gets the message also."

"You bet. I'll be right there."

Fred came to the office equipped with several large towels and a clean waitress's uniform. "I thought you might want to dry out completely," he said with a shrug, "so I brought you something to change into. Next time it rains, though, I recommend an umbrella."

"Thanks," I said. "Now give me a few minutes and

come on back in." Fred closed the door behind him and I pulled off my dripping clothes, dried myself, and slipped into the uniform. It was made of lightweight black nylon, and I smiled in remembrance as I fingered the flimsy material. The last time I wore a uniform similar to this was in the early sixties at a Midwest truck stop. It was there that I had met Max, for what I'd supposed to be the first time, never knowing that he had been the one responsible for my transformation almost a hundred years before.

"Dammit, Max, you should have told me who you were. I would have gone with you anywhere and stayed with you forever. But no, you had to wait until I met Mitch before letting me know what really lay between you and me. And then it was too late."

I looked around the office uneasily, halfway expecting Max to make an appearance. Instead, there was a knock on the door and I jumped and called, "Come in."

Fred entered, followed by a waitress I did not know, who collected my wet clothes and promised to have them dried right away. Then Fred and I sat down to discuss the business of the Ballroom. When we concluded our talk, it was only a little after eight. He had agreed to take the manager's job, as I thought he might, and I was happy to leave the club in his hands. I made it absolutely clear to him that I did not want to be involved in the day-to-day routine.

"I will, of course," I said as we ended the interview, "be stopping by from time to time. And it is absolutely essential that you keep my favorite wine in stock. Other than that, you're on your own."

"Great." He beamed his delight at the situation. "This is a good opportunity for me, and I really appreciate you giving me the chance. Max never trusted anyone and"—Fred shrugged—"since he was always here, it didn't really matter anyhow."

"Fred," I said, thinking of the ring of Max's keys still in my purse, "he couldn't have been here all the time. He must have lived somewhere else. I have one of his keys that doesn't seem to fit any lock around here. I assume it's from his apartment."

"Could be," he said skeptically, "but any time of the day or night, he was here. Keeping a separate apartment would have been next to impossible. He would never've used it."

"But he had to sleep somewhere, didn't he?"

Fred gave a wry laugh. "Max never slept. Anything else?"

"No, thank you, Fred. I'll see you later."

Just before he closed the door, I called to him. "Oh, by the way, Ron will be coming in to see me around nine or so. Please buzz me when he gets in. Other than that, I would like not to be disturbed."

"Gotcha," he said with a wink, and left.

I pulled the ring of keys out of my purse. All but one was neatly labeled. There was a key for the office, the front door, the back entrance, the desk, the cellar, and a few smaller keys that were labeled "supplies." I removed the one unlabeled key and held it in the palm of my hand, putting the rest of the ring back in my purse.

"All right, Max," I said with a trace of humor, "you and I both know that you had to sleep sometime. And you had to have a secure place to do it." I stared at the key as if it somehow held the answers to his past. Then I suddenly laughed. "Dammit, Deirdre," I scolded myself, "it is absolutely amazing that you've survived for so long with so inadequate a brain."

I got up from the desk and looked around the room. There were no heavy draperies here to conceal a hidden door such as the one that existed in my office at Griffin Designs. But it had to be here. During his life, Max had as great a need for secrecy as I still did. If he secured a safe place for himself, it would be here.

I closed my eyes and thought back to the time when Max had ruled me and this place. We were always quarreling, but he always called me back. And angry or not, I would return to him. I remembered the night I had attacked him, thinking that he had betrayed me to the police as having committed the murder of his first victim. I could feel the texture of his shirt and skin shredded beneath my nails, could still taste the blood that I licked from my fingers. He had thrown the shirt away and gotten another from the closet.

"The closet. Dammit," I said, flinging the closet door open and inserting the key into the lock mounted on the back paneling. It fit and turned with an almost inaudible click. Cautiously, I pushed the door and peered into the room. The light from the office only dimly lit the area, and I looked around for a switch.

"Come now, Max," I whispered into the still air, "even I appreciate the convenience of electricity." But there were no lights here, only darkness and dust and cobwebs. I entered the room anyway and saw a small table to the right of the door equipped with a filled candelabrum and matches. I lit them and looked around.

The room was unfurnished, totally unlike the secret apartment I had maintained for years. There was a large wooden chest up against one of the walls, but the focal point was the large stand occupied by two coffins, laid out side by side. One was larger than the other and more elaborate, but there was no mistaking either's purpose.

"Oh, Max." My laughter sounded mocking in this emptiness, and the dust, stirred by my entrance, swirled and glinted eerily in the candlelight. "How very gothic of you. But why two?"

I approached the larger one. The wooden top was

thick with two years of accumulated dust, but I could make out the ornate antique carving. I brushed my hand over the gold plate and leaned down to read its inscription—"Maximiliano Esteban Alveros—1596."

"Jesus," I breathed softly, almost reverently. "So old." As if of their own volition, my hands reached down and opened the casket. It was empty.

"Of course, you fool," I sighed in relief, "did you really expect him to be here? He's dead, dead by your own hand, and buried these two years." Even so, I studied the coffin's emptiness as if it contained the answers I sought. There was a faint aroma of Max in the room—the wood that had absorbed his scent for four centuries exhaled it now. Gently, I let the lid down and walked around the stand to the other coffin.

This one was newer, streamlined and modern. With shaking hands I flung the lid open. It was also empty and its aroma was one of newness. No one had ever used it. I dropped the lid, and when the dust flew from it I could make out an engraving of a single rose in the dark wood—a black rose.

"But this can't be mine." I denied the obvious. "I never slept in one of these." I shuddered at the thought of being enclosed here during the long summer days. But as I looked closer, there was no mistaking the name on the golden plate—"Dorothy Grey—1832–Beloved Wife."

My knees weakened and I collapsed on the floor, leaning up against my own coffin, not knowing whether to cry or laugh. I did a little of both. "Jesus, Max, if it weren't so damn perverse, the gesture might be touching." Whatever would have given him the idea that I would share his tomb with him? But as I considered the facts, I realized that there was a time when I would have done so, and willingly. Only Mitch's presence in my life had prevented that event from occurring. And Max had been responsible for our meeting.

I shook my head and pulled myself up from the floor. Everything in my life was becoming so convoluted, so bewildering, I hardly had any idea what to do. It had been a difficult situation when Max was alive, but now it was almost totally impossible.

"Quite a triangle, is it not, Max?" With one finger I idly traced the rose carving on my coffin lid. "The living, the dead, and the undead—just one big, happy family."

I moved to the large chest, found it unlocked, and was assailed by a musty odor when I opened it. Within were about a dozen large leather-bound books. I picked one from the top and glanced at the front page. It was written in Max's hand, in Spanish, and was dated from the early 1600s. Rummaging deeper into the chest, I found a fairly large gold locket. The light was too dim even for me to examine it; I slipped it into the uniform's pocket to view later.

"Deirdre?" A deep, soft voice in the doorway addressed me hesitantly, expectantly.

I dropped the journal on the floor, spun around, and peered through the semidarkness. Victor Lange stood there, the light from the office outlining his body.

"I'm sorry to disturb you, Deirdre, but Fred said you were in."

"And so I am."

His voice was smooth and confident, showing no surprise at the room he was entering. "I wondered how long it would take you to discover this place."

"You knew this was here?" The voice in my head still urged me to trust him, but as he moved toward me, I backed away. "You've been here before?"

Victor respected my hesitancy and stood still. "Of course." He smiled reassuringly. "Max invited me in, oh, around twelve years ago, to show me his new acquisition." He gestured at the coffin with my name. "But it was his private spot. It's not as if he entertained here."

I ignored his last comment. "Twelve years ago? That was about the time I moved here."

"Yes." He walked over and rubbed his hand delicately over Max's nameplate. "This is a beautiful piece of sixteenth-century workmanship, don't you think?"

"But that means you know what Max was."

He laughed in amazement. "Of course I knew what Max was. He was a vampire. As you are also."

"And still you were his friend?"

I stood too far away to discern the expression in his eyes. "To a man who has lived centuries, friendship is invaluable. Don't you have friends who know you for what you are and care about you regardless?"

Slowly I walked toward him, keeping the two coffins between us. "Well, yes, but we were talking about Max."

"Was Max's loneliness, his separateness from mankind, any less acute than yours?"

"No, I suppose not." I paused and thought. "Although Max never actually gave me any opportunity to find out. The night that I realized what he was was also the night he died."

"Murdered," Victor said abruptly.

"What?"

"You said the night he died; it was murder, Deirdre. You keep referring to his demise as if it were a natural occurrence, a heart attack or an accident of some sort." He spit his vehemence at me, his anger tangible in the dust-filled air. "Never forget that Max was murdered in cold blood by some bastard cop who wasn't fit to shine his shoes. The same bastard that I understand is now out, free and easy." Victor reached across and grabbed my wrist. "Here, Deirdre," he whispered, "here is your chance to avenge Max. Find him and kill him before he catches up with you."

"Kill who?" I twisted away from his grasp.

"Mitchell Greer, of course, the bastard who pinned him up against the wall, like some insect specimen."

In the candlelight I detected a manic gleam in Victor's eyes. He frightened me, but I stood my ground. His attitude angered me; his attack on Mitch, his worship of Max, made me want to slam him up against the wall. I felt myself tense. A snarl rose up in my throat and my canines grew sharp.

"Why would I want to kill Mitch?" The words came out through my clenched teeth. "I'm afraid you don't understand the situation, Victor. And you shouldn't meddle with what you don't understand."

"I understand that Max is dead. I understand that Greer is responsible for the snuffing out of the life of a superior being, a man with the wisdom of the centuries behind him, with the prospect of centuries of life before him."

"But Max murdered four people, four innocent lives he had no right to touch."

"The right doesn't matter." Victor's voice rose in hatred again. "He was like a god among men. Justice for him should not have been given by a human. He answered to a higher call."

The anger I held in check suddenly exploded. "Max Hunter answered to no one. He was the most heartless son of a bitch that ever lived. He deserved to die as he did. He was not a god, Victor, he was a manipulative bastard who obviously had no trouble twisting you to his purposes." I paused to collect myself. "How long had you been serving as his Renfield? What sort of rewards were you promised?" I didn't wait for his answer.

"He can't control you any longer, Victor. You're free of his evil. The world is free of his evil."

He stood staring at me in shock. I walked past him and went to the entrance to the office.

"Deirdre, you can't mean that."

I turned to face him. "I do mean exactly that, Victor. And while we're clearing the air about Max, you should know that he wasn't killed by Mitch."

My comment disturbed him, and he slumped back against Max's coffin. "But if not Greer, then who?"

I smiled at him, exposing my still-sharp canines. "You knew Max, knew his strength and his power. How could Mitch ever have killed him?"

"But all the reports said—"

"I know what the reports said, Victor. But I was here when Max died, and I know how it happened. Mitchell Greer did not do it."

"Then who?" he repeated, still confused and shaken.

I laughed a small, bitter laugh. "Never count on constancy in love or friendship among vampires, Victor. I killed Max."

Confidently, I turned my back on his stricken face and went into the office. Picking up my purse, I called to him. "This has been a most stimulating talk. We should do it again soon." I opened the door. "Oh, and Renfield"—the scorn in my voice was unmistakable—"lock up when you leave."

By the time I reached the dance floor I realized that I was shaking uncontrollably. What on earth had possessed me to speak to Victor that way? It was true that he had angered me with his talk of avenging Max's murder and his vehement hatred of Mitch, but I should have gone slower and broken the news gently, not blurted it out as if the truth were something of which to be proud. Clumsily, I pushed through the dancers toward the front door.

"Deirdre, wait." Victor's voice called out over the blare of the music, and I paused a moment to glance back at him. He was standing in the doorway, watching me, not with anger, it seemed, but with compassion. The faces of the dancers blurred in front of my tear-filled eyes, and one of the gyrating bodies turned toward me and smiled. It was a mocking smile; his face and his cologne were hauntingly familiar. Somewhere a part of my mind reacted to him with shock, but he didn't speak to me, nor did he seem to recognize me. Instead, he turned his back to me and directed his attention to his partner in the dance.

I shook my head and looked back to find him, but he had disappeared completely into the sea of bodies. Out of the corner of my eye I could see Victor moving toward me, and instantly the dancers' presence was dismissed, the nagging doubts arising within me were erased, and I concentrated only on the fact that I had to escape.

# Chapter 20

The rain had stopped and I slowed outside the front door for a moment, to decide where to go. I heard the door open behind me and someone tapped me gently on the shoulder. I spun around with a snarl on my lips, but it was only the waitress with my dried clothes. I took them and stuffed them into my purse.

"Miss Griffin," she said quietly, extending another garment, "I have a coat here that someone left in the cloak room and never claimed. I thought maybe you'd like to borrow it. Fred said you didn't have one." I smiled and thanked her, threw it over my shoulders, and began to walk.

I didn't really know where to go. I couldn't return to Mitch's place, Griffin Designs did not belong to me anymore, and even had I kept a set of keys for the offices, I was sure Betsy McCain would have changed the locks over the past two years. Sam would probably be at the hospital, and I could spend some time there, but I knew he would want to hear my life story. Then I would still need to find other shelter before the sun rose. And everyone else I had known in this city was either dead or inaccessible.

But I knew I could not stay here, and I needed a place that was close and convenient. I did not want to see Victor again, much less run into that ominous figure from the dance floor. Quickly, I began to walk toward the hotel I had occupied two years earlier. Although I probably would not get the same suite of rooms, they would hopefully have something vacant.

When I got to the revolving doors of the hotel, I suddenly realized who the man at the Ballroom resembled. He reminded me of Larry Martin. But Larry is dead, I told myself, it must have been someone who just looked a lot like him. Larry was tall, well-built, and blond, a description that could match tens of thousands of men in this city. And anyone could wear his cologne. So it was nothing more than coincidence. I could not bear the thought that I might be seeing his ghost in addition to Max's. "One ghost per person is more than enough."

I went through the doors and registered at the desk. The clerk looked at my clothing, the cheap waitress uniform and borrowed coat, and his upper lip curled slightly, as if he were thinking that I did not belong here. But when I paid for my room for three nights in advance with cash, and gave him a liberal tip, his attitude turned from condescending to obsequious. When he handed me my key, I smiled at him.

"Does Frank still work here?" I asked, realizing that I had never known the doorman's last name.

"Yes, Miss Griffin, but tonight's his night off. Do you want to leave him a message?"

Two years down the road, and here I was, back where I had started from, but now I was looking for companionship from my old doorman. The thought was pathetic, and I shook my head. "No, no message, thank you," I said sadly. "But please see that I am not disturbed during the day tomorrow—no maids, no calls, and no visitors."

He agreed, and I took the elevator up alone to my single room. The first thing I did was change back into my jeans and sweater. Then I called room service and ordered three bottles of their best dry red wine. I was halfway through the first bottle, when I decided to call the Ballroom.

Fred answered the phone and recognized my voice instantly. "Deirdre, where are you? Ron's been looking for you and so was Victor. I didn't see you leave."

"Never mind, is Ron still there?"

"Yeah, he's at the bar."

"How about Victor?" My voice trembled a bit when I said his name.

"No, he left. Although I could probably get hold of him if you want."

"No." My voice was harsh. "I don't want to talk to him again tonight. But I will talk to Ron, if you would be so kind as to get him."

"No problem." I could hear him set the phone down and waited for a few minutes.

"Deirdre? Where are you? We had an appointment, remember?"

"Yes, Ron, I remember. That's why I called. What phone are you talking on?"

"The one in your office. Why? What's going on? Why all the intrigue?"

I sighed and took another drink of my wine. "No intrigue, Ron. Victor and I had a slight disagreement and I just decided to leave." Slight disagreement? I thought. Now, there's the understatement of the century. Telling a man that you murdered his best friend is hardly slight or a disagreement.

"I see." Ron's voice sounded noncommittal. "Do you want to reschedule?"

"No, I thought you could come to me, if you don't mind."

Ron gave a short laugh and his voice lowered sensually. "Deirdre, you should know by now that I'm happy to see you anytime, anyplace, but"—a trace of exasperation entered his voice—"you do have to let me know where that is. When you didn't show, I called your other number to see if you were on your way. A very disgruntled and very drunk policeman informed me that he didn't know where you were, but if I found out, I should let him know. He was pretty offensive about it."

"Damn," I said softly.

"Excuse me?"

"Nothing. Are you sitting at my desk?"

"Yeah."

"Inside the top drawer are copies of all the documents we should need. Bring them with you."

"Got 'em."

I gave him my address with strict instructions to tell no one where I was, and hung up. Then I called down to the front desk to let them know I was expecting a visitor.

Ron arrived within an hour of my phone call, carrying a bottle of Merlot and his briefcase. "Fred sent this over"—he held the wine in the air—"with his best regards."

I looked at Ron suspiciously. "You told him where I was?"

"No, just that we'd be meeting tonight. He also asked me to tell you that Mitch called three times."

"Great."

Ron set his briefcase down on the table and took off his overcoat. "It doesn't sound great. Should I assume that Mitch is Mitchell Greer—the cop that killed Max Hunter? And that he's also the same cop you've been living with, the one I talked to on the phone tonight?"

"Yes, that is true." I gave him a sharp look. "What the hell difference does it make?"

"No difference to me, I guess." Ron shrugged. "I'm just trying to keep the players straight. You're not in trouble with the law, are you?"

I laughed humorlessly. "If only it were that simple, Ron. A night in jail might do me some good."

"But I'd bail you out." He sat down in the chair opposite me and opened his case, taking out the folder containing Max's will. "I read this over before I came. It all seems pretty straightforward to me. Either you take the money or you don't. All that needs to be done is to get your notarized signature saying yes or no. We can't do that tonight, of course, but I can make those arrangements at a later date. Maybe you'd like some more time to think about it. But"—he smiled at me—"as your attorney, I advise you to take it; it's a lot of money." He reached for the bottle of wine I had already opened. "May I?"

At my nod he poured himself a full glass and drank it. "You know," he said, his voice distant and small, "I guess I should've known about you and Greer."

"But I told you—"

"No," Ron interrupted. "You told me you were involved with a policeman, but you never mentioned his name. And for some reason it never occurred to me until tonight that it could be the same guy."

"I am sorry, Ron, I thought you knew. And," I repeated, "what the hell difference does it make? It's over."

"It could make a difference to The Cadre. They'll be losing a great deal of money, a fortune, in fact, to a woman romantically involved with the person who killed one of their most prestigious members. I could conceivably see that they might want to contest the will."

"Fine." I poured the rest of the wine into my glass, drained it, and opened the second bottle. "I told you before, I don't care about the money. If The Cadre wants it, then let them have it. I don't really want to discuss the will, or explain my actions to you or anyone else. And I especially do not want to talk about my doomed relationships with Mitchell Greer and Max Hunter. Right now I just want to do my damnedest to get drunk and forget that any of this complicated mess ever happened. Care to join me?"

"But what about Greer?"

"I don't want to talk about him. As far as he's concerned, he wishes he never met me."

"Then he's a damn fool."

"And so was I. Why I thought I could be happy involved with a, well, a man like him, I will never know. But we were not going to talk about this."

"That's right, we weren't." Ron hesitated, watching me intently as I drank.

"So," I said, filling another glass, "are you going to help me finish this wine or not?"

"And when that's all gone?"

"What the hell, we'll just order more. Didn't you know, I'm a very wealthy woman."

Ron and I wound up in bed together again. Not intimately this time, both of us were fully clothed and he seemed content to merely lie next to me with my head cushioned on his shoulder. Neither of us was very drunk, but we had reached a warm, comfortable high. We didn't talk much, and what we did say was not important. He told me about law school and some of his more interesting cases. I told him about England, how much I missed the quiet neighborhood pub and my favorite brand of port. I talked about books that I had read and he talked about movies he had seen. Before we realized it, it was nearly five in the morning.

"I guess I'd better get going," he said, shifting his weight slightly so that he could get up.

"Do you really have to? You're welcome to stay as long as you like. This has been very pleasant. It's been too many years since I've had someone I could just talk to. I don't really understand why, but I feel completely comfortable with you, as if you could know the worst about me and not ever care."

"Unlike some people, I assume, who know the worst about you and do care?" Ron reached over and lightly touched my cheek.

"Oh, he says that it doesn't matter, but deep down inside we both know that it does."

"And what is this deep, dark secret that is so horrible?" His voice was calm and comforting, and I was tempted to tell him.

Instead, I laughed. "It doesn't matter. So, will you stay?"

He met my eyes, but his expression was hard to read. "Well, I don't really have anything pressing on my calendar for tomorrow. So, if you beg me, I might stay."

"I never beg."

He laughed. "I'm sure you don't, but you could ask me nice."

"Ron." I tried to smile at him, but began to cry instead. "Stay with me, please. I don't want to sleep alone today."

"Don't cry, Deirdre. Of course I'll stay. I told you before that I was a soft touch for a lady in distress."

"Thank you."

He moved back to me and pressed himself up against me.

"Have you ever fallen in love with someone," I asked him, sniffing a bit, my head buried in his chest, "knowing from the very beginning that it would never work out? And knowing that you would never get over them, no matter how hard you tried?"

He reached down and cupped my face between his hands, drawing my eyes to his. "And we're back to Greer again, aren't we?"

"Yes, I'm afraid so. I'm sorry."

"So am I."

We lay quietly for a long while, and I thought that he had fallen asleep. I began to drift off into sleep myself, but before I did, I thought I heard him whisper.

"Yeah, I think I have."

I open my eyes to utter darkness and I realize that my limbs are restricted, that I am completely encased in a wooden box. But before the panic can overwhelm me, I feel the soft touch of Max's mind and recognize the experience as a dream. "Learn," he whispers. We melt down and merge together in the body lying in this coffin.

The year is 1850; it had been an uneasy ocean crossing, but I know now that we have docked and soon my casket will be unloaded. Not soon enough, I think, for I have been a long time without food. My body is hollow and insubstantial, and just the slightest thought of blood causes me to gasp and bite my lips. It is no help—by now they are bloodless, dry, and cracked.

Not for the first time do I wonder why I attempted this journey, why I freely accepted this agony. I had been warned. Leupold had told me what I would suffer, but I would not listen.

Or could not listen. The truth was that I could not bear one more day in his presence and would gladly accept any torture to escape from his influence. The gratitude I initially felt when he saved my life had dissipated quickly when I discovered how he had procured that reprieve, but it had taken centuries of following in his footsteps to fully realize the brutal hatred with which I now regarded him.

I cannot even bring his face to mind. Thoughts of him bring only visions of death and depravities: bloodless corpses, helpless lives lying in ruin in our wake. So I had decided to undertake this arduous journey. I will never purge myself of his evil; I had proved too apt a pupil for that, and his sway over me is too absolute to hope for my reform. There will be no repentance, no amendment of life in this new country. But at the least I will escape his constant approbation of my sins and excesses. And with that I believe I can live content.

Footsteps approach my coffin and I lie still, not daring to move or breathe for fear of discovery. The scent of the living men who carry and load me onto a carriage almost drives me mad. I can break out of my confinement with one simple movement of my arm. Their blood can be on my lips in seconds, but I restrain myself, not knowing if it is day or night. It would be a shame, I think to myself with a mocking laugh, to travel all this way only to disappear into a heap of ashes on the dock. Tonight, when I arrive at the house I have procured, will be soon enough.

Eventually, the coffin is deposited, none too gently, in a damp-smelling room, and I assume that all has been accomplished in accordance with my explicit instructions. Still, I wait for a while, listening to the sounds of the hoofs and carriage wheels moving away on the cobblestone streets. When all is quiet, I cautiously push up one side of the thick wooden lid and breathe a sigh of relief when I realize that it is night and I am alone, safe, and free at last.

The hunger will not let me stop and savor my freedom, but drives me out into the night in search of living prey. I wander the streets, taking careful note of the turns and twists I make so that I may retrace my steps to safe harbor before dawn.

A church bell chimes twice as I hurry past, urged on by the gnawing ache in my stomach and the unfaltering instinct that a victim is near. Quite near, I realize, as I round the corner and see the shadowy figure of a woman leaning up against a door frame. She is, of course, a prostitute. In this day and age no respectable woman would be out alone in the night. I am well used to this type, having used them in countless brothels for sex. But my urges now are more elemental, more basic and much darker; there will be no sexual play this night. I glide over to her, giving a courtly bow. She smiles and beckons me inside the door.

The room is dingy and sparsely furnished, the bed only a mattress set on the floor. Turning her back to me, she begins to unfasten the hooks of her bodice. Ordinarily, I would wait until she undressed, until I had possession of her body before taking possession of her blood. Ordinarily, I would not even require her life. But tonight there is no denying of what must happen if I am to survive.

I come up behind her, putting one arm around her waist, and clasping my other hand over her mouth, bend her head to one side, making her neck more accessible to my kiss. At first she does not resist, but when my teeth sink deeply into her pliant flesh, and I take my first long draw on her precious blood, she struggles, attempting to pull away. Her lips move beneath my hand, crying, perhaps in pain, calling for mercy. I have none to give.

Her blood flows into me, filling me with elation, filling the great emptiness within. I feel her heartbeat slow, then stop completely. But only when the body is drained completely do I loosen my mouth's hold on her. She hangs limp and lifeless from my arm still encircling her waist, and I drop her onto the bare mattress. I reach down to close her staring eyes gently. The words of the prayer for the dead rise to my lips as they always do when I kill, but I will not allow them to be uttered by the very mouth that took her life. Instead, I reach into my pocket, drop a gold piece next to the bed, and go back into the night.

I explore the streets of this new city until just before dawn, eventually finding my way back to my home and my coffin. As I pull the lid over me, I feel the sharp stab of pain that signals the rising of the sun, and I sleep.

# Chapter 21

It took a long time to wake from the dream. I lay in bed, eyes wide open, studying the ceiling, drifting through the state between sleep and waking. This dream had frightened me more than all the rest. It had been the first time that I had felt the glorious elation of draining a victim to death. The fact that it was not I, but Max, who had killed that woman made no difference. When I dreamed, I was Max; his emotions, his passions, were mine. I had never before realized what a precarious balance I maintained. That I could recognize myself in him, and that I could react so willingly, so naturally, to his murderous instincts, was terrifying.

I looked back on my life with disgust. I shared Max's guilt, shared it completely. That woman was dead because of me. It made no difference that the event had happened before my transformation. The seeds of a killer had been sown within me, and even if they did not grow to their fruition, I knew that their roots were forever imbedded in my soul. There could be no final salvation for one such as I.

Eventually I shook off the effect of the dream and pulled myself up into a complete state of awareness of who and where I was, and discovered that the sun had already set and that I was alone. Getting out of bed, I saw that Ron had left the will and the papers for me to sign, along with his home and work phone numbers, and a note.

*Deirdre,* it read, *I stayed all day as you asked, but had to leave around six. Tried to wake you, but you were completely out. Thanks for last night, let's do it again sometime soon. Love, Ron.* The word "soon" was underlined three times and I chuckled to myself, then sobered.

Poor Ron, I thought, he's just one more example of how twisted my life has become. I used him terribly, first for his blood, then his legal expertise, and finally for his companionship, when what he wanted from me was completely different and something I could never give him. I shook my head, picked up the phone, and called room service for a pot of coffee.

When I was on my second cup, the phone rang. I let it ring for a while. The only person who knew where I was was Ron, and if we talked, I would eventually end up spending another night with him. How long could I continue to hide out, avoiding the other complications of my life, taking advantage of a man who deserved better of me? After ten rings I answered, determined to tell him that we should never see each other again. I did not have to, because it was not Ron on the phone, but Mitch.

I could not even say hello. "How did you find me?"

His voice was quiet and sad. "If I'd been thinking straight, I would have tried this place last night. Unfortunately, I drank for four solid hours after you left, and my mind was anything but clear."

"Yes, me too. Did it work for you?"

"Other than making me feel as horrible physically as I did mentally, no. I'm sorry."

I paused, not able to speak.

"Deirdre, did you hear me? I said I was sorry, and I am. I should never have said those things to you. I'd take them all back if I could."

"And why should you be sorry for telling the truth? Everything you said was true, Mitch. What you and I have together is something that should never have happened. It can never work, and I'm glad that you've finally come to that realization. It makes my leaving much easier."

"You're leaving again?" I could hear the panic in his voice, felt my own panic rise. The thoughts of being separated from him forever tore me apart, but I knew that staying with him would be almost as bad.

"I—I—I don't know what to do," I said honestly, desperately. "I can't think straight around you; I never could. I don't know if I have the power of will to leave. But it would be much better for the both of us if I do."

"Like hell it would." He gave a tight little laugh, and I found myself smiling.

I sighed. "What am I going to do with you, Mitch?" My question was light and teasing.

"I can think of several things at the moment, and I'm sure more will occur to me when you get home." He matched my bantering tone, then grew serious. "You will come back, won't you? You can't leave me, I won't let you. If you want me to beg you, I will. I'll get down on my knees and crawl to you. I love you, dammit, and there's not a damn thing I can do about it."

"I'll come back. But we need to do some serious talking about my life and you need to do some serious thinking about how well it will fit you."

"Anything you want, Deirdre. Just come home soon."

"As soon as I can, my love. I'm glad that your mind finally cleared well enough for you to find me. I think that I must have come here so that you could."

He laughed. "Actually, I'm ashamed to say that I didn't think of it. Your attorney called and told me where you were."

"Ron called you?" That surprised me. "Why on earth would Ron tell you where I was?"

"Why wouldn't he? When he called last night, looking for you, I asked him to let me know if he located you. Or at least I think I did. Everything is pretty fuzzy."

"You did. He told me."

"And he said that you were still hopelessly in love with me, that what you needed was a good kick to make you wake up and realize it."

"Well, I'm glad that Ron thinks it's all so simple."

There was a long pause, and I thought for a moment that he had hung up. "In the end, Deirdre," Mitch said finally, "I think he's right."

I gathered up my borrowed coat and uniform. The gold locket that I had taken from Max's room at the Ballroom fell out onto the floor, and I picked it up and tucked it into my jeans pocket. Then I went downstairs and left the hotel.

As I walked on the streets, I had the feeling that I was being followed, a curious feeling in the middle of my back that someone's eyes were on me, watching my every move. I knew that it was not Max; there was none of his intimate touch in my mind. But it was familiar nevertheless, and I glanced over my shoulder for a glimpse of my stalker. There was a flurry of movement behind me, and I spun around, but he was gone. "Great," I said out loud, just what I need, another haunting. Maybe everyone I've ever known can show up all at the same time and we can have a party." I laughed at my paranoid thought but quickened my steps..

When I arrived at Mitch's apartment, I was surprised to find the door unlocked. "Mitch," I called, hanging up my coat in the closet, "where are you?"

"In the kitchen."

His voice was calm and peaceful, as if no separation had taken place.

He was sitting at the table with his back to the door and I walked over, put my arms around his neck, and gave him a kiss. Resting my head on his shoulder, I watched as he finished cleaning his gun. "The door was unlocked."

He shrugged. "Yeah, I wasn't sure if you took your keys with you." He turned around on the chair and put his arms around my waist. "Welcome home." He rested his head against my left breast, then pulled away abruptly. "Your heart is racing, Deirdre, is everything okay?"

"No, Mitch," I said with a sigh. "Not really."

"You weren't mugged again, were you?"

"No, nothing like that. But you must know that my coming back to you solves only one problem." I reached over and stroked his hair. "The problem of how I could ever live without you." I kissed him on the forehead and pulled away. "Everything else in my life is completely out of control. I don't know what to do. I don't even know how to tell you about it all."

"Well," he said, "I've a solution to one of your problems anyway." He put his gun into my hand. "This will stop you from getting victimized again."

I stared down at the revolver in my grasp, then placed it back on the table with a small laugh. "That, my love, is the very least of my problems. And I wouldn't know how to shoot it even if I had to."

"I'd teach you. We'll go down to the shooting range. I'd worry a lot less about you wandering around the city at night by yourself if I knew you had some protection."

"Mitch, I don't need a gun for protection."

"I know." He shrugged and his eyes lit with amusement. "But at the very least, you don't need to explain this kind of protection to anyone. It's a lot cleaner and simpler."

"But not as much fun," I muttered guiltily, turning

away from him to look out the window, ashamed of the delight I had experienced dealing with the mugger.

"What?"

"Never mind, Mitch. It doesn't matter. If it makes you feel better, I'll carry the gun."

"Thank you." He walked behind me and put his arm around my neck, pulling my head back to nuzzle my hair.

"Mitch," I said quietly, "we need to talk."

"I know," he said, a tinge of sadness creeping into his voice. "What really bothers me about all this is that for some reason you're afraid to tell me about it." He spun me around, gripping my shoulders and shaking me lightly. "Regardless of what I said last night, I do love you, and I want you to know that there's nothing about you I can't learn to accept as long as you stay."

I met his eyes directly and coolly. "Tell me that later, after you know everything, and I will believe you."

My stare must have unnerved him. He dropped his hands and stepped back from me. I went to the refrigerator and removed the last half-bottle of wine, poured two glasses, and handed him one. "We'll be more comfortable in the other room. This may take a while."

I let him sit down first. He chose the couch, and I sat in the chair opposite him. He gave me a questioning look, took a sip of his wine, and waited.

My voice was soft when I began, tense and choked. "The first thing you must realize, before I tell you anything, is that after receiving your letter, I never expected to see you again, never expected to have to justify my life to you."

"That damned letter," Mitch interrupted. "I've been angry about it ever since you told me."

"The letter doesn't matter, Mitch. I know now that you didn't write it, and that's the important fact. Although, I wonder who . . ."

"Chris."

"Excuse me?"

"Chris wrote the goddamned thing. He said he was trying to protect me from your influence. I nearly killed him when he told me about it that last night in the hospital. He'd no right to interfere like that."

I laughed in relief, not realizing until that moment how worried I had been about who the originator of that letter might be. "Don't be too hard on him, my love. It can't be an easy thing to discover that your father's lover is someone like me. And although he has had a few problems, Chris has actually been surprisingly civilized about our relationship."

"So you're not mad about it?"

I shrugged. "Not really. And even if I were, he's your son and not mine. He did come for me when he thought I could help you, and he was right. I think that more than balances out those two years."

"And if you hadn't received the letter? Wouldn't things have been different for you?"

Mitch's question took me by surprise. With the letter I had completely accepted the fact that he did not want me anymore and my actions had been dictated by that assumption. And yet, had I not received it, I would have assumed his answer to be the same. "No, Mitch," I said sadly, "no letter would have been just as bad as the one I received. Perhaps even worse, because I would have felt that you did not even care enough to tell me your decision." I looked into his eyes and gave him a half-smile. "Now, can we forget about the letter and who wrote it? The only important thing to remember is that I accepted it as a fact."

"And that's another thing, Deirdre, how can you believe I would do that to you?" He brushed his fingers through his hair and his eyes glinted angrily. "Goddamn it, I love you. Even now I don't understand why you thought you had to leave. And I'm still pretty mad about the whole thing. I was ready to share your life completely, and you ran out on me. I'm ready to share it now, Deirdre. All you have to do is say yes."

"Mitch," I interrupted him gently but firmly, "that is not what we need to talk about. We have time for all that later, but you must hear me out first. What I have to say might change your mind."

He said nothing, but I recognized his stubborn expression from the time he insisted that no such creatures as myself existed. Mitch needed hard proof to believe what he did not want to believe. I sighed and took a sip of my wine.

"Shortly after I arrived in England"—my voice trembled slightly—"I began to hear Max's voice, quiet yet insistent, from the back of my mind. Oh, it was only an annoyance at first, like the buzzing of a fly or static on the radio. But it seemed to grow stronger with each feeding, urging me to go further than I ever had before, to take more blood, more often. Almost as if he were living inside me, feeding off my body, and imposing his hungers and desires on me. As if I were possessed by Max's spirit."

Mitch gave a small grunt but still said nothing.

"I know. I don't really believe that theory either. But that is exactly how I feel. And no matter what the true circumstances are, I haven't been able to rid myself of his presence."

Mitch didn't smile, but cautiously glanced around his apartment. "Is he here now?"

"No," I admitted, "but he has been. And I'm sure he'll return. Strong emotions seem to bring him out—when I feed, when we make love . . ." I blushed and let my words trail off.

"I haven't seen him." I could tell from the tone of his voice that he was taking what I said seriously.

"He wasn't one of the creatures who tormented you?"

"No, I could've understood that. The vampires I saw were strangers, although some seemed familiar after a while. Maybe it was because they were making return visits." Mitch shuddered, then looked over at me with a half-smile. "I would've almost welcomed Max. At least I knew him, and had some experience dealing with him. Don't you have any idea about what's happening? I mean, you're one of them. There should be some sort of common bond or knowledge that would help you out of this."

I shook my head slowly. "No, and if what you saw was real, you've met more of them than I ever have."

"Can you ask around, find out who Max's friends were? Maybe they'll have answers.

I thought back about my discussion with Victor and gave a rueful smile. "Actually, I've already antagonized one of his closest friends. Do you remember Victor Lange?"

"Should I?" Mitch's face grew puzzled as he struggled with the name. "No," he concluded slowly, "I've never heard of him."

"You met him, Mitch. He owns The Imperial. We had dinner there one night."

"Really?" He sat for a while, his face expressionless.

"Mitch?" I reached over and touched him on the arm. He jumped and laughed nervously.

"Sorry, Deirdre, I was thinking. I have no remembrance of the man at all. He was a close friend of Max's? And you ticked him off? What happened?"

"I told him exactly who it was who killed Max."

"Jesus, Deirdre, why on earth would you do that? It could cause a lot of problems for us both. After all, I've gone on record saying that I killed him in the line of duty. Self-defense, remember?"

"And for that statement you spent two years institutionalized. I wanted to set the record straight with Victor for a lot of reasons. I don't believe he'll make trouble for me, and if he does, I can handle him. That really isn't the issue here."

"And what is the issue? You don't want to marry me because you see Max on occasion? You've been living with that for two years. I'm sure I could get used to it. It'll go away after a while." His voice was so determined, I almost believed him.

"There's more, Mitch. Unfortunately, Max was, or is, a creature of great appetites. As a result"—I stood up with my fists clenched and walked around behind the chair, trying to avoid Mitch's eyes—"I've been involved in a sexual relationship with almost every one of my victims since I left this city."

"Jesus," he swore in a whisper. "Deirdre."

I looked away, waiting for accusations and recriminations. When he said nothing more, I glanced back at him, curious as to why his usually rampant jealousy was not aroused. There was no anger, no revulsion in his expression, only sadness. My heart twisted and I wanted to go to him, to hold him, to tell him that none of this ever happened. But I could not.

"Mitch, I cannot justify my actions. It would be easy to say that all of this is Max's fault, but we both know that Max Hunter is dead and buried. I suppose that Sam would say that his appearance in my life is due to my guilt over his murder, and that the sexual episodes are revenge against you for turning me away."

I shrugged and put my hand into my pocket, coming across the locket I had put in there earlier. I pulled it out and held it in my hand, curling the heavy gold chain around my fingers. "And he would probably be right. But now I not only hear Max's voice, but I see him, plain as day and as real as you. And I dream of him, vivid dreams of his past life, a life that I experience as if I really were him." My voice sounded choked, panicked. "It scares me, Mitch, so much so that when I wake I'm not even sure who I am. I barely recognize my own reflection at times.

"So you see, we have two choices—that I'm completely crazy or that I'm possessed by Max. Either way, my life is not one you would want to share."

I sat back down in the chair, still idly toying with Max's locket. It fell open, and when I peered at the miniature within, I gasped in recognition and dropped it on the floor. "No, it can't be true."

"Deirdre?" Mitch's voice was surprisingly clear and decisive. "What is it?" He got up from the couch and picked up the locket. "Where did you get this? It's very old."

"It was with Max's things. And, yes, it is old, dating back to the late 1500s. The woman in the picture, I know her. I have never met her, but I know her. I know the sound of her voice. I remember the way she looked when she was young, how my hand fit so perfectly in hers."

He looked at the picture intensely. "But who is she?"

I ignored his question, and in panic bolted toward the door. "Oh, my God, it can't be true."

Mitch moved faster than I did, and blocked my retreat. "Who is she, Deirdre? And what possible difference can it make?" He grabbed my shoulders and pulled me to him.

Pushing away from him, I stared up into his face. "It's all true, Mitch, it has to be. But what can I do about it? I'll never be free of him."

"Deirdre." His voice was shaking, and his fingers dug deeply into my flesh. "What's this all about?"

"The woman in the locket, she's Max's mother. I dreamed of her. I know her. And if that is true, then I'm not crazy." I began to laugh, a deeply pitched laughter that echoed off the walls and sounded so much like Max that I wanted to tear myself apart. Instead, I flung myself against Mitch and clung to him like a small, frightened child. "Somehow, someway, Max lives within me. We may have killed him, Mitch, but he didn't die. And he won't die until I do."

Mitch calmed me then, his hands stroking my hair, his lips brushing delicately against my ears and neck. The pounding of my heart changed from panic into passion as he cupped my breast in one hand and placed the other on the back of my neck, pulling my mouth to his in a hard, demanding kiss.

The desperate quality of his embrace startled me, but my body responded in kind, the heat of his lips thawing any resistance I might have offered. The taste of him and the feel of his body on mine broke down the last of my inhibitions. When the kiss was over, we stood for a moment, staring at each other, both out of breath and frightened by the sudden strength of our desires.

"I don't care," he whispered vehemently. "I don't care whom you've been with or what you've done." He spun me around and roughly pressed me up to the door, holding my wrists against the woodwork. His eyes glowed with the intensity of his emotions. "I've lost you twice and I won't let it happen again. You won't run from me this time, Deirdre. We'll face this together. But you must promise you won't leave me. Ever. I don't give a damn about your excuses, your bloody morals about not wanting to share your tainted life. Just promise you won't ever leave."

I felt a smile begin to shape my lips even as the tears stung in my eyes. I nodded, not trusting the strength of my voice, and he dropped my hands, wrapped his arm tightly around my shoulders, and led me back to his bedroom.

It was like no other time with Mitch. His usual gentle

manner was gone, his hands rough as they tore the clothes from my body. But his urgency was contagious. His passion caught me up and I surrendered completely, abandoning all thoughts of what I was, what he was, what lay between us. There existed only our two bodies, our mouths and our hands, our teeth and our nails.

"Don't hold back," Mitch hoarsely urged as he pulled me on top of him. When I felt him pulsing inside me, hard and insistent, I threw my head back and cried out, snarling, howling. His labored moans echoed my lust; his hands grasped my waist and my breasts until they worked their way to my neck and forced me down. Our lips met, his tongue pushed its way past my sharpened teeth, and the brief taste of his blood drove me wild.

"Deirdre, Deirdre," Mitch repeated over and over again. My own blood pounded in my ears, in perfect rhythm with his frantic thrusts. My body undulated on top of his, writhing in that exquisite torment. And when his teeth grazed my shoulder, I began to laugh, manic laughter that both frightened and excited me. I was too far gone to recognize its source, too enslaved by this rapture to care. The rush of Mitch's blood into my mouth, his small gasp of pain, made me realize that my teeth were buried as deeply into his neck as he was in me.

I could not stop, did not want to stop, did not have the power of will to fight the demon. I rode on the tides of his blood, and the bittersweet taste of him rushed through my system, its intoxicating heat causing me to break into a feverish sweat. I wanted to devour Mitch, drain him completely, carry him inside me forever. As if from a distance, I felt his climax and my own shuddering orgasm. I gripped him tightly within me, and it was only my mad gasp for air that enabled me to release his neck from my bite.

Rolling from him, I felt the trickle of his blood on my

chin and wiped it away in revulsion. Mitch sighed and moved toward me, nestling against me, his hand resting lightly on my hips, his mouth breathing into my ear. "That was incredible," he whispered weakly. "Absolutely incredible."

"Jesus," I swore at him, hiding my tears. "Incredibly dangerous is more like it. I could have killed you, Mitch. That can't happen again."

But he didn't hear me. His shallow, labored breathing had already relaxed into a more normal pattern. He was asleep, beyond any comprehension of my panic, leaving me alone and sated with sex, blood, and guilt.

# Chapter 22

After an hour, I slid the covers from me and quietly got out of bed. The panic that I had felt had not subsided, but continued to build deep within me. I knew that if I did not escape the room, the situation could quickly get out of hand. I found my clothes in the dark and began to dress. Mitch should sleep well, and with luck he would never know that I left. But the metallic hiss of my zipper roused him slightly.

"Deirdre?" Mitch's sleepy whisper made me jump guiltily and spin around.

"Go back to sleep, my love." My voice was soft and reassuring. "I'm just going out for a little air. I'll be back soon."

"Why're you always leaving?" His petulant question only heightened my desire to leave.

"Hush, Mitch, and sleep. After all"—I walked back to the bed and smoothed his hair—"I promised. And I always come back."

By the time I finished dressing, his breathing was deep and regular again. Silently, I slid through the apartment and out the door into the night streets.

Two blocks down I found a taxi and gave the driver the address of Mitch's hospital.

A quick survey of the parking lot revealed Sam's foreign sports car, and I breathed a sigh of relief. I didn't know whether he could help me or not, but I decided it was worth trying. I couldn't live my life as it was now, torn between two men, one dead and one living, but both central to my existence. And, I thought with a sarcastic smile, he would be more than pleased with the opportunity to delve into my unusual psyche.

With my customary shudder I entered the front doors of the hospital and walked to the nurses' station. When I saw that Jean was on duty, I almost turned around and left, but she looked up from her papers and her face darkened in recognition, her expression a challenge. Formidable as she is, I thought, she's still no match for me. I smiled my sweetest smile and was rewarded by her most hateful glare.

"Good evening, Jean," I said courteously. "I wonder if I might talk to Dr. Samuels."

"Not in," she muttered. "I'll leave him a message."

"Oh, but Jean, I saw his car in the lot. And I'm sure he would be happy to talk with me. Be a dear and tell him I'm here."

She bristled at my tone, as I had expected. "And who exactly are you?"

Suddenly I grew tired of her games and reached over the counter, grabbing her chin in my hand and pulling her up to eye level. "You know damn well who I am," I said through clenched teeth. "Just call him—now."

Jean's eyes held their defiant stare for a few seconds, then dropped in failure. As her hand went for the phone, I loosened my grasp on her. "Dr. Samuels"—her voice admitted defeat—"Miss Griffin is here to see you."

"Great." I could hear the response from his office. "Send her right down."

"Thank you, Jean," I said in a softer tone. "Now, that wasn't so hard, was it?"

I walked past her, but she reached a hand out to touch my arm. "Miss Griffin?" I felt her fingers tremble slightly. "How is Mitch?"

Behind her still-obvious dislike of me I could see tears glistening in her eyes and some of my animosity toward her dissipated. "He's doing well, Jean." I smiled honestly and her expression lightened, making her seem younger, prettier. "I'll be sure to tell him you asked."

"Thank you."

I patted the hand still resting on my arm. She held it there for a minute, then moved away from me and back to her desk. Shaking my head in disbelief—it was hard to imagine that Jean had a softer side—I entered Sam's office.

"How's the shoulder?" He got up from the desk and took my hand briefly. "No complications, I trust?"

"It's fine, thank you so much." I sat down and looked around doubtfully. Now that I was there, I was reluctant to talk about my problem, not so sure now that Sam could help me.

"And how's Mitch?"

"Mitch is fine too. I left him sleeping peacefully."

Sam nodded, walked back to his desk, and sat down. He smiled at me, exhibiting just a slight bit of uneasiness. "Then what on earth are you doing here?"

"I needed to talk to you." I paused, not knowing how to proceed. I had already pushed the limits of Sam's beliefs; my next admission would probably be going too far for him.

He opened the top drawer and pulled out the cigarettes. I took one, lit it, and inhaled deeply. Closing my eyes, I leaned back in the chair and nervously licked my lips. When I raised my head, I saw that he was watching me patiently, tapping his lighter gently on the desktop.

"Do you believe in possession?" As I blurted out the question, my voice sounded light, as if I were making a joke.

But Sam knew me better than that, and glanced at me in concern. He got up, looked out into the hall, then closed the door. Taking a deep breath and exhaling loudly, he leaned back against the wall and gave a small, humorless laugh.

"Three days ago I didn't believe in vampires. Now I don't know what I believe anymore. Do you mean by possession the taking over of one person's body and mind by a hostile spirit?"

"Yes."

"And that person is you?"

"I think so." I looked down at the cigarette in my hand, took one last drag, and stubbed it out in the ashtray. "I know you can hardly be an expert on the subject, but I had nowhere else to go, no one else to confide in."

"What about Mitch? Did you talk to him about this?"

"I tried to, Sam. But he seems to think it's all an evasion on my part to avoid making a commitment to our relationship. And that is in itself another totally different problem."

"Your relationship?" Sam walked back to his desk and took a cigarette for himself. "You and Mitch are having problems?"

I threw my head back and laughed, then looked him directly in the face. "What do you think? How could we have anything but problems?" I got up from my chair and went to look out the window. "Damn," I said softly. "I was a fool to return. And I was an even bigger fool to promise to stay."

"But you love him and he loves you. I know that's true. I see it in him and in you." Sam's voice acquired a sharp edge, almost accusatory in tone. "You can't leave him again. You do him so much good."

I felt a surge of anger but repressed it as much as I could. "But that's not why I'm here. I don't mean to involve you in my relationship with Mitch. It'll work out or it won't. Either way, it has nothing to do with you."

"Sorry." He accepted my rebuke politely, professionally. "So, why don't you tell me why you think you're possessed."

"Max." I whispered the name as I brushed the condensation from the windowpane. "He never died. Max Hunter still lives."

"But you said that Mitch killed him. A stake through the heart, the only thing that works with vampires. How could he be alive?"

I walked back to my chair and sat down again. "I don't know, Sam, but I know it's true." Reaching over, I removed another cigarette from his pack but didn't light it. "And he's with me, inside me. I see him, I hear him, I feel him. I dream of his past life. I know things about him I could never know otherwise: his real name, how he became a vampire, the sound of his mother's voice. I'm afraid to sleep, afraid to do anything that might draw him out."

Sam looked over at me, his expression concerned but detached. "And you feel he represents a danger to you?"

The question seemed such a complacent textbook response that suddenly the rage I had been suppressing broke loose. I rose to my feet and leaned over him, looking him full in the face. "Don't humor me, Sam. Why will no one take this situation seriously? No, he is no danger to me, he's already done his worst to me." I closed my fist over the cigarette I had been holding and crushed it, sprinkling the shreds of tobacco and paper over his desk. "But he's a danger to everyone else I meet. Why don't you understand? Max Hunter was, or is, a bloodthirsty murderer and he can control me. I've been walking the line between reason and insanity for these past two years. And . . ." I turned my back to him. My voice trembled as I felt tears well up in my eyes. "I don't know how much longer I can keep him at bay."

"Deirdre." I felt Sam move up behind me and lay a gentle hand on my shoulder.

"No," I said, spinning around to confront him. "Don't touch me. I have to go now. I can't stay any longer. You're not safe with me here and alone. I don't want to hurt you."

Sam backed away from me. "Deirdre, don't go yet. I'll try to help you if I can. But I'll need more details to get anywhere." He sat back at his desk and opened his drawer, removing a file folder. "I could hypnotize you, maybe talk to this presence you feel. Find out why this has happened, give you some control over it."

"What is that?" I pointed at the file. "Is that about me?"

"Deirdre, calm down. All my files are kept in strictest confidence; no one but me has any access to them."

"Destroy it," I hissed at him, going to the door. I turned the knob, opened the door, and saw the patient of the other night shuffling down the hall, past the nurses' station and into the recreational area. "Jesus," I swore to myself. "Oh, not now, not again." Panicked, I slammed the door and leaned up against it, breathing hard.

Sam was staring at me, his expression a mixture of fear and hurt. I sighed, regretting my brutal treatment of him. He had done nothing to deserve it, and I had gone there looking for help, not enemies. "I'm sorry, Sam," I said with a trace of a smile, pushing back my hair from my face. "I didn't mean to frighten you. Walk me out?"

"Yes, he said slowly, "if you have to go."

"I do." I stood back while he opened the door and escorted me out. "But I can come back. Some other night perhaps."

"Tomorrow?" He sounded strangely eager for my return visit.

I shrugged. "We'll see."

"Well, I'll have some time for a little research, then." He laughed. "Though God knows where I'll find anything remotely concerning all this. As I said the first time I met you, you're a strange case, Deirdre. But I'll do what I can."

We walked down the hall and stood for a moment in the waiting room inside the front doors. He extended his hand to me, and I took it carefully. "Good night," I said softly. "And thank you." An awkward silence ensued, broken finally by raucous laughter from the recreation room. Sam looked embarrassed but kept my hand in his.

"Time for me to get to work, I suppose. Sometimes, I wonder how any of us manage to hold on to our sanity. It's a crazy world."

I nodded in response to his statement and he gave me a searching look. "Are you feeling a little bit better, having talked this out with someone?"

I thought for a moment. "Yes, I think so."

"Good, that's what I'm here for." He hesitated, still holding on to my hand, and cleared his throat. A smile crossed his face briefly. "Now," Sam said, meeting my eyes, "you say you came here for my help. Will you accept it even if you don't like what I say, even if my opinion doesn't coincide with yours?"

"Try me."

"Okay, here goes nothing. I think that your basic problem is the fact that you spend too much time running from your problems, running from commitment. This feeling you have of being possessed may stem from your denial of life. You're alone and you try to avoid loving people because you're afraid you might harm them. Your relationship with Max was the closest you ever allowed yourself until you met Mitch. And when Max died, you left immediately so you wouldn't hurt Mitch."

I pulled my hand from his. "I suppose from one point of view all that is true, Sam, but . . ."

He gave me an exasperated glance. "Don't interrupt the doctor, Deirdre. The human mind is capable of going to almost any length of self-deception." He looked around us to see if anyone was near, then lowered his voice slightly. "A good part of you is still human despite your denial of that fact. And humans aren't meant to be alone, so you've manufactured a companion, a conscience almost, to be with you. You need someone, so you take the safe way out and fall back on your unhealthy relationship with Max. The fact that he is dead and appears only periodically works out even better. But it's all gotten out of hand. Your conscious mind is no longer in control of your fantasies."

"Then I am actually crazy?"

"No, I didn't say that. Surely you know by now that insanity is a relative term. You being what you are"—he looked away for a minute—"who's to say what's the normal psyche for a vampire? The bottom line is that you must begin to live the life you've been given. And Mitch has offered to share that life with you."

"But it'll never work." My voice trembled slightly. Sam's commonsense approach and rational explanations upset me more than I wanted to admit, because I could see that he might be right.

"You asked for my advice. That's a dangerous thing if you don't want to follow through with it." Sam reached over and took both my hands into his. "Deirdre, work it out with Mitch no matter what. If any two people are good together, you two are. We can talk through more of this later, but don't throw away what works."

I nodded and pulled my hands away, then delicately grabbed his shoulders, reaching up to give him a soft kiss on the cheek.

He put his hand up and touched the place I had

kissed with a shy, pleased expression on his face. "Good night, then, and I'll see you soon."

"Thank you." I turned my back on him and hurried out into the night.

"Well, where to, lady? The meter's running."

I had flagged a cab and gotten in but did not give the driver any destination; instead, I sat silently in the back-seat. His question finally pulled me out of my brooding. "You know," I said, almost thinking out loud, "if I were smart, I would go straight to the airport."

"The airport? You sure?" The driver seemed confused by my ambivalence.

I laughed softly to myself. Why should he be any different from the rest of us? "No, I'm not sure. Just drive around for a while and let me think."

"It's your call." He shrugged and moved the cab from the curb into the street. "As for me, I don't much care. I'm on all night and it's your money."

Although I was watching out the window, I became aware that he was studying me covertly in the rearview mirror. When our eyes met, he showed no embarrassment, just curiosity. I gave him a small smile, the encouragement he was waiting for.

"You visiting someone in that hospital?"

"Well, you might say that. I know one of the doctors."

"Your boyfriend? You two have a fight?"

"No, no, nothing like that. It's more complicated than I could explain, even if we drove around all night."

"Suits me. You're better looking than most of my fares. Probably safer too. This city is getting crazier every day."

I said nothing, but he continued. "You meet all types in this job. You probably wouldn't believe some of the things I've seen from up here. But I can tell you're sad about something. And it seems a shame that a pretty little thing like you shouldn't be happy. Why, you should be living in a nice house in the suburbs, with three or four little ones running around, happily married, not cruising this city with an old, worn-out cab driver."

I looked at his license. "Are you married, Bill?"

"Was. Almost forty years, but she died."

"I'm sorry."

"Yeah, me too." He stretched his neck up so that I could see his smile in the mirror. "Probably a lot sorrier than you. When she died I was devastated. Didn't hardly know what to do with myself. It's been three years now, and I still miss her like it was yesterday."

He fell silent and I went back to the window. He stopped at a traffic light and turned around. "You decide where you want to go yet?"

"No, just keep driving. But do you mind if I ask you a question?"

"Sure, goes with the territory, you know?"

I nodded and leaned forward in my seat. "When you were married, did you and your wife ever have differences of opinion, things that you couldn't reconcile between the two of you?"

He snorted a bit. "Hell, yeah. Women and men couldn't be more different if they were two different breeds. So things that seemed real important to her didn't matter to me. And vice versa."

"But you still stayed together."

"Yep. It's a nasty world out there if you don't have someone to love."

"Then here's another question for you. If you had known, when you first met your wife forty years ago, that she would die before you, would you still have set yourself up for it?"

"The loss, you mean?"

"Yes, would you have married her regardless?"

His reply was so quick, I knew that he had put no thought into what I had asked. "Of course," he said in an injured tone, "I loved her. And how could you ever know for sure?"

"But let's say, as a hypothetical situation, you had known for a certainty that you would have only, oh, fifteen years with her and not forty. And that when she went, you would have nothing. That you knew you would never find another like her no matter how long you lived."

"Hypothetically?"

"Of course."

He thought about it this time; I could see his eyes narrow in the rearview mirror. "Yeah, it would've been hard to deal with that certainty, but I would've married her even if I knew we had only one year." He paused for a minute. "Your boyfriend sick or something?"

"Yes, I suppose you could say that. I know for a fact that I'll outlive him by quite a few years. But that doesn't seem to bother him."

"And it bothers you?"

"Yes, it does. I've already lost one husband; I have no desire to lose another."

He gave a low whistle and a chuckle. "At the risk of sounding sarcastic, lady, I gotta tell you it's a tough life. You got to take chances or you're nowhere. Marry him. You might be surprised how it'll turn out."

I sighed and settled back into the seat again, smiling to myself, watching the passing pedestrians, studying the buildings, the shops, the bars. It was the same city as ever, but suddenly, as if my eyes had been cleared, as if the city and I had been washed clean, everything changed. I realized with a deep conviction that I had a home, not just a room, but a place where I belonged, where I was wanted, loved. Like all revelations, it seemed so simple, so true, that I wanted to laugh with joy. Instead, I tapped Bill gently on the shoulder. "I know where I want to go now. Thank you." I gave him Mitch's address. "And hurry, please. I'd like to get there before dawn."

# Chapter 23

The following evening Mitch and I were married. I still had my doubts as to whether it was the right thing to do. But the revelation I had been given the night before was still clear in my mind. Sam was right, the cab driver was right. I was tired of running from commitment, sick of living from day to day in loneliness and fear. And the look of complete happiness that crossed Mitch's face when I finally agreed was more than worth any problems that might arise later. I hadn't seen that look on a man for over a century, and it felt good.

"Are you sure?" He had gripped my face in his hands and searched my eyes.

"Yes, Mitch," I said, growing more confident in my decision. "I've never been surer of anything in my long life."

"Good. We'll do it soon, okay?"

"What's the hurry?"

He laughed and leaned over to kiss me. "I'm afraid you'll change your mind."

"But don't these things take time?"

"Yeah, but you forget I'm a cop. And although I've been out of action for a while, I still know a few people who owe me big favors. They can hurry it along, and we can get our blood tests tomorrow."

"But I can't take a blood test, Mitch. Have you forgotten?"

"Oh." He had looked disappointed, then shrugged it off. "We'll figure out a way. I assume your passport is up-to-date."

I nodded and he smiled. "Well, then you get some sleep and I'll start making calls right away."

True to his word, by the time I awoke all the arrangements had been made. Sam had been enlisted to produce a valid blood test for me; his only stipulation was that he be invited to the ceremony. Mitch had even managed to produce a wedding gown of sorts, apparently with the collusion of Betsy McCain, another self-invited guest. Before I hardly knew what had happened, I was standing nervously in an anteroom at the courthouse, waiting for the arrival of the judge, wondering, as the small bridal party assembled, why the hell I had ever agreed to this situation.

Mitch reached over, took my hand, and smiled. "You know, when Betsy brought that dress this afternoon, I had my doubts. But it looks great on you."

I looked down at what little there was of my bridal gown. It was a white satin sheath covered entirely in white lace. True, it did have long sleeves, but it was an off the shoulder line, and I was afraid to move too quickly for fear of losing it entirely. Laughing, I gave a tug on the too-short hemline. "Well, if you ask me, Betsy tries too hard to save money on material. There's practically nothing here."

Mitch's eyes lit up mischievously. "Yeah," he said with an exaggerated sigh, "but what's there is wonderful."

"If you had only given me some time, I would have gotten something a little more appropriate."

"Liar." Mitch's smile never left his face.

"That is not a lie."

"Yes it is, and you know it. If I had given you more time, you'd just have found excuses to put this off. I'm not getting any younger. I've had visions of you pushing me down the aisle in a wheelchair. Or"—he pulled me to him, serious once again—"visions of you disappearing again, this time for good."

"Mitch," I whispered, "I promise you I will never leave you."

"Okay you two, break it up." Betsy McCain bustled into the room balancing several florist boxes. "You're not married yet, and you can't get married anyway without the maid of honor. And"—she flourished the boxes and set them on one of the chairs—"certainly not without flowers. Although on such short notice I had to make do with what they had."

"Whatever they are, I'm sure they'll be fine," I told her. "It was a very nice gesture." I gave her a smile as she took off her coat and hung it on the rack by the door. She looked different to me, and it took a while to recognize why. She had abandoned her normal tailored suit, donning instead a dress cut very similar to my own but with less lace and completely in black. "And you look great."

"Thanks." She shrugged off the compliment and opened the flowers. "Here." She handed me the bouquet of white roses, then removed one in black for herself. Then she stood looking at me. "On second thought, and if you don't mind breaking from tradition . . ." She handed me hers, took mine from me, and stood back, squinting critically. "I like that better—there's more contrast."

I looked doubtfully at the black roses, then began to laugh until tears formed in my eyes. "Oh, Betsy"—I choked out the words—"you could never know how much more appropriate these are."

Mitch frowned, then lightened as Betsy went to him and pinned on his boutonniere.

"Now," she said, armed with one more flower and a deadly looking pin, "where's the best man?"

"He should be here soon." Mitch looked at the clock on the wall. "He'd better be, he's got all our paperwork."

"Chris has our paperwork?" I questioned in surprise.

"Chris," Mitch said, his mouth tightening slightly, "won't be coming tonight. Dr. Samuels has volunteered to stand up for us."

I felt a flush of sudden anger. "Chris was too busy for his father's wedding?"

"No, Chris was not too busy, he just won't be here."

"But Mitch—"

"Deirdre"—he interrupted me with finality—"let it go. I don't want it to ruin our evening. He'll come around eventually."

"Stepkids," Betsy said with disgust. "There's nothing worse than sulky little brats who don't want their parents to be happy."

Mitch shrugged, but I instantly rose to Chris's defense. "He is not sulky and he is not a brat. There are issues involved that you don't understand, Betsy. And"—I softened my voice—"Mitch is right. We shouldn't let it ruin our evening."

"Okay, okay. And speaking of the evening, did Mitch tell you where we're eating after the ceremony?"

"No. Actually this entire event is pretty much of a surprise."

"Well, then," Betsy said with an obvious wink at Mitch, "I can keep a secret too."

"Secrets?" Sam came through the door, a white envelope in his hand. "Who's keeping secrets?"

"Everyone," I said with a warning glance softened by a small smile and hug. "Thanks for coming, Sam."

"Not to worry. I had tonight off. And I wouldn't miss this occasion for all the world."

Betsy sidled up to Sam and extended her hand.

"Betsy McCain, Griffin Designs. And you must be the best man."

"John Samuels." He shook her hand and accepted his boutonniere, then turned to Mitch and clapped him on the shoulder. "In this case, though, I suspect the best man is really this lucky dog. Mitch, I can't tell you how overjoyed I am about all this. You must tell me how you managed to get her to agree."

"I will when I figure it out myself," Mitch started to say, and all three began to laugh.

I stood for a while, watching their mirthful exchange, feeling a total stranger in their midst. What did I have in common with these humans other than the calling of their blood to my hunger?

"It is what you chose, little one."

I snapped my head up and saw Max, shadowed in the doorway, beckoning to me. Aware but uncaring of the others' astonished faces, I pushed through them to where he waited in the hallway.

I heard Sam's startled voice call my name, Betsy's "What the hell," and with relief I heard Mitch say calmly, "Let her go, she'll be back," but none of that seemed important.

Max was leaning against the wall, just out of view of the door. "I might have known you would be here," I said bitterly. "Have you come to talk me out of it?"

"Not at all, my dear. I've come to a grudging respect for Greer over the years, and since he has accepted my presence in your life, I can do no less."

"Accepted your presence? How on earth could he do that? He's never seen you."

"Are you totally sure about that, Deirdre? He's a lot closer to understanding than you think. And he loves you anyway. How could I stand in the way of a relationship like that?"

I laughed softly. "It never stopped you before. So, am I to believe that you are here only to wish us well?"

"Believe what you like." Max leaned over and gave me an icy kiss. "Maybe I came to give away the bride."

"Deirdre," Mitch called from within the room, "the judge is ready."

I moved into the doorway. "I'll be right in," I answered, but when I turned back, Max was gone. "Damn," I swore softly, and ran my fingers over my lips, still cold from his touch.

The ceremony went smoothly. Sam must have done a good job faking my blood test, since apparently the paperwork was in order. Although tempted, I did not run screaming from the room, and if Max was present, he at least had the good grace to stay quiet and out of my line of sight. Twice during the short time we were there though, the door had opened. The first person to enter was Chris, the second, a woman who seemed familiar, but at the time I could not quite place her and did not want to stare. I had held my breath expecting one or the other of them to interrupt at the appropriate time, but nothing had happened.

". . . I now pronounce you husband and wife," the judge intoned, and Mitch pulled me to him for a kiss passionate and long enough to make everyone in the room slightly uncomfortable. And then it was over.

Chris walked up to us, shook Mitch's hand, and hesitantly kissed me on the cheek. After the introductions were made, I looked around for the woman who had accompanied him, but she must have left at some time during the ceremony. And there was no time for questioning him; Betsy hustled us into the limousines she had rented. On the way I found out, to my dismay, that she had arranged to hold the wedding dinner at The

Imperial. When we arrived, the driver came around and opened our door.

"Well, Mrs. Greer," Mitch said, smiling at me tentatively, "shall we go in?"

I touched him softly on the shoulder. "Mitch, did dinner have to be here? After my last run-in with Victor, I doubt that I'll be welcome."

"Just a minute." Mitch motioned to the driver and closed the door. "I knew it wasn't a good idea, but Betsy made all the arrangements. I called after she told me and found out that Victor won't be in tonight. He's out on important business. So you should be safe."

"I'm not really hungry. And I can't eat anything they serve in there anyway."

"I know." Mitch reached over and patted my cheek. "But I'm starved. And the wedding dinner is almost as important as the ceremony itself. What else did you want to do?"

"Well, I thought we could just head on out to the airport. We could go anywhere you like."

"After dinner, Deirdre. Betsy was so excited to set this up, and I'd hate to hurt her feelings. She's been a real help to me. Besides, this'll give us a chance to work things out with Chris."

"Oh. I almost forgot about Chris." I sat quietly for a minute, then leaned over and kissed Mitch on the cheek. "Fine, we'll go in, but right afterward we're going to pack some things and get out of this damn city for a while."

"Great. Now, don't you think we should go in? They'll wonder what we're doing."

"Let them wonder." I took his hand and gently stroked his palm with my thumb, then held it up to my lips. "Mitch, this may sound crazy, but did you happen to see Max tonight?"

"See him, no, but I knew he was around."

"How?"

"For one thing, by the way you acted. You get this distant look in your eyes, this distracted expression when you say he's present. Now I know what that means, and when it happened tonight, I tried to pay attention. I thought I could actually feel him there, and I could almost hear something, far away and indistinct." He smiled at me. "Don't worry about it, Deirdre. It's a little spooky, but I'll get used to it." Mitch reached for the door handle, then pulled away. "So, what did he want anyway?"

"To give the bride away."

To my surprise, Mitch threw his head back and laughed. "That's what you get for putting 'Father' on his gravestone. Come on, let's go in."

We caught up with the other three in the lobby. Betsy was talking to the maître d'; Chris and Sam were carrying on a whispered discussion in the corner. They looked up guiltily when we walked in, and I knew they had been talking about us. But since Chris seemed more at ease, and smiled more freely at Mitch and me, I didn't really mind. If Sam could help him deal with this situation, it would make our lives a lot easier.

Our table was ready and Betsy claimed Mitch's arm and followed the waiter. I touched Chris gently on the arm. He barely suppressed a shudder, but Sam nodded at him encouragingly. "Everything will work out all right, Chris." I smiled at him. "I promise." He gulped slightly, tucked my hand around his arm, and escorted me to dinner.

"Deirdre, I'm sorry I didn't come sooner. Dad asked me to be best man, but I just couldn't. He was really angry, read me the riot act on the phone."

"But you finally did come," I reassured him, "and that's what matters."

Chris slowed down and looked doubtfully at the back

of Mitch's head. "I hope so. He can be real stubborn sometimes."

"Tell me about it," I said with a small laugh. "Why do you think this happened at all? For all that I love your father, and I do love him, I was not entirely convinced that this marriage was a good idea. But, Chris, it was what he wanted. He's been alone so long." As have I, I added silently, but he seemed to understand.

"I know this'll be good for you both. It's just that you're a"—he had the grace to blush slightly—"well, what you are, and that'll take some getting used to."

"Fine, we have a lot of time. But keep it to yourself tonight, kiddo. Betsy doesn't know and I'd like to keep it that way."

"And what doesn't Betsy know?" She bounded over to us, her eyes gleaming almost maliciously, acquisitively. "More secrets?"

I sat down next to Mitch and held his hand. "Only that I married the best man in the city."

"Oh, that," she said disparagingly. "I knew that. But you've got only one, Deirdre"—she settled Sam in on one side of her and Chris on the other—"and now I have two."

Chris looked embarrassed, but Sam laughed. The waiter brought and poured the champagne. I wanted to ask about the woman who had entered the courtroom and then quickly departed, but I hated to spoil what was left of the evening with an interrogation of Chris. Betsy had no such compunctions.

"So tell me, Christopher, who came in after you tonight? And why didn't she come along? One more person wouldn't have been a problem, would it have, Deirdre?"

"No, absolutely not." I glanced at Mitch, who suddenly seemed nervous.

"It was Jean," Sam interjected.

Mitch nodded and said nothing, but glared at Chris.

"Good God, so it was," I blurted out with a funny choked laugh. "I must have been really nervous not to recognize her. But who the hell invited her? She was the last person I expected to see." I looked at Sam. "Do you think she listens in on your phone calls?"

"No, she was off duty this afternoon; she works only nights. And I know I didn't mention it to her."

"Don't look at me," Mitch shrugged. "I haven't seen her since I checked out. And anyway, what possible difference can it make?"

"Who is Jean?" Betsy asked, sounding slightly annoyed at being left out of the conversation.

"A nurse at the hospital where I work," Sam said. "And like Mitch said, it's not really important, just curious that she should have shown up like that."

Chris cleared his throat. "I stopped by there this evening, looking for you, Dr. Samuels. I couldn't find you, but Jean was there and I asked if you were going to the wedding. Nobody told me not to say anything. And when she asked herself along, well, what could I do? She stayed until it was over, then slipped away before I noticed she'd gone."

Nobody said anything, and he continued in her defense. "She took good care of you, Dad, better than any other nurse there, and if she wanted to see you married, I can't see what harm it'd do."

"No harm, Chris." I reached across the table and touched his arm. "We just wondered how she knew. I think it was sweet of you to bring her along. Now, let's just drop the subject, shall we? How about some more champagne?"

By the time everyone's glass was refilled, dinner arrived and the conversation turned to other matters. I sat quietly through the meal, picking at my rare prime rib, trying to ignore the waves of nausea caused by the varied aromas of the food around me. When the waiter finally cleared the plates and provided coffee, I sighed in relief.

Mitch caught the hint, paid the bill, and got up from the table. "Thank you for your help today, Betsy and Sam. It was wonderful. But we have some packing to do before we leave on our honeymoon."

"Honeymoon?" Betsy asked blearily, the champagne having taken its toll on her. "I didn't know you were going away."

"Oh." I stood up and rubbed my head against Mitch's sleeve. "We just decided on the way over here."

"Where are you going?" Sam smiled up at us over his coffee.

"Ah, we don't actually know yet, do we, honey?" Mitch kissed the top of my head. "But we're heading straight out to the airport. We'll send you a postcard."

I walked around the table and gave them all a hug. Mitch shook Sam's hand, kissed Betsy, and clapped Chris on the shoulder. "See you later," he called, and we left the restaurant.

The limos were nowhere in sight, so we flagged a cab and when one finally stopped, we snuggled in the backseat.

"That wasn't so bad, was it?" Mitch asked me as we arrived at his apartment.

"No, it was a lot of fun, actually."

"You see, you should've married me two years ago."

"Yes, I guess so. Mitch, we have some things we still need to work out."

"I know, but it can wait, can't it? Let's enjoy the next few weeks before we get back to the harsh realities. And speaking of enjoying, we don't need to rush right off to the airport, do we?" His one hand tightened on my shoulder while the other played with the lace on the hem of my dress.

"No." I turned to face him. "We have a little time."

"Good." He kissed me, his lips crushing mine, his hand delicately moving up my thigh.

"Actually," I said breathlessly when he removed his mouth, "tomorrow night would be soon enough to leave."

"I was hoping you'd say that." The rawness of passion in his voice made me gasp, and like the night in the hospital made me forget where we were. Had it been a longer drive to his apartment, we would have made love right there in the cab.

As it was, the driver coughed and discreetly announced our arrival. When Mitch paid him, we ran up the steps of his apartment clutching each other and giggling like teenagers. He unlocked the door and picked me up to carry me in.

My head was nestled against his neck, so when he dropped me abruptly, I was taken completely by surprise by the three men, Victor Lange, Ron Wilkes, my attorney, and Fred, the Ballroom's bartender, standing in Mitch's living room. More surprising still was the fact that both Ron and Fred held rather large handguns, aimed directly at us.

# Chapter 24

"Close the door, Greer," Victor ordered. Mitch slumped for a minute, then did as he was told. He leaned up against the door; his eyes were glassy and his breathing came in short, panicked gasps.

"Mitch." I took him by the shoulders and called his name but he didn't hear me. He was absorbed in studying the faces of the men.

"What the hell is this all about, Victor?" I turned around and faced the three of them, attempting to block Mitch's body from their guns. "Are you planning to shoot me? Well"—I bared my teeth unpleasantly—"you had better give it your best shot the first time. It will be the only chance you get."

"Now, Deirdre," Victor said calmly, "we don't want to hurt anybody. And of course, if we did, it would be Mitch we would shoot. So if you'll just move away from him slowly, everything will be fine. We can talk this out like reasonable beings."

"Reasonable beings do not break into people's apartments and threaten the inhabitants with guns. What is this all about? And what have you done to Mitch?"

"Nothing. I assume he's having a little flashback from his recent mental problems. It will pass." Victor motioned to the couch. "Come here and sit down, my dear. Ron and Fred will take good care of Mitch."

I looked steadily into the faces of the two men. Fred

met my glance defiantly; Ron lowered his eyes, but not before I caught a glimpse of sadness. "You I can understand, Fred, you've always been a self-serving little bastard." He said nothing, but continued to smirk, so I turned to Ron. "But what are you doing here, Ron? I thought we were friends."

Victor laughed and beckoned me to the couch again. "As you so succinctly put to me not that long ago, 'Never count on constancy in love or friendship among vampires.' " His emphasis on the last word caused me to draw in a sharp breath that he ignored. "Rob and Fred both work for me."

"All three of you are vampires?" I dropped onto the couch with a small, humorless laugh.

"Just so, Deirdre."

Mitch made a small choking sound and slumped down onto the floor, his back resting against the door, his eyes still focused on the faces of the men.

"Ease up on him a little, boys. We don't want him passing out, do we? I think Deirdre will cooperate with us."

Some of the fear left Mitch's face and his breathing deepened a little. He managed a weak smile that wrenched my heart.

"Mitch," I said quietly. "I'm sorry. But I always said you were better off without me."

"Be that as it may," Victor continued, "he's now involved in this situation if only by association. And speaking of which, I understand congratulations are in order."

"Congratulations?"

"On your marriage." Victor's voice sounded amused.

Fred snickered, calling my attention to the two of them where they stood, their guns no longer pointed at Mitch, but still very much in evidence. Ron gave me one brief, angry glance, and his shoulders tightened. When he did speak, his tone was flat and bitter. "You don't date the meat."

"Excuse me?" But Ron made no response, so I turned again to Victor. "And how did you know we were married?"

"You'll discover that very few of your activities are unknown to me. I make it my business to know these things. And there is one member of our group to whom you have not yet been properly introduced. She's a little insecure, being only newly one of us, and I wanted her out of the way if there was trouble. But you'll be reasonable, I know." Victor smiled, not maliciously, I thought, but as if he were enjoying a joke. "And you may find out that you share many things in common; one might even say you were from the same family. Come out, Jean."

Jean stepped out of the hallway, where she had been concealed from us. One look at her pinched face and white uniform and I began to laugh, sounding a little hysterical. "Jesus, Victor, this is entirely too much. Is everyone I meet in this damned city a vampire? How many of you are there?"

"Don't you mean how many of us?" He did not wait for my answer. "We'll let that go for now. I completely understand that your ignorance of our existence was Max's doing. Ill-advised, as I said before, but Max did what he liked. And you were his responsibility."

"I take care of myself, Victor. I always have."

"And that is an admirable sentiment, my dear, one that we all admire in you. To answer your questions, there are approximately one hundred of us in the metropolitan area and no, not everyone you meet is a vampire. But of course Ron and Jean were planted, carefully cultivated for their roles. Granted, Fred had been with Max practically since the Ballroom opened. But Ron was engaged to keep tabs on you when you returned and

Jean was put into the hospital to monitor our punishment of Mitch." He looked away from me. "I must apologize for that, Greer. We had thought you had killed Max. We'll make what amends we can."

"Can you give him back the two years he lost in the institution? Can you give him back an unaltered mind?" A surge of anger flowed through me. These people were worse than Max—he at least had a personal interest in my life. And his manipulations were understandable from that point of view.

"No," Victor said gently. "But I can allow him to live, under certain circumstances, of course."

Jean gave a small gasp, then cleared her throat nervously. "Mr. Lange," she said hesitantly, "do you need me anymore? I have to be back at the hospital soon."

"No, thank you, Jean. That will be all."

She went to the door and gave Victor a sidelong glance. He nodded slightly and she looked down at Mitch. "I'm sorry, Mitch," she said, and slipped past him.

Her subservient attitude annoyed me. "This is quite a nice setup you have, Victor. Do all the vampires here serve you so willingly, or is this group your private little army?"

"No, Deirdre, you misunderstand the situation. They do not serve me so much as they serve The Cadre. But since I am the head of that venerable institution, I do command a certain amount of respect."

"The Cadre? That's the organization that inherits Max's money if I turn it down, isn't it? Is that what all this is about? Money? You can have it all. I've never wanted any of it."

"I wish it were that simple, Deirdre. The money is not the issue here. The murder of Max Hunter is. The other night you admitted to that crime. Do you want to change your statement?"

I have him a short, vicious smile. "Would it do any good?"

"No, my dear. Either way you must appear before the judicial board of The Cadre. We have no choice." Victor checked his watch. "And we must go soon. They're waiting for us."

"And if I refuse?"

Fred turned around, displaying a delighted grin and brandishing his gun. "Then we shoot Greer."

I had no doubt that he would do as he said. I stood up and smoothed the skirt of that ridiculous wedding gown. "Well, then, I can hardly refuse such a polite invitation. Shall we?"

Mitch struggled to his feet. "She's not going anywhere without me."

Fred laughed unpleasantly. "Of course, you get to come too. You're our insurance that Miss Griffin, or shall I say, Mrs. Greer, doesn't bolt."

I gave him a cold stare. "You don't need insurance, Fred. I will not bolt, as you so cleverly put it. Mitch stays here."

Fred shifted uneasily under my gaze and looked at Victor for confirmation.

"I trust you, Deirdre," Victor said with a frown, "but I'm afraid Fred is right, even if overly anxious on the trigger. Mitch will accompany us, but you have my word that he won't be harmed and that you'll both be returned here before dawn. This is merely a preliminary hearing. Certain allowances have been made for you, since you are what we call a rogue, and are unschooled in our ways. You'll be given every chance to prepare for the trial, and although you will be under surveillance, you'll still have a chance to spend a few weeks together before the final decision." Victor gently took my arm and moved me toward the door. As he opened it, he looked deep into my eyes, his eyes a curious mix of anger and sympathy. "That is the most I can promise you."

Once again Mitch and I were loaded into the backseat of a limousine, and once again our destination was The Imperial. But this time we entered through the back and rode an elevator down two floors.

Victor reached out and pushed a button on the control panel. The elevator stopped but the doors did not open. Then he turned to Mitch. "Mitchell Greer, you have been brought to a place where few humans have ever been; fewer still have left alive." His tone was formal, rehearsed. "You are here for several reasons. One, you must be cleared before the panel for the murder of Max Hunter so that others do not attempt your punishment on their own. Two, you have married one of us"—Victor glanced over at me, his eyes sparkling—"even though she will not admit that kinship. The Cadre is an ancient institution and has much respect for traditions and sacred vows. So you have been given leave to attend unharmed. But"—his voice deepened, darkened—"you must not interfere in any way. Your assistance or defense of Deirdre under any circumstances can only harm her and will not be tolerated."

"I understand." Mitch's voice matched Victor's solemn manner, but I noticed the dangerous glint in his eyes. "You've been more than fair, I suppose, given the situation. But you've also got to understand that I'll do my damnedest to keep you, or any of your thugs, from hurting her. Quite honestly, Victor, without her, my life is worthless. And I'd happily give it for the chance to take a few of you with me."

They stood appraising each other for what seemed a long time. Finally, Victor smiled and held out his hand. "You have my word," he said as they shook hands. "Deirdre will not be killed, and you won't be required to fight us for her." He took his finger from the button and the doors opened. "Despite what you might think, we're really quite civilized."

We entered a large meeting room, thickly carpeted and illuminated only by candles and torches. At the end of this room a long table stood, occupied by eight people, four on each side of the two vacant chairs in the center. On the wall behind the table, a large tapestry was hung depicting a dark night sky over a medieval-looking city. Ten small golden plates, each about six inches in diameter, resembling family crests, hung from chains on either side of the tapestry.

Victor stepped forward, motioning Fred and Mitch into chairs along the wall, and Ron moved up beside me to take Victor's place. Slowly, ceremoniously, Victor walked down the center aisle and the people seated at the table rose and bowed to him as he approached. Their eyes shone oddly in the light; none of them looked familiar to me. Victor nodded his head and walked around the table, removing two of the crests from the wall. One, he hung around his neck, the other was draped over the center of the table. He raised his hand and the others sat while he remained standing.

"Deirdre Griffin"—his voice was soft but powerful and the echoes filled the room—"born Dorothy Grey, remade in the house of Alveros in the common year of 1860, come forward."

Ron gave me a soft push in the small of my back. Trying to match the pace Victor had set, I approached the table, my hands at my sides. As I walked I kept my eyes on the center crest, recognizing it with surprise as one I had seen in my dreams of Max. *Damn you, Max,* I thought, searching for his presence and finding nothing, *why the hell did you get me involved in this?*

When I got within one foot of the table, Victor gave a slight nod of his head and I stopped. He raised his hand again. "Deirdre Griffin is brought before us on charges of murder. Do any of The Cadre wish to speak for her?"

I opened my mouth to explain that I would speak for myself, but caught the almost imperceptible shake of Victor's head and heard the footsteps behind me.

"I ask to speak for her." Ron stepped up beside me and gave me a small smile. There was shock and surprise on the faces of some of the panel, including Victor's, but when he lowered his arm, he looked strangely pleased.

"Ron Wilkes, your request is granted. This woman stands before us accused of the murder of the founder of the house of Alveros. How will she answer?"

"She cannot answer at this time. As the distinguished houses know, she is a rogue, unused to our ways. I ask that she be given two weeks in which to prepare her answer."

Given Victor's promise to me at Mitch's apartment, this defense did not surprise me. The panel members nodded and Victor raised his hand again. "Deirdre, you have been given that for which you have asked. Mitchell Greer, human and husband of this vampire, come forward."

Ron pulled me gently to one side and back a few steps as Mitch approached. He stood facing the panel, and I admired the determined way he held his shoulders and head.

"Let it be known among The Cadre that this human, who had previously, by certain evidences and by his own admission, been judged guilty of the murder of Max Hunter, is at this moment exonerated, and is to be held exempt from further punitive actions on our part, until such time as his true involvement in the crime can be ascertained."

"It has been witnessed," a female member seated to Victor's right agreed, "and it will be communicated."

"Then," Victor said, "we are adjourned."

The formality of the panel instantly dissolved at his words and everyone became more relaxed. Victor walked over to me and smiled. "See, I told you we were civilized. Now, can I offer you a drink?"

Mitch shook his head and put his arm around my shoulders. "No, but we'll take a ride home."

"Fine," Victor agreed. "I'm afraid we have rather interrupted your wedding night. Ron will call you tomorrow evening and begin your education, Deirdre. Until then, you can pretty much do what you want. You can move about the city freely and continue your activities, but"—his eyes grew stern—"stay away from the airport. Any attempts to leave town will result in your incarceration until the trial. I don't want it to come to that." He took my hand and kissed it. "Good night, Deirdre." Releasing me, he nodded. "Mitch."

We followed Victor to the back of the room, and when we reached the elevator, Fred stepped in behind us, his gun still in his hand. "Fred," Victor said, the disgust evident in his voice, "your obvious delight in tormenting your fellow beings is sickening. Put your toy away. And drive Mr. and Mrs. Greer home."

# Chapter 25

Fred remained subdued by Victor's reprimand only until we stopped at a traffic light a few blocks away from Mitch's apartment. "Good hearing, huh?" He turned around in the driver's seat and smiled at us maliciously. "You're pretty quiet, Deirdre. Don't you have any questions to ask?"

I gave him a long, cold stare. "You want questions? Fine. Just where do you fit in, Fred?"

"Oh," he said, returning to his driving, "same as you—house of Alveros. Common year 1922. There aren't many of us left from that house." He gave a cruel laugh. "And in two weeks' time there might be one less. Although"—he met my eyes in the rearview mirror—"Victor seems to like you. Maybe he'll let you live, provided, of course, you give him the proper encouragement. Play your cards right and he might even let you establish the house of Grey someday. Compared to most of Max's children, you're positively ancient. Me, I like my women younger, less experienced, if you know what I mean."

I felt Mitch tense up next to me, and putting a calming hand on his arm, I warned him with my eyes to keep his temper. I knew that Fred was merely baiting us, hoping to provoke an angry response. And I wondered how much of his self-confidence came from the weapon he carried and how much was inner strength. He was younger than I; perhaps he was weaker, perhaps he could be bent to my control. I glanced at Mitch out of the corner of my eye and shook my head almost imperceptively. He understood, and gave my knee a gentle squeeze.

I took a deep breath and leaned forward in my seat with a feigned eagerness. "So, Fred," I said, touching him softly on the shoulder, "you are one of Max's children. I suppose that makes us related: cousins, perhaps, or maybe even siblings." I lowered my voice to a sultry whisper and ran a finger along his cheek and jaw. "You must tell me," I breathed, "what exactly are The Cadre's rules on incest?"

He tensed at my touch, clenching his teeth together, but encouraged by the jump of his pulse, I continued.

"There is a lot to be said for experience, Fred. I may be over sixty years your elder, but those were sixty years spent in experimentation, pushing the natural limits. You might be pleasantly surprised at the kind of things I could teach you."

"Quit playing games with me, Deirdre." Fred's voice was curt, but his breathing quickened.

"It is no game," I whispered to him, gently nuzzling the side of his neck. I saw that we were back at Mitch's apartment. "Stop the car, Fred."

He pulled over to the curb and turned off the engine. "That's right," I encouraged. "Why don't we let Mitch go in first? We don't need him here right now, do we?"

"Get out, Greer."

I nodded and Mitch left the car. I waited until he was up the stairs and in the door before I made my next request. "And now, Fred, you can give me your gun. We won't be needing it, not now. I can give it back to you later on, after we have completed our business."

I felt his hesitation. "Please, Fred," I breathed in his ear, "give me the gun. You don't need it, not for me."

Quickly, he vaulted over the seat, landing next to me; his hands flew up to grip my shoulders. I met his eyes. "The gun, Fred. Give me the gun."

He reached into his pocket and produced the gun, handing it to me with a guttural moan. I put it into my purse and reached over to him, holding his face in my hands. "Thank you, Fred." My eyes bore into his, until I felt that I was deep inside his mind. "It's too bad that you lost your gun on the way over here. That was very careless of you. Now, open the door and let me out of the car."

Fred shuddered slightly at my intrusion but obediently opened the door for me. I smiled and, bending over, kissed his cheek lightly. "Thank you, Fred," I said again. "I will see you soon."

"Good night," I heard him call, his voice faint and confused.

Laughing at my success, I ran up the stairs, opened the door, and bumped into Mitch, who had apparently been standing at the entrance, watching. "What the hell was all that about, Deirdre?"

I looked behind me and saw Fred pull the car into traffic and drive away. "I merely wanted to see if he was controllable."

"And?" There was a slight tick in his cheek, as if he were trying not to smile.

I reached into my purse and, with a grin, produced Fred's gun, dangling it back and forth on my finger. "Like candy from a baby." I took his arm and rubbed my head against his sleeve. "Let's go inside, love. I think we'll be safe from Fred for a while."

Mitch unlocked the door and we both sighed in relief when we saw that his apartment was empty. "You know, Deirdre," Mitch started to say, removing his suit coat and tie, "I still don't understand why you felt you had to play that little scene with Fred."

I slid out of my heels and sat in the armchair, stretching my legs out in front of me and flexing my feet. "I had to know what sort of power I possess. It was not important before, because I never had to deal with beings like myself. But now . . ." Shrugging, I curled my legs underneath me and settled back. "It's important to know what I can do."

"And if it hadn't worked? If you hadn't been able to control Fred, what do you think would have happened?" Mitch came over and sat on the arm of the chair. Although he put his arm around me tenderly, I could feel the tension in his body and sense the anger he was keeping tightly in check.

Attempting to lighten his mood and diffuse his anger, I joked. "At the very least, I would have had to hire another manager at the Ballroom." Reaching up, I stroked his cheek and ran my fingers over his lips. "And at the most, there would have been one less member of the house of Alveros for us to contend with. You know as well as I that had he laid one hand on me, you would have killed him."

"Damn straight." Mitch gave a tight little laugh and kissed me on the forehead. "Now"—he stood up and began unbuttoning his shirt—"let's get changed and start packing."

"What?"

"We're supposed to leave for our honeymoon, remember? Now that you've gotten rid of Fred for the evening, I suspect that we've got enough time to get out of the city before The Cadre exacts their vigilante justice on you. I won't stand by and let them prosecute you, Deirdre. After all this time and the way I had to live without you, and after . . ." Smiling, Mitch ruffled my hair. "After you finally came to your senses and married me, I won't let anyone interfere, not the bloody pretentious Victor Lange or even his goddamned precious Cadre."

I chuckled at his accurate summation of the scene we had just been put through, then grew serious. "But Mitch, I can't leave. I promised Victor. Besides, what sort of life would we have, running and hiding from them wherever we go? The life I already lead is bad enough, but to have to avoid them for the rest of eternity?" I shook my head sadly. The decision to marry him had been an easier one to swallow, but the commitment I had finally made to face up to my problems and not run away applied as much to this situation as to my relationship with Mitch.

"No, we can't run. It really doesn't matter for me, but you, you're a different matter completely. I will not have them punish you again for something I did. And if, in the process, they were to hurt you, or drive you completely insane, or kill you, I'd be forced to take revenge on them." I sighed and wiped away a tear. "Mitch, I love you, I want nothing more than to stay with you for the rest of your life, but I'm tired of running away. I can't exist any longer at odds with the entire universe. It will stop here. Like it or not, I'm one of them and I'll accept their terms and their justice, no matter what."

To my surprise, Mitch was not angry at my statements. Instead, he smiled at me, his blue eyes almost aglow in their intensity. "Deirdre, we'll beat them together. We can get you off this charge, I'm sure of it. And if not, I'd put down money that you could take them all on single-handedly and come out unscathed."

"I wish I could be so sure. Fred was easy, but who knows how long my control over him will continue? And as for all the others, I have no experience against which to gauge their power or their reactions."

"But don't you see." He pulled me to my feet and held me to him. "You're a rogue to them, a wild card.

They have no gauge of you either. And they've all been tutored, led along the easy path, while you had to struggle and fight every inch of the way. You have an inner strength and conviction that none of The Cadre members, with all their ancient ceremonies and rites, can match."

I moved an arm's length from him and smiled. "I never thought of it that way. You may just be right. But"—I nestled up against him, sliding my hands under his open shirt, savoring the warm texture of his bare skin against my fingers—"let's not spend the rest of the night discussing this. I thought we were supposed to be on our honeymoon."

Shortly before dawn I lay entwined with Mitch, admiring the shine of the streetlights reflecting onto my wedding ring. A simple gold band, it was only a little too large for my finger. I smiled and, for those last few precious minutes of the night, watched him sleep. It has been too many years, I thought, since I allowed myself to love someone fully. And yet, he was worth the waiting.

When the sky began to lighten, I got out of bed, pulled down the blinds, and drew the heavy draperies across the window, then slid back under the covers, pressing myself against his warm body.

The dirt road I walk seems familiar somehow; a voice in the back of my mind recognizes this place even though I've never been here. I shrug the feeling away, a habit that I've become quite adept at through the centuries. What I don't understand I tend to leave alone. A soft rain is falling, and the wheel ruts in the road well up with muddy water.

I have been traveling with no purpose for some time now, ever since Leupold made the long ocean journey and found me. He remains in that city, excited by his new life and slowly building for himself a dynasty of other beings like us. I managed to convince him that I wanted no part of his empire, but helped him to locate those that I myself had transformed. There are only a few still living; whether they choose to join him or not is their decision. I have not yet met one I would be willing to spend the rest of eternity with. I tell myself that I prefer my loneliness to their inane society, prefer to commit my atrocities with no audience other than my own belabored conscience.

I hear the carriage approach long before it comes into sight. Having left a dead body behind in the closest town, I wish to remain unseen and melt into the surrounding trees. I watch them drive by, the man and the woman inside the closed coach. They are talking and smiling, and I feel a strange twinge of jealousy for a life I will never have.

When they are farther down the road, I step out of the concealing brush. I continue walking, but suddenly a bolt of lightning strikes a nearby tree. There is a deafening crash and it falls and catches the rear end of the carriage, which overturns on the road.

I wait a minute, watching the upper wheels of the carriage spin in the air. The horses rear and scream in fright. Perhaps they are spooked by the lightning, perhaps they sense my unnatural presence.

The smell of blood falls upon the air, hypnotizing, tantalizing me, and although I had already fed, the deadly hunger engulfs me again. I discover the man's dead body under the lower wheels; he lies in a crumpled heap, his neck twisted, his body crushed, and his blood uselessly mingles with the muddied rain.

But the woman, ah, the woman still lives. As I open the door of the carriage and reach in for her, she opens her eyes. There is happiness in her glance, as if she had been waiting for me. My heart twists when I realize that it is probably only relief at being rescued. But still I pull her out of the wreckage and hold her warm body close to mine, carrying her farther up the road.

She welcomes my embrace at first, responding eagerly to my caresses and my kisses. Then she looks deep into my eyes, and her fear becomes apparent. Feebly she attempts to push me aside, and I would gladly let her go, but the feeding instinct has been triggered and cannot be denied.

Her body tenses when my teeth sink into her neck; she is powerless to stop me, but still she fights. God, I think, admiring her perseverance, she is strong. As I drink, I feel a sharp pain in my own shoulder. She has clawed her way through my clothes and is answering my assault with one of her own. My own blood flows and she drinks, pulling upon me with a hunger almost as great as my own.

In my surprise, I laugh and stop feeding upon her, allowing her to drink of me. Eventually, she slows and stops; her eyes flutter shut. But I continue to hold her, cradled in my arms, until I hear the approach of another carriage. I do not want to leave her, but I have no choice. I cannot permit myself to be seen.

Reluctantly, I lay her down on the road and she opens her eyes to me once more. "If you survive, my little one," I say before fading into the night, "we will meet again."

# Chapter 26

When I woke, Mitch was not in bed. I got up, wrapped a robe around me, and opened the closed bedroom door cautiously. There was no natural sunlight in the hall, so I guessed it would be safe to venture farther. Mitch was in the living room, sitting cross-legged on the floor, sorting through a box of papers. "Good morning," I said, my voice dull and lethargic. He turned to me, smiled, and I asked, "What time is it?"

"A little before four. Sunset'll be soon, but you can sleep more if you like."

"No, I'm awake now. But how about you? You should be tired. You were awake practically all night also."

Mitch shrugged, running his fingers through his hair. "I haven't yet adjusted to sleeping all day. I guess it'll come in time. How'd you manage?"

"I had no choice, remember? It was not a conscious decision to become nocturnal. And you have no reason to adjust to it."

"No, maybe not." His voice was calm, noncommittal, consciously avoiding, I thought, this particular issue that would need to be dealt with eventually. I welcomed the development with relief, not needing another argument to further complicate our lives. Maybe this was how we would survive, avoiding the painful subjects completely until they became unimportant.

"Deirdre." Mitch's voice pulled me out of my

thoughts. "Would you like some coffee?" He stood up, and at my nod went into the kitchen and brought out a full mug.

I sat down on the couch, took a sip, and looked at the papers strewn on the floor. "What is all this?"

Mitch sat back down on the floor at my feet. "I stopped over at the station today and picked up the personal files they had kept for me in storage. It's been so long, it seems much longer than two years, and I thought I'd refresh my mind on some of the details of the Vampire Killer case. Thought maybe I could find something in here you could use in your defense."

"And?"

"Nothing yet, but who knows? The next page may just be what we need. I won't let them hurt you, Deirdre."

I sat silently and sipped my coffee. When I finally spoke, my voice sounded far away. "I had another dream."

"Max again?"

I shuddered. "Yes. This one was so real, so horrible. They're not frightening in content, but they utterly terrify me. In the dream I become a part of him, and it robs me of my self. Robs me of my defenses, of any feelings for him but sympathy and love."

Mitch looked at me questioningly, and I continued. "It's strange. I hated him for so long, never completely understanding him. But now that he's dead, I know him so much better. And when I wake, I feel empty, almost as if I've been torn in half."

Mitch reached over and stroked my leg, then laid his head on my thigh. Idly, I ran my fingers through his hair. "I just don't understand any of this situation with Max. Will I have to live with it for the rest of my life? I'm not sure I can handle that. Eternity is too long anyway." Then I laughed a little. "Did you know that Sam thinks it's all my imagination, that I've invented the entire situation to alleviate my loneliness, my guilt?"

"Yeah," Mitch said dryly, "and he thought I was crazy too."

I nodded. "I guess he can't always be right. But he sounded so sure, so authoritative."

"Forget about Sam." There was only a slight tinge of jealousy in his voice. "He can't really help you. But you should ask someone else about it, someone who might be able to give you an answer that makes sense. Victor Lange, maybe, or your attorney."

"Maybe I will."

Mitch went back to sorting his papers, methodically putting them into small stacks, glancing at each page. "Well," he said, waving one particular sheet in the air, "this one doesn't belong with the rest." He went to put it into a separate pile, then stopped and read it in more detail. "Son of a bitch, I don't remember this at all." He shook his head slightly as if to clear it, then looked up at me, an odd expression on his face.

"What is it?"

"A morgue report."

"On Max?"

"No, on Larry."

At the mention of the name, I shivered as always. "What about him?"

"Nothing much, and it's not really that unusual. Sometimes they just lose track of the final disposition papers." He read it again, slowly and thoroughly. "That must be what happened."

"What do you mean, Mitch, final disposition papers?" A cold stab of fear entered my abdomen. Vaguely I remembered the familiar face on the Ballroom dance floor. Was I destined to be haunted by everyone I touched? "Larry too?" I wasn't really aware that I had spoken it out loud.

"Larry too, what?"

"Nothing."

"Well," he said, giving me a questioning look, "I'm sure it's just an oversight. After all, he was dead. He couldn't have just gotten up and walked away."

"Are you sure?" My voice trembled. Larry's death had been nagging at me for years; something didn't seem right.

"Of course I'm sure. I shot him, remember? He was dead, all right. I suspect they shipped his body out to his next of kin and just forgot to fill out the forms. Sloppy practice, but it happens all the time."

"If you say so, Mitch." His words reassured me only slightly, but I did have other worries to occupy my mind. "Did anyone call?"

"No, you expecting someone?"

"I thought maybe Ron would set up an appointment to talk about my case."

"Deirdre, it's not sunset yet. He's probably still sleeping."

"Oh, yes, I forgot." I laughed gently. "I still don't quite believe that he's like me. That any of them are like me. I've been alone in my species for so long. I wish I had known that they existed years ago."

"I don't."

"Why not?"

"Because, if you'd known others of your kind, you'd never've fallen in love with me." He sounded a bit defensive when he said it. I looked at him for a long time, studying the lines of his face, the strength of his shoulders, saying nothing. I wanted to imprint him on my mind so that after he was dead I would never forget the fineness of him.

"What?" He smiled tentatively at me, seemingly unnerved by my stare.

"None of them could ever compare with you, Mitch, my love."

"No?" He ducked his head a bit, and busied himself with his papers to hide his pleased grin.

"No." I got up from the couch, went over to him, and sat next to him on the floor, taking his hand in mine and holding it up to my cheek. "Let's do this paperwork later and take advantage of the time we have now."

By the time Ron called, we were out of the shower. And when he finally knocked at the door, we were dressed and composed, although I was perhaps smiling more than someone accused of murder should have been.

"Hello, Greer." Ron shook Mitch's hand at the door and walked in. He nodded at me where I sat on the couch. "Deirdre."

"Would you like a cup of coffee, Ron?"

He set his briefcase on the top of Mitch's desk and opened it. "I actually prefer tea, if you have it."

I moved to get up, but Mitch stopped me. "I'll get it, Deirdre. You stay here."

I heard him running the tap and filing the teakettle. Ron removed a sheaf of papers and sat down on the chair opposite me. "Before we get started," Ron said with a wary glance at the kitchen, "I'd sort of like to apologize for my involvement in this whole affair. It's not actually my sort of thing, threatening people with guns, spying on them, you know. But Victor calls the shots, and although he seldom abuses it, his power within The Cadre is absolute. I'm too new to the life to be able to make waves."

"You don't need to apologize to me, Ron." I lowered my voice to a level that I thought Mitch could not hear.

"I just wish that I had known the kind of games you were playing those nights we spent together."

"I resent that, Deirdre. And it's not really what you think. True, I was under orders to keep you under surveillance, but I had absolutely no idea why, or even who you were. I thought maybe you were being considered for admittance to The Cadre, or were romantically involved with a member. I didn't actually realize who you were until that night in the Ballroom, when you told me you were Max's heir. But no one asked me to seduce you into my confidence. I liked you, and"—he gave me a sharp look—"as I remember, you were more than willing."

I felt my cheeks redden, from embarrassment and anger. "But that was only because I didn't know what you were. You weren't entirely honest with me and you had me at a disadvantage. And the other night, you could have told me what you were."

"And you could have told me."

"But you already knew everything about me. You lied to me through your silence, and you betrayed my trust in you."

He gave me a hard, quelling look. "No more than you did. Imagine my surprise on finding you married to a man you were never going to see again."

"But you told him where I was."

"Yeah, I did." Ron stared at me for a moment, then shrugged. "Look, Deirdre, we could talk about this all night, but we'd get nowhere. It's over and done with, so let's try to forget it and go on."

"That sounds like a good idea," I agreed. "So, what's on your agenda for tonight?"

He handed me a set of papers. " 'The Establishment of The Cadre,' " he read, " 'and the Laws and Rules Thereof.' "

The teakettle whistled, and Mitch called out, "Water's ready. How do you want it?"

"Plain will be fine, thanks."

"And how about you, Deirdre? Do you want more coffee?"

"Just bring the pot out, Mitch, and join us. You don't need to play host all night. I'm quite sure that Ron is capable of helping himself."

"There's no doubt about that." Mitch came out of the kitchen, glaring at us and balancing two mugs and the coffeepot. He handed the tea to Ron, poured himself a cup of coffee, and sat down on the couch next to me, setting the pot on the floor. Ron handed him a set of papers identical to the ones I was holding.

We all read in silence for a while until Mitch groaned and pitched the papers across the room. "Jesus, is everything The Cadre does this bloody pretentious? I don't see where a history lesson on the holy organization will do Deirdre much good at this point! Can't we get down to the facts without having to wade through a goddamned written lecture?"

Ron looked at him in surprise, then gave a small chuckle. "I guess the material is rather dry," he admitted, "but I thought you might want some of the background before we started preparing your case. Keep them anyway." He looked over to me and shrugged. "Read them later on, when you feel like it."

"Thank you, Ron." Actually the origins of The Cadre were of interest to me, but Mitch was right. Knowing how it started really did not help my case.

"The facts we really need to know"—Mitch glanced at me and I nodded my acquiescence—"are the sort of extenuating circumstances that are acceptable in the killing of other vampires and the type of punishment possible if she's found guilty."

Ron gave Mitch a look that could have been admiration. "Fine, I appreciate your no-nonsense approach. And I can answer the second fairly succinctly, so let me start there. There is no death penalty provided for by The Cadre. We're not a vigilante group out to subject the world to vampire justice. We banded together for protection and preservation of the species. As you know, our reputation among humans is deplorable. We might have a thirst for blood"—he gave a funny, twisted smile—"but we are not bloodthirsty in the way that you think. Punishment, even for the murder of one of our own, can range anywhere from exclusion from the group to a period of supervised incarceration and starvation."

He stumbled a bit over the last word, and I glanced at him in surprise.

"Starvation? That sure sounds like a death sentence to me." Mitch's voice was soft, but I could feel the anger flowing beneath.

"Actually, it isn't," Ron said, shaking his head. "No vampire has ever died from a starvation sentence. But"—he shuddered—"it is extremely grueling for both the prisoner and the keepers. A starving vampire is someone you would never want to meet or be, I promise you that. In fact, many under the starvation sentence choose suicide instead."

"How?"

Ron looked over at me again, his eyes sad. "The most accepted way is to go to a secluded but open area and simply wait for the sun to rise. Even if you should change your mind, there is hardly ever enough time to find shelter." His voice trailed away.

"But some take the starvation?"

Ron's voice took on a more definite tone. "And they survive it. After the time's up, sustenance is provided so that the weakened individual doesn't need to hunt for a while." Ron shuddered again, his eyes gaining a faraway look. Then he seemed to shake himself free of his thoughts and smiled at me. "Very few of those who've gone through the starvation need to be disciplined again. Actually"—he gave Mitch a wary look from the side of his eyes—"it's a much more humane and effective deterrent than your human judicial system."

Mitch laughed a bit uneasily. "You'll get no argument from me on that. But I don't want Deirdre to go through it regardless of the results."

"Of course." Ron nodded his agreement. "We'd all like to avoid the starvation sentence if we can. So we need to work on your motive for the murder, Deirdre. Why did you kill Max?"

I took a sip of my coffee, warming my hands as usual on the mug. "Max was out of control. He had murdered four people, and was threatening Mitch." I stopped and shook my head slowly. "No, that's not exactly true. What he did was much worse. Max attempted to coerce me into killing Mitch." My voice broke and my hands trembled, splashing coffee on me. I set my cup down and stood up, rubbing my hands on my jeans. "I understand from Victor that The Cadre does not consider the murder of humans to be a terrible crime. But I had lived all my many years hurting no one, human or otherwise. I would not even have killed Max unless he himself had brought the situation to such an impasse. He knew how I felt about Mitch, and yet he persisted. He gave me no choice." I walked around behind the couch and massaged Mitch's shoulders, easing both his tension and mine.

"Can anyone else substantiate your evidence?" Ron's expression included both interest and surprise. Apparently he had not heard the true story of Max's death. But then, I thought, no one actually had.

"I ask only," Ron continued, "because the killing of one's maker, and the founder of a house, is a serious charge, maybe the most heinous crime a vampire can commit, and yet, if you had made a case before The Cadre at that time, and told us of Max's deeds and his attempted coercion of you before you killed him, then the outcome might have been different."

"I can testify to what happened," Mitch said firmly. "I was there."

"Sorry, Greer." Ron's voice was condescending. "We can't accept the testimony of a nonvampire. You wouldn't help her case much anyway; there are too many who are opposed to marriage with humans. The fewer who know about your involvement, the better. At this point it'd be much better if you just laid low for a while. I'm stretching the rules as it is to allow you to be present at this briefing."

"And God forbid I should make you stretch the rules." Mitch stood up and walked around the chair to me, kissing me lightly on the cheek. "Deirdre, I've got to get out of here. Your attorney says so." His voice sounded calm and reasonable; only the glitter of his eyes and the set of his shoulders betrayed his anger. "And I could use a little night air to clear away the stench of The Cadre. I'll be down at the pool hall. Join me when you're done with Mr. Wilkes."

"Mitch"—I touched his shoulder—"you don't have to leave. Ron has no jurisdiction over you."

"That may be true, but I don't think I can tolerate his presence much longer. I've met him before. You see, he used to supervise some of my little trips into insanity. And every time he opens his mouth, I find myself longing for a wooden stake."

Ron shifted in his seat. "That's not really funny, Greer."

"I know. It wasn't meant to be." Mitch kissed me hard on the lips, put on his jacket, and left the apartment.

"Good," Ron said with finality as the door slammed shut, "we can talk freer now that he's gone. His presence really complicates things."

I looked over at Ron, taking in his expensive suit, his flawless features, the manicured hands that looked as if they had never done a day's work. I thought about how he had befriended me to serve The Cadre, about how he was a part of the group that had driven Mitch into madness. Trying to control my temper, I turned my back on him and silently counted to ten, gripping my hands together, telling myself that he did not know any better, that none of this was his fault. But it did not help. I spun around and confronted him, feeling anger rise uncontrollably through my body.

"Goddamn it, Ron," I snapped at him, moving quickly around the couch and grabbing the lapels of his expensive suit. "You have no right to order Mitch around. You all seem to be overstepping your bounds these days. All your regulations, all your questions, don't you understand that they mean nothing to me? I never knew about the goddamned Cadre, never even knew who Max was until the night he died." He attempted to rise, but I pushed him back down in the chair and held him there. Ron glanced around the apartment in a panic, licking his lips in fear.

"Deirdre," he gasped, "don't do this. Violence won't help your case any."

"I am not looking for help, Ron. Nobody has ever helped me. Where, at any time in my long, miserable life, was your precious Cadre to give me guidance, to read me a list of their bloody rules and regulations? And where was Max? No, you were all quite content to stand on the sidelines and let me struggle with what I had become all by myself. And damn it, I struggled and I survived, no thanks to Max or you or any of The Cadre. Mitch has been the only being to care for me, to truly love me, for a very long time, someone who stayed with me without being ordered to." Ron winced slightly at that statement, but I ignored him and continued. "And yet you feel you have the right to order him around as if he were your servant. He is ten times the man you will ever be, regardless of your superior powers and attitude. Have you ever seen the scars caused by his confrontation with the beloved and much-revered founder of the house of Alveros? Did you ever look inside the mind you tortured to find his goodness, his intelligence, his love? No, of course you didn't. Mitchell Greer deserves better treatment from you, from all of us."

Suddenly the anger I felt drained away, leaving me empty and sad. I let go of Ron, noticing as I did so that my nails had made long gashes in the lapels. He looked down at his coat in dismay, and I laughed softly. "You're a lucky man, Ron. It could have been your skin."

"Yeah," he said, his voice quavering only slightly, "but the skin grows back."

"I am sorry, Ron. Send me a bill and I'll buy you a new suit. And I apologize for my temper, it was not directed at you so much as at the entire situation. You see, I'm in a difficult position. Had I known of The Cadre's existence, my life might have been quite different. And Max might still be alive. But it's a little late for hindsight at this point. I cannot change what happened. And neither can The Cadre. So let them mete out whatever punishment they feel is necessary. I've survived worse, I assure you."

"Deirdre." Ron got out of the chair and stood in front of me, meeting my eyes squarely. "I'm sorry, too, that it should all come to this." His voice lowered. "The last thing in the world I want to happen is to see you hurt, to know myself partly responsible for that hurt. It's just that there are conventions to be satisfied, and two or three of the other house leaders are calling for blood. Your blood. But they are bound by The Cadre's decision. That's why Victor urged you to accept our justice, why he tried to impress upon you the importance of this trial. Once you have been tried by The Cadre, and their decision has been rendered, they cannot retaliate in any way, or they face the same punishment themselves."

"I suppose," I said with a twisted grin, "that Victor is one of those calling for my blood."

"No, he's not." Ron sounded so confident, and I found myself almost believing him.

"No? But he and Max were so close. Or at least that is what Victor has always claimed."

"Well," he started to say reluctantly, "they were close. But Victor was not blind to Max's faults and knew that there would come a time when Max would be held responsible for his misdeeds."

"Trial before The Cadre?" Victor had hinted at that the evening I discovered Max's coffin.

Ron nodded. "It wouldn't have been the first time for Max either. I'm sorry to say this, and I mean no offense, but there's something strange about those in the house of Alveros. They tend to be more headstrong than most, more determined to do things their own way, more vicious. Maybe it's just in their blood"—he looked away from me—"although some of us think that it's more from the tutelage they've had."

"Fred mentioned that I was one of the oldest, that there were only a few of Max's breed left. Do you have any idea how many?"

A look of concern crossed his face. "Fred shouldn't have told you that." With effort he pulled his eyes away from mine, "And I've probably said too much myself. I'm not sure how much I can actually help you, Deirdre. I don't even know why I volunteered to speak for you."

I smiled at him. "I know why: you can never resist helping a lady in need."

"Yeah"—he smiled back at me, obviously not holding a grudge about my previous actions—"that must be it. Now, I think we've covered more than enough material tonight. I'll want to look back through our archives and see what kind of loopholes there are. Maybe there's a precedent." I could see his mind working on the problem, turning over the possibilities. "If only we had a feel for what Max was trying to do with you, what purpose he thought was being served by keeping you unaware of your birthright, well, maybe we'd have a stronger case. As it is, it's only your word we have to go on."

"My word is good."

"I believe you, and I think Victor does too. But unfortunately we have eight other houses to convince." He walked over to the desk and closed his briefcase. "Well, let me see what I can do. I'll call you tomorrow evening, if that's okay."

"That will be fine, Ron." I walked over to the door with him and shook his hand. "And I am sorry that I let my temper get the better of me tonight. I won't allow it to happen again."

"I don't mind so much." He winked at me. "I like a lady with spirit. Just promise me you won't get that carried away in front of the panel, okay? They won't take it quite as well as I did." His lips brushed my mouth briefly in a light kiss and he went out the door.

# Chapter 27

Mitch was at the pool hall, hunched over a beer at one of the tables. I pushed past the crowd of people at the entrance and sat down next to him, lightly touching his hand. He looked up at me with a grimace. "I'm sorry I ran out on you. But I wasn't joking. Every time he opened his mouth I wanted to kill him, or maybe just smash his perfect face in."

"You have no need to be jealous of Ron, my love. He means nothing to me."

"Even though you and he spent nights together?" He emphasized the plural with vehemence.

I opened my mouth but did not know what to say. His name was all I managed to get out. "Mitch."

"I know," he said after taking a long drink from his bottle. "You thought I couldn't hear your discussion. And I wasn't deliberately listening in, but it's my training. When people drop their voices to a whisper, I'm naturally curious about what they must be saying. No wonder he was so quick to jump to your defense. You're a fast worker, Deirdre, only in town a few weeks and you have an instant champion for your cause. I guess I should be happy you have someone to stand up for you, but under the circumstances . . ." He took another swig of his beer and his eyes met mine defiantly. But under his anger I could see a deep sadness.

"Mitch," I said softly, "do you know that Max once said the same to me about you?"

"Really?" His voice sounded harsh and sarcastic. "And how did you answer him?"

I touched his hand softly. "I told him that I loved you more than I had ever loved anyone before. And it was true, then and now."

Mitch stared at me as he drained his bottle. "And how will you answer me?"

"Ron means nothing to me, never did and never will."

"But the same can't be said of him, I'm afraid. I've seen the way he looks at you. And I recognize that look." He signaled the waiter for another beer, then glanced back at me. "Damn it, I should recognize it. I've been wearing it around you ever since we met."

The waiter came over and brought two bottles and one glass. I didn't use it. When he left, Mitch looked at his watch and held up his beer. "Cheers," he said with no expression on his face. "Here's to a little over twenty-four hours of wedded bliss."

"Please don't do this, Mitch. I warned you what marriage to me would be like. As I remember, you didn't care at the time."

"I lied." He studied the wet bottle rings, drawing his finger through them, idly tracing designs on the tabletop. "So, when did you and Ron enjoy your little trysts? And when do you plan another?"

"There will be no other," I said firmly. "One of the nights I saw him, well, that was the first time I visited you at the hospital. You do remember, don't you?" I rubbed my jaw. "That wonderful welcome-home gift you gave me?"

Mitch looked at me with a trace of a smile. "Oh," he said hesitantly, then gave me a full grin. "Ouch, I remember. I'm sorry. Are you still mad about that?"

I returned his smile. "I was never angry with you, just hurt and discouraged. I believed that was how it was going to be between us, thought that everything was over. What difference did it make whether I went home with Ron or not at that point?" His smile faded, and I joked to bring it back. "A girl's gotta eat, you know."

"Yeah, well, I guess I can understand that, but how about the other nights?"

"There was only one other night, after you very succinctly told me that you wished you had never met me. And all we did was talk."

"Okay, maybe I'll believe that one too. But I still don't like it."

"No one said you had to like it, Mitch. But you may have to get used to it. However much I would like to, I cannot exist on your love alone. But we were not to discuss the grisly details for a few weeks, so let's drop it."

"But a few weeks is all we may have. I don't know about you, but I'm not sure I believe that The Cadre is as humane as they keep trying to convince us they are. I still say we should get out now, before they get their hands on you."

"Shame on you, Detective. Urging a criminal to jump bail and leave town." I shook my head at him, and he laughed. Then I picked up my beer and stood. "Now, I know this is not exactly the honeymoon we anticipated, but do you want to play a few games of pool before we go home?"

"No." Mitch stood up too and threw a couple of bills on the table. "Let's just go home."

He put his arm around me and slowly we began to walk back to his apartment.

"So, what did Ron have to say for himself?"

"He's going to do some research, check the archives, see if he can find any precedents. I doubt that he'll find anything. The Cadre seems to keep a strong grip on its members."

"And if he can't find anything?"

I snuggled against him for comfort. "Well, then it becomes a case of their trusting my story. I doubt that will help much either." I gave a small, bitter laugh. "If only I could get my wayward ghost to make an appearance. They would probably be more easily convinced if they had a glimpse into his . . . damn!" I stopped dead on the sidewalk.

"What is it?"

"A glimpse into Max's mind. He left a huge stack of journals behind. It's possible they may hold some answers."

"Where are they?"

I grimaced. "At the Ballroom, of course, the last place I ever want to go again. He had them stored in a chest in his secret sleeping place. I found it and them the other night, but Victor came in and interrupted me." I shivered, remembering what else that room contained, and gave Mitch a dubious look. "I don't suppose you would like to take me out dancing tonight. I really don't want to go in there alone."

He shrugged. "I don't want you going there at all, even with me, but if the journals can help, we should have them. But let's take a cab, I'm getting cold. How about you?"

I agreed, not bothering to remind him that I could not get cold. "That would be fine, Mitch."

Johnny was working as doorman again that evening, slumped against the entrance with the expression that I now recognized as his normal surliness, but he straightened up and smiled as we approached. "Hi, Miss Griffin. How're you?"

"Fine, thank you, Johnny. Listen, is Victor Lange in tonight?"

He shook his head and grunted no.

"How about Fred, then?"

"Nope, neither one's here tonight. You want me to call 'em for you?"

"No, actually I don't." I looked around; very few people were waiting for admittance. "Has it been busy tonight?"

"Nope, it's been pretty slow."

"Thank you, Johnny. Oh"—I indicated Mitch—"by the way, this is Mitchell Greer, my husband." I smiled to myself at the strangeness of that phrase, and its sweetness. "So if he ever stops by without me, you should let him in."

Mitch extended his hand and Johnny shook it, smiling. "Congratulations. It's nice to meet you." Then he dropped his hand as if he had been bit. "Wait a minute, ain't you the cop that shot the last doorman? Larry, um, what's his name?"

"Larry Martin," I said, my voice tight and nervous.

"Yeah, that's him." Johnny cringed against the door, pushing aside with one hand the lanky bit of hair that always seemed to fall into his face, rubbing the side of his neck with the other. "I don't know, Miss Griffin." He lowered his voice and glanced at Mitch with a panicked stare. "It don't seem right to let him in, not tonight."

"Calm down, Johnny. Mitch is not going to shoot anyone, especially you. I promise you."

"Well, I guess if you say so, it's okay."

"It's okay, Johnny." Mitch spoke confidently, calmly. "Larry Martin was shot while he was trying to kill Miss Griffin. I don't think you're planning to do that, are you?"

"No way, Mr. Greer."

"Then you're perfectly safe." Mitch took my arm and

led me through the door. We crossed the dance floor and entered the hallway that led to my office. "What the hell is his problem?" Mitch asked when he thought he could be heard over the band.

"Who? Oh, Johnny. He's not very bright, I'm afraid. But he seems to do a good job. On the other hand"—I opened the office door—"being unaware is an asset in this place. He's much better off not knowing about half the things that go on around here."

Mitch closed and locked the door. "Do you think he's one of them?"

I thought about that for a moment. "I doubt it, Mitch."

He gave me a humorless chuckle. "Yeah, but you couldn't tell about Victor or Fred or Ron or Jean either."

"You're right, of course," I said with only a trace of sarcasm, "but now that I know about them, I can recognize the signs. There's something about their mannerisms, their directness, their overbearing arrogance that makes them stand out. Johnny, poor boy, has none of that."

Reaching into my purse, I found my ring of keys and opened the closet door, then the secret panel. "Here you go," I said over my shoulder, "just let me light the candles and we'll go in."

Victor had apparently put everything away that night we had met there. The candelabrum and the matches were back on the side table where I had initially found them.

"Candles?" Mitch's voice echoed through the empty room. "What's wrong with electricity?"

I laughed, my voice shaking a bit. "Max was a traditionalist in more ways than one, it appears." I held the candelabrum up so that he could see the two coffins on display.

"Damn." Mitch cautiously approached the stand and bent over to read the engraved plaques. "He slept here?"

"Apparently."

"But who does the other one belong to?"

My voice was soft in the dusty darkness. "It was for me."

"Damn." He walked around and lifted up the lid of the smaller coffin, then let it down gently. "Did you ever . . ."

"No." The distaste I felt for the idea was apparent in my voice. "I never knew that this was here, how could I? Max never told me anything."

"I know that, Deirdre. What I meant was, did you ever sleep in one of these?"

"Oh, no."

"Why not?"

"By the time I had figured out what I had changed into, I had been managing to sleep quite comfortably in bed with the curtains drawn. Why on earth would I want to lock myself up in a coffin day after day?"

"I wonder why Max did?"

I could tell from Mitch's tone of voice that the question was a hypothetical one, but I knew the answer anyway. "Max was tutored, taught from his first day to choose this as his refuge. The habits of centuries are very hard to break."

"You sound pretty sure of that. How could you know?"

"I dreamed it. But let's get what we came for and get out of here. This place unnerves me." Carrying the candelabrum with me, I walked across the room and opened the chest.

"Damn it." Slamming the lid of the chest down, I swore again. "Goddamned son of a bitch."

"Deirdre, what's wrong?"

"Somebody else has been in here. The journals are gone, every goddamned one of them."

"Are you sure they were here?" Mitch questioned me patiently, as if I were a child or an idiot.

I gave him an angry glare that he was probably unable to see across the dimness of the room. "Yes, I know they were here. They were real, tangible; they weren't something I dreamed up. The box was full of them, all nicely dated, all written in Max's hand. And now they're gone."

"That's strange."

"It's more than strange, Mitch, it's goddamned convenient. My one chance to find a motive for Max's actions, something that might enable me to prove that my killing him was justified, vanishes practically overnight. How wonderfully convenient for The Cadre and that bastard Victor. All this time spent trying to convince us that they're playing fair, that they're not out for my blood, and then they do this." I brushed my hands on my jeans to remove the coating of dirt that had come off the chest, and made a move to sweep the remaining dust away with my hand.

"Don't touch it." Mitch's voice was stern and commanding; I obediently backed away. "I'll come back tomorrow during the day and see if I can get fingerprints. At least that way we could tell who else has been in here."

"Only if our thief was previously printed. What are the odds on that?"

Mitch laughed. "I've got your prints on file, remember?"

I nodded; he had taken my prints right after my secretary, Gwen, had been murdered by Larry Martin.

"Well, you can't tell me that The Cadre as a whole and Victor in particular are so careful that they haven't had some run-in with the law during their long lifetimes."

"I don't know, Mitch. It seems like such a long shot."

"It can't hurt, Deirdre. And if I come during the day, none of them can bother me."

"I'm not sure I like the thought of you being in here alone."

"Jesus, Deirdre, I'm a grown man. I was able to keep myself safe and alive before we met. I'm not your child or your pet that you need to protect. And I'm going crazy with all this happening to you and not being able to do something. This I can do; it's what I'm good at. And you can't stop me." He was extremely angry, angrier than I had seen him for a long time. But I was not upset, for, other than our lovemaking, it was the best sign that the man with whom I had fallen in love had returned.

I walked across the room and put my arms around his waist, hugging him tightly to me. Then I smiled up into his face. "I love you, Mitch. And I'm sorry if I was treating you unfairly. You do what you want, but be careful. You carry my life in your hands."

He seemed surprised but pleased by my reaction, and his mouth came down on mine in a crushing kiss. Then he pulled away from me abruptly. "What did you mean, I carry your life in my hands? You don't think I would ever do anything to hurt you, or your chances at beating this rap, do you?"

When I had reached the decision to marry Mitch, I had also decided that I would stay with him until he died and then kill myself. But I didn't want him to know that, and even if I did, this was not the time to discuss it.

"Your life is my life, Mitch," I said softly, offering no further explanation. "Now, let's get out of this tomb and go home."

# Chapter 28

The next two weeks went quickly. Ron and I worked evenings preparing our case, but without Max's journals, there was no proof available as to the state of his mind and Ron did not have any luck turning up a similar case in The Cadre's archives. Victor bemoaned the theft of the journals, admitting that they could have helped my case, but assured us that his organization would never operate in such a fashion. Mitch had found fingerprints on the chest other than mine and had spent a long time at the precinct trying to match them up with their current files, but had been unsuccessful. And both Mitch and I had, however unhappily, come to the conclusion that since Victor knew about the existence of the room, a match of his prints wasn't substantial proof that he'd been involved in the theft.

For the three nights prior to the trial, I fed. Each time, I chose a street person from different locations in the city, forcing myself to take more than I needed, to prepare for the sentence of starvation that seemed sure to follow. But I felt no elation in these feedings, no exhilaration, no rejuvenation. Instead, I felt cheapened and unclean, and the fresh, warm blood that I stole from their veins tasted more bitter than ever before.

"Have you ever wondered," I questioned Mitch when I returned from my third victim, "whether a condemned man enjoys his last meal?"

He was sitting at his desk, poring over the files he had brought home from the precinct, and he must not have heard me enter, for he jumped when I spoke. "No," he said distractedly, "I can't say that I have." Then he shook his head and smiled. "I'm sorry, Deirdre. This whole case just gets stranger and stranger. Did something go wrong tonight?"

"No, something went wrong over a hundred years ago." I did not try to disguise the bitterness in my voice. "Now my life is just one eternal picnic."

Mitch got up and held me to him tightly, stroking my hair while I sobbed on his shoulder. "It's okay, babe," he crooned, "we'll get through this. And after it's all over, we'll go away and forget that The Cadre ever existed. Don't get discouraged now. We can beat them."

I sniffed a bit. "I suppose you're right. But, God, I'm so tired, Mitch, so tired. I feel as if I could sleep for a hundred years."

He kissed me on the top of my head. "Then go to bed. I'll be just a little while longer here, and then I'll join you."

Obediently, I went back to the bedroom, stripped off my clothes, and crawled into bed, not even checking to see that the curtains were drawn for tomorrow's dawn. But I did not sleep. I wanted no dreams tonight, no visits from Max, no glimpses of lives not mine. I lay on my back and stared at the ceiling for an hour until Mitch came in.

When he settled next to me, I rolled over, pressing myself against his warm, human body.

"Hey," he said with a catch in his voice, "you're supposed to be sleeping."

I didn't answer, but put my mouth to his shoulder, taking gentle nips, my hand exploring his chest and his muscular thighs. When this preliminary love play brought no response from my feeding instinct, I grew bolder, kissing his nipples and tracing my tongue down his stomach. Shifting my position so that I lay between his thighs, I continued my attentions and he groaned softly and whispered my name.

I looked up at him for confirmation, and he nodded slightly, his eyes glittering in the darkness, but with passion, not fear. Grasping his buttocks in my hands, I took him fully into my mouth, something I had never done before for fear of my sharpened fangs. I did not think of blood or feeding, I knew only that this was Mitch, a man I loved more than anything else in the world, and I wanted to please him, tonight of all nights. It might be our last together.

So I continued, licking and kissing him, coaxing him time and time again closer to climax. Finally, when he moaned and pulled my head away from him, I crawled up his body and smiled. "How was that?" I said, kissing the side of his mouth.

"Jesus, Deirdre," he gasped, "you make me crazy. I can barely catch my breath."

Then he rolled me over and entered me quickly. I began to cry from the sheer beauty of the unity we shared, and the painful thought that we might soon be parted. But I laughed too, and whispered encouraging endearments to him in the darkness, until half an hour later we both pulled apart from each other, sated and exhausted. Mitch's body and mine were slick with his sweat. Playfully, I licked the salt from his neck and he shuddered.

"Enough," he half-laughed, half-groaned, "or you'll kill me for sure."

Then he snuggled against me, draped a hand over my breast, and we fell asleep.

Mitch woke me at five the next afternoon with a cup of fresh-brewed coffee in his hand. I pushed my hopelessly tangled hair from my face and sat up in bed, taking the mug from him. "Thank you," I said after my first sip.

"Good morning, my love." He had a smile on his face that not even The Cadre could remove. I knew because I wore the same smile.

"I'm sorry to get you up before sunset, but I thought you might want a shower."

Setting the coffee cup down, I stood up and stretched. "Yes, I do. How about you?"

Mitch shrugged. "Oh, I had mine hours ago, but"—his eyes lit with a mischievous grin—"I'll keep you company if you like."

We got into the shower together, and Mitch soaped me all over as if I were a child. He shampooed my hair, then stood back and watched me while I rinsed it. "You're so perfect," he said, his tone of voice almost reverent, "and I love you so much. I can't even begin to explain how much you mean to me, how special our time together has been." Then he reached around me, turning off the water, and kissed me full on the lips. But he did not touch me, or hold me in his arms, nor did we make love. It was as if our experience of the previous night was such a strong bonding, cementing us so firmly to each other that we never needed to make love again, but could stand forever, naked skin against naked skin, heart against heart, always together.

The phone rang and we both jumped.

"Wouldn't you know it?" he said with a twisted smile, and wrapping a towel around himself, climbed out of the shower to answer it.

I toweled my hair, then dried my body and put on Mitch's green robe, tying the sash tight around my waist. By the time I reached the living room, his phone conversation had grown animated, almost angry.

"What the hell do you mean, you don't remember?

You were on duty in the morgue that night; I have your name on the log sheet. Goddamn it, Harry, I've heard you recite the list of corpses you've handled over the years, including the dates and causes of death, and the names of their next of kin. And all that after putting away a six-pack or two. How on earth could you forget this one? Jesus Christ, Harry, he had a hole in him large enough to stuff your fist into, for God's sake."

Mitch paused for a minute listening to the agitated voice on the phone, then he nodded, discouraged. "Okay, okay," he attempted to pacify the caller, "if you don't remember, you don't remember. Thanks anyway." Nervously, he shifted the towel around his waist. "Yeah, you too." He slammed the phone down impatiently, then sat down on the couch, running his fingers through his still-wet hair.

"What's wrong, Mitch?"

He looked up at me, startled. "I didn't know you were out here. Look, I'm sorry. I really meant to tell you about this last night, but you came in so upset. And then"—he gave a reminiscent smile—"you sort of distracted me."

"Tell me about what, Mitch?"

"Larry Martin. There's no report on the final disposition of his body, and the morgue guy can't even remember seeing him"

"Does that really matter at this point?"

Mitch's eyes shifted away from me for a minute. "I think it does. Maybe not ultimately to your case with The Cadre, but it does matter, very much. You see, I finally found a match for the fingerprints in Max's room."

"And?"

"And they were Larry's."

I must have stood staring at Mitch for a full minute, taking in his statement. And when I found my voice, it was soft and desperate. "But Larry has been dead for more than two years, Mitch." Even as I said it, I realized it could not be true. Here, then, was the explanation for the sick feeling of dread I had whenever I thought of him, the familiar face on the Ballroom dance floor, maybe even for the fright on Johnny's face the other night. Larry Martin was still alive. More than that, Larry had gotten from me what I had not ever wanted to give to anyone: immortality in the form of vampirism.

"Damn," I swore softly, and sat next to Mitch on the couch.

"Is there something you need to tell me, Deirdre?" Mitch sounded stern, remembering, I thought, of how I denied him what Larry had received.

"I didn't know, Mitch, and it wasn't on purpose, believe me. When you shot him, the bullet went straight through him and into my shoulder. I couldn't tell you. You would have taken me to a hospital, and that was totally out of the question at the time. You didn't know what I was then. How could I let you find out in the emergency room?" I stared unseeingly at the floor. "It never really occurred to me, but I suppose that enough of my blood could have mingled with his to enable the change." I put my hands over my face, then looked at him. "Jesus."

We sat silent for a few minutes. Then Mitch spoke up. "We've got to find him, Deirdre. He was unstable, crazy, and I don't believe that two years as a vampire could have improved him any."

"But why would he want Max's journals? How would he know they were even there?"

"Larry Martin always made it a habit to find out what he wanted to know. As to why take the journals, I suspect that he is none too pleased with you and he did it just to hurt you. Or maybe to hurt me. Or maybe just for the hell of it, because he could. You once told me you couldn't explain the ravings of a madman. What makes you think I can?"

I shivered and Mitch put his arm around me. "I'm sorry," he said again. "I shouldn't have said anything, I guess. But don't worry about it now, nothing is going to happen. And tonight, after all this is over, you should ask Victor. Maybe he knows something. I really think he owes you that much."

As if on cue, the phone rang again. This time it was Victor. "I will be there in one hour to escort you and Deirdre to the hearing." His voice was completely audible to me, even though Mitch had answered.

"We'll be ready."

Several days ago, and much to Mitch's amusement, Ron had already surveyed my wardrobe and dictated what I should wear to the hearing. After he had made the selection and left, Mitch had started to laugh.

"What's so funny?" I had asked him.

"Obviously the breed runs true no matter how much it's transformed."

"What?"

"Ron Wilkes may be a vampire, but he's still one hundred percent attorney." Then he had sobered and looked at me intently. "I've known a lot of lawyers in my day, and I can tell he's good. I guess I'm grateful that he decided to speak for you, whatever you had to do to get him."

Now, clothed in a basic black dress, black hose, and low-heeled pumps, I had to agree that his choice was a smart one. Unfortunately the skirt was slightly shorter than I felt comfortable with. "Damn Betsy McCain," I muttered when Mitch joined me in front of his mirror.

"What's wrong? You look great."

"Damn skirt is too short, like everything else she designs."

"Oh, well," he said, patting me slightly on the hip so

that I would move out of his way while he tied his tie, "maybe they'll get one look at your perfect legs and decide to let you go scot-free."

"Chance is a fine thing."

"What?"

"Just an expression I picked up from Pete in England. I guess the American slang would translate into fat chance."

"Who's Pete?" By now it was easy to recognize the slight twinge of jealousy in his voice.

"My partner in England. I own half of a failing pub over there."

"Great," he moaned, "just what we need. Another bar owner. Don't you meet any other types?"

"But you would like him." He gave me a dubious look and I continued. "No, honestly, Mitch, you would. He's like a second father to me."

"Good God," he said, crossing the room and slipping on his suit coat, "and that's another thing we don't need. Speaking of fathers, heard from Max lately?"

"Not since that last dream."

"How typical of him. He's perfectly capable of getting you into this trouble in the first place, and then he bails out when you need him. You're not much of a judge of character, are you?"

"Oh, I don't know." I went to him and wrapped my arms around his waist. "I've done pretty well for myself this time."

"And don't you ever forget it, lady." He kissed me on the tip of the nose. "Are you ready?"

I looked in the mirror again. "I think I need some jewelry; basic black is nice, but too funereal, even for this occasion." Opening the top dresser drawer that Mitch had cleared out for me, I went through what I had. I hesitated over the ruby necklace and earrings that had belonged to my mother, when the glint of antique gold caught my eye. "This would be perfect." I opened it up and looked at the portrait of Max's mother and smiled to myself.

"Do you think that's wise?" Mitch asked doubtfully. "After all, somebody there might recognize it, might feel that you're flaunting it."

"No," I said, hanging it about my neck. "I think Max would want me to wear it. It would appeal to his ironic nature. Besides, it is a beautiful piece and she was a beautiful woman. She deserves to be remembered."

The weight of the locket pressed between my breasts was somehow comforting. I chose a simple pair of gold button earrings to match, and we went to the living room to await our escort.

# Chapter 29

Victor arrived promptly in a limousine accompanied only by the driver, who to my great relief turned out not to be Fred.

Mitch shook Victor's hand, greeting him in a pleasant voice, but his smile only thinly disguised his deep animosity, and when he spoke, all the illusions of pleasantry vanished. "Traveling without your thugs tonight, Lange?"

Victor chose not to take offense. Solicitously, he helped me into the car, then turned to Mitch with a friendly smile. There's no need for thugs, as you call them, Mitch. Deirdre is a woman of honor, I know, and I'm sure you will not attempt any useless heroics. Anyway"—he glanced in at me knowingly—"Fred has been replaced. He has proven untrustworthy as well as unnecessarily vicious."

Mitch climbed into the seat next to me and Victor walked around to get in the other side. "No, Fred will not be bothering you anymore, Deirdre." He carefully adjusted his expensive suit coat before he sat down, aligning the creases of his pant legs. "But I'm afraid you'll need to hire another manager for the Ballroom."

"Where did he go?" I was glad of Fred's absence, but also briefly angry that Victor would have released him without my consent.

"He was selected to do an overseas assignment for

The Cadre. It seemed best to get him out of your way. Especially"—Victor lowered his voice confidentially—"since he was so susceptible to your powers. That was a nice bit of control, but your timing was bad. I don't advise a stunt like that tonight, my dear."

"No stunts, Victor, I promise. Just the truth."

"Thank you." He reached over and patted my knee. "And can I assume I've your promise too, Mitch?"

"Yeah," Mitch said abruptly. "I'll stay out of it."

"Actually, you will not be allowed to be present at the questioning." Victor gave an elegant shrug. "I did my best, but too many of us are still prejudiced against your kind. Ron did explain the procedures to you, didn't he?"

"Yes." I reached over and held Mitch's hand. "I'm to be questioned by each house individually, with you acting as an impartial arbitrator."

"Not exactly impartial, Deirdre. Should the houses be divided on your decision equally, the final vote belongs to me. Hopefully, it will not come to that."

I glanced over at Victor to get some feel for what that comment meant, but his face was expressionless. Mitch's hand tensed on mine, and I leaned over and gave him a small kiss on the cheek. "It will be all right, my love," I whispered.

"It damn well better be," he muttered as the car stopped in front of The Imperial. His jaw was set stubbornly and his lips were pulled tight. "Or there'll be bloody hell to pay."

Ron met us as we got off the elevator in The Cadre's warren. The large assembly room in which we had met previously was empty and dark. I looked over at Ron questioningly.

He responded as if he had read my mind. "Oh, we won't be meeting in here."

"But this is where our paths part, my dear." Victor

took my hand and kissed it in his characteristic fashion. "Mitch and I will be waiting upstairs."

Mitch put his arms around me in a brief hug. "Knock 'em dead, Deirdre," he whispered to me, and gave me a quick, hard kiss. I watched the two of them enter the elevator, and when the doors shut, turned to Ron.

"Let's get this over with, shall we?"

All the founders of the houses of The Cadre had their own individual office, furnished in their own unique style. Any other time I would have found my surroundings fascinating and pleasant. The founders were gracious and courteous, and their manners and emotions were kept in careful control, so much so that many times I was forced to remind myself that these meetings were more than social visits. Studying the eyes of each one as I spoke to them, I found myself wondering which ones had been calling for my blood, and which were perhaps more sympathetic. But their faces might as well have been masks; they were unreadable, unfathomable, giving me no hint of their true feelings beneath.

They had each been provided with my written testimony on the death of the man I had known as Max Hunter, as well as a short biography of my life. Ron and I had spent most of the past two weeks preparing this document, and he assured me that it would be read carefully and in great detail, as the founders took their judgment responsibility very seriously.

I did not recognize any of my eight judges, and their names were not given. Most of them simply asked me questions about the night of the murder, clarifying details that seemed to me to be extraneous. But the last one, one of the two female founders, was much more interested in the biography of my life than in any details concerning Max.

"And so you woke up, in the hospital, with no idea of what had occurred?" Her voice was soft but powerful, with a suggestion of a lisp and a slight foreign accent. She was seemingly young with an amazing mass of blond, curly hair piled into an intricate fashion on the top of her head. If I had to give her an age, it would be early to mid-twenties, at least several years younger than I had been at my time of change. But the intensity of her eyes belied this apparent youth, as had the eyes of all the others.

I glanced over at Ron. None of the other interviewers had been interested in my life. He gave me an encouraging nod, and I answered her question.

"Well, I knew that there had been an accident. I knew of the loss of my husband and unborn child. And I sensed the change in my physical and mental makeup, but any memory I might have had of the transformation and the encounter with Max was buried. All I had to go on were my dreams. And"—I gave her a small, wry smile—"the fact that my father was a great lover of dreadful gothic literature."

She returned my smile briefly, then arranged her face once again in its neutral expression. "And you managed to survive long enough to piece together the facts of your vampirism without anyone to guide you or to provide you with what you needed to live?"

"I provided for myself. There was no one to help."

"You were either very lucky or very resourceful—I suspect a little of both. A pity, really, for with a mentor you could have become very powerful indeed."

I said nothing, expecting that no response was required. She nodded absently, as if to herself, then her eyes moved quickly over my features, finally fastening upon my eyes as she spoke again.

"And you had no contact with Max"—did I detect a note of scorn in that dispassionate voice? I wondered—

"until the mid-sixties, at which time he still did not make you aware of who he was?"

"That is correct. I had no idea who he was, or even what he was, until the night he died. And then, of course, it was too late."

"Yes," she said impatiently. "I have read your testimony." She picked up the document in question and dropped it into the wastebasket by the side of her desk. Then she looked at Ron. "I am the last, is that right?"

"Yes," he responded.

"Well then, I don't want to hold up these proceedings any longer." She gave a low chuckle. "I have other fish to fry this evening. A particularly delicious bellboy is waiting for me at my hotel."

Ron and I moved to the door. "Wait," she called after us. Ron tensed, but I turned around and smiled at her. She came around her desk and walked over to me. Then, ignoring Ron's gasp of surprise, she put her arms around me and gently kissed my lips. "My true name is Vivienne. You may count me as a friend, Dorothy. Walk softly this night."

"And you," I said solemnly, sensing the last as a ritual good-bye.

Her eyes searched mine again, and she smiled fully. "Your instincts are excellent. Good night." Ron stood rooted by the door, and she nudged him. "Well, go ahead, Ron, get her out of here. She shouldn't be kept waiting any longer than necessary."

Ron took my arm, and I felt him trembling, but he said nothing until we arrived at the designated reception area. When we got there, he went straight for the bar and opened a bottle of wine, pouring two glasses and handing me one before draining his completely.

I stared at him over my untouched wine. "Something wrong, Ron?"

"She surprised me. She wasn't supposed to touch you,

or respond to you in any way. And she was definitely not to tell you her name. Next to Victor, now that Max is gone, she is the oldest among us."

I sat down in one of the overstuffed leather chairs. "What difference should any of that make? You know her name, why shouldn't I? I thought she was easily the most agreeable of them all."

"And that worries me too. Vivienne has always held herself aloof from our politics. Actually, she has very few dealings with any of us: she attends when she is required and avoids us when she can. And she has always been very determined on the subject of rogue vampires." He poured himself another glass of wine, his eyes avoiding mine.

"In what way is she determined, Ron?"

"Well," he began hesitantly, taking another long drink, "she has been quoted on occasion as saying that the only way to deal with rogues is to have them killed, quickly and cleanly." Then he shrugged. "Maybe she's mellowed on the subject."

"But you don't think so, do you?"

"No, but she kissed you. And told you her name, not the name she goes by now, but the name she was born with." He shook his head as if to clear his mind. "Jesus, I wish I knew what she was up to. Victor will want to know."

I took a small sip of my wine. "Well then, tell him."

"No, I can't. It's another one of the rules, you see. Anything that I heard or witnessed must be held in complete confidence. Even you are not supposed to divulge anything about the interviews. The judges are free to speak of it, although they seldom do." He filled his glass again. "This really puts me in a bad situation."

"I'm sorry, Ron. I would help you out if I could. But other than Vivienne, how do you think we did?"

He looked at me with a rueful smile. "Honestly, I haven't got the slightest idea."

"Great," I said. "Just goddamned great." Holding my glass out for him to refill, I crossed my legs. "So I guess we just sit here and wait."

We had just started a second bottle of wine when someone knocked on the door. Victor walked in and Ron hastily placed his glass on the bar. "They've decided so soon?"

Victor inclined his head and handed him a slip of paper. Ron looked at it, then back at Victor for confirmation. Nodding slightly, Victor dismissed him. "That will be all, Ron, thank you." Ron left without so much as a backward glance at me, closing the door softly behind him.

"Ron is a good attorney," Victor said without preamble, "and he did his best for you. The papers were prepared properly, with all the right nuances and emotions. Even your biography was a masterstroke, portraying you as a romantic heroine of epic proportions, single-handedly learning to survive and grow as a vampire." Nonchalantly, he studied the bottle of wine we had been drinking. "Not a bad year, not the best, of course, but still good."

"I know you aren't here, Victor, to discuss the wine or Ron's quality as an attorney." I finished my drink and got up from the chair, walking over to the bar. Looking him directly in the eyes, I set my glass down. "They didn't buy it, did they?"

He gave an odd laugh. "I really do appreciate your directness, Deirdre. But you're wrong; half of them did buy it. That's why I said Ron was good. Your odds going into this situation were not that favorable. Now, the other half . . ." Victor's voice trailed off and he sat down. "Well, I'm afraid it's a stalemate, my dear."

"So the deciding vote is yours after all. What's it going to be, Victor?" I tried to keep all emotion out of my voice but succeeded only in sounding stilted and antagonistic.

"Sit down," he said in a sad voice. "We need to talk this out."

"In the first place," he began as I settled into the chair again, "I want you to know that I have always liked you, admired you, and I thought that Max was an ass to keep you so uninformed. But I do not have the freedom, as the other judges did, to decide this on my own emotional responses to you. As leader of The Cadre, I have responsibilities and I cannot afford to have it rumored that I decided a case of this magnitude on personal feelings. Nor, on the other hand, can the decision be made out of a desire for vengeance on my part." He gave a charming smile and shrugged again. "Quite honestly, Deirdre, I'm not sure what I should do."

I laughed softly. "I could tell you, but that would hardly be fair, would it?" As I sat back down in the chair, the chain on the locket I was wearing came loose and it fell to the floor. I picked it up and examined it, refastening the catch, and put it back on. When I looked back at Victor, he was staring intently at the locket.

"Where did you get that?"

"It was in the chest in Max's room. It seemed appropriate that I should wear it this evening. Mitch didn't think I should, but I thought that she should be remembered." My voice softened a bit as I stroked the gold. "Max would have appreciated the gesture."

Victor looked at me with a strange expression on his face. "Do you know who that is?"

I snapped the catch open and glanced at the portrait, feeling a reminiscent smile cross my face. "Of course," I said confidently. "It's Max's mother. Did you know her? She was a beautiful person."

"I never knew her." Victor's voice was flat and even. "But Max spoke of her often. He loved her very deeply. He never really seemed to get over her death." Then he stopped and gave me an intent glance. "When did she die? And how?"

I knew the answers as well as I knew my own family's history. "She died two years after Max entered the seminary, a year before the Thirty Years' War started. As to what she died of, I assume it was what we now call tuberculosis, although, in my century we would have called it consumption. What you would have called it, I have no idea."

"And when did Max transform into a vampire? And who was responsible?"

"Ten years after the war had started. He had been wounded and was going to die." I closed my eyes to avoid Victor's burning gaze and to bring the memory of the dream to the surface of my mind. When I spoke, my voice was soft and not entirely my own. "We were saved by a vampire. We were going to die, but he came along and promised us eternal life. I thought he was an angel; he worked the miracle and I thought he was an angel." I snorted angrily. "I was naive, too immersed in my religion to understand the ways of the world, and I didn't know any better. Can you believe it? I thought he was a goddamned angel. But he wasn't! He was Nosferatu, then I was Nosferatu." The word came out like an obscenity. "His name was . . ."

And I paused, searching deep within me for Max's residual memories. I knew that somewhere beneath the loathing and the depravities, past the countless dead bodies and the long centuries, there lurked a face that he had blocked from my view. Or perhaps I had blocked its recognition. Whatever the reason, I struggled to tear away the veil that obscured that identity.

Finally I found that for which I searched, and my eyes

opened wide on Victor's astonished face. "His name was"—the voice speaking was my own again—"Victor Leupold." I paused again and matched the face before me with the one my memories held. "Victor Leupold . . . Victor Lange. It was *you* who turned Max into a vampire."

# Chapter 30

Victor's face turned even paler than usual. "Max?" he whispered, searching the room as if he thought he could see him. "Max is still with you? He must be, how else would you know of these things you have told me. Why didn't you tell me that Max was still with you?"

"I have had dreams of him for years now. I have heard him and seen him. Quite honestly, I thought I was just going crazy. And I did not know it would matter to you whether he was haunting me or not, or believe me, I would have told you sooner."

"I have read of this phenomenon." Victor's voice was eager, full of emotion. "How if the bond between two vampires is strong enough, one will linger even after his death. But I never really believed it. And no vampire living today has ever experienced it. What is it like?"

"Do you want the truth?" I looked at him shyly, feeling ill at ease.

"Yes," he said without hesitation. "Of course."

"Well, there are times when he is a comfort to have around, but most times it is simply hellish." Then I laughed, surprising both myself and him. "He is actually more of a bastard dead than alive."

"But I must speak with him. Can you summon him?"

I laughed again, this time with more humor. "Have you ever known Max Hunter to come when he was called? Or to do anything merely because you wanted him to?"

Victor looked at me skeptically for a moment, then suddenly his expression lightened and he laughed himself. "No, Deirdre, I suppose not. I can't imagine that even death would change him that much."

"So, what are we to do?"

Victor stood up and poured himself a glass of wine. He gestured with the bottle, and at my nod, poured one for me.

"There is a way." He hesitated. "Not without risk to you, nor, for that matter, to me, but a way in which I can speak to Max. He must have stayed with you for a purpose."

"Other than to devil me, you mean?"

His eyes showed amusement only for a second. "That would be one reason, of course. But somehow we both know that it goes deeper than that. If I can ascertain his purpose, then maybe it'll help us both out of the awkward situation we are in."

"What are the stakes?" I was curious about why he wished to pursue this avenue so avidly.

"Your mind, maybe even mine."

"Look, Victor," I said determinedly, "I know I haven't been taking this trial as seriously as I should. But I hardly see that a few weeks or even months of starvation on my part would be worth the prospect of losing my mind. Or justify your wish to risk yours. Why not just take the sentence? It can't be so terrible, can it?"

For the first time since I had met Victor, I saw a clear, readable emotion in his eyes. It was fear, complete and utter terror. "Maybe Ron wasn't that good an attorney after all. What kind of sentence did he tell you to realistically expect?"

"A set time of incarceration and starvation. But he did emphasize that it would not result in death."

"He took it as lightly as that?" Victor looked surprised.

I thought for a moment. "Well, no, he seemed very upset at the prospect, and gave me the impression that it was a fate worse than death."

"And so he should have."

"But I don't really see—"

Victor interrupted me angrily. "What he forgot to mention is that the starvation sentence for this particular crime is rarely any shorter than fifty years. Normally it is almost twice that."

My eyes opened wide. "One hundred years?"

"Exactly so. Think it over carefully, Deirdre. Do you still wish to take your chances with The Cadre's sentence?"

I really didn't have to think very long. A hundred years was almost the entire duration of my life as a vampire. Even the mere contemplation of living those years without sustenance was painful, unthinkable. "No." My voice was shaking. I understood why Ron had neglected to tell me that one crucial fact. Had I known it at the onset, I would have been long gone, the rules of The Cadre be damned. "What do I need to do?"

"Have you fed recently?"

"Three nights in a row, actually." I gave a short, cynical laugh. "I thought I was preparing myself, you see. As if it would have done any good."

"Well, your instincts have still served you well. That will help you. Finish that"—he gestured at my glass—"in fact, finish the whole bottle. You need to be relaxed and at ease. I will do the same."

He went behind the bar and opened another bottle of dark red wine. But instead of bothering with the glass, he drank it straight from the bottle. I giggled nervously; the gesture seemed so incongruous, so out of character for someone as elegant and polished as Victor.

He gave me a stern look. I shrugged and followed his lead, draining my bottle shortly after his was emptied.

"Now," he said, pulling his chair forward so that our knees were touching, "relax and don't fight me. I need to enter into your mind and find Max." He held my hands in a tight grip and looked into my eyes. At first I felt nothing except for his cold hands on mine, then delicately at first, growing stronger and more persistent, I could feel his first tentative intrusion into my mind.

A chill crawled up my spine, and I felt the hair on the back of my neck rise. A wave of panic swelled within me, and I longed to run from this rape. But he held me, cruelly I thought at the time, with hands and eyes. And there was no escape.

"Easy." I heard his whispered thought as if it were mine. "Easy. Don't fight me."

I heard him and acknowledged the wisdom of his words, but couldn't relax, couldn't stop my fighting. I screamed, and tried to pull away from him. His hands had become shackles on my wrists, his eyes were swords driven deep into me. "No," I said. "I can't."

Then I felt a presence that was not Victor, and I struggled less, being more used to his occupation of my mind.

"Trust him," Max's familiar voice urged from deeper within my being, caressing me and calming my terror. "Trust him and let him in."

I took a deep breath and suddenly Victor's penetration became, not rape, but a warm and loving presence, like a return to a lover's embrace. I felt his gratification in his success, and his eagerness to pursue Max was as strong as my own.

I lead Victor down the paths of my life, pausing briefly at the points at which Max and I intersected.

There is the carriage and the shadowy figure that carries me from the wreckage; he hurries away and we pursue him, stopping again at a small midwestern truck stop. Here he stays longer, and we almost catch him making love in an empty field on a star-filled night. But he is farther ahead than we are. We quicken our pace to find ourselves in his office at the Ballroom of Romance. He is impaled on the door, and we watch in horror and sympathy as he bleeds out his life by my hand. Then the room blackens and we seem to be nowhere.

I call his name and suddenly we are at the same cemetery that I have walked in my dreams. But this time I do not need to search the stones for Max's name, for his blood calls to me, his being calls to me, and when we arrive he is waiting for us, as I knew he would be, leaning against his tombstone.

"Hello, Victor," Max says with a twisted grin. "It certainly took you long enough to find me." He beckons to me, and as always, I go to him. He pulls me to him, holding me closely against his chest. "Although Deirdre and I have been living such exciting lives, I sometimes did not wish it to end. But now that you are here, I know it's for the best. I'm tired." He brushes his eyes and the soft drops of his tears on my upturned cheek burn. "God, I'm tired and I'm more than ready for my rest."

"Max." Victor's voice sounds hurt; I can feel his pain. "Why didn't you come to me?"

"Ah, old friend, that hurts, doesn't it?" Max's voice is hard and cruel. "You feel betrayed, I suppose. It could even be a betrayal of the magnitude I experienced many centuries ago when you took my humanity from me. I hope so. I would be very thankful to know that I was capable of inflicting similar pain on you."

"But I saved your life." Victor is crying, his voice jagged with emotion. "I gave you everything I had. You were strong, you were powerful, you were immortal. And you owed it all to me. I loved you like a son, like a brother."

"That's true, and I was grateful, for a time, for what you gave. But over the years I learned it could never replace what you had taken." Max's arm tenses around my shoulders and his anger echoes from the surrounding graves.

"I was a man of God and with the taste of your blood I lost my one chance for salvation. There were compensations, of course, many wonderful compensations: the women, the blood, the sensations of life. But as I sunk deeper into a depravity that you encouraged, I began to hate what I was. Began to hate you. And powerful as I was, I was powerless to change.

"Then"—Max's voice becomes tender, loving—"Deirdre came to me. As trusting and as innocent as a child. She taught me to love again, not in the pure way that I loved as a priest, but as a man. How could it be a pure love? I was so depraved, so degenerate. But I did love her. And I hesitated telling her who I was. I was ashamed of my excesses, knowing that she could not forgive them, or me. I tried to guide her along the paths I had taken with you. 'Revel in your power, revel in your life' was the message I wanted her to accept. 'Be as a goddess among humans.' " Max choked out a small, cynical laugh. "It didn't work."

"Max, I'm sorry." I find that I am crying now too.

"Little one, you don't need to be. If you had accepted that path, I think that deep down I would have been disappointed. But I had to take my chance. And when I finally came to the realization that you could never accept life on my terms, I found quite simply that I did not want to live." Max sighed, then laughed. "I suppose it could have gone either way that night. You could have killed Greer and come with me. But that wasn't really what I wanted."

"Then Deirdre is innocent?" Victor stares at Max in disbelief.

"Innocent?" Max shrugs. "Oh, I don't doubt that there was a part of her that wanted me dead. Can you blame her? But I wanted to die, Victor, and I hadn't the courage to face the sun. So, as usual, I took the coward's way out, the way of least resistance, and forced her to kill me. By doing that, she gave me what I most wanted, rest from my wicked life. But her grief and remorse and love held me here." He smiles, the cynical expression that enters his eyes is so familiar, it tears at my heart. "To be honest, I really didn't fight too much, it was an interesting two years. But that time is past, and I must go." He reaches out and grabs Victor's shoulders, giving him a kiss on the cheek. "Good-bye, Victor. Walk softly this night."

"And you." Victor puts his hand to his face, then turns away, walking down the cemetery paths, leaving me alone with Max once more.

My lower lip trembles and tears stream down my face. "Max," I plead with him, "why did you never tell me?"

He holds me close to him one last time and I feel his being envelop me like black, silken wings. "And what would you have done, my little one," he whispers into my hair, "if I had?"

"I would have loved you."

"Ah, thank you for that, Deirdre." I feel his body shake slightly and look up to see that he is laughing. "I almost wish it were true. But when you met Mitchell Greer, there was no longer any room for me in your life. You had grown beyond me. You would never have given him up willingly, nor I you. And so neither of us had any choice, did we?"

"No," I say, knowing the truth of his words, "but it should have been different. You should not have died."

"Deirdre." He cups my face in his hands and kisses my mouth gently. "Victor gave me eternal life, and for that I will eternally curse him. You, my little one, you gave me death, and I will love you forever." His next kiss is longer, more passionate, but I feel a pulling away, a parting of our unity. I look deep into his eyes.

"Rest easy, my love," he says, "and sweet dreams."

"And you, Max."

He smiles. It is one of the truest expressions I have ever seen on his finely sculptured face, not mocking or cynical, but honest and sweet and loving. It is the smile I had seen the younger Max wear in my dreams. I feel despair, for I will never know that man. He touches my cheek softly and then he is gone. I am left alone once more, crying over his grave. But this time, I know, will be my last visit. The man that I know as Max Hunter, who is more than a father to me, and more than a lover, the man born as Maximiliano Esteban Alveros so very long ago, is finally dead. God rest his soul.

# Chapter 31

"God rest his soul," I whispered the prayer to darkness and I woke in a strange bed and a strange room, my head throbbing and my eyes hot and tired. Eventually I focused on the shadowy figure sitting by the side of the room, his hands pressed over his face. My heart jumped slightly. "Max? I thought you had gone."

The tortured face of Victor Lange looked up at me, sad and aged. Startled by this perception of him, I blinked my eyes. When I opened them again, I realized that his features had not changed, but his manner and stance made him appear older. The weight of his many centuries seemed to hang about his neck.

"He is gone, Deirdre."

I could not tell whether he spoke the words aloud or if some portion of him still remained in my mind. But the result was the same. I felt his pain and his loss as keenly as if it were my own. And although my empathy for him was enormous, I knew I could do nothing to help him.

"Victor, I am sorry," I started to say lamely.

"No, do not be sorry." He managed a vestige of a smile. "It was what he wanted."

Silence wrapped us for a while in its dark softness. Then we both tried to speak at the same time.

"How long have I . . ." I began.

"You've been found . . ."

We both laughed nervously. "You first, Victor."

"You've been here for well over a day. There's about three hours until dawn and you're completely free to leave whenever you want to. I sent Mitch back home when the verdict came through. He did not want to go, but I explained that you would be here for at least a day. He sat with you for a while, but when the sun rose he left." Victor waved his hand feebly. "He said something about a celebration when you got home."

"And the verdict was?"

"Guilty, but with just cause. No one could deny that yours was the hand that dealt his death. And yet, with what I learned, I could not see you unjustly punished. You do, however, have one small penance to perform. Mitch agreed to assist you if necessary." Victor stopped for a moment as if to collect his thoughts. "He's a good man, Deirdre," he said grudgingly. "Although I can't help but wish that you had chosen Max, I suppose you just did what you thought you had to."

"Victor," I began, but he did not let me continue.

"It won't help, you do understand, don't you? Nothing you can say or do will bring him back. But"—he straightened up in his chair—"as I said before, I cannot let my personal emotions interfere with my leadership of The Cadre." He looked at me again and his eyes seemed weak, drained of the energy they had always shown.

I did not try to offer my sympathy again. We were bonded so closely by his entrance into my mind, by the blood we both shared, I felt his overwhelming sadness as if it were my own. I also felt that there would be no cure for Victor. I got out of bed and walked over to him, taking his hand and silently touching it to the tears on my face.

He nodded, then smiled again. "So, your penance is this. You are required to perform one service, any service named, for The Cadre at any time we should choose to request it. May I have your promise?"

"Certainly, Victor. I'll do what I can."

"You may never be called on it, you understand. But you'll need to keep in touch with us, let us know where you can be reached at all times."

I nodded. "I can do that."

"There's one more thing." He stood and absently brushed his suit jacket, taking the pose of his former elegance. "We've a vacancy on the judicial board. As the eldest unhoused member of Alveros, you could petition to occupy it. At this point, you could even petition for establishment of your own house."

"Victor," I said slowly and deliberately, "I do not wish to take Max's place, nor do I wish to set up my own dynasty. Is it required?"

"No, no." He smiled at me again as he opened the door. "But let me know if you change your mind. Go on home to Mitch now and have a nice celebration." The final word seemed to choke him and he said no more, but walked out the door, his shoulders slumped.

I found my shoes, coat, and bag and prepared to leave. When I entered the hallway outside the room, I realized that I was still in the warren of rooms that constituted The Cadre's quarters. I recognized many of the rooms I passed from the interviews I had undergone the previous evening. The thick gray carpeting cushioned my footsteps and I moved silently, though not silently enough for the occupants of these rooms. When I reached the door that was Vivienne's, she stood there, waiting for me.

"Deirdre." She smiled at me. "Congratulations on such a favorable verdict." Her hair hung in a mass of unruly curls to her waist, and she was dressed in a filmy black negligee that left little of her lithe body to the imagination. I looked away, extremely embarrassed by her blatant exhibitionism. "I'd hoped you might join me for a drink before you leave. Who knows when we will meet again?"

I glanced back at her and the expression on her face was friendly and earnest. She seemed so young, so untouched by the life that she must have led, that it was hard to believe she was like me. But the power in her eyes, the strength and glow of her body, spoke the truth. I wanted to refuse her offer. I did not trust her, did not trust any of The Cadre, but I knew that they could not hurt me now, so I returned her smile and nodded.

"Yes, thank you, that would be nice."

"Come in, then. I promise I will not keep you any longer than an hour or so, but we've so much in common that I thought we should have a nice long talk." She moved to one side as I entered, but not so far away that I could not smell her perfume. "You see, I don't visit here very often. I find the ways of The Cadre confining at times, and I much prefer to be on my own."

She directed me to a room behind the one in which our interview had been held. It was expensively furnished with beautiful antique furniture and lit by many candles. One corner of it held a large ornate coffin much like Max's. I shuddered when I saw it, then shook my head.

"Do you all sleep in one of those?"

Vivienne followed my stare and gave a small shrug. "So we've been taught. And you don't?"

"I've never found it necessary."

"And you don't fear the sun's penetration?"

I laughed a little nervously. "Of course I do. But not so much that I care to be confined the entire day. I'm careful to protect myself in other ways."

"Ah," she said, "that is most interesting. Please make yourself comfortable and I'll pour you a drink." She indicated a brocade sofa and I took off my coat and sat down. "White or red?"

"Red, please." I watched while Vivienne worked at the sideboard that apparently doubled as her bar. Her hands were small and delicate, but the nails were quite long and highly lacquered. Not wanting to appear ill at ease, I kicked off my shoes and casually curled my legs beneath me, wondering what purpose lay behind her invitation. Ron had said she didn't like rogues, but she knew what I was and still had asked me here. Her mind was completely inaccessible to mine; I had no experience in dealing with this situation. I should just go home, I thought, and try to forget that The Cadre ever existed.

Vivienne turned around, two glasses of wine in her hands. "I will not keep you long, I promise," she said as if she had read my mind. "I'm sure you want to be back as soon as possible with your Mitch." I smiled to myself. His name pronounced in her French accent sounded so exotic, so different. Crossing the room with an almost sinister grace, she handed me a crystal goblet. "I think you will find this a marvelous vintage. I've had it set aside for many years for a special occasion."

I took a sip; Vivienne was right, it was wonderful, rich but slightly biting. I took a long drink and sighed. "Thank you." I smiled at her. "It is very nice."

"I hoped you'd like it." She settled onto a chair opposite me. "I've several others just like it, enough to last quite a while." She made a move as if to pull her negligee closer to her body, but all she managed to do was cause it to drop from one shoulder.

I felt extremely uncomfortable. "So," I said, trying to make my voice as friendly as possible, "what house are you from, initially?"

She looked at me over the rim of her glass, then took a sip but said nothing.

"I'm sorry, is that a forbidden topic? I'm totally unaware of Cadre etiquette."

"No," she laughed, but I relaxed only slightly. "I was just wondering how it could be possible you didn't know."

I sighed again, setting my glass down on the end table and pushed my hair back from my face. "Vivienne, quite honestly, I know nothing of any of this. And"—I slipped my shoes back on, stood up, and reached for my coat with a twisted smile—"somehow, I suspect I am much better off that way. Thank you for the drink."

"No, Deirdre, don't leave yet." Vivienne jumped up from her seat to prevent my retreat; her voice was low and urgent. "I forget that all of this is new to you and that you've been under a terrible strain these past few weeks. I didn't mean to make you uncomfortable. It's just that there are so few of us, female vampires, I mean, and I thought we could become friends."

I studied Vivienne as she stood in front of me. Her eyes glistened in the candlelight and she seemed sincere and honest. I fully understood her feelings. I, too, missed female companionship.

Sensing my weakening, Vivienne pressed on. "As far as my lineage, I don't mind discussing that with you. It's not forbidden and it's no secret." She leaned forward and traced her nails down my cheek, not pulling her hand away when I tensed, but grasping my chin delicately yet firmly. "I'm also from the house of Alveros," she whispered to me, an odd smile crossing her face. Her face held a strange mixture of longing and loathing, desire and hate.

I moved away from her so abruptly that she almost lost her balance. "But Deirdre," she continued, straightening herself, touching my arm lightly, "please consider. I could do so much for you. You could have power and wealth in The Cadre. After all, you and I are sisters in blood."

I met her eyes squarely and surely. "All the same, Vivienne," I said, shrugging off her touch and moving to the door, "until I know what sort of game you are playing with me, I would prefer to remain an only child."

To my surprise, Vivienne took no offense, but laughed, a light metallic laugh, so charming and inhuman, so like her. "Bravo, Deirdre," she called after me as I left the room. "Have a nice evening."

There was no limo waiting for me outside, so I walked to Mitch's apartment. I dismissed the strange episode in Vivienne's room, knowing that I didn't need to worry about her, that she was no threat to my life. With my trial before The Cadre finally over, I felt freer than I ever had before, and hummed to myself, smiling at the few people I passed.

There was no trace of Max in my mind or on the street, and although I missed his presence, I felt relieved and at peace. I would no longer be tortured by thoughts of him, for by his own admission I was free of the guilt for his death. For the first time in over a century, I did not need to fear my dreams. The demons of my sleep had finally been exorcised and were put to rest.

When I had gotten to within three blocks of Mitch's apartment, I felt a cold stab of fear and stopped dead on the sidewalk. The way the recent events of our lives had worked out seemed too simple. Would it really be possible for Mitch and me to enjoy our lives together, unencumbered by demands of the outside world? Well, why the hell not, I reassured myself, I deserve a happy ending the same as everyone else.

I counted our assets in my mind. I had enough money to last us several lifetimes, not even counting the fortune I had inherited from Max. We could go anywhere, live anywhere we liked. Freed from guilt, freed from the sentence of The Cadre, I was immortal and Mitch, well, Mitch was strong and in good health. He could conceivably live forty or fifty more years. They would be good years, I was certain, filled with love and happiness. And when death finally came to claim him, I would follow. But finally, after over a century of running away, I would be living a normal life, the life I had been denied the first time around.

I started walking again, quickly this time, for all my rationalization could not allay the terrible feeling that something wrong had happened. No, I corrected myself, beginning to run, ignoring the sharp pain of fear entering my stomach and washing over my entire body, something wrong is happening right now. Right now.

I kicked off my shoes and ran the rest of the way, shouting his name, brushing past surprised predawn walkers and joggers, the buildings and cars that I passed blurred with speed and tears.

I was almost prepared for what I faced when I arrived home. I bounded up the steps, noticing that the main door was hanging open and askew, and that one of the hinges had been torn off. Mitch's front door was battered and lying on the living room floor. The remains of a bottle of wine that he must have opened for our celebration lay in pieces on the floor. I walked over them, not heeding the pain from the broken shards beneath my bare feet.

I stopped and held my breath. "Mitch," I called tentatively, my voice quavering, "are you here?"

I heard an odd laughing sound from the bedroom, then the crashing of glass. Running down the hall, I felt the icy blast of wind from the broken window, smelled the tangy, warm scent of fresh blood, and a tantalizingly familiar man's cologne. "Larry Martin," I whispered, and knew that I could follow him out the window and easily catch up with him. But when I arrived in the doorway, the sight of Mitch occupied my complete attention.

He was bruised and badly beaten, clutching his gun with one hand and the open wound on his neck with the other. I dropped to the floor and knelt beside him. His eyes fluttered open and focused weakly on my face. His skin had the bluish-gray color that meant he had nearly been drained of all his blood. Taking his pulse confirmed this.

"Jesus, Mitch, what the hell happened? Who did this?" My voice sounded calm but inwardly I was raving; damn The Cadre and all its members! The time I had spent in Vivienne's room might well have caused Mitch's death. Even the few minutes I had spent on the sidewalk planning the perfect life would have been all the time Larry needed. And if I had been here when Mitch was attacked, I could have prevented this.

Tenderly, I touched his cooling cheek. "Mitch, talk to me, please. Oh, God, you can't die. I won't allow it."

He stared at me for a moment and coughed weakly.

"Deirdre." It was the only word he could manage, and even it cost him too much strength.

I did not think of the consequences of my actions; all I could think was that he would die too soon and leave me alone. I could not bear the thought. Taking his shoulders in my hands, I shook him until his eyes opened again and focused on me. "Do you want to live?" I said to him. "Do you love me enough to live?"

He nodded weakly, a small spurt of blood came from his neck, and he managed a ghost of a smile.

"Are you sure?"

"Yes."

Picking up one of the broken shards of glass from the window, I cut into my wrist deeply, and forced it to his mouth before the wound could heal. "Drink, Mitch, drink."

There was no pull on my blood at first. He's dead, I thought, he's truly dead. "Drink, Mitch!" I screamed in desperation, not knowing or caring if he could hear me. "You must drink."

Oh, God, I raged inside, I spent so much time away from him and we had so little time together. Don't let him die, I prayed. Don't let him die!

Finally, after an eternity of despair, I felt the delicate movement of his lips at my wrist, feeble at first and then with greater strength, as he pulled deeply on my blood. The gray color began to fade from his skin, replaced slowly by an internal glow and the appearance of health. I watched as his bruises healed before my eyes and still he drank, until I began to feel the emptiness of my own veins. Then ever so gently I pried myself away from him. He choked, spitting a small swallow of my blood back at me.

His eyes opened briefly, then closed as his body shuddered once, then again, as if adjusting to its new life. His chest moved visibly as he breathed, and I knew he would live. I got up from the floor and looked out the window. There was no one on the street below, no sign of who had broken in here. All I could see was the lightening sky. Panicked, I pulled the curtains shut, but the wind blew them back, splashing the street light on to the floor where Mitch lay.

"Damn," I swore, wondering how I could move him, how I could keep the sun from him. Then I noticed the tall dresser in the corner of the room. It would cover the window and he would be safe. Frantically, I ran to it and pushed it across the room to block the light. The noise of this movement caused Mitch to awaken and sit up.

"Deirdre." His voice sounded strong but confused.

"What happened? I can't seem to remember anything. And I feel so strange, light-headed." His eyes sought me out and linked with mine. I had always thought that their strength and intensity were one of his most attractive qualities. But nothing could have prepared me for the shock of their depth—their complete and utter transformation. I knew his eyes, but never had they bored so directly into mine, never had they been so searching, so relentless. I choked back my tears and went to his side again.

"Hush, my love," I said to him, cradling his head on my lap the way I had over two years ago, trying for his sake to hide my despair. "Everything will be fine. Sleep now."

"But I need to remember what happened. Someone broke in while I was waiting for you. He told me not to remember and I can't. Then you came. And now everything is different. What happened? Tell me, please." The urgency in his voice almost broke my heart. How could I explain in the few remaining minutes until sunrise the life to which I had doomed him? That in my fear of losing him, I had done what I had resolved never to do?

"Sleep now," I repeated. "We'll have all the time in the world to talk later."

We tensed at the same time, reacting to the rising of the sun.

His body writhed in agony and his eyes met mine. They were clouded now with fear and confusion, and in spite of my resolve, I began to cry.

"What's that?" he demanded, his voice deeper and stronger than before. "What's happening to me, Deirdre? Why are you crying? And why do I feel so different?"

"It's only the sun, my love." I put as much reassurance into the words as I could and my fingers stroked his grayed hair, trying to calm and comfort. "Now is the time to sleep."

He looked up at me one more time. His eyes were undeniably the eyes of a vampire. Then they slowly closed, the lids falling as if of their own volition, and Mitch fell into the trancelike sleep I knew so well.

And I was alone again for a time, to mourn the death of the man I loved.

# Epilogue

As soon as arrangements could be made, Mitch and I went to England. We told no one what had occurred that evening in our apartment, explaining only that we would be gone for a while on an extended honeymoon. Mitch needs time to learn, time to adjust to his new life, and I need time to calm my panic over what I have done.

Before returning to my house and the pub, we decided to travel through the country, seeing the sights at night. Stonehenge was wonderful, and we crept past the guard and the gates and lay in the center, whispering to each other, making love on the dry, cold gravel. At Mitch's suggestion, we even stopped at Whitby. From our hotel bed we listened to the waves beat on the rocks and read aloud from *Dracula,* pointing out to each other the inconsistencies of the book compared to the life we knew. As always, at the end of the story I cried when the stake pierced the count's chest, remembering with a shudder exactly how it felt to kill a man of great power and age. And he laughed and kissed away my tears.

We have found that Mitch has a great instinct for hunting, his senses having been finely honed by his many years of police work. He is as good as I, or perhaps even better, at the postfeeding suggestions, but he still approaches the feeding and the victim timidly, tentatively, as if he had no right to their blood. He senses this hesitation as a liability, and I console him that he will get better with practice.

As for me, I don't dream much anymore. When I allow myself sleep, it's become like a small death, silent and mindless. Mostly, I lie awake and watch him sleep, wrestling with his own private demon of dreams. He moans and quivers, his eyes rolling within his closed lids, and he wakes covered in sweat. I never ask who appears in his dreams, with whom he fights daily, what figure haunts his sleep. I fear his answer, sensing deep inside that I already know, not wanting to hear him say that I am the demon. So I lie, my mind pure and emptied of all former ghosts, holding him while he writhes, tormented and struggling in the darkness that is my eternal gift to him.

BITTER BLOOD was the second exciting chapter of Deirdre Griffin's story. Now the Vampire Legacy continues with BLOOD TIES.

Please turn the page for an exciting sneak preview of BLOOD TIES.

# Chapter 1

He moved through the narrow streets like a shadow, in stealth and darkness, stalking an unsuspecting prey. I followed close enough to keep him in my sight, but also hidden, my presence merging with the night. His muscles coiled beneath the black sweater, his legs, taut and powerful, and his silvery hair glistened in the moonlight. I held back a gasp at the magnificence of this creature, as I did not want to be heard. But my caution made no difference—he was oblivious of my presence. He remained a mysterious and nameless figure intent only on the quick footsteps of his chosen victim, leading him around a corner and down a darker alley. I hurried to catch up with them, not wanting to miss the moment of capture.

Standing at the head of the alley, I squeezed tightly against its rough brick wall, watching in fearful anticipation. My legs trembled and the breath froze in my throat. Then, when I thought I could stand the waiting no longer, he struck, suddenly and ferociously. His hand snaked out and grasped the young man's shoulder, spinning him around, silencing his protests with a single glance. His mouth came down on the man's neck and my hand traveled to my own throat. My pulse pounded in excitement, my breathing quickened, my tongue darted out to lick my lips. The tangy, acrid smell of blood exploded in the air, its odor enticing and invigorating.

He drank hungrily, silently, but his pleasure was almost tangible, as easily heard as the strangled moans of his victim.

"Ahh." The slight whisper escaped my lips involuntarily, and although it was barely audible, he heard and pulled away to face me. His mouth was bloodied, his canines sharpened and lethal, and the ecstasy of feeding shone on his features. *I do not need to fear him,* I thought. *He is of my own kind.* But the internal reassurances did no good, and, in spite of myself, I shrank away from him in awe and fright. A look of puzzlement seemed to flash across his face, then he smiled and his eyes, with their intense blue glow, met mine and broke the spell under which his presence had held me.

"Mitch." I murmured his name and slowly moved toward him, claiming my place at the man's neck. Delicately, I placed my bite within the marks he had left and pulled deeply on the strong, rich blood. As I drank, Mitch stroked my hair with one hand. His other arm held me and the victim in an iron embrace until I finished my feast. Then with a few hoarsely spoken words, he calmed the man, urged him to forget, and gently deposited the now-sleeping form on the sidewalk.

We linked arms and walked back down the alley to return to the pub. I nestled into his strong arm and glanced up at him, smiling. He kissed the top of my head and I sighed. Mitch had adjusted to his new life better than I had ever expected.

"So how'd I do?" It had been his first solo stalking since his transformation, and the apprehension he had shown before we came out was now replaced with an exhilaration I knew all too well.

"At first I thought you would have been better off with someone older, someone slower perhaps. But you picked well. He was young and strong and you . . ." I sighed again. "You were perfect, Mitch. No, more than that, you were magnificent. You took my breath away."

"Well"—he shrugged and pulled me closer to him—"I had a wonderful teacher."

"Yes," I said. "I suppose I should offer professional tutoring in bloodsucking. Such a valuable skill." I tried to make my voice light and teasing, but the acid of the words splashed through.

We walked in silence until we were about a block from the pub. Mitch stopped and turned me around to face him. "What's wrong, Deirdre? You've been edgy and nervous all day. It's crazy, but I can't help but think it has something to do with me. Are you tired of me this soon?" The anger and hurt in his voice made me want to cry.

"No, my love." I reached a hand up to stroke his cheek. "It's not you. I wish I knew what it was. I am tired, perhaps that's all."

"But we slept all day and just fed pretty well. You should feel great. I know *I* do."

I gave him a sidelong glance. "You slept all day, you mean. I don't sleep much anymore."

"Why not? Do I snore?" His voice was slightly indignant.

"No, that's not it," I said with a small laugh, then sobered instantly. "I feel uneasy, like something is nagging at my mind, but I can't pinpoint it." I glanced up at the night sky, mentally numbering the remaining hours until dawn. "We'll have to leave here soon, you know."

"I know. Pete's expecting us back at the pub soon so he can go home. It was nice of him to stay while we ran out for a bite." He winked at me and I smiled, but shook my head slightly, for both the bad joke and his misunderstanding of my words.

"No, I meant that we'll need to leave England soon."

"But we just got here. And everything is just starting

to fall into place—the house, the pub, and you and me. What else could we possibly want?"

"More than four hours of darkness at night would be nice. You've never spent a summer at this latitude. I have and it's an experience I am not eager to repeat."

"Oh, yeah." He paused a minute and ran his fingers through his hair. "I was never real good at geography. Where should we go, do you think?"

I shrugged. "Anyplace is as good as another, I suppose, as long as we get at least seven hours of darkness. Any less than that and we might be in for trouble. What would you think about Spain?"

"Sounds fine to me." Mitch's face lit up with a mischievous grin. "I hear they have some great beaches there. You know, the ones where you can get a really good tan."

A sharp wave of panic struck me. I remembered too clearly my own initial longing for the sun, how, after over a century of living in the night only, I still missed the warming rays and the brightness of summer days.

"No beaches, Mitch." My voice was imperative and harsh. I reached over and grasped his arm tightly. "You have to promise me, no beaches."

"Okay, okay." He disengaged my fingers from his arm but kept my hand in his. "Bloody hell, Deirdre, I was only joking."

"Please, Mitch, never joke about that."

He must have heard the despair in my voice and said no more, but pulled me close to him, rocking me slightly for a few seconds.

"Feeing better?" His breath tickled my ear and I smiled into his sweater.

"Yes, thank you. Now, we'd better get back to the pub."

* * *

"Dottie, and Mitch my boy." Pete's boisterous voice greeted us as we opened the front door. "Back so soon? I was just saying that you'd be a while longer. Trying to make a liar of me, are you?"

I shook my head slightly and smiled, knowing that it did no good to interrupt him. Mitch laughed, clapping Pete on the shoulder, and stood next to him behind the bar.

"Sure," Pete continued, "and now I suppose you'll be sending me home right as I was in the middle of making the acquaintance of a new visitor, telling him the story of how you returned here with a new name, a new husband, and without an extra ounce of fat on your bones. Not that they're not fine bones, mind you"—he nudged Mitch, giving him a small wink—"but you both could do with a little fattening up."

I tensed slightly at his mention of a visitor and glanced around the bar, seeing no one but the regulars. Catching Mitch's eyes, I shrugged and asked the question I knew Pete was waiting to hear. "What new visitor?"

He looked around in confusion. "Why, he was just here, wasn't he, boys?" The men around the bar nodded and Pete continued. "Probably stepped off to the gents. He'll be turning up soon, no doubt. Real eager to see you, he was. Says he knew you both in the States." Pete's eyes narrowed in a fake scowl. "Seems to me, Dottie, the last time that happened you took off and left me for another man."

"But I came back, Pete."

"And that you did, Dot." He drew himself a glass of stout and walked around the bar, lighting a cigarette.

"But this wasn't the same man that dragged you away before. This one is older and has a trace of an accent, not American, mind you, but someplace foreign."

As he settled himself onto a stool to finish his drink, I moved back behind the bar with Mitch. "Do you remember his name, Pete?" I asked with a smile, leaning toward him. "Or did you forget to ask?"

"Now, Dottie, don't give me grief, I get enough of that from the missus owing to my poor memory. Vincent, it was or something close to that."

"Victor Lange."

I knew Mitch well enough to hear the undercurrent of tension in his voice, but Pete merely nodded and announced triumphantly, "Yes, that's the chap. Know him, do you?"

"Unfortunately." This time the anger in Mitch's voice was unmistakable.

"Well, fortunate or not," Pete said, glancing curiously at Mitch, "he's here somewhere." He drained his glass, stubbed out his cigarette, and stood. Taking off his apron, he tossed it to Mitch, then reached over to give me a delicate pat on my cheek. "Now, Dot, don't you go running off on me again without notice."

Although I knew Mitch and I would both be leaving soon, I nodded my head, thinking that we had at least a month before the nighttime hours would begin to dwindle enough to force us to move on. "Well, Pete," I began, "we won't . . ." But the rest of my answer went unsaid. The air seemed to thicken over me; the hair on the back of my neck rose. I could hear nothing, but felt the presence of someone standing close behind me as clearly as if a hand had been laid on me. I quickly looked over my shoulder and around the room, but could see only those who had been there a second earlier, no one else.

Mitch walked over next to me and wrapped an arm around my waist, his familiar touch calming me only slightly. "Don't worry," he said, "we won't leave you in the lurch. Now, if you don't go soon, your wife'll be mad."

Pete's contagious laugh roared over the pub and almost rid me of the unsettling feeling of the invisible presence. "Right you are, my boy. See you tomorrow night."

The rest of the evening passed uneventfully. I was still nervous. I thought that the patrons spoke too loudly and that the smoke of their cigarettes was unnaturally heavy, curling thickly through the dark corners of the room. I breathed my relief when last call had been made and the doors were finally locked. Mitch silently poured me a glass of port, handed me Pete's cigarettes, and began to clear the tables.

When I finished the wine, I lit one of the Players and sat at the bar to watch Mitch wash the glasses and the stems, admiring the grace of his movements and the strength of his hands. He looked up at me, his eyes met mine, and he smiled. "What?"

"Nothing," I said. Suddenly the nervousness fell aside and I felt at peace with myself for the first time since Mitch's transformation. "I just like to watch you. You do that so well."

Mitch laughed. "I know, you brought me all the way here just so I could wash dishes for your pub."

I returned his laugh. "That's right, my love, regular dishwashers don't come cheap, and you know how Pete is about spending money."

He gave a noncommittal grunt and completed his work behind the bar. Then he pulled out a glass for himself and filled it and mine with tawny port. He took both glasses and sat down at the closest table. I followed and sat down next to him.

"So"—his voice had lost all of its humor and was intense and serious—"what exactly was that?"

"You mean right before Pete left? I don't know. I've never experienced anything like it."

"Wasn't Max, was it?"

After having lived with the ghost of Max for nearly two years, I discarded that theory immediately. "No, it didn't have his imprint, somehow."

"I didn't think so."

I turned to him in surprise. "You felt it too?"

"Yeah." He ran his fingers through his hair in a tired gesture. "But it was vaguely familiar." Then he shrugged and touched my hand. "Another thing, what the hell is Victor Lange doing here? And where in bloody hell do you suppose he disappeared to?"

I shook my head and my eyes drifted to a corner of the bar, where the smoke of the night had collected and the darkness was impenetrable. Rubbing a hand on my face, I looked again, and a shiver of amazement flowed over me. "Why, that son of a bitch," I whispered in a trembling voice. "He never left at all. He's been here all night."

"What?" Mitch looked at me in surprise, then glanced over his shoulder. When the figure behind the bar began to materialize into an almost recognizable form, Mitch jumped out of his chair, knocking his glass to the floor in the process. Its crash was the only noise for what seemed a long time. Then there was the sound of footsteps, and suddenly Victor stood in front of us.

"Good evening, Deirdre," he nodded, "and you too, Mitch. It's good to see you again."

Mitch and I just stared at him. Neither of us ever had any inkling that what Victor had just done was even possible. Mitch cleared his throat and tentatively held out his hand. Victor shook it, grinning.

"Jesus, Victor," Mitch said with a touch of both anger and awe in his voice, "how the hell did you do that?"

# Chapter 2

"Forgive me for the theatrics," Victor began, ignoring Mitch's question. He brushed a spot of invisible lint from his impeccably tailored jacket and sat down at the table. "I did think that our meeting would best be conducted in private. We have a lot to discuss, we three."

I glanced at Victor uneasily, then glanced away, feeling, as I usually did in his presence, shoddily dressed in my jeans and black sweater. He exuded an elegance and a confidence as easily felt as the power and magnetism of his being. Mitch was still staring at him, and I could almost hear the questions racing through his mind. Was what Victor had done possible for us? And if so, how was it accomplished? But where I shrank away from the inhumanity of such a trick, Mitch, I knew, would pursue this new power effortlessly and relentlessly, as he had so readily embraced the unnatural life he had been given.

I shuddered and looked down at the tabletop. Victor reached over and lifted my chin. "Cat got your tongue, Deirdre? I do apologize for the abruptness of my appearance. I didn't mean to alarm you."

"No." I found my voice and was amazed that it sounded even and calm. "It was just a surprise, seeing you appear like that. After all, we had been told you were here."

"Yes, well"—Victor looked over to Mitch—"what if

you pour me one of whatever you two are having and we'll get down to business."

Mitch walked back behind the bar to get the bottle and another glass for Victor. My mouth curved in an almost smug smile as I watched him. Victor might be elegant and powerful, but he could never be a match for the utter intensity and sensuality that Mitch possessed. A low noise escaped my throat, almost a purr, and I blushed, but Victor merely laughed.

"He is developing nicely, my dear. You've done a good job with his training."

"What do you mean?"

"Come now, Deirdre," Victor admonished, "I do have eyes and my senses are even more finely honed than yours. The glow of transformation still lingers over him. He'll do well, and for what it's worth, I approve."

Mitch came back to the table and handed Victor his wine. "And exactly what is your approval worth, Lange?"

Victor looked up at him calmly. "Quite a bit, actually. As head of The Cadre, I have the final decision on most transformations, especially one such as yours, since you now both fall into the house of Leupold. Never underestimate the ties of blood, Mitch. As you grow older, you will eventually lose your human family, but your blood clan will continue. And"—Victor gave a low chuckle—"like it or not, I am the head of that clan."

"I'd like it a lot better if you could teach me that little trick you entered with." Mitch sat down and leaned back casually in his chair. "How on earth do you do it?"

Victor gave me a puzzled look. "Deirdre should be able to teach you. It merely requires concentration and practice—years, or more properly, decades of practice. I wish I could take the time to teach you, but I'm afraid my business here is not pleasant and my time is short. I'm needed back at The Cadre before tomorrow evening." Victor stood up and brushed at his pants again.

"And, although I hate to interrupt your honeymoon, you two must accompany me."

"Why must we?" Mitch still sat in his relaxed pose, but the glitter of his eyes and the set of his jaw betrayed his animosity.

Victor glared coldly at him and leaned over the chair, his posture threatening, his tone of voice even more patronizing than usual. "You do remember when you promised to perform a service for The Cadre at our discretion? Well, quite simply, Greer, we are now calling in our marker, and as you value your life and Deirdre's, you will not refuse. A private jet is waiting for us at the airport and we will leave in an hour and a half. Be there."

Victor turned to me, and the anger in his eyes faded, replaced by something that could have resembled tenderness. Taking my hand, he kissed it, then he spun around and was gone.

Mitch looked where he had been standing and shook his head. "Do you suppose he's actually left?"

I laughed. "Your guess is as good as mine, my love. Shall we close up now and go home and pack?"

"Just drop everything and do as we were ordered? Give me one good reason why we should have anything to do with Lange."

"I can give you several reasons, Mitch. We did promise to do the service for The Cadre, whatever it may be. I know that we were hoping never to have anything else to do with them, but so be it." He nodded reluctantly, and I continued. "And Victor is right about the bond among the three of us, there is no way to deny that." I stood up and smiled at him, reaching out for his hands. "Plus, if you stay in his good favor, he might even teach you his little parlor trick. I have no inclination to dissolve myself. And even if I did, I have no idea how to go about it."

"Okay, okay, you've convinced me. But you'll have to break the news to Pete." He pulled me to him and kissed me, his lips cool against mine. Then he held me out and studied my face. "Deirdre, if whatever we are called to do is dangerous"—he gave a small, humorless laugh—"as I'm sure it will be, I want you to promise that you'll let me bear the brunt of it. Don't take any chances. I don't think I want to exist eternally without you."

"Nor I without you."

"So then, we're agreed."

"No"—I shook my head with a small smile—"not at all. But let's not fight until we know what the situation is."

"Okay, I guess I can live with that, but only for a while. And we'd better hurry, as I'd hate to keep Mr. Lange waiting."

We made it home, and were almost through with our packing when I finally asked, "Why do you hate Victor so much?"

Mitch looked up at me from his suitcase. "It's not really Victor, you know. I could almost like him if it weren't for—" He paused for a minute, staring at me. Then he looked away. "It's the whole hierarchy of The Cadre. They sit in their underground warren, spinning their devious little webs, meting out their arbitrary justice."

He folded his last pair of jeans, crammed them into the suitcase, and snapped it shut. "They almost succeeded in making me crazy. They would've left me in that institution for the rest of my life and not thought a thing about it. They could very easily have doomed you to a hundred years of starvation and never once bothered to ascertain the fairness of the sentence. They're immoral, inhuman parasites living off innocent people, and I wouldn't care if the entire lot died tomorrow."

Well, I told myself as I watched him stack our suitcases by the bedroom door, you asked for it. But I said nothing, and walked across the room, picked up the phone, and dialed Pete's home number.

"Pete," I said when he answered, "it's Dorothy. I am afraid I have some bad news for you."

"Leaving again, are you?" He sounded more amused than angry.

"Yes, I am sorry."

"And didn't I know it when that Vincent chap turned up asking for you. I suppose you'll be taking your husband with you too, leaving me with no help at all?"

"Yes."

"Dottie darlin', you know, if you didn't own half the pub, I'd be firing you right now."

"I am sure you would, Pete. I'll call you when we get there."

"I'd appreciate that. But don't you worry, I'll do fine."

"Thank you, Pete. You take care now."

"And the same to you, my girl. God's speed."

I hung up the phone, stood for a minute with my back to Mitch, and wiped away a few tears. A horn beeped on the street, and still I didn't move until Mitch came up behind me and wrapped an arm around my neck, kissing me softly on the ear. "We'd better get moving, Deirdre, the taxi's here. Are you ready?"

I nodded and we went downstairs. We locked the house, loaded the trunk of the taxi, and made it to the airport with five minutes to spare.

The plane Victor had chartered was a small, sleek Gulfstream, and Mitch and I were the only passengers evident. The seats were plush and comfortable and I settled in by one of the windows. Mitch sat next to me with a grim smile, outwardly relaxed and at ease, but I could feel the keyed-up tenseness of his muscles as he stretched his legs out. Even though Victor was nowhere in sight, the plane began its acceleration down the runway almost immediately and made a smooth leap from the ground into the night sky.

My sigh from the window was easily audible. Mitch reached over and took my hand. "Nervous?"

"No," I said softly, turning to him, "not at all. I love to fly. But I was just wondering what it would feel like without the plane, how it would feel to just be picked up by the wind and carried away." I gave a small laugh to compensate for the emotional outburst. "I guess we would find out soon enough if we were to crash."

"Do you think we'd survive?"

"You know, I have no idea."

Mitch was silent for a while. "My guess is we would. Unless"—he chuckled a little—"we happened to land on a picket fence somewhere."

I studied the view from the window. "I think we're safe from that. We're over the ocean already. But I suppose if you really want to know, we could ask Victor. I wonder where he is."

Mitch gave a noncommittal grunt. "What is it with you and him anyway? All of a sudden the two of you seem pretty chummy. You jump to his commands, express concern over his whereabouts. Personally, I don't know why he even bothers with the damn plane at all. Why doesn't he just turn into a cloud and float back?"

"Mitch"—I turned from the window again and looked into his eyes—"don't start. There is nothing between Victor and me. I married you and intend to stay married to you. I'm here to fulfill my commitment, nothing else. After that we're free to do whatever we like, go wherever we want."

"Okay." He shrugged, giving me a boyish grin, so at odds with his silvered hair. "I'm sorry. I just don't like the guy."

"I think you've made that more than evident." My mouth twisted in a dry smile. "But"—I reached up, kissing him on the cheek—"just put up with it for a while, for my sake."

Mitch returned my kiss, then moved away from me and laughed. "I will say one thing for Lange though"—he gestured around us—"he sure knows how to travel. This is quite a setup. How much do you suppose this put him back?"

"Actually, Mitch"—the door to the cockpit opened and Victor came out—"I own this plane. And believe me, the convenience far outweighs the cost." He went to the back of the compartment and opened another door. "Now that we're safely airborne, may I offer you a drink?"

Before Mitch and I even had a chance to agree, Victor had poured drinks and brought them over: red wine for me and a scotch on the rocks for Mitch. When I saw Victor's choice for Mitch I started to laugh.

"What?" Mitch looked at me after taking a long drink. "Is something funny?"

"No, but Victor has a surprisingly good memory. He actually remembered what you drink when you're angry."

"Oh." Mitch shrugged sheepishly. "I see."

"Not that you don't have the right to be angry." Victor's voice was smooth and conciliatory. "After all, you've hardly been away for more than a few months, and I've called you back. I do apologize for the inconvenience, but I want to assure you that this trip is necessary. And it was not just my decision to call you, it was a unanimous vote from all the founders."

Mitch gave a snort. "And what could possibly be so

difficult for that esteemed group to require our involvement?"

"We have our reasons, Greer, as I will explain when you give me the chance." Victor gave him a warning glare, then turned to me. "In the first place, at least six murders have occurred that lead us to believe that we are faced with a dangerous rogue vampire. Since we became acquainted with you, Deirdre, most of us have come to the realization that we've been weakened by our ritualized training.

"You"—Victor nodded at me—"have the advantage of being able to approach situations such as this from a fresh viewpoint. Being a rogue of a sort yourself, we hope that you can outthink our culprit, or at least anticipate his moves. In addition, Mitch, there is your police training—a highly valuable asset in this situation. Although, I must admit that your transformation has come as something of a surprise. We had hoped that you could cover the daytime and root this vampire out of his lair. But I suspect your new skills will only enhance your old detective instincts."

Mitch shrugged. "And?"

Victor looked down at his hands for a moment. "And as you know, The Cadre has strict rules governing the killing of one of our own. None of us can attempt to catch and kill this vampire without incurring the impact of our laws. But you two, since you are not officially part of the organization, can be given special dispensation in this one case only."

"How convenient," Mitch drawled. "I remember it otherwise."

Victor bared his white teeth in a threatening smile. "Different circumstances, Mitch. We're not talking here about an established house founder, but about an undisciplined murderer."

"And Max wasn't?"

"Max would have been dealt with our way. Let's not begin to rehash a situation that, regretful as it may be, is now over and done with."

Hearing the pain in Victor's voice, pain not diminished by the time that had passed since Max's death, I looked over at Mitch and pleaded with my eyes for him to drop the subject. Then I took his hand in mine and turned again to Victor. "All of that seems reasonable to me, Victor. We'll do our best to help you."

"Thank you, Deirdre. I knew you would. But I'm not quite through with the story. And this part may not be pleasant for you, my dear, but it is the most telling reason we wanted you." Victor stood up, opened the overhead compartment, and brought out a large manila envelope. "The murders began to occur shortly after you and Mitch left town. Obviously, you personally cannot be held accountable for the deaths, but it seems that you are involved. All of the victims were last seen at the Ballroom of Romance."

"What a surprise." Mitch gave a small, derisive snort. The Ballroom had belonged to Max, been passed on to my ownership through his estate. And it carried nothing but bad memories for us both.

Victor sat back down and passed the envelope to Mitch. He took it but did not open it. Instead, he set it down on the seat next to him, as if leaving it unopened could delay the inevitable decision to cooperate with The Cadre. "You're involved with the Ballroom too, Victor," Mitch said evenly. "After all, you've been managing it for Deirdre in her absence."

"Actually, I turned it back over to Fred. After you left town, there was no need to keep him in exile, and he does a good job."

"But," I said, "Fred is not a rogue."

"That is true," Victor chuckled, shaking his head. "And Fred, even with all his faults, is definitely not responsible for the deaths. We have"—he cleared his throat—"screened all The Cadre members. None of them are involved."

"So where does the Ballroom enter into this?" I did not really need to ask. From the sickening twist of my stomach, I realized suddenly that I knew who the rogue was. I glanced over at Mitch, and his grim nod confirmed my thoughts. But neither of us said a word—we just let Victor continue.

"Ever since the unfortunate occurrences there, rumors have abounded that the club is haunted." Victor raised an eyebrow in a half-smirk. "Humans, who can figure them out? Business is better than it's ever been since the rumors started. Even the murders haven't kept them away, but only added to the mystique."

"Haunted?" Victor's choice of words threw me off balance. "How could it be haunted? Max is gone." Mitch looked away from me and drained his scotch, tensing at the tone of sadness in my voice. I couldn't help myself; not a day had gone by since his true death that I did not miss him.

"Deirdre"—Victor's voice wavered only slightly—"it's not Max who haunts the Ballroom of Romance. It's Larry Martin."

## ENTER THE WORLD OF KAREN E. TAYLOR'S VAMPIRE LEGACY

### BLOOD SECRETS (Book One)

Allow me to introduce myself. My name is Deirdre Griffin and I'm a vampire. Currently I'm living in Manhattan and I spend my evenings at the Ballroom of Romance, where I satisfy my blood lust with weekly feedings. Unlike other vampires, I *never* drain my victims, but it seems there's another vampire on the loose, only this one *is* draining his victims—and pointing the finger of suspicion at me! What's a woman to do? If you're a vampire like me, you use your feminine wiles to hunt him down . . .

### BITTER BLOOD (Book Two)

Remember me? Deirdre Griffin, *vampire?* After living in London for two years, I'm back in my favorite city. But life in New York's no picnic in the park. It seems that a group of vampires want revenge against me for killing their leader. What's worse, they're using my ex-lover, Detective Mitch Greer, as bait, and the only way I can save him is by converting him into a vampire like me . . .

### BLOOD TIES (Book Three)

It's me again: Deirdre Greer, *vampire.* When we last met, my husband, Mitch Greer, had finally become a vampire. Now we're back on the streets of New York, at the request of The Cadre, a secret society of ancient vampires, because another series of murders is taking place. It turns out this guy isn't just killing humans, he's also killing vampires . . .

### BLOOD OF MY BLOOD
### (Book Four—Coming in October 2000)

I'm back. Deirdre Greer, *vampire*—formerly Deirdre Griffin. I promised to love Mitch for all eternity, but now he's vanished from our backwoods Maine cabin. As I embark on a search for my beloved, traveling to the French Quarter of New Orleans, I uncover a baffling trail—a trail supposedly left by me. Who is the shadowy, eerily familiar figure lurking on the fringes of my life? What does she want of me? And what has she done with Mitch?